REUNITING
SECRETS

SHAE MARTIN WORTHY

REUNITING SECRETS

Five Sisters, Five Secrets

Worthy Publishing

This book is a work of fiction. Names, characters, places and incidents either are products of the author's imagination or are used fictitiously. Any resemblance to actual events or locales or persons, living or dead, is entirely coincidental.

Cover design by Shae Martin Worthy

Dedications

This book is dedicated to my daughter Ariel, who always inspired me. It's also dedicated to my mother and father, Barbara and Vonzell Nash who never let me give up on my dreams.

This book is dedicated in loving memory of my wonderful "Granny" Mildred McCloud Worthy, who always believed in me. It is also dedicated to my aunts Rosie, Novella, Garnett, Elvira, Mattie and my uncle Preston, whose names all inspired my characters.

To the memory of Timothy Fitts, a wonderful fiancé and great loss who was truly the love of my life.

To my sisters Kim, Sheila, Dee Annamarie, Merideth, my brother Mickey, and my cousins Kenya, Kisha, DJ and Jarell, thanks for being so supportive over the years.

I love you all!

And thank you GOD Almighty for Your wonderful blessings and the gift of writing. I love You first and foremost.

Chapter One
Nora's story

My eyes were closed as I lay on my stomach. I wanted to drain away the stress before tonight, and my masseuse was doing a wonderful job. She came three times a week, and this was the day for my hour-long massage. None too soon either, especially considering the party we were throwing tonight. Although my relaxation room, as I liked to call it, was quiet with nothing but the soothing sounds of nature around me, and the perfectly dimmed lights, I could still hear the phone ringing in the distance. I heard my maid answer. She's an incompetent idiot, and she was extremely close to being fired. She'd only been with me a few weeks after my capable Sarah went off and got married. It had taken two years to whip Sarah into shape, and she was the perfect maid. Now, I would have to start all over again, and this girl was off to a rocky start.

"Riley residence. One moment please," the maid responded.

Surely, she had sense enough not to come in here. I just know the new girl has learned that I hate being disturbed during my 'me' time. 'The new girl.' Ironically, I don't even remember her name. But, considering I could hear her footsteps treading towards my relaxation room, she'll be dumb enough to interrupt me.

"Mrs. Riley?" She poked her head in timidly, completely destroying the calming ambiance my masseuse had created.

"You know, I thought by now you'd figured out that from 10 a.m. until 12 p.m. I am not to be disturbed. Yet, somehow, you've found a way to do it. Now, what in the hell do you want that couldn't wait another 47 and a half minutes?"

"I-I'm sorry, Mrs. Riley. You have a phone call. It's from South Carolina according to the caller ID, so I thought you might want to take it."

"South Carolina? It has to be Millie," I sighed. "Tell her I'll call her back." I closed my eyes as my masseuse hit a tender spot on my shoulder. "Oh, that feels great."

"It's not a 'her,' ma'am; it's a 'him.'"

"Fine. I'll be there in a minute. Tina, let's finish this up later," I said to my masseuse. I got up from such a comfortable spot. My masseuse gave me my robe to put on. Damn him. It had better be important. The one thing I didn't want in my relaxation room was a phone. At this point, it seems as if maybe that was poor judgment on my part. "Hello?"

"Nora? It's Clayton."

"Hello, Brother-in-law. To what do I owe the

2

pleasure?"

"I wanted to call to let you know that Millie's in the hospital," Clayton said.

"Hospital? What happened?" I asked. My heart skipped several beats.

"Nora, Millie has cancer," Clayton responded.

At that moment, the words echoed in my ears. I kept trying to think of a snide remark, but all it could think of was the fact that my sister had a fatal illness. Millie's the 'good girl' out of the five of us. She thrives on being the one to solve everyone's problems, and be the 'go to' person for advice and help. She's a goody-goody, and I try to have as little use for her as possible.

"Cancer?" As much as I wanted to think of something else to say, I could only choke out one word. The selfish bitch has cancer. Just another way to get attention from everyone.

"Yeah," Clayton sighed. He sounded almost in tears.

"So? What am I supposed to do about it?" Better than to tell him the thought of losing Millie scared the hell out of me.

"That wasn't exactly the response I was hoping for," Clayton retorted.

"What's her prognosis?" I asked, almost distant.

"Not good," Clayton said.

"When did she find out?" I asked.

"A year ago."

"A year ago?" I said, not sure if I was more astonished or pissed that she didn't tell me. "My sister wouldn't dare have a terminal illness for a year and not tell anyone. What is she? A martyr practicing for sainthood?"

"I don't know why I called you. I thought that even you would have a little bit of decency and at least want to come and see her. This could be the end for her."

"No it's not. She's too stubborn for that. She'll be fine. Thanks for calling, but I won't be coming. Tell Millie I hope she feels better." Before my brother-in-law could respond, I hung up the phone quickly.

I ran off to my bedroom, willing the tears away. When I entered the room, I broke down. I sat on my bed, wondering what I was supposed to do if Millie died. How could she? A year with cancer? A year and not a word? What was supposed to be the hint? Her death? Boy, she really pulled a fast one on me this time. Millie's not supposed to die, she's supposed to live forever. I got up and went to the closet quickly to pack my bags for the airport. I stopped, thinking there was no way I was going to South Carolina. It's not fair. How could she do this to me?

After changing out of my robe into a silk lounger, I sat down again and sighed. This was going to be the most difficult decision for me. Sometimes, I had no idea how I felt about my sisters. At times, I wished they all would just fall off the face of the earth. Especially Ellen. That's another story, though. I'll get to her later. Before I could make up my mind, my husband Bill walked in. He was here just in time to make me once again question why I ever married such a moron. Then, I thought about it. It's because the son of a bitch is loaded. I knew when we started dating while I was in high school that he'd amount to something. He was a junior in college when we started dating. I wouldn't give him the time of day because he'd courted my sister five years before he even knew I existed. When she chose someone else over him, he dated around a little, but, when I turned 17, he took notice and pursued me. I was determined not to play second fiddle to anyone, especially my sister. But, I found out he had a trust fund. That was an attractive enough quality for me to reconsider going out with him.

"Hi, Sweetheart," he smiled. He leaned down to kiss me slightly on the cheek. I wryly thought about the fact that I have another cheek he can kiss. His touch makes me cringe.

"My darling husband," I sighed monotonously.

"Don't get so excited," Bill said sarcastically.

"No threat of that. Being with you is like watching paint dry."

"I'm not exactly doing cartwheels at the sight of you. The only reason I came home early was to see how much preparation you've made for John's party."

"Don't worry. The caterers will be here soon. Your precious partner's birthday party will go off without a hitch. I've been practicing my loving wife routine for tonight. You know, I don't need you here to check up on me. I'm quite capable of planning a party."

"That's about all you're capable of," Bill shrugged.

"Oh, I can do a lot more than that."

"Damn, I left my briefcase at the office," Bill said to himself, ignoring me.

"Serves you right. You didn't have to come home. You could have called."

"Maybe I just wanted to bask in a little of your sunshine," Bill said sarcastically.

"I doubt that seriously," I said. "By the way, I'm going to South Carolina tomorrow." I'm not sure when I made up my mind, but, somehow I did. Maybe it was to get away from Bill.

"Oh? To visit Millie?"

"Yeah, she's got cancer," I said matter-of-factly.

"What?" He seemed shocked. If I didn't know better, I'd think it bothered him.

"You don't hear so well, do you? Millie has cancer. Was that clear enough for you that time?!"

"I'm coming with you," Bill said.

I looked seriously at my husband, trying to read him. "You're still in love with her," I observed.

"There will never be another woman like Millicent," Bill responded.

"Hmm, she threw you over for Clayton. Yeah, you picked a real winner there, Bill," I laughed.

"On her worst day she's a hundred times more human than you are, Nora."

"Must have been a real let down when you came home for the summer and found out she'd fallen for Clayton. How did you feel, knowing he was screwing her and she never let you get near her?"

"Still twisting the knife, huh?" Bill said.

6

"You make it so easy, Dear. But, if it makes you feel better, Millie was a virgin when she got married."

"How would you know?" Bill asked sarcastically.

"Sisters talk. Plus, Mama had 'the talk' with her on her wedding day."

"I'll bet she didn't have to have 'the talk' with you when we got married," Bill laughed.

"We eloped, remember? And considering I was already pregnant, what would have been the point?" I shrugged.

"Well, for the record Nora, it's been 27 years ago since I dated your sister. She's happily married to Clayton, and I'm happy for her."

"Oh, please! If Clayton left her, you'd be there with open arms!"

"I sure as hell don't have anything here to stop me! I've tried to tolerate you for the sake of our children, but when Matthew graduates from high school, I'm leaving you."

I laughed at his declaration. "Haven't you heard the phrase 'it's cheaper to keep her'? To save yourself the agony of court, just leave your checkbook here and you're free to go."

"I'm a lawyer, remember? There's not a judge alive who would reward you for being a two timing tramp," Bill said.

"If I'm a two-timing tramp, it's because you made me that way. Your bedroom skills leave a lot to be desired," I lied.

"Go to hell, Nora," Bill said, frustratingly

taking off his jacket and tie.

"Besides, why would you think I cheated on you?" I shrugged.

"Because you're breathing. I think it's pretty safe to assume you'd screw anything with a pulse," Bill said nonchalantly.

I watched him as he got completely undressed. I'll give him one thing. He's sexy as hell. I started to want him right then and there as he stripped down to his briefs. I've always loved a briefs man. He looked at me with smoldering glance. I smiled at him seductively, lifting my foot to caress his leg. He pushed me back on the bed forcefully and ripped away my lounger. I wanted desperately to resist as he kissed me. I felt his manhood harden against my thigh, and I wanted him to take me. Whenever we disagreed, our lovemaking was always more passionate. Over the past few years, that's all we ever did. It seemed to make him better in bed somehow. I moaned softly as my husband entered me. He had a lot of pent up anger against me, and to my advantage, he let it out with every passionate thrust. After it was over, he got up and went to the shower. I laid there, disgusted at the thought that I'd allowed him to even touch me.

Later that night, we hosted a party for 100 of our closest friends for his law firm partner's 50th birthday. John was an attractive guy and he didn't look a day over 40. But, he was a little too honorable for me. After knowing him for almost 20 years, he'd never made a pass at me. He actually seemed happily married to his wife. Everyone of course asked about our children. We had two: Jessica, 20 and Matthew, 17. At least, I had two. It was questionable about whether Jessica was really Bill's child. If the truth ever came out about her real parentage, there would be hell to pay. One of my sisters might not ever forgive me. Of course, it really doesn't matter. They've always been jealous of me anyway. I always wanted to throw it in my sister's face that I'd had her husband years before, but, I wasn't about to take a chance on losing my own gravy train just to hurt her. So, I kept my mouth shut. Knowing his little girl might not be his little girl might push him over the edge. As much as I hated to admit it, Bill was right. I might not get a good settlement if we divorced.

Jessica was my pride and joy. Matthew was his father's son. I suppose he was a good boy, but, sometimes I felt that my son was a little too nice for me. He was like a doormat half the time. Hard to believe he was able to be star running back on his high school football team. Jessica was prima donna all the way. I kept her in beauty pageants, well, because she's a beauty. She won just about every one of them. The one time she didn't win was, pardon the pun, poor judgment on the judge's part. Rumor has it that one of the moms of one of the contestants was a little too friendly with one of the judges, if you know what I mean. My little Jessica was now a junior at Yale, and in the top five percent of her class.

I looked around anxiously for Jessica who said she would try to be there. Matthew was still in Switzerland with friends for a couple of weeks this summer. I insisted that he go, because he's not as outgoing as he should be.   A trip abroad was just what he needed.   Of course, if football didn't toughen him up, going to another country probably wouldn't either. But, he'd be away from his dad, and maybe, just maybe he'd finally lose his virginity.   Who ever heard of a 17 year old virgin these days anyway?   He was a good-looking boy, and the girls were constantly after him.   I know he could have gotten one of them into bed by now if he wanted to.   After looking around, I finally spotted my daughter, flirting shamelessly with the bartender.   I observed her body language.   It was perfect.   Not too obvious, but, quite welcoming. With my daughter's looks and attitude, she always had men eating out of the palm of her hand.   Which is exactly the way it should be.   Although, a bartender wasn't every mother's dream for her daughter.

Jessica and I had a few problems a few years back, but, we're past that now, I think.   I suppose it wasn't everyday a daughter comes home with friends and finds her mother having sex with another man.   I fault her for that, because she shouldn't have come home early.   Why not go to the mall and spend more of her daddy's money like every other rich girl would do?   She didn't tell her father, but she made me pay for it constantly, by bringing it up to get her own way. Can you believe that little minx?   Trying to blackmail her own mother.   I suppose I taught her too well.   I debated about interrupting her, and decided what the hell?   After all, it's my house.

"Hello, Sweetheart, I'm glad you could make it," I smiled, hugging her slightly.

"Mother," Jessica said, almost as dryly as the

10

hug I'd given her.

I taught my daughter a long time ago never to get too emotional in the public eye, unless it was to get her own way. I looked at her hand holding her drink. An apple martini. Just like her mom, but, mine was always minus the apple. She looked beautiful with her jet black hair pulled up. She had beautiful green eyes that were almost haunting. The black cocktail dress was perfect, just as I told her it would be when I purchased it for her. Bill hit the roof. He thought it was too short and too revealing. If a woman can't show it off, then what's the point of having it? I wasn't going to let my 20 year old with a perfect figure dress like a nun. If Jessica and I didn't agree on anything else, we agreed on clothes. The more they cost the better.

"Can I get you anything, Mrs. Riley?" the bartender asked.

"Dry martini," I said.

"Yes ma'am," he said.

"So, where's Ethan?" I asked. I think that's the guy's name.

"Eric, Mother," Jessica sighed frustratingly.

"Sorry," I smiled.

"Sure, Mom. But to answer your question, he's not here," Jessica said.

"Well, I gathered that," I said.

"He's probably 'hanging out with the fellas,'" Jessica said sarcastically.

"Trouble brewing?" I asked, picking up the drink the bartender made.

"Sorry to disappoint you, but, we're fine.

11

Even if we weren't, I wouldn't tell you," Jessica said.

"Smart move," I laughed. "You know I'll never let you live it down. He's not of our social climate, Dear, and I think you could do so much better. What about John's son, Andrew? He's been pining over you for years."

"Andrew's a drunken playboy," Jessica rolled her eyes. "Besides, he's really not that good in bed."

"Well, that can be a damper on things," I shrugged. "But, he's worth a fortune. John's worth millions."

"Mom, my trust fund isn't too shabby. Or did you forget that Daddy's loaded?"

"But, combining your daddy's money with John's money could be a real powerhouse," I said.

"Look, you married for money. I have no intention of doing the same. I'd rather walk on hot coals than be anything like you," Jessica said.

"Hot coals are too overrated, Honey," I said jokingly. "Taking after me is something you're going to do whether you like it or not. We're cut from the same cloth, Jessica. You're beautiful like me, you're smart like me, and you can have whatever you want by--"

"Mother, please don't finish that statement," Jessica sighed, holding her hand up.

"What? Jessica, you really need to think about your future," I said, shaking my head.

"I thought attending an Ivy-League college and being in the top five percent in my class was doing just that," Jessica argued.

"It is, Sweetie. But, you're majoring in

psychology. What kind of money can you make like that? You need to consider marrying well."

"Such gems of wisdom from someone whose only skill is lying on her back," Jessica retorted, sipping her drink.

"Don't knock it 'til you've tried it, Sweetie," I smiled. "Looks like it paid off for me."

"Whatever," Jessica sighed. She looked across the room. "There's Daddy." She smiled as she waved to get his attention.

"Who cares?" I shrugged. "The further away from me he is, the better."

"I'm sure he feels the same way. Tell me something, Mother, have you ever loved him?"

"Love doesn't pay the bills, Jessica."

"That doesn't answer my question. Did you ever love my father?"

I was glad that before I could answer, my husband interrupted. I had to give it to him. He looked dashing in his tuxedo. I can honestly say I've never been ashamed to walk into a room with him. He's a handsome son of a gun. I didn't like him, but I'd play the loving wife role to a hilt if I needed to. I guess some may wonder why we share the same bed. Mostly because of what people would say. Image is very important to the two of us, and we didn't need for any of the hired help to get wind of the fact that we didn't share our bed. Considering Bill's status in Washington, DC, they'd sell the story for sure. Especially now, since Bill made the decision to run for congress. I loved being rich, but being an important politician's wife held even more notoriety.

"Hi, Daddy," Jessica smiled, hugging Bill tenderly. She never hugged me like that.

"Hi, Sweetheart," he flashed that gorgeous smile of his. Funny, he never smiled at me like that. "So, you wore the dress." He looked at her disapprovingly.

"I thought you liked it," Jessica pouted.

"No, I never said that," Bill said, shaking his head.

The two of them were so different, but, Daddy's opinion was very important to Jessica, and Bill was very protective of his daughter. They had a bond that made me jealous at times. Not enough to treat him better, but just enough to resent him.

"Dance with me, Daddy," Jessica said, pulling him away.

I looked a few feet away and saw Andrew dancing with some girl. I smiled as I walked over to him.

"I know it's not customary for the woman to ask a man to dance, but I haven't seen Andrew in ages," I smiled. "May I cut in?" I smiled, looking from him to his dance partner.

"Mrs. Riley, of course you can," the girl smiled. She stepped back as I joined Andrew.

As we danced, I struck up a conversation about Jessica. I knew my daughter would thank me later.

"So, who's your date?" I asked.

Andrew smiled. "She's not my date. She's Dr. Grayson's daughter. I'm surprised you don't know her."

"Was that Fallon? I haven't seen her since she

14

was in braces," I smiled. "That girl had the ugliest smile I'd ever seen. Braces were invented with her in mind. And those feet. They're still bigger than any horse's I've ever seen."

"I don't know. I think she's turned into a beautiful young woman," Andrew protested.

"The Ugly Duckling turned into a beautiful swan?" I responded coyly.

"Something like that," Andrew laughed.

"I must say, the real beauty in this room is Jessica," I said, looking in her direction. "Don't you just love that dress?"

"She does look good," Andrew smiled. I noticed that he seemed to be undressing my daughter with his eyes.

"She's quite fond of you, you know," I whispered.

"Oh? I got the feeling that she wasn't interested," Andrew said.

"Not interested? Oh, nothing could be further from the truth. We women have to play hard to get sometimes and my Jessica's no exception." I leaned in closer to whisper in his ear. "She told me about the two of you. Said you were like a stallion."

Andrew pulled away surprisingly. He looked embarrassed. "Sh-she told you about that?"

"Andrew, my daughter tells me everything. How would I know about the two of you being intimate unless she told me?" I said.

"Hmm. Maybe I should give her another shot," Andrew smiled.

"Go for it, Andrew. Eventually, she'll give in

15

to what she is feeling," I encouraged. "Why don't you go and ask her to dance?"

"What if she says no? She's dancing with her dad."

"I'll take care of Bill," I said. We stopped dancing and I grabbed Andrew's hand. "Come on, Andrew." We made our way through several people dancing and got to Jessica and Bill. "May I cut in?" I asked.

"Mother, I thought you were tired," Jessica said dryly.

"Oh, no. The night is still young," I smiled.

Bill looked at me venomously, until he noticed Andrew. He quickly turned his icy stare into a smile as he reached out to shake Andrew's hand. "Andrew, my boy, how are you?"

"Just fine, Mr. Riley, just fine. I bought a new thoroughbred last week. Maybe Jessica can come out to the ranch for a ride with me," Andrew said.

"I hate riding," Jessica said in protest.

"Jessica, you're an excellent rider," I said.

"I'd have to agree with your mother on that one," Bill smiled.

"So, it's settled? Why don't I pick you up tomorrow?" Andrew asked. "In the meantime, let's dance." He then grabbed Jessica's hand and led her away before she could protest further.

Despite Jessica's feelings towards him, the two of them went off to dance the night away. Jessica had drink after drink, which is probably why she was still willing to spend time with Andrew. After what seemed like an eternity, the party finally came to an

16

end. John had fun, and he got lots of gifts. Everyone's limo had come and gone, and the hired staff was cleaning up in the ballroom. I was exhausted.

When I got up to my room, I picked up the phone to call the airline. It was after 1 a.m. already, so I figured I'd better get a late flight. They had a flight leaving Washington, DC at 3:38 p.m. and arriving at 6:54 p.m. in South Carolina. I hope my sister gets a kick out of disrupting my life. But, I wasn't going to be the one not to show my support. I could only hope that Ellen wasn't going to be there. Of course, I hadn't gotten into a good catfight in a long time. That simple bitch makes it so easy. I don't think I'll ever forgive Ellen for what she did to me years ago. Any amount of hell she may be suffering through is still too good for her.

The next morning I awakened, glad that I was going to be getting away for a few days. I didn't want to see Bill, and Jessica worked my last nerve most of the time, so it would be nice to get away from her. She was home for the summer, and I would be so glad when it was time to go back. I loved her, but, I could only take my daughter in small doses. Matthew would be back tonight, and it wouldn't bother me not to see him either.

My oh-so-capable maid helped me to pack. I watched and shook my head as this idiot put sweaters into my suitcase. It was the middle of July.

"What are you doing?" I asked in frustration.

"Packing your bags, ma'am," she said, somewhat frightened.

17

"It's the middle of July. Why are you packing sweaters?" I asked.

"Well, because you're going to Myrtle Beach, ma'am. The beaches can be cool at night," she explained.

"This is not a pleasure trip! If I need sweaters, I'll buy them when I get there! Now, pack something more appropriate! God, how difficult is it for you to do one simple thing? Just pack the damned bags!"

"Y-Yes, ma'am," the maid said. She was almost in tears. Serves her right. Maybe she would finally learn to do what I tell her.

As What's-her-name was packing my bags, Bill came in. One of the drawbacks about Saturdays was that I couldn't get rid of him unless he was playing golf at our country club.

"Well, I see you're getting ready for your trip. I'm going to miss you so much, darling, until I'm coming with you," he said, kissing me on the cheek lightly.

I looked at him. "What?"

"I'm coming with you," he repeated.

"But, Sweetheart, you're a busy man, and I don't know how long I'll be there," I protested through clenched teeth. This miserable bastard was trying to ruin my plans. I looked at our maid. "Go on, I can finish up here," I said, wanting for her to leave. She nodded and walked out the door. As soon as the door closed I whirled around towards Bill. "What in the hell do you mean you're coming with me?"

"I'm going to see Millie for myself. There's nothing you can do to stop me. I've already called the

18

airline. I'll be in first class right next to my sweet wife," Bill said sarcastically.

"You know what? I hate you!" I said, lifting my hand to slap him. He grabbed my arm forcefully before I could slap him.

"If you slap me, Nora, it'll be the last thing you ever do," Bill said calmly. "Now, whether you go or not, I'm going. And there's not a damned thing you can do to stop me."

I jerked my hand away from him and massaged my wrist. Damn him! How could he do this to me? I wanted to get away from him. I'd gotten myself into a situation, because I really wasn't that interested in seeing my sister. I just wanted to leave for a few days. After a few moments, there was a knock on the door.

"What?!" I yelled.

"It's me, Mother," Jessica said.

"Come in, Sweetheart," Bill smiled, looking at me with steely eyes.

Jessica walked in, and looked at the two of us. She saw my suitcases on the bed. She smiled. "So, Mother, are you leaving."

"Don't sound so upset about it," I said. "But, I'm sorry to disappoint you. I'm going to South Carolina to visit your aunt."

"Well, considering there's no love lost between you and Aunt Millie, there has to be a more serious reason for your going to visit her," Jessica said as she sat on the sofa.

"She has cancer," I said.

"Wow, that's a bummer," Jessica said

nonchalantly. "For you to be going to see her, she must be about ready to check out."

"I'm sure my brother-in-law exaggerated a bit, but, I suppose I should check on her," I shrugged.

"Hmm, maybe I should go, too," Jessica said.

"You don't even like Millie," I said, turning up my nose.

"So? Neither do you and you're going," Jessica said.

"So much love in this room," Bill smiled, shaking his head.

"Oh, shut the hell up!" I said.

"Don't yell at Daddy! Let's make this a family thing," Jessica smiled.

"The two of you really know how to screw things up, don't you?" I said. "Now, why do you all of a sudden want to go?"

"It's either that or spend time trying to get rid of Andrew. This will be the perfect excuse for not going riding with him today or any other day. I need to see my precious aunt," Jessica sighed mockingly as she stood up.

"No, you need to see Andrew. If you're not careful you'll end up being nothing more than a spinster," I said.

"Nora, leave her alone. If she doesn't want Andrew, we sure as hell aren't going to force him on her," Bill said.

"You stay the hell out of this! This is between me and Jessica!" I yelled.

"Not when it involves you trying to push our daughter off on my partner's drunken son! She's not in love with Andrew!" Bill yelled.

"So? I'm not in love with you, and I'm still here!" I said. I got a small degree of satisfaction from the glint of hurt he tried to conceal.

"At least you finally admitted it," Bill said calmly. He then looked at Jessica. "The last thing I want is for my daughter to be as miserable as I am. Sweetheart, I'll call the airline and make you a reservation."

"Thank you, Daddy," Jessica smiled at her father. She then looked angrily at me. "As for you, Mother Dear, stay the hell out of my life! I'm going to pack." She then turned on her heel and walked out of the room.

I looked at Bill. "Do you have to pacify her all the time? You've turned her into nothing more than a spoiled brat!" I yelled.

"At least she's not useless, which is more than I can say for you," Bill said calmly as he dialed the number to the airline.

I fumed as I listened to him make a reservation for Jessica. As if things couldn't get more confusing, an hour later, Matthew got home. His best friend's dad dropped him off at home. He didn't need to find out about Millie, because for some reason, he thought she was the greatest thing since apple pie. Of course, at this point, what the hell? My husband and daughter had already ruined my trip. My only hope would be that Matthew was too jetlagged to want to board another plane the same day. He noticed Jessica's luggage in the foyer. "You going back to school, Jessie?" Matthew asked.

21

"Nah. Mother, Daddy and I are going to visit Aunt Millie. Say, why don't you come along?" Jessica said, nudging her brother. She then looked at me. "Mother would love to have you."

"Yeah, about as much as she would love living in poverty," Matthew laughed.

"Always a smartass comment," I said. "What in hell are you doing here so early?"

"Well, I'm glad to see you too, Mom," Matthew said. "But, to answer your question, we took an earlier flight."

"That's obvious," Jessica shrugged.

"It was a unanimous agreement to return early," Matthew said. "I'm jetlagged, and I just want to go to bed."

"Well, I'm glad you got back early," Bill said, patting Matthew on the back. "We were flying out this evening to South Carolina. Since you're jetlagged, I understand if you don't want to go with us."

"Is something wrong?" Matthew asked seriously.

"It's your aunt Millie. She has cancer," Bill said somberly.

"What?" Matthew said, shocked. My son was genuinely upset. "H-how is she?"

"She's sick, how do you think she is?" Jessica sighed.

"Shut up, Jess," Matthew said, looking at his sister. He then looked back at Bill. "Dad, book me on the flight with you."

"Are you sure? You just had a long flight,"

Bill said.

"Forget that," Matthew said, shaking his head. "I want to see Aunt Millie."

"Okay," Bill said, pulling out his cell phone. We listened as he made another reservation for Matthew. After he hung up the phone, he smiled. "Well, Son, I was able to get you on the flight in first class with the rest of us."

"Thanks, Dad," Matthew smiled.

"Wow, Dad, we're really going to rack up a lot of frequent flyer miles on this one," Jessica shrugged.

"Don't be a smart ass," I said.

"Don't be a bitch," Jessica retorted.

"Well, I see everything else is pretty normal around here," Matthew smiled. "The blissfully miserable Riley family going away together. I'm going to go upstairs and unpack some of this stuff and pack again. Where's Caroline?"

"Who?" I asked.

"The maid, Nora," Bill sighed. "She's in the kitchen. Caroline!" Bill called out.

She appeared out of nowhere, undoubtedly listening to our conversation. "Yes, Sir?"

"Matthew needs help getting his things unpacked. He's going with us, so if you could please help him pack clothes for the flight to South Carolina, I'd appreciate it," Bill smiled. "Yes, Sir," Caroline smiled, picking up one of Matthew's suitcases. They then went upstairs.

"Why are you so nice to her?" I asked.

"Because she's nice to me. You're the one with all the psychotic episodes, not me," Bill said.

"You don't have to say 'please' to someone you pay to do a job," I said.

"To put up with you, I get the feeling I don't pay her nearly enough," Bill said. "I'm going into my library until the limo arrives to take us to the airport." He then walked off to his private library, a place in which he allowed very few people.

One thing for sure, this was going to be a very interesting trip. The strange part is, we had no idea when we'd be back. I knew that Jessica had to be back at school in a couple of weeks, and Matthew's practice would be starting pretty soon. I wasn't going to put my life on hold for Millie when she didn't even have the decency to call and tell us about this herself when it first happened. The limo arrived around 2 p.m., and we all left for the airport. As I was getting in the car, I had a wave of uneasiness. Something told me that after this trip, my life would never be the same.

Chapter Two
Rhonda's story

As I lay there in pain, the shrilling ring of the telephone didn't help. I sighed as I sat up slowly to answer it. My ribs hurt. I held my side as I reached over to the bedside table to answer the phone. At this point, breathing hurt. I looked at the caller ID. South Carolina. Must be Millie. She can read me so well. I mustered a smile before answering the phone, as if she could see me. Millie always knew when something was wrong. But, after all these years, I'd gotten hiding wounds down to a science.

"Hello?" I answered, wincing slightly in pain.

"Rhonda? It's Clayton," my brother-in-law said. He sounded upset.

"Hi, Clayton. Is everything okay?" I asked.

"No, I'm afraid it's not. Rhonda, I called to let you know that Millie's in the hospital."

"The hospital? What happened? Was she in an

accident?" I asked, sitting up straighter.

"No, it wasn't an accident. She has cancer."

The words were like a knife piercing my heart. It was worse than any amount of abuse Aaron could ever inflict on me.

"C-Cancer? Oh, God, Clayton! What kind of cancer? When did she find out?" I asked. I had a million questions.

"It's a form of leukemia, and she was diagnosed a year ago," Clayton said.

"A year?" I asked, astonished, as a tear rolled down my face. "Well, why didn't she tell me?"

"She didn't want to worry you. Rhonda, I know its short notice, but, she needs her big sister now," Clayton said.

"I'm catching the first available flight. And, Clayton, tell Millie that I love her," I said.

"She loves you, too," Clayton responded. "Listen, if you call when you have a flight itinerary, I'll pick you up at the airport."

"No, that's okay. I'll rent a car at the airport," I said. "I know how proud and stubborn my sister can be. I'm the oldest out of the five of us, but Millie's always been the stronger one. How are you holding up?"

"I don't know at this point. The days are running together, and I'm exhausted with worry. I don't know what I'd do without her," Clayton said, his voice shaking. My brother-in-law was almost in tears.

"I'm going to be there for both of you. How are the kids holding up?" I asked.

"Kirsten and Kyle are fine. But, they're adults. Kirsten's a nurse, so, she's trained to know what to expect."

"She may be trained, but this is her mom, not just any patient," I said.

"You're right, but she's been great. The ones I'm worried about are Tim and Shauna," Clayton said.

"Yeah, but, they're strong kids," I encouraged.

"I know you're right, but why should they have to be strong? Millie's the last person who should be suffering like this."

"I agree. Millie's always been my rock," I said.

"Well, look, I'm not going to hold you. I'll let you make your travel plans. Call me the minute you get to Myrtle Beach," Clayton said.

"I will. Clayton, be strong for her," I said.

"Thank you, Rhonda."

"Do you need for me to call the others?" I asked.

"No, I'll take care of it. I've already called Nora, and that was a complete disaster. I don't think she even has a heart," Clayton said.

"My sister Nora's heart is pure ice," I said.

"She told me that she wasn't coming, and to tell Millie she hopes she feels better."

"That sounds like Nora," I sighed. "Look, don't take her words personally. Let me call her."

"No, don't worry about it. I thought about it after I hung up with her. Maybe it's for the best that she not be here. She'll only cause trouble and confusion."

"You're probably right. I'll call you later with my flight plans," I said.

"Okay, Rhonda. I'll see you soon," Clayton said.

"Bye, Clayton."

"Bye, Rhonda."

After hanging up with Clayton, I rose slowly from my bed. I was still really sore this time. I went to the closet and pulled out a suitcase from one of the shelves. I then looked up the number to the airline and called them. I was able to get a flight out the next afternoon. I was glad because maybe I could get away from Aaron for a few days. I looked at myself in the mirror. My eyes were puffy, and I looked a lot older than 45 years of age. It hadn't always been that way, but, after being with Aaron, abuse tends to age a person. He always said it was for my own good. I loved the lifestyle. I've never worked a day in my life, and my husband is head neurosurgeon at the best hospital in Colorado. He's so good, in fact, that they built an entire wing to coax him to stay five years ago. No doubt, he was the best doctor in his field. But, he failed miserably at being a husband. Hard as it is to believe, he is actually a good father to the children. Ginny and Aaron, Jr. have never wanted for anything. I angrily thought about the fact that neither does the illegitimate child he conceived 12 years ago with his longtime mistress. I'd been married to this man for 27 years, and the abuse was evident from the very beginning. I managed to keep it quiet from everyone, including my own children. Aaron was smart. He never punched me in the face, but he would slap me because they don't bruise as bad. He wanted his 'model wife' to always look the part.

As I packed, I breathed a sigh of relief. I could get away from him for a few days. While I hated that my sister was sick, it was the perfect excuse to leave without his getting mad. My hands were shaking with nervousness and anxiety. I knew that I was taking the coward's way out. I wanted to have my bags packed, but, I didn't want to tell my husband yet. I wanted to be safely in South Carolina before telling him. I'd given our housekeeper, Agnes, the day off, and I knew that Aaron would be home late. She spied on me for him. She told him everything I did. It was like living in a prison.

At least our children were adults now. Ginny is 25, the same age as Clayton and Millie's son Kyle. Aaron, Jr., or AJ as we call him, is 22, which is a year younger than their daughter Kirsten. I'm so proud of the both of them. Ginny is climbing the corporate ladder as one of the youngest associates at her marketing firm. AJ is getting ready for medical school. He'd already been accepted, and is now at orientation. He will be starting in a few weeks in Arizona to study anesthesiology. I hope that being a doctor is the only way he will follow in his father's footsteps. After getting my bags packed, I took them down to the garage to place them in the trunk of my car. Agnes would be back tomorrow, and I didn't need for her spying on the fact that I was carrying luggage to my car. I'd leave my car parked at the airport. After getting everything stowed away in the trunk, I went to the salon for my weekly hair appointment. My beautician, Darcy usually cheered me up.

"Hi, Rhonda! Right on time!" Darcy smiled. I marveled at how she didn't seem to have a care in the world.

"I always am," I smiled as I sat in her chair.

"Oh, honey, I've got to do something about all this breakage! You've got such beautiful hair, but who can tell with the way it breaks off!? I'm going to cut it, okay?" she asked, looking at me for approval.

"You know I don't like to cut it," I sighed.

"Rhonda, look, you're beautiful, but who's going to know it with bad hair? Now, I've been avoiding cutting it for months. It won't be much, maybe three inches, four inches at the most," Darcy reasoned.

"O-Okay," I smiled.

"Good! Now, sit back, relax and let me take care of you," Darcy said.

I sighed, as my chair reclined so that she could wash my hair. Aaron hated short hair. Maybe he wouldn't notice. After all, he barely seemed to notice me anyway when he wasn't beating on me. I stayed at the hairdresser for another two hours while she worked her magic. I was very pleased with the result when I saw myself in the mirror.

"Well? What do you think?" Darcy smiled.

I smiled slightly as I looked at my reflection staring back at me. "I love it."

"Good," Darcy smiled. She placed her hands on my shoulder lightly. "Rhonda, is everything okay?"

"I just found out some very disturbing news today," I said.

"Anything you want to talk about?" Darcy asked, as she put the finishing touches on my hair.

"My brother-in-law called today. My sister has cancer," I said tearfully.

"Oh, I'm so sorry!" Darcy said. "What kind of cancer does she have?"

"It's some form of leukemia," I said. "I don't know all the details yet."

"Janice Frye's sister had a form of leukemia," Darcy said. "And remember? Janice donated bone marrow to save her sister's life."

"I'd forgotten about that," I smiled slightly, looking up at her. "I wonder if that's an option for Millie?"

"It could be. You never know, you might be a perfect match for her," Darcy said encouragingly.

"I'd do it in a heartbeat. Millie deserves every chance to beat this," I said, reaching into my purse to pay her. "I'm going to fly out to see her."

"Thank you," Darcy said, as she retrieved the money. "So, when are you leaving?"

"Tomorrow," I sighed. "I just hope I can help her."

Darcy smiled as she looked at me. "I'm going to keep good thoughts."

"Thank you," I smiled. "Look, I have to go and get dinner on the table before Aaron gets home."

"Are things better at home?" Darcy asked.

"They'll never get better," I said solemnly, standing from the chair. "I have to go."

"Okay, and good luck to you," Darcy said.

"Thanks. I may not be in next week according to how my sister does."

"Well, good luck. I'll see you whenever you get back," Darcy smiled.

"Okay," I smiled. "Bye, Darcy."

I left the salon with a ray of hope for my sister. I quickly drove home to fix dinner. I was still determined not to tell Aaron about Millie yet. I worked peacefully for the first time in ages in my own kitchen. I was still so worried about my sister. I mean, what if the bone marrow transplant isn't enough? As I was preparing dinner, Ginny came by.

"Mmm, something smells good," she smiled as she leaned in to kiss me slightly on the cheek. She stepped back and observed my new hairdo. "I love your hair! You got it cut and it looks great!"

"Thanks, Dear. So, what brings you by to visit your mom?" I smiled.

"Just wanted to see how things were going. I'm meeting Keith for dinner tonight, and your house just happens to be on the way to the restaurant. I suppose now that AJ and I are out of the house, you and Dad can have a lot more romantic nights," Ginny smiled.

I mustered a smile. "Something like that."

"Is everything okay? You look upset," Ginny said seriously.

"I got a disturbing phone call earlier," I said.

"Well, who was it from?"

"Your uncle Clayton. He told me that your aunt has a form of leukemia."

"What? Aunt Millie has cancer?" Ginny said, astonished. I could see the tears welling up in her eyes. "What's her prognosis?"

"Not good, from what Clayton was telling me. I'm taking a flight out tomorrow morning to visit her for a few days. I'm going to talk to her about being a bone marrow donor for her if it's an option."

"Let me come with you," Ginny offered.

"No, dear, that's not necessary," I said.

"Mom, I insist. You know how much I love Aunt Millie. I want to be there for her," Ginny said.

"But, what about work?" I asked.

"I've got vacation time I need to use anyway," Ginny smiled.

"Okay," I smiled. "I'll call the airline and reserve your ticket."

"Is Daddy going?"

"No. I haven't told him yet," I said a little too anxiously. Ginny looked at me strangely. "Would you do me a favor?"

"Sure, anything, you know that," Ginny said.

"Don't mention this to your father," I said.

"Why not?"

"Please don't ask questions. Just, please, keep it quiet."

"Mom, is everything okay between you and Dad?"

"Of course, it is. Your dad's just under a lot of stress at work, and I want to make things as easy on him as possible."

"But, you're leaving for South Carolina tomorrow. When are you going to tell him?" Ginny

33

asked.

"I'll call him once we get there," I said.

"Why?" Ginny asked suspiciously. "Why on earth would you wait until you've gotten out of town before telling your husband unless you're running away from him?"

"Sweetheart, don't read too much into it," I insisted.

"Mom, you can tell me anything," Ginny said, covering my hand gently with hers.

"I-I'll be fine," I smiled, fighting back the tears that were threatening to fall.

She looked at me intently, wanting for me to confide in her. Finally, she conceded.

"I'll be by here first thing in the morning, or do you want for me to meet you at the airport?" Ginny asked.

"Just meet me at the airport," I mustered a smile.

I looked earnestly at my daughter. It was as if she knew, but refrained from pushing me about it. Did she know? Did my daughter know that her father was abusing me? I've always tried desperately to hide it from her. But, she's a smart girl. She'd been on her own since she graduated from college. Even then, she stayed in the dorms or in an apartment off campus. So, it had been easy for the past seven years to keep it from her.

After visiting with me for a few minutes more, and after calling the airline to see if we could get her on a flight with me, she left to meet her boyfriend for dinner. I sighed heavily as I wondered what type of mood my husband would be in tonight. I'd been abused just about every day since we'd been married. Even when I found out about his mistress, he turned the tables on me, telling me that if I were more of a woman, he wouldn't have turned to anyone else. He told me that he married me under false pretenses, because when we met, I was in pageants, and I modeled quite a bit. I quit doing that after we got married because he demanded a lot of my time. Even though he's the one who went into a jealous rage every time a man looked at me, he managed to make my quitting all my fault. When I decided to become a fulltime housewife, I still made sure I looked good every day. I always wore makeup, I dressed in nice clothes, I kept my hair in excellent condition. Ironically, my hair had been breaking off from stress, which was caused by my husband. Despite everything I did to be a model wife, it was never good enough.

My children don't even know that their father killed two of their siblings. Before I had Ginny, I was pregnant. My husband beat me so terribly, kicking me in the stomach, until I miscarried. I was also pregnant again after AJ, and once again, he beat me causing me to have another miscarriage.

Aaron played such mind games with me. He would tell me to dress provocatively for him on some nights by the time he got home from work. I'd do it, and he would show up with friends of his to watch a football game. I'd be so embarrassed by it. He'd belittle me for dressing that way, although it was his suggestion. He has humiliated and hurt me on more occasions than I can even remember.

I was brought back to reality when I heard Aaron pull into the garage. I closed my eyes and let out a deep sigh as I prayed that he would be in a good mood tonight. I nervously chopped tomatoes for a salad, and I realized my hands were trembling. I had a glass of chardonnay to calm my nerves, and I had jazz playing in the background. Maybe in a relaxed atmosphere, he might be in a better mood. I had his cognac patiently waiting in a brandy snifter for him. I waited for what felt like an eternity before he finally came through the door. He walked in calmly, not even speaking.

"Hello," I smiled slightly, picking up the brandy snifter from the counter. I passed the drink to him with frigid, shaking hands. He reached for it and downed the brown liquid. I breathed a sigh of relief. Usually, he was in a better mood once he'd had a drink before dinner. "I-I made your favorite. Beef burgundy and asparagus spears with a hollandaise sauce."

"Whatever," Aaron sighed. He tossed his newspaper on the counter as he walked into the dining room with his drink. "Anything interesting happen today?"

"No, nothing," I said, as I placed the asparagus into a serving dish.

I'd already set the table and placed warm rolls out. I finished putting the dinner out as Aaron watched me. He loosened his tie, as it seemed to hold all the stresses from the entire day.

"Hurry up with dinner," he demanded, as he sat

at the head of the table. "Where's Agnes? I swear, it takes you forever. You have nothing to do during the day, and yet you still act like getting a simple meal is rocket science."

"Everything's ready," I said. I stood next to him and fixed his plate with shaking hands.

"I hope it tastes better than it smells," Aaron barked.

"I-I know it's your favorite," I said.

"Yeah, it was until you started cooking it," Aaron mumbled.

I sat down at the other end of the table after serving him. He ate quietly, never once looking at me. I wanted desperately to talk to him about Millie, but, he wouldn't understand what I was feeling. I loved my sister, and if I could help her, I was determined to do just that. Aaron looked at me after he finished his meal. He tilted his head ever so slightly as he just stared at me.

"You cut your hair," Aaron observed.

"It-it was badly damaged," I said timidly, reaching up to stroke my hair.

"Hmm," Aaron shrugged. "It looks good," he smiled.

I let out a huge sigh of relief. I watched as he got up from his chair and walked over to me. Maybe he'd feel more attracted to me. I smiled, thinking that for once in a long time I'd pleased my husband. He stared at me eerily. With one swift move, he slapped me hard across the face with the back of his hand. It was done with enough force to knock me to the floor. As I lay there, he reached down and pulled me up by

37

my hair.

"Ow! Pl-Please, Aaron!" I cried.

"I told you never to cut your hair!" Aaron yelled, slapping me hard again.

"I-I'm sorry, Aaron! I pr-promise not to cut it again!" I sobbed.

"You lying, pathetic piece of trash! When I tell you not to do something, you don't do it. You understand me!?" At that moment, he kicked me in the stomach several times. "You bitch! Don't ever defy me again!"

I started to cough, wanting desperately to die. I watched in horror as Aaron took the serving dishes off of the dining room table and smashed them to the floor.

He was breathing hard. "Now, clean this mess up and come to bed!" Aaron said, walking out of the room.

I lay there and cried. I tried so hard to please him. This beating only reiterated how much I was looking forward to getting away from him. Aaron had managed to destroy everything in me. I stood slowly from the floor, overwhelmed by sharp pains in my stomach. I immediately fell to the floor again, crying. I sat up slowly, resting my back against the wall. As I cried, I looked around to survey the damage. I had half a mind to save it for Agnes, but, I knew that Aaron would come back downstairs to see if I'd cleaned it up. I couldn't take him hitting me again. After sitting there for another half hour, I slowly got up. I started to pick up the large pieces of my beautiful serving dishes off of the floor. I loved those pieces. They were a wedding gift from my parents, and to me they were priceless. I cried as I cleaned the mess up. By the time I finished cleaning my beautiful hardwood floor in the dining room, and trying to get stains out of the Oriental rug, I was exhausted. After getting the dining room in perfect condition, I still needed to clean my kitchen. Once the dishwasher was loaded and everything was done, I was finally able to go upstairs.

Every step was a precious gift because I was in so much pain. When I got to the bedroom, I paused slightly before opening the door. I sighed heavily, not sure what awaited me. I could see the light was still on underneath the door. I turned the knob and walked in slowly. He was lying in bed reading innocently. He looked in my direction and took off his glasses.

"Go and take a shower; get cleaned up and wear that," he said, pointing to a negligee he'd draped over the chair.

I walked slowly to the chair, retrieved the negligee with shaking hands and made my way towards the bathroom as a stream of tears rolled down my face. I wasn't sure how much longer I would be able to take this. I went into the bathroom and got into the shower. While the hot water soothed my soreness, he'd broken the skin on my side, and I didn't realize it until the hot water hit it. I wanted to yell out in pain, but I knew he'd take immense pleasure in knowing how much he'd hurt me once again. So, I winced quietly in pain. As my tears blended with the water from the shower, I wondered what I'd done to deserve this treatment from him. He'd gotten progressively worse towards me over the years. I wanted desperately for my shower to last all night, or at least until he fell asleep. Obviously, that wasn't an option. After prolonging it for as long as possible, I stepped out and dried myself slowly. As I put on lotion and the perfume he always made me wear, I looked in disgust at the negligee. If I thought my husband loved me and that it would please him, I would have put it on without hesitation. Aaron wanted to degrade me, make me feel like a whore. I felt the tears welling up again as I stepped into the negligee. When I came out of the bathroom, he looked at me, closed his book and placed it on the night table. I walked slowly to the bed and pulled back the covers.

"Not yet," he said. "Take it off."

"B-But I just put it on," I said.

"Take it off," he said with more force. There was no love, no passion, just hateful demands.

I reached to my shoulders and slowly pulled the straps down, crying as the negligee fell from my body.

"Aaron, please don't do this to me."

"Shut up. Come here," he said.

I stood still and cried.

"Dammit, I said come here!" he yelled. "You're pathetic. Just look at you. You should be thankful I want to touch you at all! A model. You've let yourself go, Rhonda."

"I-I'm sorry, Aaron," I cried.

"Sorry isn't good enough. Now, come to me," he said again.

I got in next to my husband, who I noticed at that moment was naked. He pulled me to him hard and entered me. His thrusts were hard and painful, and I got no pleasure in his making love to me. Making love. It wasn't making love; it was sex. Thoughtless, heartless, impassionate sex. My moans were not from pleasure but from pain. Tears streamed down my face as he continued his onslaught. No one should have to be treated this way. When he finished emptying himself in me, he turned over on his back.

"Go take another shower. Get that stench off of you," he said cruelly.

"Aaron, I'm tired," I cried.

"I don't care! Go take another shower! Make it a good one. I don't need you smelling like a whore while lying next to me," he said. "I'm going to sleep." My husband then turned his back to me.

I sighed heavily as I got up and went back to the bathroom. I took another shower, still hurting from earlier, only to have the added pain of rough sex. I was numb. I couldn't even cry anymore.

"Only a few more hours," I said to myself.

At that moment, I made the conscious decision that I would not be coming back. I went over in my mind what I needed to do. I knew the moment he discovered my leaving that he'd cancel my credit cards. I decided to get cash advances and go to the bank to make a large withdrawal the next day. Our flight was due to leave at 12:30 p.m. I thought about the fact that I probably shouldn't have put our plane tickets on my credit card. It wouldn't matter, because once I was away from him, I'd never come back. I'd packed the most important things to me, and anything else, I'd worry about later. After I finished my shower, I put on something I was most comfortable in. He wouldn't care at this point, because he'd gotten what he wanted for the night. I wryly thought about the fact that his mistress must have been out of town or angry with him. Sometimes, I preferred for him to spend the night with her. It was the only time I got any peace. But, Agnes reported everything to him, so I was still a prisoner in my own home.

The next morning, I awakened to an empty bed. Thank God. He'd gotten up and left around 5:30 a.m. It was a Saturday, but, he was at the hospital anyway to check on his patients. He was such a dedicated surgeon. If only his patients and colleagues knew how he really was. If only his children knew how he really was. I knew that if I spoke up I could ruin him. Did I love the opulent lifestyle at any cost? Obviously, I did. I'd endured the abuse for 27 years, never leaving him. What did I think would happen if people found out? He could go to prison, lose his license. We'd be ruined financially. I couldn't even give myself the excuse that I'd done it for our children. I did it for them, but, I did it for myself also. I was so afraid of what the outside world had to offer. I even wondered now what I expected by going to Millie's. I knew I wanted to be with my sister, but, she couldn't protect me from Aaron. I wouldn't want her to. Did I really think Aaron wouldn't embarrass me in front of my family? Of course he would. I was getting scared, because I would possibly have to come back to this maniac. I really hadn't thought anything through. But, I had to do it. I'd rather roll the dice and see what happens than endure another day of his abuse. With that thought, I got up from my bed and looked at the clock. It was 7:30 a.m. The banks would open at 9 a.m. As I was getting my thoughts together, AJ called.

"Hello?" I answered.

"Hey, Mom," AJ's cheerful voice was just what I needed to hear.

"Hi, Sweetheart! How are things?"

"Great. My orientation is just about over, and I'll get to come home for a couple of weeks before medical school starts. I talked to Ginny last night. She told me about Aunt Millie."

"I'm so worried about her," I sighed. "Ginny and I are leaving this afternoon to see her."

"Listen, I finish up here today. I'm going to fly down there as well tomorrow morning, okay?"

"I think your aunt would like that," I smiled.

"Mom, are you okay?"

"I'm fine, Sweetheart," I said.

"Ginny's worried about you," AJ said.

"Just Ginny?" I probed.

"Well, maybe I'm a little worried, too," AJ said slowly.

"Don't worry about me. I'm fine," I lied. If only he knew. I was far from fine.

"I worry because I love you, Mom."

"Well, I love you too, AJ. But, I want you to concentrate on medical school. That's what's important now."

"Has Dad left for the hospital?"

"Yes, he left around 5:30 this morning," I said.

"I'm excited to talk to him about the medical school here in Arizona. I know he wants for me to do my residency in his hospital, but, they've got an excellent facility up here."

"Son, do what makes you happy. Don't conform to other people's expectations of you, not even your father's when it comes down to your peace of mind."

"I know, you're right," AJ sighed. "Well, I've got a little while to think about it."

"Exactly. Well, listen, Sweetie. I have a million things to do today before our flight leaves. I'll call you when we get to South Carolina."

"Be careful, Mom."

"I will. I'll talk to you later."

I then hung up with AJ, hoping he wouldn't talk to his father before I was safely in South Carolina. I don't know why I didn't tell him not to tell his father of my whereabouts. I suppose I knew he'd ask me a million questions. AJ was like my father. He wanted to know everything. It was easier just to hope he wouldn't talk to Aaron until later tonight.

I was finally able to leave home around 8:30, and I went straight to the banks to wait for them to open. I went in and withdrew funds from three different banks, and got advances on all of my credit cards. Thankfully, I was on the accounts with no restrictions. I now had enough cash to help me get started if I needed to. I was a little nervous about carrying around so much cash, because I typically used

44

credit cards to pay for everything. I called Ginny from the car around 10 a.m., and she told me that she was about to head to the airport. I had the money split between my purse, pockets, and carry bag. Maybe the airline security wouldn't question it with it not all being together. I almost felt like a criminal trying to smuggle in money.

As I stood in line to retrieve our tickets, I spotted Ginny. She made her way through the crowds and hugged me. She looked at all of my luggage and then at me.

"Why are you taking so much luggage?" Ginny asked.

"Well, I don't know how long I'll have to be there. If Millie needs a bone marrow transplant and I'm a good match, I might be there for a while," I explained.

"Mom, are you leaving Daddy?" Ginny asked pointblank.

"Ginny, please, don't take it so extreme," I smiled lightly.

After we finished getting our luggage checked in, we went through security with no problem. I looked at my daughter and wondered what she was thinking. I knew that there was going to come a time really soon when I'd have to explain it all to her. Now just wasn't the time. I needed to be there for my sister. In order to do that, I had to put my own problems aside. As we settled into our seats, I sat back and breathed a sigh of relief. I'd gotten away. My eyes became misty as I realized I'd finally done it. I'd left my husband. Somehow, I felt that after this trip, my life would never be the same.

Chapter Three
Ellen's Story

I awakened wondering where I was. My head was clouded with vague memories of what happened the night before. I looked around, realizing I had no idea where I was. I was about to get out of the bed when I noticed that I was naked. I heard the shower running in the bathroom. Did Jim and I go out of town? Where was I? I looked around for my clothes, and saw three empty liquor bottles. My clothes were strayed on the floor, and I saw a pair of jeans and a dingy white t-shirt lying there as well. I looked on the night table and there was a gun with a silencer. I knew it wasn't mine because I didn't own one, and Jim's looked nothing like that one. I quickly got out of the bed and reached down to retrieve my clothes. As I started to dress, I hadn't noticed that the shower had turned off. The man stepping from the bathroom startled me.

47

"Hey, Doll!" he smiled.

I jumped as I turned around. "Wh-Who are you?" I asked.

"You don't remember me?" he asked, almost surprised.

"No, I don't!" I yelled. My heart was racing. I'd spent the night with a man who wasn't my husband.

"I'm Ray. We just had four hours of great sex, and you don't remember me?"

"I-I slept with you?" I asked, with tears in my eyes.

I'd hit rock bottom. No matter how much I drank, I'd not cheated on my husband. At least, I didn't remember cheating on him. I suppose I should say I've never been slapped in the face with the truth about cheating on him. I've gone on drunken binges before, and there are days of my life that I don't even remember. But, this? This was a nightmare. I knew exactly what happened. I shook my head, desperately trying to make sense of it all.

"You don't remember sleeping with me? Come on, Doll, let me refresh your memory," Ray said, pulling me roughly to him, kissing me hard on the lips.

I fought to get away from him, pressing hard against his chest, trying to push him away from me. Eventually, I got him to let go of me. I backed away and wiped my mouth. "I'm a married woman!" I yelled.

"Married? Who cares? So am I, and you don't see me crying over it! We had a good time last night," Ray shrugged.

"I-I don't even remember meeting you," I said, shaking my head.

"We met at Casey's Bar last night, and you were looking good, Doll," Ray laughed.

"Casey's Bar? I-I went in for one drink," I said softly.

"One drink? Doll, by the time I approached you, you were ripe for the picking. I watched you from a nearby table, and you downed five drinks in 10 minutes. I offered to buy you another one, you accepted. Next thing I know, we're buying three bottles of vodka, and checking into this hotel as 'Mr. and Mrs. John Smith,'" Ray laughed. "You were a barrel of fun, Doll."

"'A barrel of fun'? You took advantage of me!" I screamed.

"Nah, Doll. You took advantage of me, or don't you remember?" Ray said, reaching up to touch my face.

"Get your hands off of me!" I said, slapping his hand away.

"You were an animal!" Ray smiled. "Now, I'd like a replay of last night." He then grabbed me again.

"No!" I yelled.

"Shut up, you slut! You were all over me last night!" Ray yelled.

He then slapped me across the face and pushed me down on the bed. He dropped his towel to the floor, as I noticed his manhood was hard. He got on top of me and ripped off my underwear. He then

49

entered me hard, raping me.

"No! Pl-please, don't!" I cried. "No!" My mind then wandered back over twenty years before. "Daddy, no!"

"Yeah, that's right! I'm your daddy!" Ray moaned, misunderstanding what I said.

"St-Stop it!" I said, pushing him hard. I looked over at the night table and spied the gun. I stretched my arm and reached for it. I cocked it in his face. "Get off me!" I demanded, holding the gun on him.

He immediately stopped his thrusts, obviously startled. He then smiled. "You're not going to use that, Doll."

"Get off of me, or I will blow your head off!" I said through clenched teeth.

"Fine! You weren't that good anyway!" Ray said, getting up. "Stupid bitch! Only reason I'm here is because you paid for everything! Hell, you're not even that good looking!"

"Get out before I call the police! You raped me!" I screamed as tears ran down my face.

"I'll get out, you pathetic drunk! You're not worth it! Look at you! No one would believe I raped you!" Ray yelled.

At that very moment, Ray morphed into Daddy, and I thought back to Daddy saying the exact same thing to me after he raped me.

"No one would believe I raped you!" Daddy's voice echoed in my mind.

I shook my head as I tried to get the image of Daddy out of my head. When I couldn't take hearing his voice over and over, I fired a shot, directly into the wall, only inches away from Ray. At that very moment, I realized what I'd done. It startled Ray enough to stop him from talking. Thank goodness I was a terrible shot, or else I could have killed him.

"Look, Doll, if you want to leave, go ahead," Ray said, his voice shaking as he held his hands up.

"G-get out of my way!" I said, putting on my pants, still holding the gun.

"Alright, alright," Ray said. "Just calm down. Put the gun down."

"As soon as I get out!" I said. I grabbed my purse and keys. I motioned for him to move with the gun. "Get away from the door."

Ray then moved from the door with his hands up. My hands were shaking as I opened the door and rushed out. My car was parked in the parking lot. I got in and drove off quickly. I didn't look back, as the tears streamed down my face. What had I done? I'd cheated on my husband, and I'd been violated again. I'd almost killed a man, all because of my drinking. I stopped at a nearby dumpster and wiped my prints off the gun before disposing of it. Before long, I found myself in Manhattan traffic. I wanted to get home to my family. My daughter, Amanda and I were already on shaky ground, and now my staying out all night wouldn't help matters any. I wondered if I had it in me to be a good mother. I should be a good example for my daughter instead of always making excuses for my screw-ups.

How would I explain not coming home last night? Jim was probably worried sick about me. I pulled into the parking garage and caught the elevator up to the 24th floor, where our penthouse apartment was located. We used to have a housekeeper, but because of my drinking problem, we were in financial trouble. Between rehab and bail, not to mention the destruction of property, he'd paid out so much money just to keep me out of trouble. Thankfully, we didn't have to give up our home. When I went in, my daughter was in the kitchen preparing lunch. I made a beeline straight upstairs to my bedroom, because the last thing I wanted was a confrontation with her. Jim wasn't there. I went into the bathroom immediately to shower. I felt dirty and cheap. I wanted to get rid of all reminders of what I'd done the night before. As I showered, I started to think about what I was doing to my husband. I seemed to be making matters worse and worse for him. As if he didn't have enough stress. Jim is a pharmacist, who now owns a pharmaceutical company. Instead of being there as a good wife, I continuously made matters worse for myself. He has always been a loving and supportive husband, even when I didn't deserve it. He'd even surprised me with my own coffee shop a few years before. Because of my drinking, unfortunately, it was running itself more than I did. I had a good manager and staff, but, I honestly had no idea about anything going on.

Now, I may have pushed the envelope a little too far. When my husband came back to me after our separation a few months before, I swore I'd not drink again. But, this might be too much. When I finished showering, I put on my robe and stepped out into my bedroom. I suddenly became overwhelmed by everything. I sat on my bed and cried. As I sat there, Amanda came in.

"Well, the epitome of loving mothers comes home," Amanda said sarcastically.

"Not now, Amanda," I sighed, holding my head.

"What? Are those tears? Daddy's been out all night looking for you. You're destroying his life! I hate you! I wish you would just die!"

"Amanda, no, please don't say that," I cried, shaking my head.

"Go back to your bottle, you pathetic bitch! I wish he would leave you! You don't deserve him!"

"Honey, I--"

"I don't want to hear it! Daddy's been worried sick about you. Although, you're not worth worrying about. I wasn't worried. I figured you'd crawl out from that bottle at some point and resurface your pathetic face!"

"Amanda, that's enough," Jim said from behind her.

I looked in my husband's direction as tears fell down my face. He looked tired and emotionally drained. He was hurt by me once again. How much longer could our marriage last like this?

"But, Daddy, she did it to us again! Why do you keep forgiving her?"

"I said that's enough Amanda. Leave your mom and me alone. She and I have to talk," Jim said, looking at me.

Amanda looked at me disgustedly and sighed.

53

She then looked at her father. "Okay, Daddy. I have lunch ready for you." She then hugged Jim and kissed him on the cheek.

"Thank you, Sweetheart," Jim said.

Jim then closed the door, and sat down on the sofa in our bedroom. He looked at me and sighed.

"I-I know I hurt you, Jim. I-I'm so sorry," I cried, shaking my head.

"I've had it, Ellen. I want a divorce," Jim said quietly.

"P-please give me another chance!"

"For what? More lies? More drinking binges? Why don't you tell me where you were all night?"

"Casey's Bar," I answered.

"Casey's Bar closes at 4 a.m. I know because I've been there enough times looking for you. It's almost noon. What have you been doing since then?" Jim asked.

"I-I--" I was at a loss for words. How do I tell him I spent the night with another man?

"Looking for the right lie to tell?" Jim asked sarcastically. He held his hand up. "You know what. Save it. I don't think I could stand another one of your lies."

"No, Jim, I need to be honest with you," I sighed. I closed my eyes, trying to find the words to tell him about my infidelity. There were times when I've been out all night and at hotel rooms, but, this was the first time I knew for a fact that I'd cheated on him.

"I'm listening, because it will definitely be a first," Jim said, folding his arms as he leaned back on the sofa.

"Jim, I was with another man last night," I said quietly.

"What did you say?" Jim asked, as he sat up.

"I-I slept with a man I met last night at Casey's Bar," I said, as tears fell down my cheek.

I could see tears welling in Jim's eyes. It killed me to say those words to him, but, I owed it to him to be honest. It's something I'd not done in a long time.

"How do you expect for me to respond to that?" Jim asked calmly. "I shouldn't be surprised. You've stayed out all night so many times, and I always knew there was the possibility that you'd cheated on me. Now, at least I know the truth."

"But, it's not me, Jim. It's the alcohol. I love you," I cried.

"Who do you think is drinking the alcohol? It's you, Ellen! It's you all the way! Alcohol is a crutch for you! You won't stay sober despite what it's doing to your family! Did you hear the hate in our daughter's voice a few minutes ago? She hates you, Ellen! Your child, the child you gave birth to, hates you! Doesn't that do something to you!? Doesn't it do something to you when you break my heart over and over again?"

"Jim, I'm so sorry! What can I do to make this up to you?"

"Nothing, Ellen. You've tried rehab, and it obviously didn't work. We don't have a marriage anymore," Jim whispered. At that very moment, the phone rang. I wanted to ignore it, but Jim answered it. "Hello? Hi, Clayton. How are you? Yeah, she's right here," he said, holding the phone out to me. I got up from my bed and went to sit next to Jim on the sofa as I retrieved the phone.

"Hi, Clayton," I smiled slightly.

"Ellen, how are you?" Clayton asked.

"I'm fine. Is something wrong?" I asked.

"Yeah, there is. I'm calling about Millie. She has cancer," Clayton said.

"C-Cancer? Wh-what? Wh-what kind? When was she diagnosed?" I was shaking. At that very moment, I desperately wanted a drink.

"She has leukemia," Clayton said.

"Well, how long has she known?" I asked.

"For almost a year," Clayton responded.

His words were like an echo in my ears.

"Almost a year? How could Millie have cancer for almost a year and she not tell me?"

"She didn't want to worry any of you. Things aren't looking too good, and I thought it would help her to see you."

"I'm catching the first flight out," I said, looking at Jim. "Clayton, I'm so sorry this happened. Have you talked to the others?"

"I've talked to Nora and Rhonda. Nora's not coming, but, Rhonda will be here as soon as she can get a flight out. I haven't called Gina yet," Clayton sighed.

"Do you want for me to call her?" I offered.

"No, I need to do it myself. I'm just glad you're coming. I know Millie would love to see you," Clayton said.

"I would love to see her, too. We've not been together since--" I stopped in mid-sentence.

"Not since your father's funeral ten years ago," Clayton finished.

I couldn't bring myself to mention that horrible man, but, Clayton didn't know anything about what I'd endured at my father's hands. For that matter, neither did my husband.

"How are my nieces and nephews holding up? I know this has to be hard on them."

"It is. Kyle and Kirsten are strong, and they've been such a big help to me. I'm worried about Tim and Shauna, though."

"Well, Shauna's only 12. I'm sure she has to be scared out of her mind that she's going to lose her mother. And as far as Tim's concerned, let's face it, 15 year olds deal with things a lot different from the way adults do," I said.

"I know you're right. Well, listen, I have to go. Call me when you find out your flight itinerary, okay? Either Kyle, Kirsten or I will pick you up at the airport."

"No, I'll rent a car at the airport or catch a cab. Don't worry about me. I'll be fine," I smiled. "Is Millie in the hospital right now?"

"Yeah, but, she's going home tomorrow morning. She's been doing rounds of chemotherapy and steroids, and she's had a couple of complications. But, they're letting her out tomorrow."

"I'll be there for all of you, Clayton. Tell Millie I love her and that I'll be there as soon as possible."

"I will. I'll see you when you get here, Ellen. Talk to you soon."

"Bye, Clayton," I said, hanging up the phone.

"Millie has cancer?" Jim whispered.

"Yeah," I said, breaking down into tears.

Jim reached out to hold me, as I buried my face in his chest. "It's going to be okay. I'll go to South Carolina with you."

I sat up to look at him. "Jim, you don't have to. I know you hate me right now, and I deserve every bit of it," I cried.

"I don't hate you, Ellen. I love you. You have to stop doing this to yourself."

I laughed slightly through my tears. "You know, out of all of us, Millie was the one perfect child? Outside of an occasional social drink, she never touched the stuff. And look at me. I'm a falling down drunk and I can't seem to get it together. Why is she the one that's sick? It should be me fighting cancer right now!" I cried.

"Don't say that, Ellen. Look, I'll make flight arrangements for the three of us."

"Amanda's not going to want to go," I said.

"Amanda doesn't have any say in the matter. After what she's done the past couple of years, we can't trust her yet, Ellen. She might go kicking and screaming, but she's going to be on that flight with us," Jim smiled slightly. "Don't worry, Ellen. Everything will be just fine."

"What did I ever do to deserve you?" I asked. "How can I make any of this up to you?"

"Stop drinking. We're going to have to go to

58

counseling if we stand any chance of saving this marriage. Get back into rehab if that's what it takes. Go get tested. We don't know anything about the man you were with," Jim said.

"I'll do it all," I said anxiously. "Thank you for not closing the door on us."

"Clayton's call did it. I thought fleetingly about how I would feel if that were you. I'm willing to try if you are."

"Yes, Jim! I'm willing! I love you so much!" I smiled, hugging him.

After talking for a few minutes more, Jim called the airline to reserve tickets to South Carolina. Maybe this trip to see my family was just what we needed. New York held too many temptations for me, and I needed to get away for a while. When I think about what could have happened to me, I realized how blessed I was to still be alive. That stranger I was with could have killed me.

Jim was able to get a reservation for the following morning. I was looking forward to seeing Rhonda. A part of me was glad that Nora wouldn't be there. Nora and I haven't gotten along since we were teenagers. I never understood my sister's hate towards me. I tried to love her, but, she made it hard. None of my sisters knew what I'd gone through in life. They were all so lucky. Nora was married to a successful attorney who cherished her, Rhonda was married to a top neurosurgeon in Colorado who loved her. Millie had a loving husband who worshipped the ground she walked on, and Gina was a successful architect. They all led such normal lives, while I was

59

constantly fighting alcohol on a daily basis, and fighting to keep my marriage together.

From the time we were kids, there was an unspoken competition between us all. Nora had always been beautiful. She's a brazen beauty, as Mama put it. But, Rhonda's beauty exceeded anyone's. Rhonda had the most haunting eyes, and a smile that would put anyone to shame. Millie was so sensitive to other people's needs. She always put everyone else ahead of herself. Gina was the youngest, and she had more guys after her than she knew what to do with. She had confidence enough not to marry the first guy to come along. All of us were blessed enough to have choices. Jim courted me from high school, but I had a tough time committing to him at first. He was so patient with me. I often wondered why he waited on me. He had no idea why I had such a hard time with intimacy early in our relationship. But, somehow, we'd managed to stay married for almost 20 years.

Later that night, when we sat down to dinner, Amanda wouldn't even look at me. She picked over her food. Jim looked at me and then at Amanda.

"Amanda, Sweetheart, your mother and I are going to try to work things out," Jim said.

"What? You're going to forgive her again?! Why are you such a glutton for punishment? She'll only hurt you again," Amanda said.

"Your mother is getting help. And, the three of us are going to South Carolina tomorrow," Jim said.

"The three of who? I know you're not including *me* in that little equation!" Amanda yelled.

"Yes, I am. Your aunt Millie is very sick and we're going to check on her. It'll be nice for her to see you," Jim said.

"Look, I'm sorry Aunt Millie's not feeling well, but, I'm not going along like everything's okay in our family. Aunt Millie's not going to miss me. We're not close at all, so, I'm not going," Amanda said.

"You don't have a choice in the matter. After dinner, go upstairs and pack your bags," Jim said.

"This is your fault!" Amanda said, looking at me. "Daddy had just about come to his senses and left you for good! Once again you win! Well, I'm not going to sit and watch Daddy make a fool of himself again!"

"You watch your tone, young lady!" Jim said. "Now, we're going to South Carolina and that's that."

"How long are we supposed to be there?" Amanda asked.

"I don't know. A few days, maybe a week," Jim said.

"A week? But, what about my friends? I have plans, Daddy!" Amanda whined.

"Then, you'll have to change your plans. You're only 16 years old, and you'll do as we say. This trip is important," Jim insisted.

"Amanda, we're a family, and we need this time together," I said.

"What do you know about anything? Every problem our family has ever endured has been because of you!" Amanda said.

"Amanda, I know you're angry with me, but, I

want you to give our family a chance," I said.

"Why? You'll only ruin it again!" Amanda yelled.

"Amanda, I won't. I promise," I said.

"We've heard that before! I may have to go to South Carolina with you, but I don't have to like it! I'm going to my room!" Amanda then threw down her napkin and stood abruptly from her chair, storming out of the dining room.

"Amanda," I called after her. Of course, she ignored me. I looked at Jim. "I'm sorry, Jim."

"Sweetheart, we'll figure our way through this thing somehow. Amanda's just angry. She'll come around, but you've got to give her reason to. Every time she gets her hopes up that things will get better again, you fall off the wagon. You can't keep doing that to us, Ellen," Jim said.

"You're right. I know that I have to be strong for you and our daughter," I said.

"You have to mean it, Ellen. Your relationship with Amanda won't survive any more letdowns."

"You're right," I sighed.

I looked at my plate, but I wasn't hungry. I tried to make things seem normal by cooking dinner for the three of us. If it weren't Amanda half the time, she and Jim probably would have starved on more than one occasion. There were so many nights when I was either passed out in bed, or out at the nearest bar. I was getting worse and worse.

After all I'd endured, it was nothing compared to what Millie was going through. She didn't deserve this. She was the best one out of all of us. She's always been the glue that held our family together. She'd tried to call a family reunion a few years ago, but, no one was interested. The more I think about it now, the more I realize we should have done it. It would have been nice to come together for a happier occasion. We would have had a lot of arguments, because our family's been estranged for a long time now. Everyone kind of went their own way and forgot about the family. When we finished dinner, I went upstairs to our room. When I walked into the room, I looked around, thinking about the fact that I could have been lying in a gutter somewhere dead right now instead of here safe at home. At that moment, I knew that I'd been spared because God had a greater plan for me. Although, I didn't know what that plan was, I was sure it would become quite clear when the time was right. I pulled out my gown and went into the bathroom to take a shower. I still felt dirty after what I'd done the night before. Somehow, this entire incident stirred something in me that I didn't know existed. For the first time in a long time, I had a true desire to quit drinking. Maybe because for the first time, I knew without any doubt that I'd cheated. At least when I drank myself into a drunken stupor in the past, I was able to avoid thinking I'd cheated simply because I couldn't remember. Now, the reality of it all hit really hard; hard enough for me to finally face up to my mistakes and what they've cost my family and me.

When I finished my shower and getting ready for bed, Jim walked in. He'd been in his study while I was in the shower. I sat at my vanity table and brushed my hair. I was nervous with each stroke, because I felt awkward around my husband. I could barely face him after everything. He quietly went to take his shower without saying a word. Although he defended me and agreed to go with me to South Carolina, there was still something very wrong with our marriage. It was me. All of my mistakes may have taken their toll on us. I suppose I'd know soon enough where things stood between us.

As Jim showered, I got into bed and picked up a book I'd been neglecting for a long time. I'd read through several pages by the time he came out. I smiled at him, thinking how forgiving he'd been. I know he said it was Clayton's call that prompted him to forgive me, but I have to believe that his love for me played an even bigger part in it. I closed my book when he approached the bed. When he lied down beside me, he let out a big sigh. I cuddled close to him, as I reached up to caress his face with my hand. I kissed him seductively on the neck. I wanted desperately for my husband to make love to me. The moment was broken when he pulled my hand away from his face.

"Ellen, please," Jim whispered.

"What? What's wrong, Sweetheart?" I asked.

"Everything's wrong," he said, looking at me earnestly.

"Honey, I know making love can't fix everything that's wrong, but, it could be a good start," I said.

"Don't you get it, Ellen? I can't make love to

you."

"Why not?" I asked.

"Because every time I see you, I think about the fact that you were with another man. I keep thinking about the fact that he touched you, kissed you, did all the things we've done."

"You think I'm filth?" I asked, astonished.

"No, Ellen, I don't think you're filth. This is just too new right now. You have to give me time to wrap my mind around all this."

I turned away from him, as tears rolled down my cheek. "You don't want me anymore."

"Ellen, I want you," Jim said, reaching out to touch me. "But, I have to be honest with you, just like you were with me."

"I know you're right. It just hurts to hear it," I sighed.

"I'm sorry if this hurts you, Ellen. That's the last thing I wanted to do."

"After everything I've done to you, this is child's play. We'll get through it," I said, trying to muster a smile.

"I would like to hold you, if that's okay," Jim whispered.

"I don't want sympathy," I said.

"It's not. It's simply a man wanting to hold his wife," Jim said. "I love you, Ellen."

"I love you too, Jim," I smiled, moving closer to him as he held me.

It was probably the first peaceful night's sleep we'd had in a long time. For the first time in a long time, I didn't feel the urge to sneak downstairs and raid the liquor cabinet. I knew this was temporary for now, because I felt safe with my husband. But, what would happen when it was time to face up to other hardships in my life?

The next morning was a beautiful Saturday, and a perfect day for traveling. We finished packing for our trip to South Carolina. Our flight was due to leave around noon. I tried to call Rhonda, but her maid told me she was out. I was unable to reach Gina as well. I didn't want to talk to Nora, because we would have simply been at odds. She more than likely would not have welcomed a call from me.

When I went downstairs, Amanda was sitting on the sofa texting on her phone. I sighed, thinking my daughter really hated me. I suppose I couldn't blame her. A lot of Amanda's ways were my fault. I'd never really been there for her as a mother. So, I took the verbal abuse from her because I deserved it. I sat down next to her, in hopes of having a civil conversation.

"Hey, Sweetheart," I said, stroking her hair.

She stopped texting at looked at me angrily, forcefully pushed my hand away. "Leave me alone! Why are you making me go on this trip?"

"Well, your dad thinks it could be good for all of us. Maybe offer support to Aunt Millie and her family."

"What do you know about offering support? You have to be sober to do that," Amanda said.

"Why do you hate me so much?" I asked quietly.

"Because you've done nothing but ruin my

life! My friends know you drink! You're never home! And I can never come to you because you're drunk half the time! The only time you didn't drink lasted about a minute! You're nothing but a liar!"

"I don't mean to lie to you. I always intended to stop drinking, but, it's an illness. Some things can't be helped, Amanda."

"No, Aunt Millie having cancer can't be helped. All you have to do is put down the bottle," Amanda said.

"It's not that easy, Sweetheart."

"If you really want to do it, if we really mean anything to you, you'll do it."

"I'll do whatever I have to in order to make things better between us," I said.

"You want to make things better?"

"Yes, I'll do whatever it takes for you to believe me," I said.

"Then go to the bar, dump every bottle of alcohol you and Daddy own right down the drain."

"Is that what it'll take to prove to you I'm serious?"

"Yes."

I stood slowly and walked towards the bar. There were several different bottles there. Some half full, some never opened. I took the first bottle, opened it, and was about to pour it out and I couldn't do it. I sat the bottle down and sighed.

"See? I knew you couldn't do it," Amanda said, storming out of the room.

I looked at the bottle sitting on the bar. I got a glass from underneath the bar and poured a drink. I needed it. I was about to get on a plane, Amanda hated me, my sister was sick. I had a lot of reasons to drink a small drink just to take the edge off. It wasn't going to hurt. I was determined that after we got back, I wouldn't touch another drop. One drink eventually turned into two. Two turned into three, and before I knew it, I'd had four drinks. The only thing that stopped me from having more was Jim coming in. I was sitting on the sofa as he walked in.

"Hi, Sweetie. Our car should be here soon to take us to the airport. Where's Amanda?" Jim asked, looking into a drawer for something.

"She's upstairs," I said, sneaking a spray of breath freshener while he wasn't looking.

"Are you okay?" Jim asked, looking at me seriously.

"I'm fine. Just argued with Amanda and I'm worried about Millie."

"Amanda's going to be fine. As for Millie, all we can do is pray for her."

"I know you're right," I sighed.

"Hey," Jim said, grabbing my hand and pulling me up close to him. "It's going to be fine. Are you nervous about seeing your sisters again?"

"That's putting it mildly. Of course, as long as Nora's not there, I'll be fine."

"You know, some day you and Nora are going to have to face up to whatever it is that sparks all this hate between the two of you," Jim advised.

"I want to love my sister, but she makes it impossible."

"She can't control your feelings. If she hates

you, that's between her and God. You don't have to give in to that. Love her anyway," Jim shrugged.

"I wish it were that easy. I don't even know why she hates me so much," I sighed.

Jim looked at me intently. He then looked at the table where my empty glass rested. "Have you been drinking?"

We were interrupted by the doorbell before I could answer. I walked to the front door to answer it. It was our doorman.

"Dr. and Mrs. Loweman, your car is here," the doorman said.

"All of our luggage is over there," I said, thankful that I didn't have to answer Jim's question. I knew, however, it wasn't the last of it.

The doorman loaded our luggage as Jim went upstairs to get Amanda. By the time we got down to the limo, I became more nervous. Jim looked at me but didn't say anything. Amanda scowled at me, but didn't say anything. The tension was very high in the car. I wasn't sure what I was about to encounter on this trip, but, I had an eerie feeling. I had the strangest feeling that after this trip, my life would never be the same.

Chapter Four
Gina's Story

The alarm clock going off next to my bed was way too early. I looked at it. 6:15 a.m. I had a million things to do. I had to get the final drafts of the new office building out by the end of next week. Since this was Friday, things were going to be hectic. I sighed as I realized my life was like a runaway train. So much to do, so little time. I turned over on my side. Alex. My beautiful, sexy Alex. I reached over to stroke her hair lightly as I watched her sleep. It was her day off. I wished we could lie in bed together all day without a care in the world. But, reality was, I needed to get going. Alex stirred slightly at my touch. She smiled when she opened her eyes.

"Keep that up and I won't let you go to the office today," Alex said.

"There's nothing I'd like more than to be here

with you all day," I said.

"Well, give me something to look forward to," Alex smiled, reaching over to pull me close.

I kissed my lover passionately, wondering why I wasted so much time dating men. My family doesn't know that I'm a lesbian. My sisters would have a fit. Especially Nora. Somehow, she'd make my being with a woman all about her. I'm the youngest of the McAlray sisters. The spinster of the family. I'm only 28, but, they all think that by now, I should be married and starting a family. Little do they know, I almost took a walk down the aisle. But, after the disastrous relationship with Mark, I decided on a change in lifestyle.

"Stop it, Alex, or I'll never get anything done!" I laughed.

"Gina, you're head of your department. Can't you delegate authority?" Alex asked, as she nuzzled my neck.

"This is my project, Alex. You're really making this hard," I sighed.

"That's my plan," Alex said, as she caressed me.

As Alex continued to caress me, I became aroused, wanting desperately to make love to her. Despite the fact that I had a million things to do, this would take top priority. After we finished making love, I got up to take a shower. I looked at the clock, and it was almost 7:30 a.m. I'd been planning on being half way to the office by now. But, given Alex's little distraction, I was running an hour behind. After getting ready for work, I left home ready to fight

Los Angeles' rush hour traffic. My office was only 15 minutes away, but, by LA's standards, it easily turned into 45 minutes.

As I drove along, I thought about how happy my life was, yet, how afraid I was to share it with the rest of my family. Alexandria was a wonderful woman, and I cared for her deeply. She was someone I trusted completely, and she understood about my being afraid to tell the whole world about our relationship. She'd known she was a lesbian from her early 20's after dating men that never seemed to fulfill her. She and I met at a party a couple of months ago. I had no idea she was gay. I was trying to get over Mark, so when a friend invited me to a party, I went. Little did I know how profoundly that one party would affect my life. When we met, she was just coming out of a bad relationship as well. Initially, she was a good friend to talk to, until she told me about the feelings she was developing for me. In spite of myself, I felt something for her as well. It was so new to me, and I wondered if it was real, or if I simply wanted to experiment with something different. So far, I'm enjoying my new lifestyle. I was even able to stop using birth control pills. No need to worry about getting pregnant now. Maybe now I'll lose that extra ten pounds I've been trying to get rid of since being on those things.

It was almost 9 a.m. by the time I arrived at the office. I was head of my department at Carlisle Architectural Firm. My ex-fiancé, Mark and I work together. Since the breakup, it's been difficult, but I refuse to leave my job. His father owns the firm, so let him leave. Mark's father owned a conglomerate of several businesses that might spark his interest. I've worked very hard to get to my position. I started interning with the firm during my senior year in college, and they were so impressed with me, until I was offered a job immediately after graduation. At age 23, I started with the firm, and by age 26, I was head of my department. I earned the right to stay in my job.

Mark's been trying to reconcile since I broke up with him. It's been flowers and candy almost every day. He has no idea that I'm involved with Alex. It would just be another way for him to have something on me. I refused to give him any kind of leverage. Although I wasn't ashamed of Alex, I was still a little uncomfortable with the fact that I was now sleeping with a woman. But, more importantly than that, it wasn't his business. I walked in and was greeted by my assistant.

"Gina, Parker and Freeman called. They need the final draft by next week. And, we have the layout for the Calloway Building. It's in the drafting room," my assistant Jennifer said, walking with me towards my office. She held out a cup to me. "Here's your coffee."

"Thanks. Where's Vicki? She was supposed to make sure those proofs were sent out to Morgan two weeks ago, and he contacted me yesterday. No proofs," I said in a chiding voice.

"Vicki's on vacation," Jennifer answered.

I sighed heavily. "Get Morgan on the phone, get a messenger up here now so we can get those proofs over to his office."

"Will do," Jennifer said, leaving out of my office.

I put my purse down, ready to get started with my day. Before I could, in walks Mark.

"Well, Beautiful Lady, how are you?" Mark flashed that gorgeous smile of his.

"Fine, and yourself," I said in a monotonous tone.

"Ooh, so cold, so unfeeling," Mark said, further walking into my office.

"I don't remember inviting you in!" I said.

"I own the building," Mark smiled, closing the door.

"No, your *father* owns the building. You're nothing but a spoiled brat, who hopes to one day inherit your father's empire."

"You're in love with this spoiled brat," Mark said, leaning over my desk.

"Mark, what do you want? I have work to do," I sighed.

"I wanted to invite you to a play tonight," Mark said, holding up tickets.

"*A Lifetime in the Making*," I said, looking at the tickets. "I'll pass. I heard the reviews weren't that good."

"It's had excellent reviews," Mark said.

"Well, maybe it did, but, being in your company wouldn't make for exactly a terrific evening. Why don't you ask Nikki?" I said sarcastically.

"When are you going to let that rest?" Mark asked.

"Let's see? How about never," I said, looking coldly at him.

"Gina, I made a mistake. Haven't you ever done something you've regretted?"

"You know, you're right. I have. I got involved with you!"

"You love me, Gina McAlray. Go ahead and admit it," Mark said. He used that seductive tone that has weakened me many a days.

"No one loves you as much as you love yourself, Mark," I said.

"I'll weaken you soon enough," Mark smiled.

"Not in this lifetime. Damn sure not while I'm sober," I said.

"We'll see," Mark smiled.

"Mark, if you don't mind, I have work to do. Unlike you, I actually come to this firm to work," I said.

"I'll leave you alone. But, I'll be back. See you later, Beautiful."

"I hope not," I said.

With Mark finally gone, I was able to concentrate on work. I began working non-stop, desperately trying to keep deadlines. I was working on one when my phone rang. "Yes, Jennifer," I answered.

"There's a Clayton Welby holding for you. He said it's important," Jennifer said.

"Clayton?" I repeated. My heart skipped several beats. For my brother-in-law to be calling me at work, something had to be wrong. "I-I'll take it, Jennifer."

"I'll transfer him," Jennifer said.

"Clayton?" I said.

"Gina, how are you?" Clayton's voice responded.

"I'm fine. Is everything okay?"

"Not really. Millie's in the hospital. She has cancer, Gina," Clayton said.

"C-Cancer? There has to be some mistake, Clayton," I said, as tears welled up in my eyes.

"I'm afraid not," Clayton said.

"Wh-What kind of cancer does she have?" I asked.

"She has a form of leukemia," Clayton said.

"Leukemia? Well, what are the doctors saying?" I asked.

"That's partly why I'm calling you. She's not doing too well, and I thought it was time you knew, in case you wanted to see her. I think that seeing her would do her a world of good," Clayton said.

"Oh, Clayton," I sighed. "I've got a million things going on at work. It'll be so hard for me to break away."

"Gina, I'm not trying to pressure you. I just thought it would be nice for her to see you, but I know you have your obligations."

"You know nothing comes before my family, Clayton. I'm just under a lot of pressure," I explained.

"Gina, you don't owe me any explanations. It's just that Millie's time is so limited."

"How long has she known?"

"Almost a year. She didn't want to burden

any of you. We thought she'd be able to get treatments and it would be enough. Unfortunately, it wasn't."

"I wish she would have said something before now. Look, I'll see if I can break away in a couple of weeks for a few days."

"There's an important reason Millie needs you to come before then, Gina. Her life depends on it," Clayton said.

"Is it really that serious, Clayton?" I asked, as a tear streamed down my face.

"I'm afraid it is. Look, Gina, I don't want to turn your life upside down, but, Millie needs her family right now."

"Does anyone else know?"

"I've called everyone else. Nora's not coming, but Rhonda and Ellen will be here tomorrow."

"Why isn't Nora coming? As if I need to ask," I said.

"Nora's just being Nora," Clayton sighed.

"Clayton, I'll see what I can do, but I can't make any promises," I said.

"Good. Normally, I wouldn't have called you at work, but, apparently, your cell phone number has changed."

"Yes, I changed carriers and decided to get a new number. I just got it a few days ago, but I forgot to call you guys with it."

"That's fine. I called your apartment, someone named Alex gave me your work number and told me it would be fine to call you. I didn't know you had a roommate," Clayton said.

"She's not my roommate," I said slowly. "She's my girlfriend." I couldn't believe that I was willing to reveal that to Clayton. I'd always trusted him, and I knew he wouldn't say anything.

"Oh. Well, she seems really nice," Clayton said.

"She's wonderful. Clayton, I'd appreciate it if you wouldn't tell Millie or anyone else about Alex."

"It's not my business to tell. But, if you're serious about her, at some point, your family is going to have to find out. If you want Millie to know, you can tell her yourself when you feel the time is right."

"Thanks, Clayton," I said. "I've always been able to depend on you."

"That's what I'm here for, Gina."

"I'll try to come out next weekend," I said.

"Good. Let me know once you finalize your plans. Millie will be so happy to see you. It might do both of you a world of good."

"Do you think it would be okay to bring Alex?" I asked.

"I don't see a problem with it. But, if you choose to do that, let Millie know. Don't spring it on her without warning."

"I wish I knew how to tell her."

"Just like you told me. Look, the decision is yours in the end on how you handle it. If you don't want her to find out until you get here, that's your choice. I won't say a word," Clayton said.

"I appreciate it. You know, you're the only one who really treats me like an adult. Everyone else seems to think I'm still a little girl," I said.

78

"They just haven't been around you enough in your adult life to get used to the idea that you're a grown woman. Maybe that's something you can work on when you get here," Clayton suggested.

"Maybe so," I smiled. "Well, look, I really need to go. I have a million things to do. I'll call you as soon as I have definite plans."

"Sounds good. I'll talk to you soon, Gina."

"Oh, before you go, my new cell number is (213)555-3526."

"Okay. I've written it down and I'll store it in my phone," Clayton said.

"Okay. You'll be hearing from me soon. Bye, Clayton."

"Bye, Gina."

After hanging up with him, I wondered how I would deal with it if Millie died. She was such an important part of me. When I graduated from college, she and Rhonda were the only ones to attend the ceremony. Nora and Ellen are such at odds, until they refused to come. I was really disappointed that they thought so little of me to even come. I eventually got over it, but I never forgot. I don't know that I would go rushing to Nora's side if it were her that was stricken with cancer. I know that sounds pretty bad, but, it's the way I feel. I wish I felt differently towards my sister Nora, but she has the tendency to bring out the absolute worst in people.

I sat there at my desk trying hard to concentrate on my tasks ahead, but, all I could think of was Millie. Could she be cured? Was she in any pain? How much was my sister suffering? What if I went to her too late? Do I drop everything to be at my sister's side? Deep down, I knew she was worth it.

Somehow, I mustered my way through the day after telling Jennifer I wasn't to be disturbed, and turning my cell phone off. I didn't want any interruptions. Before long, it was almost 7 p.m. I looked in my wallet at a picture of Millie and Clayton that they'd sent me a couple of years ago. My beautiful sister. She's the last person in the world who deserved a fate like this. As I sat on the sofa in my office, I started to cry. Most of the staff had gone home for the evening. I was so concerned with deadlines and dates, until I was about to ignore the one thing that was most important. I sighed deeply as I lay on my sofa in my office. Before long, I was interrupted by Mark.

"Hey, Beautiful," Mark smiled, coming into my office.

"Not now, Mark," I cried, as I sat up.

His smile faded, as he came over to sit on the sofa. "Gina, what's wrong?"

"Nothing you'd understand! Just leave me alone!"

"I want to help if I can. What is it?"

"Oh, Mark!" I cried, leaning on him.

"What's wrong?" Mark said in a soothing tone.

"My sister's sick! She's been diagnosed with cancer, and they don't know if she's going to make it!"

"Gina, I'm really sorry," Mark said, hugging me. "Is there anything I can do?"

"No, there's nothing anyone can do," I sighed. "Outside of a miracle, my sister's going to die."

"Don't give up yet. Doctors don't know everything. Are you going to see her?"

"My brother-in-law wants for me to come, but, I've got so much to do around here. How can I possibly break away?"

"It'll be fine here. Your family's more important, Gina. Charles can take over your projects until you get back."

"I can't put that on him," I sighed.

"It's alright. I'll talk to him about it tomorrow. Now, you really should go to see your sister."

"I'm scared Mark," I cried softly.

"Shh, it's okay," Mark soothed, rubbing my hair.

He then tilted my chin up for me to look at him. He gently wiped away my tears, and as I looked into his eyes, I saw the man I'd fallen in love with. Slowly, our lips met. A soft kiss soon turned passionate, and something in me yearned to be as close to him as possible. He kissed my neck, caressed my breasts, and I loved it. I loved his touch, and until that moment, I didn't realize how much I missed him. I found myself yielding to his touch, letting him rain kisses all over me. He slowly unbuttoned my blouse, as I unbuttoned his shirt. I could feel his manhood hardening against me. I wanted him. I wanted for Mark to make mad, passionate love to me. He leaned me back on the sofa, lighting a fire in me that I thought was long gone. Before long, he was entering me, taking me just as he had so many times before. I loved the feel of him. With every thrust, I remembered my love for him. At the moment we both reached climactic heights, I was hit with the realization that I never stopped loving Mark. Making love to Mark was natural. It was what I wanted, it was what I needed. When it was over, Mark sat up, breathing hard. He was smiling, as he caressed my cheek. He leaned over to kiss me again. We lied back down on the sofa, cuddled close together underneath the blanket I kept in my office.

"I still love you, Gina. I know I hurt you, but, I want for us to find a way to be together again. Please don't close the door on us," Mark pleaded.

"Mark, I don't know if I can trust you. You hurt me," I whispered.

"I know I did, and I know that I deserve for you to turn your back on me and never look back. Can you honestly tell me that this little episode between us was just sex?"

"Honestly? No, I can't say that. But, Mark, sex doesn't make a relationship. Trust and honesty are important factors. You destroyed that with your infidelity," I said.

I immediately thought about Alex. Didn't I just cheat on her? Was I any better than Mark? I mean, Alex trusted me to be faithful to her. Sometimes, I didn't know what I wanted. I loved the feel of Mark, but, Alex seemed to know what I needed in a relationship. I felt that I'd found that in her. Now that Mark and I had made love, I was more confused than ever.

"Gina, I was wrong to be with Nikki. I'm sorry about everything that went down with her. Her child may be mine, and I'll take care of that child, but, my heart is with you.   I haven't been with Nikki since you ended things with me," Mark said.

"So, am I supposed to be grateful?   A little too late, Mark.   You should have thought about that before you started sleeping with her in the first place!" I said, sitting up.

Mark sat up next to me.   "My mistake with Nikki will forever be a part of my life because of my child with her.   But, I want my future to be with you."

"I-I need time to think," I sighed.   I looked at him earnestly.   "Will you give me time to sort things out?   Without any pressure from you?"

"Fair enough.   Just promise me you won't shut the door on us forever," Mark said.   "I know I joke around a lot with you, but, my feelings are all true.   I still want you to be my wife.   After you threw your ring at me, I kept it, just hoping you'd wear it again one day.   Will you, Gina?"

"Please don't pressure me, Mark.   Give me time to think about it."

"I'll wait forever if I have to," Mark said.

I smiled.   "It won't be forever, I promise."

"Good.   Because forever is a long time," Mark smiled.

"Look, I need to get home," I said.

"Well, why don't I come with you?" Mark asked.

"No, I need to be alone tonight," I said.

"But, you're hurting, and I want to spend the night with you.   Even if it's just to hold you," Mark said, stroking my face.

"No pressure, remember?" I reminded him.

Mark smiled. "That's not pressure. I just don't think you should be alone tonight."

"I'll be fine, Mark."

For some reason, I didn't want to tell him about Alex. Was this thing with Alex real? I couldn't even acknowledge her to people. No one knew of our relationship; no one except Clayton. If I loved Alex, wouldn't I want the world to know? When Mark and I started dating, everyone knew. We kept our engagement private for a couple of months, but, the relationship was very public otherwise. Maybe I wasn't being fair to Alex nor myself if I couldn't even admit that the relationship existed. I got up from the sofa to put on my clothes as Mark watched me. I looked in his direction as he smiled at me. His eyes roved my body, and I could tell he wanted me again. He reached out for me, pulling me back to him.

"Come here," he smiled.

"Mark, I really need to go," I said, not too convincing.

"I'll let you go in a minute," he said, kissing me on my neck.

"You know, we could get into a world of trouble if we're not careful," I said, once again being drawn in by his kiss.

"Not trouble; just pleasure," Mark said. He leaned in to kiss me passionately, and once again, we were lost in each other's love.

After making love again, I knew I had to get away from him. This was only making matters worse. Once again, lying in the afterglow, Mark tried to convince me to give our relationship another chance. As much as I wanted to make things work with him, I owed it to Alex to be fair.

Finally, after another hour had passed, I was able to go home. Obviously, there wasn't much more that I could do that night as far as work was concerned. When I got home, it was fairly dark, so I figured maybe Alex had gone to her own apartment. I walked in and was about to turn the light on when Alex spoke up, startling me.

"Don't turn it on," Alex said. She sounded upset.

"What? Why are you sitting here in the dark?" I asked, reaching for the light switch. When I turned it on, I saw that Alex had been crying. I rushed to her and tried to hold her. "Alex, what's wrong?"

She rebuffed my concern. "Leave me alone! How dare you?" she cried.

"What's wrong with you? Why are you mad with me?" I asked.

"Where have you been all night?" she asked suspiciously.

"I was at the office. I've had a lot going on," I said.

"So, all this time, you've been at the office working?" Alex probed.

"Of course. I've had a very hard day."

"I tried to call you."

"My brother-in-law Clayton called about my sister. I had a hard time concentrating, so I told my assistant not to disturb me and I turned my cell phone off."

"I was really worried about you, Gina. Worried enough to come down to your office tonight," Alex said calmly.

I started to wonder if she saw me with Mark. Surely, I would have known. My imagination was running wild with worry.

"I was pretty busy, Alex," I said, standing.

"I saw you Gina," Alex said calmly.

"Alex, what are you talking about? Saw me where?" I asked, playing dumb.

This reminded me of the time when I confronted Mark about Nikki. Here I was lying to someone I claimed to care about. I was on the defensive, and I handled it just the way Mark did when he was in the same situation.

"In your office," Alex said.

"Well, I told you I had a lot going on at work today."

"Do I look stupid to you?" Alex asked.

"No, you don't look stupid. But, I'm trying to figure out why you're upset."

"Seeing my girlfriend having sex with her ex-boyfriend tends to make me a little upset. I thought things were over between the two of you!"

"They are," I cried. "I-I'm sorry, Alex!"

"Sorry you got caught! Would you have come home and told me? Or would you let me go on thinking that you were faithful to me?"

"Alex, I was worried about my sister, I was stressed out, and I--"

"You what? Made a mistake? After I saw you, I wanted desperately to confront both of you.

86

Instead, I stood outside your office, listening to the two of you. You didn't even tell him that you were involved with me! Are you ashamed of our relationship? Is that it?"

"No, I'm not ashamed of you! Mark and I got swept up in a moment. He was comforting me after I found out about Millie. You have to believe that! He doesn't mean anything to me!"

"Typical lying response. He doesn't mean anything to you. I wasn't born yesterday, Gina. If you're still in love with him, just at least be woman enough to tell me. I deserve that much!" Alex cried.

"Alex, there's nothing to tell. What will it take to prove my feelings for you?"

"Show me that you're not ashamed of me," Alex said.

It occurred to me that the best way to do that was to introduce her to my family. They're the ones I was most afraid of accepting my relationship with her. Without even thinking, I made a suggestion.

"Come with me tomorrow to South Carolina," I blurted out.

Until that moment, I wasn't sure when I would get to see Millie, but, my first mind seemed to have made the decision for me. I really wanted Alex with me. It would give me the chance to see who I really wanted: Alex or Mark. Alex and I had never been away together, so maybe we needed to spend some time out of Los Angeles.

"South Carolina? To meet your family? Are you crazy? There's no way in hell I'd go anywhere with you!" Alex spit out.

"Please, Alex. I really want for you to go with me because I care about you. You know how much you mean to me."

"Save your sympathetic declarations of love or whatever it is you feel, Gina! I've never been with a woman who felt sorry for me, and I'm certainly not going to start now! Why don't you invite Mark to South Carolina? Wouldn't he be more fitting to meet the family?" Alex asked sarcastically.

"I want for *you* to meet my family. If I wanted Mark, I'd be with him right now," I said, grabbing her hand.

"Gina, you slept with Mark tonight," Alex sighed. "How are we supposed to get past that? How to I forgive you?"

I looked deep into her eyes. "Do you care about me?" I asked her earnestly, touching her face.

"You know I do. I love you," Alex whispered with tears in her eyes.

"Then, come with me to South Carolina. I want you with me," I said softly.

Alex closed her eyes and sighed. "Oh, Gina, that won't solve our problems."

"No, maybe not all of them. But, it could put us on the right road. I want to show you off to my family. I'm not ashamed of you. I'm not ashamed of our relationship."

"Then why haven't you told Mark about us?"

"Mark is my boss's son. I don't know what would happen if he finds out I threw him over for a woman. Let me take things slow on my job as far as we are concerned. Just give me time," I said.

Alex smiled. "I must really love you, Gina. Because despite everything that's happened tonight, I still want to be with you."

"So, you'll come with me to South Carolina?"

"Yes, I'll come with you," Alex smiled.

"Good," I smiled. Then, I kissed her passionately, wanting to prove my feelings for her. A part of me felt more confused, but, I felt that this trip could answer all of my questions about what I should do.

I called the airline to make a reservation for the two of us. Then, I emailed my director to let him know I'd be away for a week or so on a family emergency. Alex contacted her supervisor to let her know the same thing. Within an hour, Alex went home to pack her things for our trip the next day. We decided to meet at the airport the next day for our afternoon flight. As I was packing, my phone rang. I assumed it was Alex, so without looking at the caller ID, I answered. "Hello?" I answered.

"Gina, hi, it's me," Mark's voice came over the other line.

"Mark," I responded. My heart skipped several beats at the sound of his voice. Why did this man have such a hold on me?

"I just wanted to see if you were okay," Mark said.

"I'm fine, thanks."

"Gina, I'm glad about what happened tonight. It gives me hope for us."

"Mark, tonight was a mistake."

"A mistake? How can you say that?"

"I was upset about my sister, and overcome with emotion. Somewhere in the mix, I needed to feel close to you. But, the more I think about it, tonight was all about closure."

"Closure? Tonight wasn't about closure. The woman I made love to tonight wanted me just as much as I wanted her. You know we're good together, Gina. I thought you said you'd consider giving us another chance."

"Mark, I wish I could. But, deep down, too much has happened. I can't get past the infidelity. I don't trust you."

"So, where does that leave us?" Mark asked.

"It leaves us nowhere. We're over Mark. Over for good," I said firmly.

"Why did you get my hopes up tonight?"

"I didn't mean to lead you on. I've got a lot on my mind right now. I've decided to leave town for a few days to visit my sister and her family."

"Let me come with you," Mark suggested.

"No, Mark. It's over. Please respect that. What we had at one time was beautiful, and I'll always be grateful to you for loving me."

"I don't want your gratitude. I want your love."

"A part of me will always love you," I said. "I just don't know if I'm still *in* love with you."

"Gina, don't do this," Mark pleaded.

"I-I'm sorry, Mark. I know we have to work together, but as far as I'm concerned, that's the extent of our relationship now. Please don't call me again," I said. "Goodbye, Mark."

"Please, Gina!"

"Goodbye, Mark." I then hung up the phone.

I had to focus on my relationship with Alex. If we were going to work, I had to do my part. I'd hurt her deeply, and I regretted it. She didn't deserve that. I wanted to make it up to her and prove how much she meant to me. For the first time, I didn't care what others thought. The most important thing was that I was happier with Alex than I'd ever been in my entire life. Being with her was the right decision for me.

The next morning, I awakened to the sun shining, and I knew it was going to be a wonderful trip. I wanted to see my sister, introduce her to the wonderful person in my life, and be there for her when she needed me. Taking Alex with me was more than just taking my lover on a trip. It was a milestone for us. Taking her to meet my family was a huge step for me. I knew with everything in me that in order for me to feel comfortable enough to do that, I must really care about her.

After I finished getting my luggage loaded into a cab, I called Alex on my way to the airport. She told me she was heading that way as well. I smiled thinking that finally things were going to go right in my life. I didn't know what to expect when I got to South Carolina, but, I knew that with Alex by my side, everything would be okay. Although, the closer we got to the airport, the more I felt a sense of uneasiness. I wasn't sure why, but a chill went all over me. Was this a sign? Was I making a mistake by going to South Carolina? What was I facing by going across the country to see my family?   I had the strangest feeling that after this trip, my life would never be the same.

Chapter Five
Millicent's Story

I stirred slightly, still somewhat out of it from the medication my nurse had recently administered. I was growing tired of it. I wanted to be home, with my family to die in peace. But, because of my children and my husband, I fought to hold on. My precious children, my beloved Clayton. All a part of a neat little package I'd cherished for years. They were my world. It was a shame that I might have to leave them so soon.

My life was serene, as close to perfect as anyone's when I was hit with the news almost a year ago. I was diagnosed with aplastic anemia after a routine checkup. My doctor noticed a low red blood cell count. After running more tests, it was confirmed that I'd fallen prey to a deadly cancer. Me being one for not giving up, I immediately started fighting the fatal disease, determined to beat the odds. It had been almost a year of drugs, chemotherapy, and long hospital stays, and now, I was about ready to give up.

Although a part of me was ready to meet with the fate that was obviously in God's plan, my Clayton wasn't so willing to give up on me. He and all of our children were tested to see if they would be viable bone marrow donors for me. None of them were a close enough match for it to be a successful transplantation. I now wanted for things to be over quickly, so that my family would no longer have to suffer. My doctor suggested that I contact my siblings to see if they'd be viable donors, but I refused. I'd not contacted my sisters when I first found out about the cancer, so I figured they'd not welcome my crawling to them now asking for them to donate bone marrow on my behalf. I was ready to die peacefully, with my husband and children around me. Little did I know, it wouldn't be that easy.

I noticed Clayton sleeping in the chair next to my bed, with a book resting open faced down across his chest. He looked so tired. I felt sorry for him. He'd been at the hospital every single day. I suppose he took that 'in sickness and in health' thing literally, because my husband had not left my side. I felt guilty taking him away from work and rest in order to be with me. Over the past year, he'd taken family medical leave from work, and had waited on me hand and foot. I suppose it helped that he was one of the top executives at his brokerage firm, rumored to be next in line as Vice President of Operations. I was always so proud of him. He'd made me so happy over the past 26 years. I suppose it couldn't last forever. No one should have had as perfect a life as mine. I was blessed beyond deserving.

I laid there and stared at him. He looked so comfortable. I didn't want to disturb him. It was as if he could feel me watching him, because he awakened.

"Hey, Sleepyhead," he smiled.

"I should say the same thing to you," I joked.

"Oh, I wasn't asleep; I was just resting my eyelids briefly," Clayton said.

"Is that what it was?" I smiled.

"Of course. How are you?" he asked, getting up to come and sit on my bed.

"Ready to go home," I sighed.

"Well, today's the day," Clayton smiled.

"I know. But, sometimes it seems hopeless, Clayton," I sighed.

"We still might find a donor from the national donor list," Clayton encouraged.

"Yeah, but, when? Time isn't exactly on our side."

"Millie, I still don't understand why you're hesitant to ask your sisters to be tested."

"Oh, Clayton, how would that look? Me asking them to be tested when I didn't even have the heart to tell them that I'm sick. Yeah, I'm sure that'll go over really well. Especially with Nora," I said, rolling my eyes.

"They may be more receptive than you think," Clayton shrugged.

"I doubt it. Trust me, I know my sisters. Rhonda will be upset about it, Ellen will be hurt, Gina will be too busy with her career and Nora will be downright mean."

"I still think you may not be giving them enough credit," Clayton sighed.

At that moment, we were interrupted by a brief knock and then Dr. Tracer entering the room.

"Good afternoon, Millicent, Clayton," Dr. Tracer smiled. "How are you feeling today?"

"Ready to go home," I smiled.

"Well, I think you are ready," Dr. Tracer said. "Everything looks good. So, you get to go home today around 4 p.m."

"For good?" I asked.

"Well, unless we find a candidate to donate bone marrow," Dr. Tracer said.

"Seems unlikely that will happen," I said.

"I still think you should talk to your sisters," Dr. Tracer said.

"Have you been talking to my husband?" I smiled.

"Great minds think alike," Dr. Tracer smiled.

"I'm going to take my shower," I said.

"Now, Millicent, don't overexert yourself. Stick to your strict diet," Dr. Tracer instructed.

"I know the routine," I smiled.

"Have you heard this before?" Dr. Tracer joked.

"Only a million times from you," I chuckled.

"And you'll hear it a million more if necessary," Clayton said.

"My husband, the worrywart," I smiled.

"He's concerned, just as I am. Now, you need to follow up in a few days, okay?"

"I've done this all before, remember?" I

laughed lightly.

"I'll see you in a few days," Dr. Tracer smiled.

At that moment, my nurse came in. "So, Mrs. Welby, you're leaving us today," Sandra smiled.

"Hopefully, for good," I said.

"Well, if we find a viable donor, you'll be back. But, that's a good thing, right?" Sandra asked.

"I suppose," I shrugged. "I've just about given up."

"Well, don't do that. I see miracles every day, and you're no exception," Sandra said.

"Thanks, Sandra. You've been wonderful, you know that?" I asked.

"Thank you, Mrs. Welby. You've been a great patient. I'm going to miss you," Sandra smiled.

"Come here, I want Clayton to take a picture of us," I smiled.

Sandra came closer to the bed, and Clayton got the digital camera and took a picture of us. Since I'd been back and forth, the staff was like a family to me. I'd gotten to know all of the nurses, assistants, clerks, doctors, everyone. Over the past year, I'd been admitted no less than five times, ranging from a few days to a couple of months each time. Despite the fact that the staff was amazing, I really missed home. I was looking forward to sleeping in my own bed, sitting at my own dinner table, relaxing in my special sunroom.

After getting the last of my results, I got ready to go home. I was at peace, because I'd made the conscious decision that I would not be admitted again. I knew that Clayton didn't want to give up on me, but,

I was tired of going back and forth so much. I had to handle things with him as gently as possible, to try and get him used to the fact that I no longer had the energy or will to fight.

A few minutes after we'd gotten my things together, I was surprised by the arrival of my children. The four of them had been through so much since finding out about my illness. Kyle and Kirsten both were mature minded enough, but, how do you prepare a fifteen year old and a twelve year old? Tim was under enough pressure just being a teenager. Shauna was just starting her teenage years. These were supposed to be the best years of their lives. I felt that I was ruining it for them.

After almost an hour, Patient Transport came to take me to the discharge area where Clayton had pulled the car around. When I got outside, I noticed that it was a beautiful Saturday. I smiled as I took it all in. Little things like the sun shining, or soothing patter of rain against the window, were all so precious now. Things that a year ago, I took for granted. The trip home seemed long, maybe because I was so anxious. I wanted to see my home, which I'd been away from for over a month.

When I got home, Erin, my new daughter-in-law was waiting, along with Miriam, our housekeeper. Clayton pulled into the circular driveway, and it was a welcoming sight. I'd instructed him not to pull into the garage. I wanted to look at my beautiful home for a few minutes. Kyle, Kirsten, Shauna and Tim all waited patiently while I took in the breathtaking sight.

After I got inside, I had a lot of restless energy. My maid, Miriam was about to put my things away when I insisted upon doing it myself. After I unpacked, I went to sit in the living room. Sadly enough, I never utilized my living room. It was always more formal, for company. Never did I sit in there on a fall morning to read a book, or just play something on the piano. I smiled as I walked over to the piano. I sat down and started to play. It was a soothing sound, because I'd not played in years. That along with my desire to draw had faded somewhere into the back of my mind. Even more so since I found out about my cancer.

I was interrupted by the doorbell ringing. I assumed it was probably one of Tim's friends coming over. I wanted to believe that life had gone on completely as usual during my absence. Clayton called from another room.

"Millie, could you get that, Sweetheart? Miriam's helping me," Clayton yelled.

I sighed, looking around, realizing that none of my children were around. I got up from the piano and went to the front door. When I opened it, I was completely shocked by the faces staring back at me. It was my sister Rhonda.

"Rh-Rhonda?!" I whispered, as I covered my face with my hand. "Rhonda!" I yelled, opening the door to let her in. I embraced my sister, as tears flowed down my face.

"Millie!" Rhonda said, smiling as she hugged me. "How are you?"

"I'm fine. How are you?" I said, smiling at

99

my sister.

"It's so good to see you! I have missed you!" Rhonda said.

"Let me look at you," I said, stepping back. "Still beautiful!" I felt the tears welling up in my eyes. "My sister! My sister's here with me! This is such a wonderful surprise! Ginny, how are you?" I said, hugging my niece.

"I'm fine, Aunt Millicent. How are you?" Ginny asked.

"Oh, I'm okay," I said. "There's so much to talk about. Well, come on in! Let's not stand out here in the doorway!" I excitedly opened the door further, as Clayton, Miriam and our children emerged. Obviously, this was a surprise that all of them were in on.

We all went into the living room and Miriam brought in a tray of appetizers. We all sat around talking, catching up on old times. I noticed that AJ and Aaron weren't with them.

"Where are my nephew and brother-in-law?" I asked.

"Aaron had to work, and AJ will be here tomorrow," Rhonda answered.

"How long can you guys stay?" I asked.

"As long as you need me," Rhonda said, reaching out to touch my hand.

"Oh, Rhonda," I said, hugging her.

Everyone looked as my sister and I shared an emotional moment together. I was so afraid for her to find out about my cancer. Obviously, my pride cheated me for the past year. After a little while,

Rhonda and I went out to the gazebo and talked. The view was beautiful. Our gazebo sat on a hill, overlooking the ocean. We could hear the waves crashing against the shore. It was such a clear, warm July evening. I looked at my sister. I knew she had a million questions.

"Millie, why didn't you tell me?" Rhonda asked, hugging my shoulders.

"I don't know," I sighed. "I suppose I didn't want to burden you."

"Burden me? You're my little sister and I love you," Rhonda said, with tears in her eyes.

"I know you're right. I don't know what I was thinking keeping something so monumental in my life from you," I sighed. "Can you forgive me?"

"There's nothing to forgive," Rhonda smiled.

I studied my sister carefully. "Rhonda, is everything okay?" I asked.

"Everything's fine. Why would you ask?"

"I don't know. You just look like you have a lot on your mind," I said.

"Well, let's see," Rhonda looked thoughtful. "My sister has cancer, and she forgot to tell me. Maybe that's it."

I smiled. "That's not what I meant, Rhonda. This is a lot more than something you just found out about. Seems like there's something else going on," I observed.

"Millie, things are great."

"You'd tell me if something was wrong, wouldn't you?" I asked. "You may be the oldest, but I'm still here for you."

101

"Of course I would tell you if something was wrong," Rhonda said, unconvincingly.

"Are things okay with you and Aaron?" I asked.

"They're great," Rhonda said, half-smiling. She let go of me, and walked to look out over the water.

Even in the dusky sunset , I could see the sadness in her eyes. My sister was hurting. The wind from the ocean waves blew against her face, and I remember thinking how beautiful she was. I always envied Rhonda's looks, but never in a bad way. More in an admiring way. I hate that she wasn't able to become a model like she wanted. Mama wanted her to do it, but Daddy wouldn't hear of it. When the opportunity arose for her to get into modeling, Daddy refused to let her. He always said he never wanted to set his little girl up for a huge disappointment if it didn't work out. Daddy thought he was doing what was best for her. Maybe in some ways he was right. But now, Rhonda will never know what could have been. She was a rare pick, always winning pageants and being voted 'Most Beautiful' in high school.

"Are you sure? You two aren't having problems, are you?"

"Aaron's a good father. He takes care of me, he's put both the kids through college, and he works very hard. He's a well-respected doctor whose patients adore him. What more could I ask for?"

"So, who are you trying to convince, me or yourself?" I asked bluntly.

"What do you mean?" Rhonda said looking at

me.

"I mean, it's good to know that Aaron's a wonderful father, but you've failed to mention one thing."

"What's that?" Rhonda asked.

"You haven't mentioned that you're happy," I commented, walking closer to her.

"Who wouldn't be happy with all that I have?"

"Rhonda, you're talking around the subject. Is everything okay?" I touched her shoulder.

"Millie, you always worry too much. I'm fine," Rhonda said, smiling.

"I'll leave it alone. But, please, know that you can tell me anything."

"Millie, you have enough on your mind with your illness."

"Trust me, Big Sis, I need a distraction. My life has been about nothing but cancer over the past year. If I can be here for you, I'd feel like I was being productive."

"Millie," Rhonda sighed. "Everything's fine between my husband and me."

I looked at Rhonda closely. I knew her well enough to know that something was wrong, but I also knew she'd tell me when she thought the time was right. We spent another hour there just talking about old times when we were younger. It was wonderful talking with her about so many things, things I'd long ago forgotten. Looking at her, I wondered how I survived without having her near. I also wondered how she was surviving. Was my sister as happy as she pretended, or was it all just a cover up? What was the real reason my brother-in-law didn't come? Aaron had a mean streak when they were dating, and I terribly hoped it never spilled over in their marriage, although somehow, I had my doubts. Ironically, her marriage was the one Daddy seemed to encourage over all of ours. I suppose it had to do with the fact that she was the oldest, and she had to set an example. Plus, he felt it would take her mind off of modeling.

After talking for almost an hour, we went back into the house, where Ginny was visiting with Kirsten, Kyle and Erin. As Miriam prepared dinner for us, the doorbell rang again. I looked at Clayton, who feigned innocence by giving a little shrug and a smile.

"Let me guess. Miriam's busy again?" I laughed.

"Well, you wanted to be more useful after getting out of the hospital," Clayton smiled.

I sighed and smiled as I got up from my seat. "Come on, Rhonda, let's see what else my husband has in store for me."

I walked to the front door and opened it. To my complete surprise there was Nora, Bill, Jessica and Matthew. Once again, I couldn't stop the tears from flowing. I squealed in excitement.

"Nora!" I said, hugging her.

"Millie, Dear, how are you?" Nora asked. "Why didn't you tell me you were sick?"

"I-I'm sorry," I said. "Please, come in!"

"Nora!" Rhonda smiled, hugging her sister. "I didn't think you were going to make it."

"Plans change," Nora smiled. "It's good to see you, Rhonda."

"It's wonderful to see you, too, Nora," Rhonda smiled.

We all went into the den where everyone else was waiting. Nora was a beautiful woman, and it was always a fact that never escaped her. She had gray eyes like me, and her hair was jet black. She wore her hair long all the time. I looked at her flashing that beautiful smile, which unveiled that mischievousness she carried naturally and charmingly. Nora got away with being bad because she was so good and charismatic with it.

She looked at Clayton. "Hello Brother-in-law," she smiled.

"Hello, Nora. How are you? Glad you were able to make it after all," Clayton smiled, as his tone held a slight note of sarcasm. Nora and Clayton have never gotten along as well as I would have liked. Clayton always thought of Nora as obnoxious and over-bearing. "Bill! How are things in the political spectrum of the country?" Clayton asked.

"They're good. I'm thinking of campaigning for Congress in the next election," Bill stated.

"That would be wonderful!" I smiled. "My brother-in-law, a congressman."

"Don't pop the cork on the champagne bottle yet. I'm only *thinking* of running. But, left up to my wife here, I'd be on the ballots already!" Bill laughed.

"You'd be great. Besides, you already have quite a few important people backing you," I encouraged.

"And you know we're behind you 100%," Clayton said, patting Bill on the back.

105

"Thanks, Brother-in-law," Bill smiled.

"Auntie Nora, Uncle Bill!" Kirsten smiled, reaching to hug Nora.

"Kirsten!" Nora said. "My goodness, you've grown! And where's that young man of yours?"

"He'll be here later," Kirsten smiled.

"So, Kyle, this must be your new bride," Nora said, looking at Erin.

"Aunt Nora, Uncle Bill, this is my wife, Erin," Kyle smiled.

"Hello, Erin," Nora said shaking her hand.

"Hi," Erin smiled.

"Erin," Bill said, shaking her hand next. "I'm sorry we couldn't be here for the wedding."

"That's okay. It was so nice of you to send us that state-of-the-art cookware set. Now, if I can just get my wife to use it, we'll see how well it works!" Kyle joked.

Everyone laughed, except for Erin. I stopped laughing when I noticed how my daughter-in-law took offense to Kyle's joke. I got the terrible feeling that my son would have to deal with the aftermath of that little comment later.

"So, how are things going in school, Jessica?" I asked.

"I'm still in the top five percent," Jessica said smugly. "That won't change."

"Well, I'm sure it won't. You've always been a smart girl," I said.

"Tell me something I don't know," Jessica sighed in an annoyed tone.

The moment my niece made that statement, I

realized that some things never change. Jessica was her mother's daughter through and through. I thought about the fact that she was simply following in her mother's footsteps. Nora had never been known for being humble, and Jessica was the same way.

We all visited in the den for another few minutes or so, when once again, someone was at the door. I realized that Clayton must have been responsible for my sisters showing up like they did. Although I was tired, I couldn't have been more pleased that they were there. Rhonda walked with me to the front door. This time, it was Ellen, her husband Jim and their daughter Amanda.

"Ellen!" I smiled. I immediately opened the door and hugged her. "How are you?"

"I'm fine," Ellen said. "It's so good to see you!" she said not wanting to let go.

"It's been a long time," I said.

"Ten years is much too long," Ellen said.

"Hi, Sis!" Rhonda said, interrupting.

"Ron! How are you?" Ellen said, hugging her next.

"I'm just fine. Just sorry it took something like this for us to all come together," Rhonda said.

"Come on into the den. Everyone's in there," I said.

Miriam helped to get their luggage inside. Poor Miriam. Unfortunately, with all that was going on, she was quite busy. But, she handled it professionally. No doubt, Clayton had informed her that we were going to be having company. When we walked into the den, there were hugs all around for

Ellen and her family.

"Hello, Ellen," Nora said dryly.

"Nora," Ellen said, attempting to hug her.

"I didn't know that you were coming," Nora said, backing away, rebuffing her sister's hug.

"Well, I didn't know that you were coming either," Ellen said.

"The important thing is that we're all together," I smiled.

"Yeah, right. This ought to be an interesting trip," Amanda said sarcastically. "We all know there's only one reason we're together. We all think you're going to die."

First Jessica, now Amanda. I was starting to wonder how in the world I would be able to deal with two of them in my house. At least Amanda's tongue ring matched her nose ring. My niece always had a way of 'making a statement.' I often wondered what possessed teenagers to do the things they did. I remembered Ellen mentioning that she'd gotten the piercings without permission, as a form of rebellion. Ellen and Jim really had their hands full with her.

"Amanda! How dare you speak to your aunt that way? I didn't raise you to be disrespectful!" Ellen said.

"Doesn't look like you did much raising at all," Nora commented.

"Oh, and you're one to talk. Tell me, is Jessica still the same self-centered brat she always was?" Ellen shot back.

"Of all the nerve! At least my daughter attends an Ivy-League college. Do you think yours will stay in school long enough to graduate?" Nora said.

"Alright! Enough you two!" Rhonda said.

"See what I mean? Look at us. We can't even stand the sight of each other!" Amanda said.

"Well, I hope you can manage to enjoy the visit a little bit. We have a lot to catch up on," I reassured my niece.

"Tell me something Ellen, why did you even come? This could have been a pleasant visit if you'd not come," Nora said.

"Same goes for you, sister dear. I was told that you were too self-absorbed to even want to come. What ran you out of DC?" Ellen said, looking Nora square in the face.

"Nothing had to run me out of DC. I'm here because I care about my sister!" Nora shouted.

"Please, you two! I can't deal with this!" I cried. "Is this entire visit going to be nothing but the two of you sparring at each other?"

"I'm willing to be adult if she is," Ellen said.

"Whatever," Nora sighed, rolling her eyes. "Just stay the hell out of my way, Ellen. Don't talk to me, and I sure as hell won't talk to you!"

"You know, it really touches me that the three of you were willing to come and visit me like this," I smiled, trying to change the subject. "It's been the best medicine for me."

"If we'd known, we would have been here a long time ago for you," Rhonda said.

"I know that now," I smiled. "I shouldn't have been too proud to tell you what was going on. I hope you can all forgive me. I'm going to assume that my husband ignored my wishes and called all of you."

"He called me yesterday," Ellen said.

"Me, too," Rhonda said. "I told him I was taking the first available flight out to see you."

"I wish Gina could be here," I said.

"Knowing your husband, she will be," Rhonda smiled.

"I wish she would find a nice guy to settle down with. I don't want for her to be alone," I sighed.

"Oh, Gina won't be alone. That girl could have any guy she wants," Nora shrugged. "Why are you always so worried about her?"

"Because she's our baby sister living out in Los Angeles all alone," I said.

"Millie, she'll be fine," Nora sighed. "That's been her problem all along. We baby her too much."

"It's not about babying her. It's about the fact that she should be ready to settle down. It's long overdue," Rhonda said.

We were in the den, trying to find unbiased conversation for a few moments when Miriam came and told me that one more guest had arrived. I got the sneaking suspicion that it was Gina. I walked outside along with my sisters, and to my pleasant surprise, Gina got out of the passenger side.

"Gina!" I yelled, hugging her. "It's so wonderful to have you!"

"Millie! Oh, Millie, why didn't you call me and tell me what was going on with you?" she asked with tears in her eyes.

"Gina, I'm sorry," I said, as I cried right along with her. "I'm so glad you came!"

"I am, too. And from the looks of it, I'm not the only one to show up. Hey, Guys!"

She smiled that beautiful smile that I'd missed dearly as she hugged each of her other sisters.

"You cut your hair!" Nora smiled.

"Yeah! You like it?" Gina smiled, giving a little pose.

"I love it!" Nora said.

"Everyone, I brought a very special friend with me. Alex!" Gina said turning towards the car motioning as the driver's side door opened.

I wasn't expecting what I saw next. A beautiful woman in her mid-twenties stepped from the driver's side. Everything seemed to move in slow motion as she walked around the car. Gina reached down as they linked hands, leaning slightly against her.

"Alex, this is my sister, Millicent, my sister Rhonda, my sister Nora and my sister Ellen. Guys, this is Alexandria Franklin, the love of my life," Gina said, smiling.

My sister had fallen in love with a woman.

Chapter Six

Needless to say, everyone was shocked beyond belief. I was the first to speak.

"H-hi, Alex. It's a pleasure to meet you," I said, smiling politely, holding out my hand to shake hers.

"Hi, it's nice to meet you, too," Alex smiled, shaking my hand. "I've been looking so forward to this!"

"My God, you're a woman," Nora said.

"Nora!" Rhonda said.

"Well, she is! This is the 'love of your life'? When did you become a lesbian?" Nora was never known for mincing her words.

"That's my fault. I didn't tell you because I knew you'd react this way," Gina stated.

"So, you decided to bring you girlfriend across country to meet us? Have you lost your mind?" Nora

112

asked.

"Listen, I think everyone's getting a little worked up right now. Why don't we all go inside?" I suggested.

"No, Alex and I will go to a hotel," Gina said.

"You'll do no such thing. You and Alex are both welcome to my home," I said. "Please come in."

"Well, if they're going to be here, my children won't!" Nora exclaimed as we walked inside.

"Nora, be reasonable. It's not like your children are totally innocent. Jessica's 20 and Matthew's 17," Rhonda said. "This is Gina's decision, and we have to respect that. Alex, I'm Gina's oldest sister, Rhonda and it's very nice to meet you." Alex and Rhonda shook hands as Rhonda smiled at her.

"And I'm Ellen. It's nice to finally meet someone who will make my sister happy," Ellen said, smiling as she shook Alex's hand.

"Why don't we go into the den and sit down?" I suggested.

We all sat in stifled silence for the first few minutes until Ellen spoke.

"So, Alex, what do you do?" Ellen asked.

"Here it comes," Gina smiled. "The 'interrogation.'"

"I'm a physical therapist," Alex replied.

"So, how did you two meet?" Rhonda asked.

"At a mutual friend's party," Gina stated.

"What, one of those parties for gays?" Nora asked sarcastically.

"Nora!" I exclaimed.

113

"Oh, come on! Like no one else was wondering the same thing!" Nora said. "You're sleeping with a woman. Since you insist upon revealing that to us, you might as well tell it all."

"Would you please learn to use a little tact?" Ellen spoke up.

"If memory serves me correctly, I thought I told you not to talk to me," Nora stated.

"Same spoiled brat as always," Rhonda sighed. "Nora, please behave."

"Oh, shut up, Rhonda. My husband's entering politics. I don't want his 'wayward sister-in-law with the alternative lifestyle' to surface during his campaign," Nora said harshly.

"Nora! Was that really necessary to say?" Rhonda asked.

"Maybe not, but if Gina insists on doing what she wants, I can say what I want," Nora said defensively.

I sighed and shook my head. I smiled inside, because even though we were disagreeing, we were together, and I'd missed that over the years. We were interrupted by Clayton, who wanted us to join him in the media room. Clayton had transferred a lot of our old home movies to DVD and brought them to me at the hospital to cheer me up on several occasions. He thought everyone would like to see times from our childhood. The home movies were setup in the media room. We decided to watch the movies after having the dinner Miriam had worked so hard to prepare. I gave her the rest of the night off to spend with her family because she'd been working so hard; she

114

deserved it.

After dinner, we sat in the theater and watched movies from our childhood. There was a special scene between Daddy and Nora when she was child. She'd fallen off of her bike and skinned her knee. Daddy had been recording it because she'd started riding without her training wheels. Daddy positioned the camera so that he could film himself tending to Nora's wound. She stopped crying the moment he picked her up and hugged her. Nora had been sitting next to me in the media room. She suddenly got up and left the room. I immediately went after her. She was in the sunroom crying.

"Nora, what is it?" I placed my hand on her shoulder.

"I'll be okay," Nora said tearfully.

"Please, honey. Tell me what's wrong," I pleaded.

"Millie, how can you be so upbeat after everything going on in your life? And why do you and your husband keep digging up these old skeletons? Leave them dead and buried," Nora cried.

"What are you talking about? I thought you would have loved seeing footage of us with Mama and Daddy. You were always Dad's favorite," I smiled.

"Yeah, in more ways than you can imagine," Nora murmured.

"What's that supposed to mean?" I asked.

"Nothing. Look, I'm going for a walk on the beach. I need to be alone right now," Nora said.

"Are you sure? Why don't I come with you?" I offered.

"No, I want to go by myself," Nora insisted. "Besides, your immune system is not supposed to be compromised. You don't need to go walking on the beach."

"I know all too well what I'm not supposed to do, but I'd chance it if it would give us time to talk," I said.

"No, thanks. I'll be fine. I need some time alone, to think about a few things," Nora said.

I looked at her skeptically.

"I'll be fine," Nora reassured. Nora then looked at me. "What?"

"Nothing," I shook my head.

"Do you think I'm going to off myself by jumping into the ocean? 'Put myself out of misery'? Come on Millie, I'm too arrogant to ever end my own life," Nora smiled.

"Well, I know that. I just thought you'd want a little company," I smiled.

"Maybe another time. I'll be fine. I promise," Nora reassured.

"Okay," I said.

She left out of the sunroom and went out to the beach through the backyard. I went back into the media room and noticed that Ellen was now missing in action.

"Where's Ellen?" I leaned over and whispered to Clayton.

"She left out a minute or two before you came back. Is Nora okay?" Clayton asked.

"Yeah, she said she was going for a walk on the beach," I said. "I just don't want for those two to run

116

into each other without a referee."

"Everything's going to be fine," Clayton said, covering my hand with his.

Ellen eventually returned ten minutes later. She seemed in much better spirits. Probably because Nora wasn't there. We enjoyed the rest of the night laughing and reminiscing about our childhood. Ellen was notably more relaxed with Nora's absence. She was almost cheerful, which was something I'd not witnessed since her arrival earlier. There was still so much bad blood between Ellen and Nora, and I wondered would they ever make things right between them.

Bill was understandably concerned about Nora. He excused himself to go and look for her. Almost an hour later, the two of them came through the door. They were laughing as they came in, holding hands. Soon after the movie, everyone decided to turn in for the night. As luck would have it, I had room for everyone in my home and guesthouse. In a seven bedroom house, and a guesthouse with two bedrooms, we were able to house everyone comfortably. As I sat in my sunroom to read a little, the doorbell rang and I remembered that Miriam was gone. All of my sisters were here, so I wondered who it was. I looked at the clock, noticing it was almost 11:30 p.m. Clayton came down the stairs and we went to the front door together. To my surprise, Aaron and AJ were at the front door.

"Aaron!" I smiled, hugging my brother-in-law.

"Hello, Millie. Is my wife here?" Aaron smiled, as he reached to shake Clayton's hand.

"Yes, she is! Wow, this is a wonderful surprise! Rhonda said you couldn't get away from the hospital!" I said.

"Aaron, I'm glad you were able to make it," Clayton smiled.

"Some things can be arranged when it's important enough," Aaron smiled.

"Oh, that's so sweet!" I said. "And AJ! How are you?" I said, hugging my nephew.

"I'm fine, Aunt Millie. The bigger question is how are you?"

"I'm great now that my entire family is here! Rhonda's going to be so glad you were able to make it after all! Come on in! I'll get Rhonda."

"I'd like to surprise her, if that's okay," Aaron smiled.

"She'd love it! She's in the third room on the right once you go up the stairs," I said, pointing the way. "AJ, would you be okay bunking out in the guesthouse with Tim and Matthew? Jessica and Ginny are staying with Kirsten at her apartment. If you'd like, I'm sure Kyle and Erin would gladly let you stay there," I said.

"The guesthouse will be fine, Aunt Millie. Where are Kyle and his new bride, by the way?"

"They left about 20 minutes ago. He'll be back tomorrow, so you'll get to see him then."

"I hate it took this for us to come together, Aunt Millie, but, I'm glad we're here," AJ said, hugging me again.

"I thought you were at orientation?" Clayton asked.

"I was, Uncle Clayton, but, we finished today. I talked to Dad earlier and told him that I was coming here to join Mom and Ginny tomorrow. Dad didn't want to wait, so he caught a plane from Colorado and I decided to catch an earlier flight from Arizona. Our planes arrived here about a half an hour apart. I met up with him at the airport, we rented a car and came on over here together," AJ explained.

"Well, we're just glad you're here," Clayton smiled, patting AJ on the back. "Come on, I know you're tired, so I'll show you to the guesthouse."

"Man, I have quite a few fond memories in the guesthouse! Kyle and I used to get into a lot of trouble in there, especially with the Connor twins one summer!" AJ laughed.

"Don't let your aunt hear you say that. She'll lock it up until Shauna's 25," Clayton laughed, as the two of them walked off.

I smiled at them as I watched them walk out onto the patio. Even a little joke like that made me sad. I probably won't be here when Shauna turns 25. But, I had to focus on what was important: my family. Everyone was here, and I loved it. I'd always wanted to call a reunion, but I'd never been able to get anyone to cooperate. I just hate that the only reason they're coming together is because of my illness. It's almost unfair, because I know we have a lot of love to offer each other if we'd just try. I sighed as I turned and went up the stairs to get ready for bed.

I'd not realized how tired I was until I ran my bubble bath. I felt like pampering myself, so I lit candles and put on a jazz CD. Clayton had already

119

taken his shower. I leaned back onto my bath pillow after immersing my tired body into a jetted tub full of bubbles. I simply wanted to escape from the day's events. I thought about when we were growing up. We were so close when we were younger, always vowing never to let anything or anyone come between us. We protected each other from bullies, from boys who got a little too close, everything. What happened along the way? I suppose at some point, we just simply grew up and those little things weren't as important anymore. At times, I'd give anything for those days again.

My mind wandered back to the present, as I sat and thought about my sisters. I'd allowed myself to be consumed by the problems with Ellen and Nora. God, give me the strength to bring us together. So many demons to fight, so much anger and resentment. Lord, how could we work through it all? My time was so limited. We seemed to be so far apart. No matter how successful we were in other ways, we were failing miserably at being a family. There were so many emotional scars to heal, emotional scars I had no idea about. I was almost afraid of what was next. It seemed like with every passing moment, there was some sort of issue with them. Rhonda seemed so sad; Gina was here with a woman. Not to mention how Nora and Ellen seemed to hate each other more than ever. I know Clayton meant well by bringing them together for my sake, but, he may have asked for more than what he bargained.

I'd sat in the tub so long, until eventually, I drifted off to sleep. I was awakened by the soft brush of Clayton's lips on my forehead, as his hand caressed my cheek. I didn't open my eyes immediately, but he knew I was awake from my smile.

"That bed's kind of lonely without you," Clayton smiled. "I've missed sleeping with you in there these past few weeks."

"Don't worry. I didn't slip away," I smiled, opening my eyes.

Clayton immediately straightened up, looking serious. "Don't say it like that, Millie," Clayton whispered.

I soon realized how careless I'd been with choosing my words. Clayton always hated how cavalierly I'd refer to dying. "I'm sorry, Honey. I didn't mean anything by it," I said, placing my hand on his.

"I know. If you weren't sick, I wouldn't have given that statement a second thought," Clayton sighed.

In the candlelight, I saw a tear roll down his face. This was so hard on him. The love of my life was suffering and there was nothing I could do about it. Ironically, he felt the exact same way.

"I've been meaning to ask you something," I said.

"What is it?" Clayton asked.

"When I introduced Alex to you and the other guys, you were the only one who didn't seem surprised or uneasy by the fact that she was a woman," I said.

"Well, what was I supposed to do? Pass out from the shock?" Clayton chuckled.

"No," I said hesitantly. "But, I know you.

What gives?"

"I wasn't surprised. I already knew about Alex."

"How did you know?"

"When I called Gina's apartment, Alex answered the phone. Obviously, I thought it was a roommate. When I called Gina at work, she told me who Alex was when I brought it up. I told her that I wouldn't tell you, and I'd leave the final decision up to her as to when she revealed it to you."

"Well, it was quite a surprise. It may not be the decision I wanted for my sister, but, she's an adult, and Alex seems nice enough," I sighed. I then held my hand up. "Come on, help me out of this tub."

Clayton gently took my hand and helped me to step out of the tub. He looked at me passionately. Despite my illness, my husband still desired me intimately. He reached for the towel resting on the chair and wrapped it around me, trapping me in a circle of his arms. It was at that point I realized he didn't have a shirt on. I put my arms around him as he leaned in to kiss me. Our kiss became more passionate, as he lifted me into his arms. He carried me to our bed, laying me down gently. Now, when we were intimate, he always treated me more fragile, as if I was going to break. As the music played in the background, my husband made love to me. We became lost in our own world, as if no one else existed. I suppose at that moment in time, it was true. He was so gentle and loving with every touch. Afterwards, as I lay in his arms, tears ran down my face without my even realizing it. Clayton felt my tears on his chest.

He gently tilted my chin up.

"What's wrong?" Clayton asked.

"I wish it could be like this forever," I said, looking into his eyes.

"It will be," Clayton whispered. "We can make the memories last a lifetime."

"A lifetime isn't as long as it used to be," I said somberly.

"Maybe it's longer than you think. I believe with everything in me that we won't be apart for long."

"I don't want to be apart at all," I whispered. "I'm afraid. I think so often about what it will be like when I die. I mean, will I remember you and our children? Will I be able to see how you're surviving? Let's face it, no one knows what really happens when a person passes on."

"Sweetheart, let's not dwell on that. Not now," Clayton said. "I want for us to enjoy every moment we have without it constantly being darkened by what the future may hold."

I pulled away slightly. "Clayton, you know as well as I do what's going to happen. I thought we'd both accepted it."

"I can't accept losing you. I'm going to hold on to you as long as I possibly can." With that statement, he pulled me back to him. "I'm not letting you go without a fight."

I smiled. "My hero. I guess I'd better not go out without a fight either, huh?"

"That's my girl," Clayton smiled. "We've fought the odds for a year. Let's go for another 20, or even 30."

"Do you really believe that, Clayton?   That I can beat this thing?"

"I can't afford to believe anything less," Clayton commented.   "I love you too much to accept less than forever with you."

"I wish I shared your optimism, but I've finally accepted reality, Honey."

"The reality is, as long as you're alive, I will continue to fight to keep you that way."

"I love you, Clayton."   What else could I say? When my time comes, he's not going to handle it well. I prayed that God would give him the strength to carry on.

"I love you too, Millie."   He then kissed me gently, and we fell asleep in each other's arms.

Chapter Seven

Early the next morning, we all got up and went to our church. I figured the one thing we needed more than anything was prayer. This was the first time my entire family had come together to honor God in a long time, and I intended to make the most of it. We had a wonderful service, and I felt as if we all left feeling a little more uplifted. When we got back home, Miriam had a wonderful late lunch waiting on us. We all sat out on the patio and ate, while we talked and enjoyed each other's company.

After we'd been there for a while, one of Tim's friends, Anthony, came over. He was 16 and typically brought along some sort of confusion. God knows, that was the last thing we needed. To add fuel to the fire, he was showing a lot of interest in Ellen's little Amanda. The two of them together would almost immediately spell trouble. He came from a good family and his parents were pillars of the community. All I could do was pray that no problems would arise with him being present. For the most part, he behaved. Although they were there because of my illness, everyone seemed so relaxed and happy. Unfortunately, I got the feeling that it was just on the surface.

As we were talking, I looked around and noticed that Amanda and Anthony were both missing. No one seemed to know where they were, and then we realized that Anthony's car was gone. He and Amanda had left together, and were gone for over two hours. When he dropped her off, he left her alone to face the music. Amanda came around to the patio, and had clearly been drinking. She was stumbling slightly, and had a glazed look in her eyes.

"I'm going to have a talk with her," Jim said to Ellen.

"No, let me handle this," Ellen said.

Ellen went to Amanda and pulled her aside. They were clearly arguing as their voices became louder and everyone became quite uncomfortable. Amanda stormed off from Ellen, almost losing her balance.

"Don't walk away from me young lady!" Ellen shouted.

"I'll do whatever I please! I'm warning you! I'll run away again! Leave me alone!"

"Amanda!" Jim yelled, pulling her by the arm. "Watch your tone! What in the world made you go off with a boy you just met?!"

"I'll do what I want, when I want! At what point did you even realize I was gone? Probably not until I got back!"

"We realized it two hours ago!" Ellen yelled.

"Yeah, right! You don't give a damn about me!"

"That's not true!" Ellen yelled vehemently. "What have you been doing with that boy?"

"None of your business! We were having fun, and that's all you need to know!"

"What does that mean?" Jim asked.

"Just what I said! The boys down South aren't as bad as I thought they were!" Amanda smiled.

"Wow, Ellen, you really raised a little whore, didn't you?" Nora laughed.

"Go to hell Auntie Nora!" Amanda shouted, running into the house.

"Ellen, you need to control your daughter. It's true what they say: 'the apple doesn't fall far from the tree,'" Nora said in an exasperating tone.

"Leave me alone, Nora!" Ellen cried running into the house. "Amanda!"

"Why do you do that to her? Just leave her alone!" Gina yelled.

"Oh, you stay out of this, you queer! You should have kept your 'alternative lifestyle' out west!" Nora said.

"What? You want for me to 'keep up appearances' like you? You're about as phony as anyone I've ever met!"

"Phony or not, at least I lie next to a man every night! You remember what that is, don't you?" Nora snapped. "That's the one with a–"

"Nora!" Rhonda yelled, cutting her off.

"Damn, you're awful!" Gina said, running into the house.

"Nora! Will you please behave? My goodness, I feel like I'm talking to a child! Why do you alienate everyone around you?" Bill said.

"Bill, I'm warning you!"

"And just what are you going to do? You haven't worked a day in your life! Let's face it, I don't exactly need you for financial support!" Bill said. Bill then stormed into the house.

Nora looked stunned. She was humiliated by Bill, but she deserved it. Maybe she'd actually start treating her husband with the respect he rightfully deserved. Somehow, though, I seriously doubted it. I hate sometimes that Bill ended up with my sister. Even when we dated years ago, I always felt in my heart that he wasn't the one for me. When I found out he was interested in Nora, I felt a little uneasy. Not jealous. Just uneasiness about my sister's behavior. Nora had always been brazen, speaking her mind with a very sharp tongue most of the time. Bill was too nice for that.

"I'll take care of him later," Nora said venomously.

"What's that supposed to mean? Bill's your husband and he had every right to say what he said. My goodness, Nora, wake up! You're acting like a spoiled child!" I yelled. "Oh, what's the use? You'll never learn!" I then walked off, going into the house.

"Oh, no, you don't!" Nora yelled, following me. "You're the reason we're all here, so, you deal with the consequences!"

"Dammit, Nora, I didn't plan to get sick! Get that through your thick head! You fight us all on everything! Haven't you had enough misery in your life!?" I yelled.

"Oh, I've had enough misery to last a lifetime! Not that any of you would care!" Nora yelled, as we walked into the den. Our other three sisters were there as well as Alex. Everyone stared in our direction. "What are you all looking at?"

"You, and your continued desire to make a fool of yourself!" Gina yelled.

"By the way, why are you and your lover still even here?" Nora snapped.

"Because they are welcome guests in my home!" I shouted.

"Millie, you'd better make a choice: them or me! I won't stand for Gina's need to make our family look bad!" Nora said.

"Like you give a damn about anyone but yourself looking bad! You've made it quite clear that you want no part of this family!" Ellen yelled.

"No, you miserable toad, I don't want any part of you!" Nora shot back.

"Please! This has gone on long enough! I'm tired of this!" I said, with tears in my eyes. "My husband contacted all of you, and you came. Look at you. My sisters are here with me," I smiled through my tears. "The four of you came because you love me, and I know that deep down, you love each other."

"Stop living in a fantasy land, Millie," Nora sighed annoyingly. "We're not children anymore. We've not been together in years, and to be quite

129

honest, I like it that way."

"You don't mean that, Nora. Tell me something. If you don't care, why did you come?" I asked.

"Oh, you don't want to know the real reason I came!" Nora said.

"Yeah, I want to know. If you didn't come for my sake, then why are you here?" I asked.

"I came to get away from my husband. But the annoying son of a bitch wanted to fly out with me. And you want to know why? Because he's still in love with you!"

"What? Nora, don't be ridiculous!" Rhonda intervened.

"You think I'm being ridiculous? Ask him! His concern for Millie went way beyond brother-in-law concern," Nora said.

"Nora, Millie and Bill have been over years ago. Millie's in love with Clayton and Bill's in love with you," Rhonda argued.

"Oh, shut up! You've got a perfect husband who worships the ground you walk on! What would you know about anything?" Nora asked Rhonda.

"I know that you have no idea what you're talking about half the time. Let's face it, most of the time you're completely unreasonable," Rhonda responded.

"Look, this is about to escalate into something more than what it is. It doesn't matter why we're together. The important thing is that we are. Let's try to make the most of this visit," I pleaded. "I'm not giving up on the fact that we're all together right now.

Please, you guys, let's try to be civilized towards each other. Can we at least agree on that?" I asked.

"I'm willing to try," Gina spoke up.

"Me, too," Ellen said.

"And you know I want to get along," Rhonda said to me.

I looked at Nora. "Well? Are you willing to try and be civilized?"

"The only reason I'm staying is because you all would probably be happier if I left. I'm not letting you all run me off," Nora said.

"Whatever the reason, I'm glad you're staying," I smiled.

"Yeah, right," Nora sighed. "I'm going upstairs." Nora then walked out of the room.

"What? Are you going to kill her with kindness? Because I can't think of any other reason why you're so interested in her staying," Gina said.

"I'm interested in her staying because she's our sister. Her anger is on the surface. There's something more going on with Nora, and I think this visit will be a good way to get to the bottom of it," I said.

"I can tell you one thing. I've reached a whole new level of respect for you," Gina sighed.

That evening, we decided to cook out, so Miriam fired up the grill and cooked everything in the freezer. Everyone had a wonderful time, and I suspected that even Nora and Ellen were not as revolted by each other's company as they had been. Of course, after the fiasco earlier in the day, things could only get better. I was just so glad that this visit gave us all a chance to get reacquainted. Nora and Ellen did their best to be civil towards each other, which was hard for both of them. Ellen was also disappearing a lot, as if she wanted to be alone. There was so much to resolve, yet she seemed to be pulling away from the family. She seemed to want to stay away from everyone for some reason. I knew that she and Nora had their differences, but why was she being this way towards everyone else? At this point, I was tired of speculating.

Miriam was always so efficient, and she knew my kitchen better than I did. Citing that fact, I only did what she told me to do, which was very little. She, like everyone else, wanted me to do as little as possible. I looked around the backyard. Here I was, with my family, laughing and talking; not a care in the world. Life didn't get much better than this. My thoughts were interrupted by Clayton, who was looking for his deck of cards. He was going to play a game of poker with his brothers-in-law. They used to play together years ago, and Clayton usually won.

"They're upstairs. I'll go up and get them," I said.

"No, I can find them. Stay and visit with your sisters," Clayton offered.

"No, you stay here. I know exactly where they are. It'll only take a minute," I said.

I left everyone and went upstairs after stopping by the kitchen to see if Miriam needed my help. She playfully shooed me away, so I ventured on to my bedroom. Every step up the stairs was a chore, and as I neared the top of the staircase, I suddenly became too weak to stand. My breathing became labored, and for a brief moment I feared that this was the end for me. I managed to make it to my bedroom, and I sat there for a few minutes to get my bearings. I guess I must have sat there longer than I realized, because eventually Clayton came looking for me.

"Honey, I was worried about you. Is everything alright? Are you feeling okay?" Clayton asked, sitting next to me.

"I'm fine," I smiled. "Just tired."

"This has been too much for you. Why don't you lie down, and I'll go down and let everyone know you're not feeling well."

"No, that's not necessary. I'm fine," I smiled.

"Okay. Are you sure you don't want to lie down?"

"I'm sure. Here, let me get your cards," I said, standing. Suddenly I felt lightheaded, and almost fainted.

Clayton immediately took notice. "That's it. You're getting into bed right now. Maybe it was a mistake, my asking your sisters to come. You've been stressed since their arrival."

I immediately reached out for his hand. "No, Honey, I thank you for it. It's going to be the best medicine for me," I insisted. "And I'll be fine. I've gotten my second wind, so I can go back and visit a little more."

"No arguments, Millie. You're going to rest and I don't want to hear another word about it. I'll go downstairs and let everyone know. Come on, let me help you get ready for bed."

I was extremely weak, and despite the fact I'd insisted I was okay, I was so glad Clayton was there to help me. He went into my dresser and retrieved my nightgown while I undressed. He helped me to put on my gown and pulled the covers back on the bed. I got in, and he tucked me in like we used to do our children. He sat there and stared down at me. Looking into his eyes, I thought of how blessed I was to have him in my life.

When we first met, I couldn't stand him. Clayton's mom taught at my high school. Clayton had graduated from there a couple of years before me. I was a sophomore when he was a senior, and he thought he owned Creighton High. He played football, and could have pretty much had any girl he wanted. Unfortunately, his favorite extracurricular activity was making my life miserable. He used to put notes on my back saying 'kick me' and he'd make fun of me constantly. Amazing how all of that changed when he asked me to his senior prom that following spring. I thought it was a big joke at first. I didn't believe he really wanted to take me to his prom until his mom, who taught me geometry, asked if I was going to go with him to the prom. I told her that I didn't know that he was serious about my being his date. She smiled and told me that her son was very serious about taking me. At the time, I was dating Bill, who graduated a semester early and was in basic training in the military. When I talked to him, he was okay with my going to the prom with Clayton. Little did I know how monumental that date would be. So, we double dated with his twin brother, Payton and his

134

girlfriend. That so-called hate quickly turned into love, and the romance started from there. Since then, he's been making me the happiest woman alive. I realized that I'd loved him all along. Bill was nice, but, we both knew we weren't meant to be.

"What were you thinking just now?" Clayton asked.

"About when we first met, and how miserable you made me," I smiled.

"I was only acting out because I liked you so much," Clayton smiled. "You know, I think I fell in love with you that first day you walked into study hall. I'd never seen a prettier girl."

"And then I dropped my book," I smiled.

"Yeah, and when I picked it up for you, you became defensive and told me you could get it yourself," Clayton said.

"I was nervous. I mean, here was the most popular boy in school paying some attention to me. Of course, at the time, I had no idea how much attention I would get from you," I laughed.

"Sorry I made life so miserable for you," Clayton said.

"Are you kidding? I loved every minute of it," I joked.

"You're still the most beautiful woman in the world to me." Clayton stopped smiling, and looked very serious. "My Millicent, how will I go on without you?" Clayton said suddenly. There were tears in his eyes. "I can't lose you, Millie!"

"Honey, let's not dwell on it," I whispered, reaching up to caress his face with my hand. "You have made me so happy over the years. Remember what you said to me last night? You're not letting me go without a fight."

"I remember," Clayton smiled.

"To be honest, I want to go first. Because I honestly don't think I could live a day without you."

"Millie," Clayton whispered. He leaned down to kiss me lightly on the lips. "I love you so much."

"I love you, too," I said. "Now, you'd better go downstairs. In fact, just carry on without me. I'll be fine. I don't want to see everyone's evening end because I'm not feeling well."

"I'll be back shortly," Clayton said, standing from the bed. I lied there thinking about my life, and how precious every moment had been for me. How would Clayton make it? I know he's part of what makes me a whole person. God, I'm not ready to leave my husband. I started to cry just thinking about all of the uncertainty in my life. Yes, spiritually, I felt I was ready, but how could I leave? There was still so much to be done because my family was in turmoil. My youngest sister had lost her way, and Ellen was dealing with her own share of misery with her daughter. Just a little more strength, God, a little more time. Deep down, I knew it wouldn't be long now, but I just needed to hold on a little longer. Before long, I drifted off to sleep, praying once again that I would see tomorrow.

Chapter Eight

That Monday morning when I got up, I noticed that almost everyone had gone out. Clayton had gone to his office for a little while and all of my sisters were out. Kirsten had taken my nieces and nephews to the new mall that had just opened up, so they were out as well. Maybe my sisters realized they'd gotten on my nerves, and they wanted to give me some time alone. I welcomed it, even though I was a little bored. I went into the sunroom after taking a long shower. I wasn't really supposed to be around fresh flowers, so Miriam removed all of them from the house. I looked longingly out the window, wishing I weren't so limited on what I could do. It depressed me terribly. I was sitting there drinking a cup of coffee when Alex came in. She noticed my mood.

"Hey, are you okay?" Alex asked.

137

"I've been better. I have cancer, remember?" I smiled slightly. "I'm surprised you didn't go out with the others. Please, join me." I patted the seat beside me.

"Thanks. I'm still a little jetlagged, so I decided to stay in," Alex said, as she sat down next to me. "I'm curious about something."

"What's that?" I asked.

Alex then poured herself a cup of coffee. "Why haven't you talked to your sisters about being a bone marrow donor? It could save your life," Alex said. She stirred her coffee after adding cream and sugar and turned towards me. "You are going to ask them, aren't you?"

"No, I'm not," I said.

"Why not?"

"Because I don't want to burden them. I've had cancer for a year, and I never even bothered to tell them. What kind of person does that make me?"

"You're a wonderful person, Millie. That's why your sisters flew hundreds of miles to see you. Don't you think they'd help if given the chance? Even Nora?" Alex smiled lightly.

"Maybe so," I smiled. "But, I have no right to ask them. Being a donor would disrupt their lives. I can't do that. Besides, there's no guarantee that either one of them will be a match."

"And there's no guarantee that they won't be a match either," Alex reasoned.

"How did you know about the bone marrow possibility?"

"I work in the medical field, remember?" Alex

138

smiled. "Besides, I'm on the national bone marrow donor list."

"Really? I had no idea," I said. "What made you become a donor?"

"My brother," Alex smiled. She suddenly seemed distant, as if she drifted into another world. "He needed a transplant. I wasn't a match, but our sister was. After she got tested, but before we found out she could donate, she was killed."

"No!" I said quietly. "What happened?"

"She was robbed at gunpoint. The crook panicked and shot her. She died instantly," Alex said with tears in her eyes.

"Oh, Alex," I said, reaching out to hold her hand. "I had no idea. So, what did your brother do? Did he ever find a viable match?"

"No," Alex shook her head slowly. "He died eight months after my sister."

"That's terrible! I'm so sorry you went through that. How long ago did this happen?" I asked.

"Three years ago. You know, I haven't even admitted this to Gina."

"You should. Gina's very understanding."

"I know she is. It's just really hard to talk about sometimes," Alex sighed.

"You talked to me about it," I said.

"That's different. You can relate because you're going through it," Alex commented.

"That's true," I smiled. "I admire your courage."

"I'm not courageous," Alex sighed, shaking

her head slowly. "I've just lost two people I love, and I'd hate for you and your sisters not to make peace before its too late."

"I hope we can," I smiled slightly. "We take so much for granted, don't we?"

"Always," Alex smiled. Her smile then faded. "I wish I could be a donor for you. But, if you've researched the national list, I would have come up if I were a match for you," Alex said.

"That's so sweet of you," I smiled. "But, I've pretty much given up on finding a donor."

"And you still refuse to ask your sisters?"

"I can't, Alex," I sighed.

"It sounds like you're more willing to accept help from a complete stranger than from your own family," Alex observed.

"Terrible, isn't it?" I asked. "But, I suppose that's the case. Look, I don't think they're even aware that a bone marrow transplant could help me. I'd appreciate it if you wouldn't say anything."

"Millie, that puts me in an awkward position. If Gina ever found out I knew and didn't tell her, she'd never forgive me."

"The last thing I want to do is cause problems for you and Gina, but, I really don't want for any of them to know."

"You have a brother-in-law who's a doctor and another one who's a pharmacist. Your sisters probably already know."

"Well they've not mentioned anything," I said.

"You're an admirable woman, Millie," Alex sighed.

"Not admirable. Just realistic. There are no guarantees that either of my sisters will be a match. I just don't want to go through the heartache of finding out they're not. And even if I find a donor, I could still die. I mean, the odds are against me either way."

"Oh, Millie. You have so much to look forward to in life. Don't you want to be here to see your grandchildren? To see Kirsten and Robert married? Heck, even to see Shauna married."

"Now, that's stretching it a bit," I smiled.

"No, it's not. This thing doesn't have to beat you. You can beat it, Millie. But, it'll take more than your doctors or Clayton or your sisters. It will take you," Alex encouraged.

"You know, you should be a motivational speaker," I said.

"Only if it worked. Did it?"

"It worked enough for me to think about it. How's that?"

"It's better than nothing," Alex smiled as she shrugged.

"I have a doctor's appointment tomorrow. I'll discuss it with Dr. Tracer."

"Good for you," Alex smiled. "Meanwhile, let me show you a little hobby of mine that always relaxes me," Alex said, standing.

"Okay. What is it?" I asked, standing.

"Scrap booking," Alex smiled, as we walked out of the sunroom.

We went into the den where Alex already had her kit laid out. I'd never seen so many materials for one hobby. We worked on a book for over three

141

hours, and I must say I've never found anyone as serious as she was about it. We had a wonderful time, and for the first time since my sisters' arrival, I felt as if I was relaxed and at peace. It was shameful that it took the caring and understanding of someone I'd only known for a couple of days to help me through a difficult time. I really admired Alex. While I'd never been one to hate those with alternative lifestyles, a part of me wished for something more traditional for my sister. But, Alex was starting to prove me wrong, showing me that love has nothing to do with gender.

Alex and I spent the better part of the day together, having lunch after we finished our scrap books. Then, I showed her some of the art I'd done in the past, including a painting I did of Gina when she was younger. Alex loved it, so I gave it to her. She refused to take it at first, citing how much it must have meant to me. But, I insisted that she take it, because she and Gina meant so much to each other.

My sisters finally got back home that night around 7 p.m. I had no idea where they'd been all day, and they didn't seem anxious to tell me. I felt it best not to pry. Knowing Nora, she'd found the new mall the others had gone to. That night gave me a sparkle of hope that we might go an entire day without arguing. Let's face it, we'd found just about everything to fight about. What more could there be?

Miriam prepared a wonderful dinner for us that night. Everyone was laughing and talking when Aaron's cell phone rang. He excused himself from everyone to take his call. Rhonda looked upset, yet she tried to cover it. Something was obviously wrong. After Aaron had been gone for 15 minutes, Rhonda went to see if everything was okay. Rhonda stayed gone for quite a while, and I was beginning to worry. While everyone went out on the patio, I decided to go and check on Rhonda. I know she's my big sister, but the vibes just hadn't been right between the two of them since Aaron arrived. Was I imagining things? Maybe paranoia was working overtime because the evening had gone so well. They weren't in the den, so I decided to go upstairs to see if they'd gone into their bedroom. I didn't want to interrupt an intimate moment, although I got the sneaking suspicion that the last thing those two had on their minds were a few stolen romantic moments. As I went up the stairs, I heard yelling. I rushed up to the door, wondering what was going on. I didn't want to eavesdrop, but my feet were glued to the floor. I stood frozen outside their room.

"Don't you talk to me that way!" Aaron's voice was filled with so much rage. "I've had it with you!"

"Aaron, please don't be this way!" Rhonda was pleading with her husband. "We're here in my sister's home!"

"Like I give a damn! You should have stayed your ass at home! Trying to leave without my knowing about it! Look at you! You disgust me!"

"Aaron, please," Rhonda said.

"Let go of me! I'll talk to who I want, when I want! Do you understand me?!" Suddenly, I heard a thud, and him slam her against the dresser. "You stay the hell out of my business!"

"Aaron, please don't hurt me anymore! I'm sorry!" Rhonda was crying.

I covered my mouth to avoid crying out. Rhonda was being abused by her husband.

"Get up, you miserable bitch! You're so pathetic! And don't think I don't know about the hefty withdrawal you made from the bank! What are you trying to do? Leave me? You wouldn't last a day! I would have left you a long time ago if it weren't for the fact that you'd try to get everything I have! And I did not work hard all those years just to let some pathetic, know-nothing twit walk away with half!"

"Aaron, don't do this to me!" Rhonda cried.

"You bitch! Had me running half way across the country to find you! If it weren't for AJ calling, I wouldn't have known where you were!"

I couldn't take anymore. I knocked at the door, interrupting.

"Wh-who is it?" Rhonda stammered.

"It's me, Millie. Is everything okay?" I said.

"Everything's fine. We'll be out in a minute," Aaron said calmly.

"Rhonda, would you open up please? I need to talk to you," I said.

It took a while, but Rhonda finally opened the door. I could tell she'd been crying, but somehow she'd mustered a smile.

"What is it, Millie?" she smiled.

"We're having tea out on the patio. Will you join us?" I asked. Any excuse to get her away from Aaron. Her next words surprised me.

144

"No thanks. Aaron and I were just about to turn in," Rhonda said.

It was as if she didn't want to get away from him. I looked at her. Why wouldn't she come with me? I assumed she didn't want for anyone to know about what happened. He was dangerous and abusive, and I really wanted to get my sister away from him.

"Are you sure?" I whispered.

"Yes. We'll see you in the morning," Rhonda smiled again. Then, she gently closed the door in my face.

This is what Rhonda didn't want to tell me. Aaron's been abusing her. My goodness, how long has this gone on? It took me a moment to gather my thoughts. What could I do? How should I even approach Rhonda? I went to my room and sat on the bed for a minute and thought about her situation. The last thing she needed was to be in an abusive marriage. She and Aaron had been together for so long. Their children were around the same age as mine and were old enough to understand their parents splitting up. Rhonda was scared and she didn't want to leave him. What could I say to her? My sister had always been so strong. What made her yield to such torment? Rhonda was always very pretty and she could have had any man she wanted. She didn't have to settle for this, so why was she? There was so much going on with her that I had no idea about. How do I tell Clayton? He'll never stand for Aaron being here if he finds out. Would Rhonda resent me for getting involved? I was so afraid for her, but I was torn as to

145

how I should handle it.

****

The next morning, I woke up with Rhonda on my mind for obvious reasons. I'd tossed and turned throughout the night. God, when would all of the worrying end? Clayton had already gone down to breakfast. After I'd taken my shower and gotten dressed, I went to knock on Rhonda's door. No answer. Then, I saw Miriam, who was about to make up the beds.

"Miriam, have you seen Mrs. Harmon?" I asked.

"Yes ma'am. She and Dr. Harmon are out on the patio having breakfast," Miriam said.

"Thank you," I smiled.

I went downstairs and joined everyone else. After breakfast, I had a doctor's appointment. Clayton went with me and stayed the whole time. This particular appointment lasted the better part of the day. I was so tired of the appointments, but, they were a necessary part of my treatment. I wanted desperately to give up, and be left alone to die peacefully. My family refused to give up on me. After my examination and the usual lab work, I talked with Dr. Tracer.

"So, Millicent, how have you been feeling the past few days?"

"I've been getting weaker."

"Well, that's to be expected from time to time. We may need to admit you if I don't see a bit of an improvement in your lab work. You've got a slight

146

low-grade fever that I'm a little concerned about. And you know what happens when you have a fever, right?"

"I get admitted," I sighed.

"But, it's not quite high enough for me to admit you, so you're safe for today. Maybe we'll find you a donor soon and we can get you on the road to recovery."

"Dr. Tracer, I really don't want to have to be admitted again. I mean, what's the point? We already know the end result. It won't matter."

"Even if we find you a donor?"

"Come on, Dr. Tracer. If there was a donor to be found, he or she would have surfaced by now."

"That's pretty pessimistic of you. But, as your doctor, I'll be more optimistic because I have to put your health first."

"And I have to put me first," I said.

Dr. Tracer smiled. "I understand. How's that new medication working out for you since you left on Saturday?"

"It's been fine. I haven't experienced as much nausea as before."

"Good. I think we'll keep you on that for a while. Have you had any dizziness? Shortness of breath?"

"Nothing out of the ordinary. Dr. Tracer?"

"Yes?" Dr. Tracer responded, as she made notations in my chart.

"How much longer do I have?" I asked.

Dr. Tracer looked at me. "Millicent, I can't assess an exact date as to when you will die."

"I know that, but, based upon your expertise, how long do I have? Do I have a few months? A few weeks? A few days?"

"Honestly, I don't know. It could be a couple of weeks, or it could be a couple of months. You could miraculously survive for another year. It's too hard to pinpoint. If we can find you a donor, you can go on to live for years, Millicent. But, you seem adamant about not pursuing that anymore," Dr. Tracer sighed.

"After this past weekend, sometimes, I think I'd be more at peace if I were no longer here."

"Now, what brought that on?"

"My sisters," I sighed. "They came here because Clayton contacted them about my illness."

"Not that it's any of my business, but why would that be a problem for you?" Dr. Tracer asked.

"Because I didn't want for them to know."

"Is it really that bad, Millicent?" Dr. Tracer asked.

"More than you know," I said.

"You know, your sisters might surprise you," Dr. Tracer said.

"Not in this lifetime," I smiled.

"Well, I really hope things work out for you."

"Me, too," I smiled.

****

We arrived back at home around four o'clock that evening. I'd still not had a chance to talk to Rhonda about what had happened because Clayton and I had been gone the entire day. We got home in time enough to enjoy a nice dinner with the family. Afterwards, I noticed Rhonda sitting in a lounge chair. She was alone, and I figured now would be a good time to talk to her. I honestly didn't know what to say to her because she'd always guided me. She looked so happy on the surface, but I knew that she was far from it. She had such sadness in her heart. I knew what she was dealing with because I'd witnessed it firsthand. I walked over to where she was sitting.

"Mind if I join you?" I asked.

"Anytime, you know that," Rhonda smiled.

I sat in the lounge chair beside her. "How are you, Ron?" I asked.

"I'm fine. Are you feeling okay?" Rhonda asked.

"Oh, I'm about as well as to be expected. Can we talk?" I asked.

"Of course we can. I always have time for you," Rhonda said.

"Maybe we should go somewhere more private, like in the sunroom," I suggested.

Rhonda looked at me, and immediately knew. She became very uncomfortable. "Um, maybe we should just talk later," she said.

"Please, Rhonda. Later is not to be taken for granted. It's a luxury I don't have," I said.

Rhonda sighed as she put her iced tea down and stood up. "We may as well get this over with."

She walked into the house and I followed her. We went into the sunroom and I closed the doors.

"Rhonda, last night, I heard–" I started.

149

"You heard my fight with Aaron," Rhonda finished.

"Yes, I did. Did he hit you?" I asked, already knowing the answer.

"Oh, Millie, couples argue; it doesn't mean anything," Rhonda said lightly.

"Don't patronize me, Rhonda. Did he hit you?" I repeated.

Rhonda suddenly became very serious and her eyes became misty. "Yeah, in the stomach. He didn't want to 'bruise my face' in the company of others, so he slapped me," Rhonda smirked. "Slaps don't bruise as much as punches."

"How long has this been going on?" I asked.

"How long have we been married?" Rhonda responded.

"Rhonda! He's been abusing you for 27 years?" I asked surprisingly.

"No, not the entire time. It just feels like it," Rhonda sighed. "It started out because he was frustrated all the time when he was a resident. The attending physicians treat residents pretty shabbily, and my husband was no exception. He had no one else to take his anger out on at work, so he took it out on the closest thing to him, which was me. I took it because I felt that as his wife, it was my job to be there for him through the bad times, even if it meant being verbally or physically abused. I felt that at some point, after he'd gotten past the stress of his residency, it would stop. Unfortunately, it never did; it simply became a way of life."

"It doesn't have to be," I reassured.

"It's easier said than done."

"Why didn't you leave him?" I asked.

"I couldn't, although he'd stopped loving me a long time ago. I knew my husband didn't want me. After he finished his residency, I suddenly became a 'liability' for him. He was tired of me, and really wanted out. But, when he went to see an attorney, he decided against divorce."

"Let me guess: money," I said.

"Exactly. He found out that I would be entitled to half of what he makes, plus child support since the children were still minors. If he left, it would be abandonment, and he wouldn't stand a chance." Rhonda ran her hand distractedly through her hair. "I was afraid to leave, because I had no idea what Aaron would do to me. So, I stayed, and I endured. But, a few days ago, I finally got the courage to leave him. Although I desperately wanted to see you, a large part of my drive to come here was because I wanted to get away from him," Rhonda said, her voice shaking. She started to cry, and I held her.

"Ginny and AJ are adults now, and it's all going to work itself out for the best," I soothed.

"No it won't. He doesn't even care about the fact that I'm here with my family. I don't even know why he followed me here. He doesn't want me, so why not leave me alone? I wish I could understand why my husband hates me so much," Rhonda said.

I realized my sister was talking about something I couldn't relate to. The love Clayton and I have for each other is so monumental. How can I fathom an unhappy marriage? "Has he cheated on you?" I asked.

Rhonda looked at me. "You mean has he cheated on his mistress with me?" she said in a malicious tone.

"What?"

"Aaron has been keeping the same mistress for years. She even has a daughter for him."

"Oh, Rhonda. I'm so sorry!" I said.

"It's so embarrassing. We belong to the country club at home, and everyone there knows what type of man I'm married to. He's had affairs with just about all of the women I'm supposed to be friends with."

"I'm glad you came here. At least now, you realize you've got to get out of this marriage," I said.

"I wonder about that. I mean, I left him the other day, but, realistically, how can I leave him for good? I've no skills to get a good job, I've nothing on my own!" Rhonda cried. "I'm too old to model now!"

"Nonsense! There are a lot of women your age who model," I argued.

"Not starting out. Why did Daddy stop me? Sometimes I feel like if I'd been allowed to follow my dreams, I would never have married Aaron Harmon. The only good things to come out of our marriage are our children."

"Do they know?"

"No," Rhonda shook her head.

"Oh, Rhonda," I sighed. "Well, don't worry, because you can stay here. And you have to tell Ginny and AJ."

"I will. Before I left, I managed to withdraw almost $100,000.00, in hopes that I wouldn't have to go back to him," Rhonda said. "But, let's face it. I can't survive forever off of it; not after being accustomed to life as a neurosurgeon's wife for so many years."

"Forget about the money, think about your life!" I yelled.

"I-I'm scared, Millie!" Rhonda cried.

"I know you are," I said, hugging her.

We'd been so engrossed in our conversation, until we didn't realize that Nora and Gina had opened the doors, looking for us. They stood in the doorway.

"What's going on?" Nora asked, looking serious. "Rhonda, why are you crying?"

I looked at Rhonda. "It's nothing," I said.

"No, it's time they knew," Rhonda spoke up. "I'm getting a divorce."

"What? Why? After all these years?" Gina asked.

"My husband's been abusing me for years, he has a daughter by another woman, and he's still cheating on me. I guess that about sums it up," Rhonda said. "Now, don't you think I have grounds to divorce him?"

"My goodness, how long has this been going on?" Gina asked.

"It's been so long I can't even remember," Rhonda stated.

"Why didn't you ever tell us?" Gina asked.

"Gee, I don't know Gina. Why didn't you tell us about your sleeping with a woman?" Rhonda said defensively. "I didn't tell you because it wasn't your damned business! Just like your having a girlfriend wasn't ours! You show up here from LA without warning with a woman and expect us all to accept it with open arms!"

"Rhonda!" I said.

"No, it's alright, Millie. She's right. It wasn't my business. Of course, she should take her anger out on that lousy husband of hers instead of me. Just because you've been too much of a coward to stand up to him is no reason for you to lash out at me! My lifestyle has nothing to do with any of this, so you just keep Alex out of it!" Gina turned and stormed out of the sunroom.

"Well, I guess this has really turned into an interesting visit after all. Rhonda, how could you allow such a thing? You're too strong for that," Nora stated.

"Why are you coming down on me?" Rhonda said.

"Because you need a swift kick in the ass. Oh, but I forgot, your husband's already doing that! I'm not going to feel sorry for you. If you don't have enough common sense to leave the SOB then don't cry on our shoulders!" Nora yelled.

"I wasn't crying to you! You were eavesdropping!" Rhonda said.

"Look, it doesn't matter how anyone found out; please let's just calm down," I said.

"Perfect Millicent. Always the voice of reason. Why are you petting her? She didn't have to go through this," Nora said.

"Maybe not, but she did, and you should feel a little bit of sympathy for her," I said.

"No, I don't want her sympathy," Rhonda spoke up.

"Don't worry. You weren't going to get it. You're an adult, so act like one!" Nora said.

"Nora, do you always have to be so crass about everything?" I asked.

"Forget it, Millie. Nora doesn't know any better. But, she's right. I shouldn't be in an abusive marriage, just like she shouldn't be carrying on a feud with her own sister after all these years!" Rhonda spoke up.

"That doesn't have anything to do with your situation. Ellen knows why I hate her, and we'll just leave it at that. But, why is your husband abusing you? Wake up, Rhonda! Quit being stupid about the situation!" Nora said. Then, she turned and walked out of the room.

"I'm sorry, Rhonda. I can't believe they just reacted that way," I said.

"No, they're right. And I can't believe I just talked to Gina that way. I insulted her decision to live her life her own way. How could I have done that? Gina's always been very supportive, and I turned on her. I have to make this right with her," Rhonda said. "Thank you, Millie, for being here for me." She then hugged me again and left the room.

Chapter Nine

I stood there thinking that this was another setback. Every time I think we've moved forward a step, we seem to get knocked back two. Afterwards, I went out to find Clayton. He seemed to be the only sound, stable person in my life at the time and I needed him desperately. He was outside talking with Bill and Aaron. It was so hard to look at Aaron with anything other than contempt. He'd disgusted me so after finding out what he was doing to my sister. I wanted to say something to him, to lash out at him, but I knew it wasn't my place to do so. I purposely interrupted Aaron's attempt to brag about how he'd saved some patient's life.

"Can I borrow my husband?" I asked.

"Is everything okay?" Clayton asked.

"Yes, everything's fine," I responded, glaring at Aaron. I could tell by the way he looked that he knew that I was aware of what was going on. Clayton and I walked away from the rest of them. "Why don't we go for a walk on the beach for a minute?" I asked.

"Sure, whatever you want," Clayton smiled. We held hands as we walked, just like when we were dating. The sun was starting to set. We'd walked along in silence for several minutes. I was so deep in thought, until I'd forgotten about the fact that I wasn't alone.

"Honey, what's bothering you? You've been upset about something since last night. You know you can talk to me," Clayton said.

I stopped walking, hit with this sudden urge to simply have him hold me. I sighed, as I leaned my head on his chest. Clayton put his arms around me.

"Sweetheart, what is it?" He rubbed my back.

"It's Rhonda," I cried.

"Rhonda? What about her?"

"She's being abused by Aaron."

"What?"

"Last night, when I went upstairs, I overheard the two of them having an argument. I heard him hit her, and talk so terribly cruel to her. She was pleading with him, and he kept on! How could he be so cruel?" I cried on my husband's shoulder.

"I had no idea! How could he do that to her?! He has to go! I will not stand for a coward taking his frustrations out on a woman!"

"I feel the same way. I talked to Rhonda about it today, and she's agreed that she needs to leave him. I told her she could stay with us, if you don't mind," I said.

"Of course she can stay here. She can stay as

157

long as she needs to. Do Ginny and AJ know what's going on?"

"No. They haven't a clue. To make matters worse, Aaron has another child by his mistress. He seems to have so much contempt for Rhonda."

"Why doesn't he just divorce her?"

"Because it all comes down to money. He knows that if he walks, she gets half of everything he has, and he refuses to let that happen. What should we do?"

"Well, for starters, I think you, Rhonda and I need to sit down and talk. Before that, I'm going to go and tell Aaron he has to leave," Clayton said.

"Do you think that's wise? He's going to cause a scene," I said.

"So? This is our home, and he doesn't have any rights to be here if we don't want him here. Let's see him try to hit me like he does Rhonda. I'm not afraid of Aaron Harmon. Come on. Let's walk back up to the house," Clayton said.

Before we could even get to the patio, we knew that something was wrong, yet again. Clayton ran to see what was going on. Bill and Jim were holding Aaron back, and Kyle and Robert were holding AJ back. Rhonda was crying, while Ellen was comforting her.

"What's going on?" I asked.

"This bastard's been abusing my mother!" AJ yelled.

"What happened?" Clayton asked.

"Rhonda is trying to turn my children against me!" Aaron yelled.

"I'd never do such a thing!" Rhonda said.

"I knew something was wrong!" Ginny cried. "Daddy, how could you do this?"

"Tell them, Dad! Tell them how you've been using Mom as a punching bag!" AJ said.

"Aaron, I want you out of my house," Clayton said calmly.

"With pleasure! Just know, Rhonda, that money you stole from me the other day? That's the only money of mine you will ever get! So, you'd better make it stretch! And I want you out of my house! Let's see how you get along without me!"

"She doesn't need your house! I've already offered her a place to stay," I said.

"Fine! I'll send the rest of her things to you! Finally, one less headache in my life! It's taken a lot of years to get rid of you!"

"Did you tell your children about your other daughter?" Gina spoke up.

"What!?" Ginny yelled.

"Yeah. It seems your daddy has another child, a daughter by his loving mistress," Gina said.

"Is this true?" Ginny said, with tears in her eyes.

"Yes, it's true," Rhonda murmured.

"Ginny, it's not what you think! Your mother's trying to poison your mind against me!" Aaron said.

"Is it true, Daddy?!" Ginny asked again.

Aaron looked around at everyone. Then he looked at Ginny. "Yes, it's true. But I need to explain–"

"There's nothing to explain! How could you?! You disgust me! Look at what you've done to our family, to our mother! All this time, I've been thinking that she never gave you the benefit of the doubt! Now, I know you've been the problem all the time!" Ginny cried.

"Whatever! I don't care anymore! You'll never get a dime from me, either! Neither one of you! Your mother's never been worth all the years I spent trying to make her a woman!" Aaron shouted.

"Why you miserable– " AJ lunged at his father, pushing him over a lounge chair, into the pool.

"Someone, stop them!" I yelled.

"Stop it, you two!" Clayton yelled.

He and Bill along with Jim and Robert jumped into the pool to pull them apart. AJ was trying to drown Aaron. He wouldn't let him up for air. I feared that my nephew would do something out of anger that he would deeply regret later. They finally managed to get AJ away from his father. Aaron was coughing as Jim and Robert pulled him out of the pool.

"You stay away from me!" Aaron shouted, stumbling as he stood to his feet.

"I'll kill you before I let you ever lay another hand on my mother!" AJ threatened.

"She's not worth it! None of you are! All of you are crazy and the sooner I can get away from this family the better off I'll be! I'm sure Bill can relate, considering he's married the whore in the family!"

"You miserable coward! You leave my wife out of this!" Bill said.

"Why? She never liked to be left out of

160

anything! Yeah, Rhonda! I had your sister, too!"

"What?" Rhonda said, looking at Nora.

"I slept with Nora! Bill, you might want to get a paternity test on Jessica! You never know!" Aaron bragged.

"He's lying!" Nora yelled.

"Oh? Remember when your little sister came to stay with us for a week during spring break? She brought more pleasure than you ever did!"

"Dammit, Aaron, you would stoop to any level! How could you say such a thing about my sister?!" Rhonda shouted.

"Because it's true!" Aaron shouted.

"Aaron's crazy! Don't listen to him!" Nora cried.

"I'm not crazy and you know it!" Aaron laughed.

"My sister may be capable of a lot of things, but she wouldn't do that to me!" Rhonda yelled.

"Oh, yes! She would!" Aaron laughed.

Rhonda looked at Nora. "Is there any truth to what he's saying, Nora? Did you sleep with Aaron?" Rhonda asked.

Nora shook her head, crying.

"Answer me! Did you sleep with my husband!?"

Nora covered her face with her hands, as she cried.

"Bill, doesn't your wife have a heart-shaped birthmark on her left cheek?" Aaron smiled, looking at Nora.

Bill looked alarmingly at Nora with utter

disgust in his eyes.

"It-it was a long time ago! Bill and I had broken up briefly!" Nora cried. "I was weak, and it only happened once!"

"Is Aaron Jessica's father!?" Bill yelled, grabbing Nora. Nora shook her head slowly as tears streamed down her face. Bill shook her. "Is he!?" Bill asked again.

"I-I don't know!" Nora cried out.

"I-I don't believe this! You took advantage of my wife!" Bill yelled.

Before anyone could stop him, Bill went for Aaron. He pushed him to the ground and started choking him. This evening was beginning to be more than I could handle. I was crying by now, because everyone was falling apart. Clayton and Jim pulled Bill off of Aaron. Bill looked at Aaron with so much hate.

"What's the use? You're not even worth it," Bill said, breathing hard. "I'm leaving!"

"Bill! Please wait!" Nora said, running to him. She placed her hand on his arm.

"For what?" Bill jerked away from her. "For more lies? Our whole marriage has been nothing but a big joke to you!"

"Bill! I'm sorry! I was young and foolish! Please forgive me!" Nora cried. For the first time in my life, I actually heard Nora beg.

"Daddy!" Jessica cried. Jessica ran to Bill and hugged him.

"Come on, Jessica and Matthew. We're leaving," Bill said calmly.

162

"Bill! Please don't go! It was a long time ago!" Nora cried.

"Bill, wait a minute," I said.

"Please, Millie. I know you're trying to help, but I've nothing more to say. I'm going upstairs to change out of these wet clothes and then my children and I are taking the first flight back to DC!" Bill said.

"Well, you finally did it! You finally destroyed our family! I'll never forgive you for this!" Jessica yelled. "You never deserved Daddy and I'm so glad he's leaving you! I only wish it would have happened a long time ago!"

"How could you?" Matthew asked. "I never thought I could be so disgusted with you! I always wondered if you were faithful to Daddy, but it's worse than I thought. Your own sister's husband? That's a new level of low, even for you!" He shook his head and looked at his mother with so much anger and disgust.

Bill then walked into the house, as Jessica and Matthew followed him. Nora sobbed loudly as she fell to her knees. Gina and Alex went to try and comfort her.

"Let me try to talk to Bill," Clayton suggested. "Take care of Nora and Rhonda."

"Thank you, Clayton," I said. "You'd better change, too, before you catch cold."

"I will." Clayton then looked at Aaron. "Aaron, go upstairs, pack your things and leave."

"Gladly!" Aaron smiled.

Robert and Jim still held AJ back from going after Aaron. I suggested that they all go and change.

AJ went to the guesthouse to change, and Kyle had something he could loan Robert since they were around the same size. Ellen was with Rhonda, who was completely stunned by everything that had just happened. Kyle and Kirsten were really concerned about how I was feeling. I assured them that I was fine. I went to Rhonda to check on her.

"Rhonda, are you okay?" I asked.

"I can't believe her! She had an affair with my husband! My own sister! How could she!" Rhonda cried.

"I don't know," I sighed. "Come on. Let's go inside."

"I'll check on Ginny and AJ for you," Ellen offered.

"Thank you, Ellen," Rhonda said.

We walked past Nora who was still crying.

"Rhonda, I-I'm sorry!" Nora cried. "It was so long ago!"

Before uttering a word, Rhonda spit on Nora. She looked venomously at Nora.

"You're trash to me, Nora. You are dead as far as I'm concerned. I hope you lose everything. I'll never forgive you for this," Rhonda said calmly. Then, she walked off.

I looked at Nora, as she wiped her face. I didn't have to say a word to her. My facial expression was enough for her to know how disappointed I was in her.

What kind of person was Nora? Her own sister's husband? I was truly disappointed in my sister. It's as if she wasn't raised by the same people

164

as the rest of us. We were raised to respect each other, and definitely not to go after each other's spouses. Rhonda and I went into the sunroom. She sat down, and massaged her forehead with her hand.

"How could she Millie? It's hard enough knowing Aaron's never been faithful, but to know that one of the women he's been with is my own sister?"

"Honey, I wish there was something I could say to make this easier on you," I said as I sat down next to her.

"I know you do," Rhonda smiled. Then, she reached out and covered my hand with hers. "So much for us coming here to be here for you. Seems like all we've done is argue since we've been here, haven't we?"

"Seems like it," I smiled. I looked at her. "I knew that beautiful smile of yours was in there somewhere."

"Oh, Millie," Rhonda sighed, as she stood and walked to the window. She looked out and saw Nora. "Look at her! Crying those crocodile tears! As if she's actually sorry for what she did!"

"Maybe she is," I reasoned.

"No, she's sorry because Bill's going to divorce her," Rhonda said. "And it would serve her right, too."

I had to agree with Rhonda. Nora was so unbelievably selfish until I seriously doubted if she cared about the fact that she'd destroyed her marriage. It was all about status. Nora loved being the wife of an important man. I still wanted to give her the benefit of the doubt.

"She seemed sincere when she apologized to you," I said.

"Ha! That was just for show. Nora being overly-dramatic Nora!" Rhonda smirked. "You know our sister has always had a flair for the dramatics. She should have been an actress!"

I smiled. I admired how Rhonda still tried to make a joke out of the entire situation. I stood and walked over to the window next to where she was standing.

"How did all of this happen? Clayton and I went for a walk on the beach. We come back and chaos everywhere," I said.

"Apparently, Aaron picked up on the fact that you knew something by the look you gave him. He came and confronted me. AJ witnessed him hitting me."

"Oh, my goodness!" I exclaimed.

"AJ tried to stop him. My son looked at me and asked how long Aaron had been abusing me. I told him the truth. And 'the rest' as they say 'is history.' You and Clayton pretty much witnessed everything else."

"Oh, Honey," I sighed, hugging her shoulders.

"You know, maybe it's for the best. I came here because I knew I'd have to get out of the marriage or he'd kill me. He's such a manipulator! He always wants to have sex after he uses me as a punching bag. Last night was no exception."

"Well?" I asked, looking at her.

Rhonda sighed. "I did it. Usually, he forces me anyway. I'm always too scared to say no. Then,

I forgive him for everything. But, this was the eye-opener. Sex with my sister? Not even I'm stupid enough to forgive that one!" Rhonda laughed slightly.

"Don't worry, everything will work out. You have a home here as long as you need one."

"Thank you," Rhonda smiled, reaching up to touch my hand. "I don't know what I'd do without you." Rhonda must have instantly realized what she said. She turned immediately to look at me. "I'm sorry, Millie."

"Why are you apologizing? I'm still here," I smiled. "I'm not gone yet. I'll be here for you as long as I can."

Rhonda looked at me intently. "You really are at peace with this, aren't you?" she whispered.

"Yeah, I think I am. I've led a good life. I have a wonderful husband, four beautiful children, a beautiful home, and four sisters whom I love dearly, no matter how crazy they may drive me," I smiled. "I'm ready," I whispered, looking into Rhonda's eyes.

"You are a much better woman than I am," Rhonda whispered tearfully, hugging me. "You're so calm, knowing you could be dead tomorrow. I don't want to lose you!"

"Shh, it's okay," I whispered, hugging her tighter. "You'll never lose me because I'll always be in your heart. Okay?"

"I-I want my sister here!" Rhonda cried.

I pulled away to look at her. "I am here. I'm afraid, but I've accepted God's plan for me. I need for you to be strong. I can't leave if you're not going

167

to be strong."

"Then I'll stay weak if it means keeping you here." Rhonda smiled through her tears.

"Sweetheart, I wish it were that simple," I smiled, wiping the tears from her face. We were interrupted by a knock at the door. It was Ellen.

"Are you okay?" Ellen asked gently.

"Yeah, I'm okay. Has Aaron left yet?" Rhonda asked.

"He just left," Ellen said.

"Good riddance," Rhonda said. "How are AJ and Ginny?"

"They're fine," Ellen reassured. "Kyle and Robert took AJ for a ride so that he could cool off. Erin and Kirsten are in the guest house with Ginny to make sure she's okay. I'm worried about you."

"Just hurt pride, I guess. The hitting doesn't hurt anymore. He destroyed my soul a long time ago," Rhonda said. "I've grown numb to the abuse. It's just so embarrassing!"

"Why? We're your family. We'd understand," Ellen said.

"You obviously didn't hear Nora earlier today," I said.

"Oh, come on! Nora? She's as crazy as they come anyhow. Who cares what she thinks?" Ellen said.

"I sure don't. Not anymore," Rhonda said. "As far as I'm concerned, Nora Riley doesn't exist."

"You don't really mean that, do you?" I asked.

"Of course I do!" Rhonda insisted. "What if it were you that she did this to? Are you telling me you can just forgive and forget?"

"Honestly? No, probably not. But you've said yourself that you came here because you want out of the marriage," I reminded her. "Maybe this is just the thing to give you the courage to go through with a divorce."

"I know, but just the thought that this secret has been kept from me all these years. She could have told me."

"Oh please! And taint her image as a 'model wife'? Nora doesn't expose her own faults, just everyone else's," Ellen said.

"But this supposedly happened before she and Bill were ever even married," Rhonda said. "She could have been honest with me. I mean, my husband could be Jessie's father. And we all know the real reason behind her getting pregnant with Jessica," Rhonda said.

"You know, all these years, we've speculated that it was to get Bill to marry her because of his money. But, maybe she really got pregnant by accident," I tried to reason.

"Now you don't really believe that, do you?" Ellen asked.

"Can't we give our sister the benefit of the doubt?" I asked.

"Millie, you have one of the most gullible hearts of gold," Rhonda said.

We sat in the sunroom talking for quite a while. Nora never had the courage to come in and try to talk to Rhonda. Eventually, AJ and Ginny came in to check on Rhonda. She decided to go off and talk with the two of them; to try to explain everything that had transpired over the past years. She told Ellen and me goodnight, leaving us in the sunroom. I looked at Ellen, still concerned about her after what had happened with Amanda.

"How are you holding up? I know Amanda's been a handful," I said.

Ellen sighed. "Like you wouldn't believe! Millie, I don't know what's wrong with that girl. She's gotten wilder and wilder with each passing day. She's been kicked out of school. When school starts back, she's going to be attending an alternative school."

"I had no idea!" I said.

"Jim and I have really tried with her. She's been sleeping around, and I'm so afraid for her. And you don't know the half of it! But, it seems like the more we chastise, the more we punish, the worse she gets. I'd bet my last shiny nickel that she had sex with that boy the other day. Why does she keep doing this to herself?" Ellen said tearfully.

"Maybe she should see someone professionally," I suggested.

"Oh, we've tried that. It didn't work. She told her therapist exactly what she wanted to hear."

"How long did she go?" I asked.

"For over a year. It's sad, Millie. She sneaks out of the house constantly. We've been thinking of leaving New York. I think it's too fast of a city for her."

"Do you really think that will solve the problem?" I asked.

"Probably not," Ellen sighed. "I'm sorry to be putting all of this on you."

"Nonsense! I'm here as long as you want to talk," I said.

"I don't know what I'd do without you!" Ellen cried. Then she hugged me.

I sighed. Lord, what could I do? My sisters need me. They were drifting so much already. God, please don't take me away from them. Not now. It was at that precise moment I knew I wasn't ready to go. How could I fight? I was so weak already; so tired of fighting. Ellen and I sat talking a while longer until Jim interrupted. They soon went up to bed and I sat there quietly. I dimmed the lights in the sunroom. Since we'd had this house built, this had always been my most favorite room. It gave me a sense of peace and escape.

I went into the kitchen and fixed a glass of warm milk. I went back into the sunroom, and sat there, thinking about my life. I seemed to be doing that a lot lately. I also took the time to write in my journal. I kept a journal for my future grandchildren. I'd already written letters to each of my children as well as Clayton. I had so much to say and so little time in which to say it. This was my 'me' time. I sat there pondering over all that had transpired, and I cried. I cried because all this time, I thought I was the one with the problems. Although I knew I was dying of cancer, my sisters were suffering even more. I'd not even considered writing letters to them, but now, I felt compelled to do just that. Where would I start?

Dear Rhonda,

I'm writing this letter on the same night you found out about Nora and Aaron. It's around 10 p.m., and I started thinking about what I'd say to you, what type of words I would have for you after I'd gone. I won't dwell on what's happened between you and Nora, because I feel with all of my heart and soul that it will be worked out for the best. You love each other, and I hope that you can look beyond everything and become a family again. I do have a favor to ask of you. When I'm gone, I want for you to be a mother to my daughters. Especially Shauna. She's so young and impressionable. It's so unfair to think that my little girl will have to grow up without her mother. Be a mother to her, love her as you have your own daughter. She's going to need guidance through puberty, boys, prom, graduation; so many things. Things that I was able to guide Kirsten through. Although Kirsten's an adult, she'll need you, too. I know that she gets along well with Robert's mother, but, she needs someone she can turn to no matter what. When she argues with Robert, I need you in her corner, even if it's just to tell her she's wrong. It's my belief that Clayton will be there for our sons, but, if by some terrible twist of fate he's not able to be there for them, nurture them as well. Teach Tim that he should never treat a woman the way you've been treated. I pray that we've instilled proper beliefs in our children, but I need you there as a constant reminder. Be strong, Rhonda. Be happy, no matter what. Take care of yourself, and always remember how much I

172

love you.

Love,
Your Little Sis, Millie

Dear Nora,

I'm sitting here writing to you, trying to find the words to say from beyond the grave. As you've probably figured out, I'm instructing that this letter not be given to you until after I've passed on. With everything in me, I'm praying that by the time you read this, you will have made amends with your sisters. I know you will. But, Nora, if it takes my death to bring you all together, then so be it. As a dying request, if you've not made amends, I beg you to do it. I love you so much, Nora. You've done some things that I know you're not proud of. Just know that I don't hold those things against you. I've never judged you, no matter what you may think. You're so strong. You're about as feisty as anyone I've ever encountered, which is a part of what makes you special. It's not too late, Nora. It's never too late to be happy, even if it's just for the last day of your life. Everything will work out for the best. Maybe you've taken some things for granted in your life, things that now may seem threatened to be lost. It could be your wake-up call to be the woman that you were meant to be. Bill's angry tonight, but you have to fight for your marriage. You're a fighter, and I know it's worth it. Your whole family is worth it, no matter what you say. Be the loving wife, mother and sister that it's in you to be.

173

Be a family again, and never forget how much I love you.

All my love,
Millie

Dear Ellen,

Gosh, where do I even begin? I guess I should just begin by telling you how much I love you. I know that we are in the middle of what has been a very trying reunion for us all, but, I get the feeling it won't be in vain. I know you all came because of Clayton's call, and that alone tells me there's so much love between the five of us. The four of you have challenged me beyond my wildest dreams, but I've come to the realization that anything worth having is worth fighting for. So, I've not given up on you guys yet. I can't tell you how much it means that you all came here for my sake despite our ups and downs. At least it gives me the chance to etch in my memory your beautiful faces. I hope I can remember these things after I'm gone. I will look in on you guys from time to time, just to see my wonderful family happy and content. It's coming. I don't know when, but I do know it's going to happen. You and Nora will be sisters again, that I can assure you. I don't know if it will happen during the course of this reunion, but you will love each other as you did years ago. It's not impossible, Ellen. Just know that no matter what, I love you and I will always be here for you, even after death.

Love always,
Millie

My Dearest Gina,

I think I'm happiest writing this letter, because it's to my little sister, the one I'm most proud of. (Don't tell the others, but, you've always been my favorite!) Despite everything that's happened during this reunion, the one thing I'm happiest about is that you are here. I may never lay eyes on you again after this, but I will always smile, knowing that you were an important part of my life for the past 28 years. I remember when you were born. Mama and Daddy had so many plans for you. I wonder if they can see just how well you turned out. I'm saddened to think that of all of my sisters, I've had the least amount of time with you. You're a precious part of my life that I will miss dearly. If you are happy with your decision to be with Alex, you have my blessing. But, make sure it's your decision, not anyone else's. Alex is a wonderful woman, and although a part of me pictured you with a husband and children, I will never hate or judge you for the decision you've made on how to live your life. Live it to the fullest, Gina. Never let one day be wasted on regrets and anger. If you've learned nothing else from your sisters' influences, let the one thing you learn be that anger, hate and regrets can plague a family and destroy it worse than any cancer. Be happy, my little sister, and know that I will always love you and protect you.

175

Love,
Your Big Sis, Millie

After writing those letters, I sealed them in individual envelopes with the appropriate sister's name. I wrote that they were not to be opened until my death. I put them in my keepsake box, which is where I kept the other letters I'd written. Those tasks complete, I was able to feel as if I'd completed another chapter in my life. This cancer had taken its toll on me. I just wanted more time with my family. A few minutes later, I heard the clock chime midnight. I'd sat there for over two hours before I knew it. As if on cue, Clayton came in looking for me.

"I thought I'd better check on you," he smiled. "Are you okay?"

"I'm fine. Just needed a little 'me' time," I said.

"Do you want to be alone?"

"No, I'm glad you came in," I smiled.

Clayton sat beside me on the sofa. He stroked my hair as he stared at me intently. "What have they done to my Millie?" Clayton asked.

"They've tried me beyond belief," I sighed.

"I'm so sorry," Clayton whispered.

"For what?" I asked.

Clayton sighed. "I really thought I was doing the right thing by bringing the five of you together. Maybe I should have left well enough alone."

"Don't feel that way. I couldn't be happier that they're here. It gives me a healthy distraction," I said.   "If it weren't for you calling them to come here, these destructive secrets wouldn't have come out, and we might not ever heal," I said, leaning on Clayton. He hugged me.

"I know you're right.   But the one thing I want to make sure of is that you don't worry yourself over their problems.   Each one of your sisters is an adult. It's time they started acting like it.   Maybe now that all of this is out in the open, they can deal with it and move on.   But, I don't want for it to be at the cost of your happiness and health," Clayton said.

"Why do they have to fight so much?   We didn't disagree this much when we were younger," I said.

"They didn't have the problems they have now. They have to learn how to deal with the things going on in their lives.   Now that Rhonda knows what happened, she can try to find a way to forgive Nora," Clayton said.

"But, we still don't know why Nora hates Ellen.   She won't reveal that.   What could have happened to make her feel the way she does?" I asked.

"Beats me.   Maybe she'll open up now that she's on the receiving end of the anger.   Maybe this will do her relationship with Ellen some good."

"I doubt it.   How did your talk with Bill go?" I asked.

"Not good," Clayton shook his head.   "He's heading back to DC as we speak.   Jessica hates Nora, and Matthew is so disappointed in her.   I don't know if they'll ever get past all of this."

"I hate to say this, Clayton, but Nora pretty

177

much deserves what she's getting right now. She's treated Ellen so terribly bad over the years, without explanations why," I sighed. "I wonder about something."

"What's that?" Clayton asked.

"Nora also has animosity towards Daddy. Do you think there's a connection?"

"What do you mean?" Clayton asked.

"I mean, something happened between the three of them that Nora's not talking about. I don't know, I could be totally wrong," I said.

Clayton and I sat there for the rest of the night. Eventually, we snuggled really close together on the sofa and fell asleep. I'd dozed off in Clayton's arms, but I woke in time to see an absolutely spectacular sun rise from the sunroom. I gently nudged Clayton to wake him.

"Clayton, look," I said, pointing out the window.

Clayton stroked my shoulder as he looked out the window. "It's beautiful, isn't it?" Clayton asked.

"I wish I could capture this in my art," I said.

"Does that mean you're ready to start painting again?" Clayton asked.

I looked at him. I used to love to do oil paintings, but somewhere, that part of me died after finding out about my cancer.

"I don't think I can."

"Why not? You're such a talented artist. Don't give up on that part of your life. Maybe that's just the thing you need to get back on track," Clayton said.

"'Get back on track'? How, Clayton? Have you not been here the past year? I'm dying. There's no 'getting back on track' for me." I realized after I said it, that I was feeling sorry for myself. In the year I'd known about my cancer, I'd desperately tried not to do that.

We sat there quietly for the next few minutes, simply enjoying each other's company. That was the beauty of being together so long. Neither one of us felt the need for idle chitchat to try to entertain or impress the other. We got up and went upstairs to shower and change when we heard Miriam come in. She always got there promptly at 6:30 a.m. every morning. I wasn't looking forward to the day ahead because I knew there would be a lot of animosity. This was getting to be more than I could handle. If it weren't for Clayton being there to keep me sane, I honestly didn't know what I would do.

By the time we got back downstairs onto the patio, Nora and Rhonda were already at each other's throats. Thank goodness Kyle and Kirsten had taken the others out to breakfast that morning. So, along with my four sisters, there was only Clayton, Alex, and Jim.

"You think you're better than everyone else! That's always been your problem! I hope you choke on it!" Rhonda shouted.

"How dare you? I've tried to apologize for what I did! It was a long time ago!" Nora said defensively.

"Oh? Apologizing makes it okay? You're a

miserable piece of trash who deserves whatever bad comes your way!" Rhonda said. "You want me to forgive you, but you won't even forgive Ellen for whatever it is she supposedly did!"

"That's not your concern! That's between Ellen and me!" Nora shouted, looking in Ellen's direction.

"But you won't even be woman enough to admit what it is you're so mad about! Do I look like a psychic to you?!" Ellen spoke up.

"How could you forget what you did?" Nora asked, looking surprisingly at Ellen.

"What did I do!?! Dammit, Nora, just tell me!" Ellen demanded.

"You watched him do that horrible thing to me!" Nora cried.

Ellen looked confused. "What are you talking about? Watched who do what horrible thing to you?"

"Oh, you are really playing this one to the end, aren't you?" Nora asked.

"My God, Nora, if you're not going to tell me, then let it go!" Ellen said.

"You watched Daddy rape me!" Nora screamed.

Chapter Ten

Wh-what?" Ellen was completely stunned, just as we all were.

"You stood there, and watched him rape me! And you did nothing! I yelled for you to help me, and you completely ignored me. Then, you ran away! I hate you, Ellen! I'll never forgive you for doing that to me!"

"Are you sure about this?" I asked.

"Millicent, I couldn't be more sure about anything in my life! My own sister stood by and watched our father rape me! I was only 15! How could you?!" Nora shouted, crying.

"I-I never saw such a thing!" Ellen said defensively.

"And now you have the gall to stand here and lie about it!?! I looked right at you! You saw it all and then you ran away like the coward that you are!"

181

Nora said.

"No! It can't be true! I never would have stood by and watched such a thing! Never!" Ellen said, starting to cry. "Nora, you have to believe that. I wouldn't do that to you!"

"Oh, yes, you would! I ought to know! Remember? It happened to me," Nora said.

"Oh, Nora! I-I'm sorry!" Ellen said, sitting down in a chair as she cried.

Rhonda sat down beside Ellen and held her. "Its okay, Ellen," Rhonda whispered.

I looked at Nora, who was crying.

"My goodness, Nora, is this true? Did this really happen to you?" I asked.

"Why would I lie about such a thing?" Nora said, looking at me.

"Oh, Sweetheart, I'm so sorry," I said, reaching out to hug her.

"I-I tried to get him to stop, but he wouldn't!" Nora cried.

What could I do? My sister had experienced something so traumatic, and it was done by someone I'd admired my whole life. What kind of monster was he? It certainly explained a lot, considering how Nora had behaved over the years. Was this why she slept with her sister's husband? My heart went out to my younger sister, and I truly had no idea how to help her. At least now it was out in the open so that maybe she and Ellen could start to mend their relationship. Was this something they could get past? What I didn't understand was why Ellen denied witnessing what Daddy did when Nora was adamant about it.

Was there some sort of misunderstanding? Something wasn't right because Ellen would never have been so heartless. Nora continued to cry on my shoulder. She and I walked into the house and went into the room Nora was using. We sat down on the bed.

"Do you want to talk about it?" I asked softly.

"Oh, Millie, I've kept this bottled up for almost 25 years," Nora sighed. "I don't know if I can bring myself to talk about it."

"Honey, this has eaten away at you for so long. It's time to start the healing process. Please, Nora. Talk to me," I soothed.

Nora gave a deep sigh. "It happened one summer in late August, after you and Rhonda were married and out of the house. Ellen and I were the only two at home because Mama had taken Gina to the doctor that day. I'd been out in the backyard practicing cheers with some of the other girls from my cheering squad. Ellen came out of the house and told me that she'd be next door at her friend Katie's house practicing for their baseball game. Later, after my friends left, Daddy came home early from work." Nora wiped her tears as she spoke. "I was in my room dressing after my shower. Daddy called for me, and I told him that I would be out in a minute. He didn't wait, and he came into my room. He had this strange look in his eyes, and it really frightened me. I was only half dressed, and embarrassed. He pushed me down on the bed, and tore my blouse away. I kept yelling for him to stop, and he wouldn't. He ripped off my underwear and raped me. I was crying, and

183

begging for him to stop. My window was open, and while he was on top of me, I saw Ellen peeking into the window. She had on that stupid red baseball cap that she wore everywhere. I begged her to help me. She looked at me, then she ran away! I mean, how could she? How could she run away after seeing what he was doing to me?!"

"Are you sure it was Ellen? That's so unlike her to do such a thing," I reasoned.

"You really think I'm lying, don't you!?! H-how could you?" Nora cried.

"No, no, no, I don't think you're making it up. I just think that maybe there's more to this story than you're aware," I said.

"What more could there be? Our sister saw our father rape me, and she did nothing, absolutely nothing. She never even came to me and admitted what she saw. She didn't apologize. She acted as if it didn't even happen. She didn't even care if I was okay or not," Nora yelled.

"Did you ever tell Mama?" I asked.

"No, because Daddy told me that if I did, she wouldn't believe me. He called me a whore and said that they knew I wasn't a virgin, so there was no way Mama would believe a word I said. And you know what? He's right. I'm not worth it! I've done some awful things, thanks to him!" Nora said.

"Oh, Nora," I sighed, hugging her.

A part of me wondered if now Nora would automatically blame this for her constant erratic behavior. This was her new 'trump card.' I was by no means making light of her suffering, but my sister has always blamed others for her problems, even before this ever happened. Was I being unsympathetic? After all, she's my sister, and I love her. I sat there with her to comfort her, but what could I say? I hated what she'd gone through, but Nora had done so many things to hurt other people. She'd lashed out and destroyed everything in her path. Nora immediately stood from the bed.

"I can't stay here, Millie. I have to go home, to my husband, to try to salvage what's left of my marriage," Nora stated, grabbing her luggage.

"What about Ellen? Don't you think the two of you should talk things through?" I suggested.

"Talk what through? She's denying it ever even happened. There's nothing more to say to her," Nora said, as she tossed things into her suitcase.

"There's still the situation with Rhonda that needs to be dealt with," I said.

"Rhonda's not ready to forgive me. When she is, she'll contact me," Nora said cavalierly.

"So, that's it? Just up and run away?" I challenged.

"'Run away'? I've tried to apologize to Rhonda, and she won't listen! What do you want for me to do? Tie her down and make her accept my apology?" Nora asked sarcastically.

"No, but she does have the right to know why you had an affair with her husband!" I shouted. It was unbelievable how selfish Nora was! What was she thinking?

"She doesn't want to hear anything I have to say!" Nora shot back.

"Make her listen! You have a knack for getting everything else you want, so talk to your sister! Talk to both of them! I'm so tired of your attitude!" Why did she try to make everything about her problems, or her wants and desires? She acted as if no one else's feelings mattered. "Does anyone mean anything to you?" I asked.

"How dare you judge me!" Nora yelled.

"Listen to yourself! You've slept with your sister's husband, you refuse to forgive or listen to your other sister, you've judged your youngest sister for her lifestyle, yet you have the nerve to stand here and say something about someone judging you?! You've managed to somehow hurt everyone in your path!" I yelled. "I'm ashamed to even be associated with you!"

"Well, well, well. It's finally happened. Millicent Welby's finally found something on me to make her feel better about her own misery! You've appointed yourself my judge and jury."

"What?! Is that what you think!? Do you think I've gone looking for something on you so that I can judge you?"

"Let's face it, Millie, you always look down on everyone else. No one's life is as perfect as yours, is it? You're so high on your horse! When you fall, and believe me you will, you're in for a painful landing!"

"Oh, Sweetheart, I've landed! And I didn't have far to fall because I've never been condescending to others, unlike yourself! Now, it's time you grew up! Gosh, you are unbelievable! So, who do you blame for what you did? Bill? Rhonda? Daddy? Ellen? Or maybe you blame me?" I challenged. "Tell me something, Nora. Was Aaron the only one? Was he the only time you ever cheated on Bill?"

"For someone who is no longer in love with Bill, you sure are protective of him. Don't forget, he's my husband!" Nora shouted.

"What's that supposed to mean?" I shouted.

"You know damn well what it means! I figured you out a long time ago! Little Miss Innocent! You love to play both sides against each other! Bill and Clayton! You treated Bill like dirt!"

"I did not! I fell in love with Clayton, but I never mistreated Bill. Can you say the same?"

"Just stay the hell out of my life! What I do isn't your business!"

"You know, you're right! What you do isn't my business! But it's your husband's business, and considering you slept with Rhonda's husband, it's your sister's business. Because those are the ones you've hurt the most by your selfish indiscretions!"

"I've been hurt, too! What about what I've been through!? But, you don't care about that, do you? I was young, and our father took advantage of me! But, that doesn't matter, right? As long as I apologize to Rhonda, and forgive Ellen! Why are their feelings more important than mine? Why is their hurt more painful than mine? Talk about a double standard!"

"Nora, no one ever tried to belittle your pain, but you've got to stop this! Daddy's to blame, and he's not here! So, talk to your sisters, and try to get

187

on with your life!"

"Ellen's to blame, too!" Nora said. She was determined not to be wrong, not to accept responsibility for her actions.

I threw my hands up in desperation. "Oh! I give up!" I walked out, and slammed the door. I stormed downstairs, where Clayton met me.

"Honey, are you okay?" Clayton asked, rubbing my shoulders.

"I'm so tired, Clayton," I sighed. "Despite everything that has happened, Nora seems to show very little remorse. She still insists upon blaming others for her problems."

"I'm sorry, Sweetheart," Clayton said.

"I just wish I could do something to bring them together," I said.

"There's nothing you can do until they're ready. I know you want to, but, you have to let them work this out for themselves."

"I know you're right, but it just hurts to see them at odds like this. Have you seen Ellen?"

"She's out on the patio with Jim and Rhonda," Clayton said.

"I need to talk to her," I said, walking away.

"Are you sure you're up for it?" Clayton asked, pulling me back to him.

"I have to be," I sighed, resting my head on his chest.

"Oh, honey, I hate to see you like this," Clayton said, stroking my back. "If I'd known this would happen, I never would have called them."

"No, Sweetheart. We have to work through

this.   I'd like for us to face this while I'm living.   But, time isn't exactly on my side."

"It'll work out, Millie."

"Easier said than done," I smiled.

Clayton and I walked out to the patio.   Rhonda and Ellen were in a deep discussion about Nora.

"Rhonda, I swear I didn't see Daddy do anything to her!" Ellen cried.

"I believe you," Rhonda soothed, rubbing Ellen's hand.

"What do you think may have happened?" I joined in.

"She's lying!"   Rhonda shouted.   "My goodness, Millie, can't you see what our sister's doing?"

"That's a pretty serious thing to lie about.   Not even Nora would lie about something like that," I reasoned.

"Yeah, and I never thought she would have slept with my husband either, but she did," Rhonda stated.

I hated to admit it, but Rhonda had a point. But, how far was my sister willing to go to get attention?   Knowing Nora's hunger for attention and sympathy, it is surprising that she's kept such a horrible secret bottled up for so long.   Was I actually ready to accuse my sister of lying about such a terrible thing?   I sat down in a nearby lounge chair and listened as they talked about Nora.

"Ellen, I know you would never do something like that.   You're the innocent in all of this.   Nora's a manipulator and a tramp.   She'd say anything to get

189

her own way," Rhonda said.

"Why would I keep that from Mama? It's a terrible, terrible thing! She's wrong! I-I can't believe her! Why would she say it?!" Ellen cried. She was shaking terribly.

"Ellen, please calm down," I said. I stood up and walked over to her.

"Sh-she's determined to hurt me! H-how did she know?!" Ellen said hysterically.

"What are you talking about?" I asked.

"Sh-she's saying it to hurt me! H-he was so mean to do that to me!" Ellen cried. She wasn't making any sense at all.

"Ellen? Sweetheart, what are you saying?" Rhonda asked.

"Oh! H-How could they hurt me like this?!" Ellen yelled. Ellen jumped to her feet and ran into the house.

"Ellen!" Jim said, running after her.

I looked at Rhonda. "Rhonda, is it just me, or is Ellen hiding something?" I asked.

"She's definitely keeping something from us," Rhonda said. "What do you suppose it is?"

"I don't know, but I'm going to find out," I said.

Rhonda, Clayton and I went into the house and I went to Ellen as we walked into the den. Gina and Alex were already there, watching Ellen curiously.

"Are you okay?" I said, rubbing her arm.

"I-I'm fine," Ellen smiled through her tears. "I need a drink." Ellen made a beeline for the bar.

"Ellen, maybe you shouldn't–" I started,

following her.

"Shouldn't what? Take a drink? Why not? I at least deserve that much, don't I?" Ellen said.

Ellen poured cognac into a brandy snifter. She downed the brown liquid without the slightest flinch, only to be followed one after the other, until she'd consumed four. Watching her made me wonder how accustomed she was to drinking.

"Honey, maybe you should slow down," Jim said.

"Slow down?" Ellen smiled, pulling away from him. "For what? So that I can listen to my dear sister once again rake me over the coals? How could she?" Ellen suddenly was crying. "I-I'd never watch Daddy do that! Especially after all I've gone through!"

"What do you mean?" Rhonda asked.

"N-nothing. Forget I said anything," Ellen said, as she poured another drink.

"Ellen, drinking is not going to solve anything," Gina said, attempting to take the drink away from her.

"Oh no? Well, neither is sleeping with another woman, but that hasn't stopped you, now has it?" Ellen laughed. "How pathetic are you?"

"Ellen, you're drunk, so I'm going to ignore what you're saying. Why don't you go upstairs and sleep it off?" Gina said calmly.

"Sleep what off? You can't sleep off all those years of pain!" Ellen said. "You know nothing about what I've gone through, Little Girl! So, stop trying to psychoanalyze me! Why don't you go out and find a man, and leave this woman alone?!"

"Ellen, you really need to calm down," Jim stated.

"Calm down? Why? Isn't it time we got everything out in the open!?" Ellen yelled.

"Ellen, this isn't the time or the place," Jim said calmly.

"Why not? After all the revelations that have come about over the past few days, why stop now? This family has been on a roll!" Ellen laughed.

"Ellen, please," I said. "Don't say something you'll regret."

"Did you know that my husband's going to leave me?" Ellen laughed, ignoring me.

"What?" Rhonda said.

"Yeah, he hates me because I'm an alcoholic. The only reason he's with me right now is because my sister's sick!" Ellen laughed, while crying at the same time.

"Ellen, I'm sorry," I said.

"Oh, save your sympathy! You've never been sorry before! All the turmoil I've gone through! You never cared enough to tell us you were dying! Of course, I guess I should be thanking you. Your dying is keeping me out of divorce court right now!" Ellen yelled.

"Ellen, watch what you're saying!" Rhonda yelled.

"Why should I? It's true, isn't it?" Ellen snapped. Her brown eyes pierced through me. "Isn't that the reason now for all of us to come together? To feel sorry for you? To sympathize

192

with you? You never tried to reach out to us! And then for you to have cancer for an entire year and never mention a word of it? What were you thinking? So, now, everyone is supposed to disrupt their lives because the 'perfect life' of Millicent McAlray Welby has been turned upside down." Ellen walked towards me, looking me straight in the eyes. "What gives you the right? Why didn't you just die and let your husband call us when it was over?"

Without thinking, I slapped my sister across the face. I fought so hard to hold back the tears that threatened to fall.

"H-how dare you! H-how could you say something like that to me? My God, after all I have done, this is how you repay me?" I yelled.

Ellen held her face, and looked at me as tears streamed down her face. "'Repay you'? Repay you for what? For not having the decency to tell us about your illness? The only reason we're here now is because your husband called us to tell us something you should have told us a long time ago. 'Saint Millicent.' You hypocritical bitch!"

"Now that's enough!" Jim shouted, pulling her away. "Ellen, go upstairs and calm down!"

"Not until I finish what I have to say!" Ellen looked at her husband, pulled away from him and then looked around the room. Jim sat down in a nearby chair, clearly frustrated with Ellen. "You think Nora is the only one who's been violated by that monster?"

I walked towards Ellen. "What are you trying to say?" I asked.

"Forget it," Ellen said, stumbling away.

193

"No, Ellen. Tell us," I said, turning her towards me.

"Get your hands off of me!" Ellen jerked away, almost falling.

"Not until you tell us the truth!" I yelled.

"What for? For you to feel sorry for me!? I will not give you the satisfaction! This," Ellen picked her glass up from the table and held it up, toasting the air. "Is all I need!"

"How long have you been drinking?" I asked.

"What difference does it make?" Ellen asked.

"Answer me!" I yelled.

"Long enough to know it's exactly what I need to take my mind off of my troubles! You try living with a spoiled brat like Amanda! She's violent, she's wild, and she's made it quite clear that she hates me!" Ellen yelled.

"Amanda doesn't hate you," I whispered.

"Oh, spare me! Don't try to solve my problems with my daughter! You know nothing about my issues with her! You know nothing about my life! And that's because you haven't tried to find out! Now that you see how pathetic our lives are, maybe you can find solace in your own disastrous life! I'm going upstairs to share in company with the only thing that can help me through this," Ellen said, clutching a bottle of cognac to her.

"Ellen, this is not the way," I said.

"Will you leave me alone!?" Ellen yelled. "Damn, you are such a nuisance!"

"Fine, if you think you can find answers to your problems at the bottom of a bottle, then be my

194

guest!" I said.

"Finally, you're making sense," Ellen smiled. Ellen then stumbled out of the den. Jim was sitting down, with his hands clenched together in front of his face. His eyes were closed. How long had my brother-in-law been dealing with this?

"I'm going to follow her. She doesn't need to be alone," Gina said, running to catch up with Ellen.

"Jim, how long has this been going on?" Rhonda asked, touching his shoulder.

"Entirely too long," Jim sighed. "Ellen's had a drinking problem for the entire time we've been married. Apparently, she had the problem before then, but she kept it well-hidden. I found out by accident one day several years ago, when I discovered a liquor bottle hidden in a cedar chest in our bedroom."

"Has she tried to get any help?" I asked.

"She's been in and out of rehab facilities. She just plays the game long enough to get in and out. She was mandated by the courts to attend rehab on two occasions for driving under the influence, not that it matters to her. She shuts me out and our marriage is totally falling apart. She was telling the truth about us. I'd just told Ellen I wanted a divorce right before Clayton called the other day. It made me realize how much I still love her and how much I want to help her," Jim said calmly. "We're going broke because of all the problems her drinking has caused. I may have to sell her coffee shop. She doesn't have much to do with its success anyway because she's always drinking."

"My goodness, I had no idea," I said.

"Jim, what can we do to help you through this?" Clayton offered. "You're family and we want to help if we can."

"I don't know what else can be done. I'm tired of fighting with her. She's left home for a week at a time, and I'd be going crazy trying to find her," Jim said.

"Why didn't you ever say anything?" I asked.

"I didn't want to worry you. Remember last year, I called you out of the blue, asking how things were going?" Jim said.

"Yes, I remember that," I recalled. "I thought it was a little strange for you to call like that. I remember asking where Ellen was, and you told me she was at the coffee house."

"I was fishing around to see if she'd contacted you. I soon realized that you had no idea that she wasn't with me," Jim said.

"I remember you calling me as well," Rhonda said.

"I tried all of you, except Nora. I knew that was the one person she wouldn't reach out to," Jim said.

"Jim, I'm so sorry. I wish we'd known," I stated.

"There's nothing you would have been able to do." Jim smiled. "It looks like we all have our own private hell to deal with, doesn't it?"

"Looks that way. I wish you would have told us. You shouldn't have had to go through this alone," I said.

"I know that now. I've come to realize over

the past few days that keeping secrets only destroys people," Jim said.

"We'll get her more help," Clayton said. "In fact, I know the name of a good therapist who's a client of mine. I'll call him, if you'd like."

"At this point, I'm willing to try anything if it will keep her off of this self-destructive path she's on," Jim sighed.

We were all still in the den when Nora's cab arrived to take her to the airport a few minutes later. He blew his horn and waited patiently. We knew she was coming because we heard her slam the door to her bedroom. She stormed down the stairs with a carry-bag and a suitcase. Miriam was following behind her with her other suitcases.

"The sooner I get away from this God-forsaken house the better!" Nora yelled. Nora was so busy fussing, until she lost her balance coming down the stairs. "Aahh!" Nora screamed. We helplessly watched as my sister tumbled down last six steps of the staircase.

"Mrs. Riley, are you okay?" Miriam asked.

"Do I look okay to you?! Help me up, dammit!" Nora yelled.

"Nora!" I yelled, going to her. "Are you okay?"

"I'm fine! Leave me alone!" she yelled once again, jerking away from me. Nora started to stand up, and immediately toppled once again, yelling in pain. "Ow, my leg!" Nora cried.

"Let's get her to the sofa in the living room. Miriam, take her things back upstairs," Clayton suggested.

"Yes, sir," Miriam said.

Jim and Clayton helped Nora to the sofa. Shortly thereafter, the doorbell rang. I answered the door. It was the cab driver.

"Did someone need a cab?" the driver asked.

"Not anymore," I said. "Here's something for your trouble," I said, giving him twenty dollars. I then joined the rest of them in the living room. Alex was there, and she was trying to get Nora to relax her leg.

"Nora, you have to relax," Alex sighed impatiently.

"Easy for you to say!" Nora yelled. "Just remember, I like men!"

"Ha! Yeah! Anybody's man!" Rhonda laughed.

"Trust me, Nora, you're safe," Alex shot back. "Now keep still so I can check your leg." Alex moved her leg.

"Ow! That hurts dammit! What are you trying to do, kill me?!" Nora yelled.

"Don't tempt me," Alex said.

"Just leave me alone! I'll be fine! Get away from me!" Nora demanded.

"Nora, sit still and stop acting like a spoiled brat!" Alex yelled.

"How dare you!" Nora yelled, pushing Alex's hand away. She tried to stand. "Ow!" she said, falling to the floor once again.

"See? Now, sit still. I'm trying to see if it's broken," Alex said.

"Do you know what you're doing?" Nora asked.

"Yes, I do," Alex replied.

"How do I know you have the sense to cross the street and back?" Nora retorted.

"Well, I have sense enough to know how to walk down the stairs without falling. After all, I'm not the one lying flat on my ass with a possibly broken leg, now am I?" Alex said.

I had to hand it to her, Alex was handling Nora's sarcasm in the best way possible. She was quickly learning what being a part of Gina's family would be like.

"Of all the nerve!" Nora yelled.

"Look, Nora. I'm trying to help you, but you are starting to get on my nerves!" Alex said.

"Nora, will you act right?" I asked.

At that moment, Gina came in. "What's going on?" Gina asked.

"Nora fell," Clayton said. "Who's with Ellen?"

"Miriam. She came up and said Nora hurt herself."

"I'm going upstairs to check on her," Jim said.

"Okay. Nora, are you okay?" Gina asked.

"Ask your girlfriend here. She's trying to kill me!"

"How's her leg, Alex?" Gina asked.

"It's broken," Alex said. "We need to get her to the hospital."

"You don't know what you're talking about! I'm going home today!" Nora said.

"Not until we get you to the hospital," I reasoned. "I sent your cab away."

"I didn't ask you to do that!" Nora said.

"Tough. Clayton, go and pull the car around," I said.

Nora glared at me with contempt. Could my sister be any more ungrateful? I was growing weary of her constant discontentment. She wanted for everyone to be as miserable as she obviously was. Clayton, Alex and I took her to the Emergency Room. She complained all the way to the hospital. They brought out a wheelchair, and she refused to get into it. She tried to walk, and almost fell. Two nursing assistants helped her. This was obviously going to be a long day. We stayed in the ER for the next three hours waiting. When the doctor came out to talk to us, he told us that Nora's leg was indeed broken, and that she'd have to wear a cast for the next few weeks and would be on crutches. He'd given her something for the pain that would make her sleepy, but that he was going to let her go home after her cast had been set. He wanted to send her to an orthopedic physician in a week to check her leg to make sure it was healing properly. We thanked the doctor, and waited a while longer before they brought her out. She was definitely drugged, because for once, Nora was quiet. She seemed almost friendly. I was tempted to ask for more of whatever they'd given her, so that we could slip it to her every day. As I jokingly thought of doing so, the nurse handed me two prescriptions to fill for her. She explained that they would make her sleepy, and that she just needed to stay off the leg for a while.

They instructed that she would need therapy, but that the orthopedic doctor would be scheduling that for her.

Whether she was trying to or not, Nora once again would be the center of attention. At least this way, she couldn't just up and walk away while someone was trying to talk to her. We finally were able to leave the hospital that evening. When we got home, Clayton and Kyle helped Nora up to her room. Miriam helped her to undress and get into bed. It had been such a long day. That night, somehow or another we had dinner together as a family, with exception of Nora, Ellen and Jim. Nora slept through it and Ellen and Jim stayed in their room. The younger crowd all went to see a movie afterwards. Everyone else turned in early.

After I took my shower, I went into the den and pulled out several photo albums. Where had we gone wrong? I looked through an album that had pictures from when we were children. There were pictures taken at family picnics, school plays, Christmas plays, Halloween; just about everything imaginable. I ran across a picture of Nora and her cheering squad. I realized this particular picture was taken a few months before she was raped by our father. Raped by our father. What kind of monster was he? I looked at the picture, and saw how happy Nora seemed. She was smiling, as she had her arms around some of the other girls. As I sat there, I didn't realize that Ellen had come into the room.

"Am I interrupting?" she asked, almost embarrassed.

"No, Ellen, come on in," I smiled. "I'm just

looking at some old photos. Why don't you join me?"

"Are you sure you want me to? After the fool I made of myself earlier today?"

"We're all entitled," I said gently.

"Dammit, Millie! Get mad! Yell at me! Do anything but be nice to me!" Ellen demanded.

"Why, Ellen? What will it accomplish? You had some things to get off your chest earlier, and you did it. Let's just let it go."

"Oh, Millie," Ellen sighed, as she sat down beside me. She covered her face with her hands. "There's so much to tell you. I don't even know where to begin. I'm sorry for the way I acted earlier. I had no right to treat you that way."

"That's okay, Ellen. I'm sorry for slapping you," I said, hugging her.

"I deserved the slap, but why are you always so good to me? That I don't deserve," Ellen stated.

"Maybe not," I smiled. "But you're my sister and I love you."

"I heard about Nora. How is she?" Ellen asked.

"Sleeping. Whatever the doctor gave her knocked her out, thank goodness. I don't think I could have taken much more of her today," I laughed slightly.

Ellen smiled, then she looked at me seriously. "Millie, about what Nora said, I would never have watched Daddy do that to her. You believe me, don't you?"

"Of course, I believe you, but Nora thinks you saw her."

Ellen sighed. "I know. I just don't understand that. After what happened to me, I wouldn't want to see that happen to–" Ellen stopped. I looked at her.

"What are you talking about?" I asked.

"Nothing. Just forget it," Ellen said, standing. She walked over to the window.

I stood up and walked next to her. I put my hand on her shoulder. "Ellen, what were you about to say? What happened to you?"

"Forget it," Ellen said. She looked dazed as tears rolled down her face.

"Ellen, what's wrong?"

"Millie, there's so much I want to tell you! You're the only one who would understand!"

I turned Ellen towards me. "Just tell me, Ellen," I said gently.

"I-I can't!" Ellen cried.

"Yes, you can. I'm here for you. Please let me help you," I said.

"Oh, Millie! Nora's not the only one who's been violated by Daddy!"

"Ellen, what are you saying?"

"Daddy raped me, too! I-I was pregnant!" Ellen sobbed. She laid her head on my shoulder and cried. I hugged her tightly. A pain totally unrelated to anything I'd ever felt ripped through me as I cried with my sister.

"Oh, my goodness," I whispered.

"I was only 15!" Ellen cried.

"I'm so sorry Ellen," I said.

"H-he raped me, Millie! He raped me four

203

times!"

"Come on, let's sit down," I said, leading Ellen back to the sofa. We sat down, and I held her as she cried. "Did Mama know?"

"No. I never told her. Daddy threatened to put me out. He told me that Mama would never believe me!"

"Was Daddy the father of your child?"

"Y-yes," Ellen whimpered. "H-he made me abort the baby and threatened to kill me if I ever told!"

"You poor thing! You could've have come to me."

"How? Daddy had me so frightened. I didn't know what to do."

"How did you have an abortion and Mama not know?"

"Daddy told her that I was going to summer camp out of town for a week. She believed him. She never questioned him about anything! He took me to Georgia to have the abortion. He told them that I'd gotten knocked up by my teenage boyfriend. Since he was my father, he could give legal consent."

"That was probably the only smart decision Daddy ever made," I said.

"What do you mean?"

"That would have destroyed you, having to carry and raise a child that was a result of your father doing something like that to you. Not to mention the deformities the child probably would have had from incest. I know Daddy's reasons for it were purely selfish, but it was the best thing."

"I know you're right. But, having to go

through an abortion was probably one of the hardest days of my life."

"I wish I'd known. You could have come and lived with Clayton and me."

"You had two small children. You didn't need me there to burden you."

"Nonsense! You're never a burden to me."

Ellen sat up and grabbed a tissue to wipe her face. "After Daddy made me have an abortion, I started drinking," Ellen said calmly. "It helped to forget everything that happened. Then, I got hooked. From that point on, every time I had the slightest crisis, alcohol became an escape for me. After a while, I needed to forget everything, everyday."

"But you seemed so together. You're running a successful business. You're so strong, Ellen."

Ellen laughed slightly. "You know, I stopped drinking for a while. I'd been in detox and I was determined to make things right. I wanted to strengthen my marriage, become a good example for Amanda. All of this came about when I realized I'd hit rock-bottom."

"When was that?"

"Three years ago. I woke up one morning and didn't know where I was. I was alone in a hotel room. I had no idea how I got there or who I'd been with. My credit cards and money were gone, my car was gone."

"My goodness, Ellen. You could have been killed!" I said.

"I know," Ellen sighed. "That was when I realized that I had to change."

205

"What did Jim do?"

"Well, I frantically called my husband. He came and got me." Ellen sighed heavily. "Oh, Millie, you should have seen the hurt in his eyes. Amazingly enough, he stuck by me. I have no idea how he did it, but he forgave me. I didn't know if I'd cheated on him or not. After seeing how hurt he was, I decided I needed to talk to someone. I'd been required by the courts to go into a rehab program twice before, but I never took it seriously. But this time, things were going to be different. I started in a detox program, which, of course, required seeing a counselor. My counselor told me I needed an outlet. The owner of a coffeehouse was retiring and wanted to sell the business. Jim knew it would be the perfect therapy for me. So, he surprised me and bought the business."

"Which obviously was a good move," I encouraged.

"Yeah, you'd think so. Things were great for the next couple of years. Then, it happened again. You don't know this, but my shop was robbed last year," Ellen revealed.

"Oh, Ellen!" I cried. "Did anyone get hurt?"

"No. Actually, I was there alone. When my last employee left, I was too busy to go behind her and lock the door. A guy came in and held a gun to my face. I'd never been so frightened in all my life," Ellen cried.

"What did you do?"

"I emptied the cash drawer, he grabbed the money and made me lie down on the floor. I was so scared because I thought he was going to kill me. But, I was blessed because he ran out. I got up and frantically called Jim and the police," Ellen explained.

"Did they catch the guy?" I asked.

"No, they didn't," Ellen shook her head. "He had on a ski mask. Actually, from what the police said, that saved my life."

"How?"

"Because if I could identify him, he would have killed me on the spot," Ellen said.

"I suppose you're right," I commented.

"When that incident happened, I became a recluse all over again with the bottle as my best friend. I didn't know how to handle it." Ellen tried unsuccessfully to wipe the tired lines from underneath her eyes. "A month after it happened, I left home for a week. Jim had no idea where I was. I hit every bar in New York. God really watched over me, because I rented a hotel room, drank myself into oblivion every night, and never once called my husband. I took faceless men back to my room. I have no idea if I slept with them or not."

"Boy, talk about nine lives! Ellen, why did you do such a thing?"

"I don't know. When I finally showed up at home, Jim packed his bags and left. He'd had enough. He'd spent an entire week looking for me. He filed a missing persons report. Once again, I'd let my husband down. We were separated for three months. I stopped drinking again, because I really wanted us to work things out. He came back home by the time the holidays rolled around last year. I

207

promised him that I'd never drink again."

"Was today your first time drinking again since you made that promise?"

Ellen looked at me and shook her head. "No. I wish it were, but, I've been drinking again. Millie, right before I came here, I spent the night with a man after drinking all night. For the first time, I was hit with the reality that I undoubtedly had cheated on my husband. The man I was with got rough with me, trying to get me to have sex with him again. When I tried to refuse, he raped me, Millie."

"Oh, Ellen," I sighed.

"I've been a terrible mother and wife. Yet, I wonder why Amanda is like she is," Ellen smirked. "Since we've arrived here, I've been going off to get a drink in order to deal with Nora."

"Don't let Nora intimidate you. Trust me, it's not worth it," I said.

"Sometimes I think she's right about me. I'm nothing," Ellen said tearfully.

"Don't beat yourself up over this. You have an illness. You can change, Ellen. This doesn't have to rule you for the rest of your life."

"That's easier said than done."

I listened as my sister continued to unburden herself. She'd suffered so much. My sister was on the verge of death so many times, yet God chose to spare her. I prayed she could see what a blessing this was. God still had a reason for sparing her life.

"Does Jim know about what Daddy did to you?" I asked.

"No. I never told him. On our wedding

night, I was afraid for Jim to touch me. He thought it was because I was a virgin. He had no idea it was because of the horrific experiences I'd endured."

"Ellen, you have to tell him. This is destroying you," I said, rubbing Ellen's shoulder. "It'll destroy your marriage completely if you don't do something about it. You know where the root of your problem stems from. It's time to face it head on, Sweetheart. Your husband obviously loves you very much. Are you willing to keep pushing the envelope? He's forgiven you so many times. If you're not careful, there will be a time when he won't forgive you. Don't keep risking your marriage. Get help, Ellen."

"I know what you're saying is right, Millie, but how do I do it? How do I tell my husband about this? It was hard enough telling you."

"I know it was, but I'm so glad you did."

"Promise me you won't say anything to Jim," Ellen pleaded.

"I promise. Although, I can't stress enough how important it would be for you to tell him."

"I know it's important. Knowing he's with me now is encouraging, but, what happens when we go back to New York? He's going to leave me again, I just know it," Ellen said.

"If Jim didn't want the marriage to work, he could have still left you, Ellen, phone call from Clayton or not. But, no matter what, I want you to always remember you can talk to me whenever you need to. Anytime, day or night."

Ellen looked at me and started to cry again.

"How can you say that? You're so weak, Millie. I can't put all of this on you."

"That's what I'm here for," I smiled.

Ellen smiled as she dried her eyes again. "You know what? I have to stop feeling sorry for myself. It was a long time ago and I want to change the subject. Let's talk about something else."

"Are you sure?"

"Yes, I am. I needed to talk, and I'm glad you were here for me, but I can't keep dwelling on it. So, let's see what pictures you were looking at when I came in." Ellen picked up one of the books I was looking in.

"I was just reminiscing. Gosh, we were all so young," I said, as we looked through the album.

We ran across a picture of Ellen holding her baseball bat. She had her arm around her best friend Katie, who was holding a ball in her gloved hand. They had on matching baseball caps and were dressed almost identically.

"You and Katie were inseparable. When was the last time you spoke with her?" I asked.

"You know, I haven't talked to Katie in over 5 years."

"Did you ever confide in her about what happened?"

"She and I shared just about everything, but I never divulged that secret to her. She and I drifted apart somewhat after she went off to college. We tried to keep in touch, but it got harder. She married Michael Spearman right out of college and they had a couple of children. I really wish I could see her

210

again."

"Does she still live in Alabama?" I asked.

"As far as I know she does. Our class reunion was last year, but I didn't go. I talked with Brenda Gillman, who recently moved to New York. She told me that Katie and Michael were at the reunion, and that they are running Katie's dad's business since her dad retired a few years ago. So, they must still be there."

"You should call her," I suggested.

"What's the point? I'm such a mess. I'd be too ashamed."

"That's crazy, Ellen. You run a successful business, you have a husband who loves you. Why would you be ashamed?"

"I'm also a drunk who was molested and impregnated by my father. I have a daughter who seems to hate everything about me. And as far as the successful business goes, my staff runs it; not me. We're in so much financial trouble because of my drinking. I wouldn't want her to see what my life has turned out to be like."

"She was your best friend. She'd never judge you," I said.

"I'm not willing to take that chance," Ellen said.

"I understand." I smiled slightly.

"Do you think I'll ever make things right with my daughter?" Ellen asked.

"Give it time. Amanda's only 16. At her age, children always hate their parents."

"But she loves Jim," Ellen argued.

"Then give your daughter something to look up to," I suggested. "You keep crying over how your daughter doesn't respect you. You have to set a good example, Ellen. Staying out at bars and not coming home for days at a time isn't the way to do it."

"I know you're right," Ellen sighed. "I just don't know where to begin."

"Staying sober would be a good start," I smiled slightly.

"I think I missed the opportunity to do that," Ellen stated.

"What do you mean?"

"Before we came here, Amanda dared me to pour out all the liquor in the house, and I couldn't do it."

"That was probably too drastic too soon. Rome wasn't built in a day, so you can't expect to turn away from it like that. Start doing other things. Spend more time at your business, spend time doing things with your husband. Put something between you and that bottle until you have the strength not to lean on it so much," I shrugged.

Ellen smiled. "You have the answer for everything, don't you?"

"Well, maybe not everything," I laughed.

Ellen smiled, but seemed unconvinced by everything I was saying. We sat there talking for the next hour, during which time we heard the kids pull up. Tim and AJ went out to the guest house, and Amanda went upstairs with Shauna. Erin and Kyle left to go home and Ginny left with Kirsten and Robert. We told everyone goodnight, and went back into the den. I think Ellen and I needed this time together. My time was so precious now and I wanted special time with each of my sisters alone. Sadly enough, 'special time' with them seemed to be about revealing heartbreaking secrets. Ellen and I cried and laughed for the better part of the night. How can there be so many contradicting emotions? After sitting there a while longer, Ellen decided to turn in for the night. I went into the kitchen and fixed some warm milk. As I was in my kitchen, my mind went back to something Nora said earlier:

"My window was open, and while he was on top of me, I saw Ellen peeking into the window. She had on that stupid red baseball cap that she wore everywhere. I begged her to help me. She looked at me, then she ran away!"

"That's it," I whispered to myself.

I took my glass back into the den and pulled out one of the albums. I looked at the picture of Katie with Ellen. I suddenly had the feeling that this was the key. It was Katie. She and Ellen could almost pass for twins. They dressed alike, had the same build, even their hairstyles were similar. I immediately called information for Katie and Michael Spearman in Birmingham, Alabama. I looked at the clock. It was after 1 a.m. I knew it was too late to call, so I decided to call in the morning. Maybe Katie could shed light on some of the things that had happened. After I put the albums away, I turned off the lights and went to bed. Clayton was lying in bed reading. He took off

213

his reading glasses and smiled at me when I walked in.

"I was going to come looking for you if you didn't show up soon," he commented.

"Ellen and I were downstairs talking. I didn't forget about you," I smiled. I sighed as I sat on the bed.

"Is everything okay?" Clayton asked, rubbing my shoulders.

"If only you knew." I reached up to caress Clayton's hand.

"What is it, Sweetheart?" Clayton asked.

"I didn't think it could get much worse," I told him.

"What's happened now?" Clayton sighed.

"Ellen confided in me tonight. Daddy molested her."

"What?"

"It gets worse. He got her pregnant."

"Oh my goodness! Are you serious?" Clayton asked disbelievingly.

"My little sister was only 15. It seems like 15 was the magic number, since Nora was the same age."

"I can't believe this, Millie."

"Daddy doing that to her caused her to start drinking."

"He was really a monster, wasn't he?"

"Hard to believe, isn't it? I looked up to him, admired him. What made him do this?" I shook my head.

"Who knows what goes through a sick person's mind? I admired your father, too."

I suddenly thought of Gina. I looked at

Clayton in horror. "Clayton, what about Gina? Do you think he did this to her?"

"Has she ever indicated anything?"

"No. I mean, he never molested me, and as far as I know, he didn't molest Rhonda either. I'm praying he never touched Gina. I hate that Nora and Ellen endured such pain," I said, leaning back against Clayton. "Maybe one good thing can come out of this."

"What's that?" Clayton asked surprisingly.

"Ellen's friend, Katie. I'm going to call her tomorrow."

"Why?"

"I get the feeling she knows something."

"I don't understand," Clayton said, in a confused tone.

"She and Ellen were inseparable. What if *she* witnessed Nora's rape?"

"That's a little farfetched, isn't it? I mean, you could be grasping at straws."

"Not really. I'm going to follow my instincts on this one."

"Does Ellen know about this?"

"No. I didn't want to tell her yet."

"Sweetheart, don't be disappointed if you don't get the outcome you were hoping for," Clayton advised.

"I won't. After all that's happened, I have to try something."

I got under the covers with Clayton and snuggled close to him. We lay there in silence, each consumed by our own thoughts. I knew he was worried about me, but this was something I had to try. I thought of Ellen's situation with Nora. Maybe if Katie could offer some light, the two of them could mend their relationship. My worrying about my family caused me to have a restless night. I hoped I wasn't about to make a big mistake by bringing someone else into this. I eventually succumbed to sleep a little after three a.m.

Chapter Eleven

The next morning, I woke with a start. Clayton was in the shower because I could hear the water running. I looked at the clock and noticed it was 9:30 a.m. I decided to try to reach Katie before going downstairs. I had no idea how she would receive my calling her about such a sensitive matter.

"Hello?" a woman answered.

"May I please speak to Katie?" I asked.

"This is she," Katie responded.

"Katie, I don't know if you remember me or not, but this is Millicent Welby. I used to be Millicent McAlray."

"Oh, hi! I remember you! You're Ellen's sister!" Katie said, cheerfully.

"Yes, that's right," I smiled.

"It's good to hear from you. How are you?" Katie asked.

"I'm fine."

"Is Ellen okay? Has something happened to her?"

"No, no. Ellen's fine. I'm calling about a rather sensitive matter."

"Excuse me?" Katie asked.

"Um, Katie, we just found out some rather devastating news about our family," I said.

"I'm afraid I don't understand what that has to do with me."

"Well, it could, believe it or not, be something that you could help us to figure out."

"I still don't see what could be going on in your family that would relate to me."

"Katie, this is very hard to talk about. I guess the best thing to do is to just say it. Twenty-four years ago, Nora was raped by our father. Nora has hated Ellen for years because she thinks Ellen witnessed it and never said anything. Do you know anything about it?"

"Why would I know about it?" Katie was clearly agitated.

"Well, you and Ellen were very close. The problem is Ellen doesn't remember witnessing such a horrific thing. I'm just wondering if you know anything that could help."

"What are you implying?"

"I'm not implying anything. I'm just wondering if you might have seen anything."

"Are you asking if I saw Mr. McAlray rape Nora?! How could you ask me such a thing?"

"I'm sorry, Katie. I just thought–"

"Well, you thought wrong! How dare you call and interrogate me about something like that?"

"Katie, please. I'm not trying to accuse you. You and Ellen were only 14 at the time. It's understandable that you might have been frightened and not wanted to say anything."

"You have a lot of nerve calling my home and accusing me of something so terrible!"

"Katie, I'm not accusing you."

"Oh, yes you are! Look, don't call me anymore!" At that point, Katie hung up on me.

I quickly realized that calling Katie was a big mistake. Obviously, I was wrong. After chastising myself, I realized I couldn't dwell on it. As long as Ellen never knew I called, there wouldn't be a problem. I figured it would be better for me not to tell her. I couldn't believe how far off base I was. I really thought Katie might have been the one Nora saw, but she wasn't. So, why couldn't Ellen remember it? None of this was making sense. Would Nora lie about such a thing? I tried to put everything in the back of my mind as I got dressed. Maybe this was a sign that I needed to mind my own business.

As if I was a glutton for punishment, I decided to check on Nora. She'd slept all night, and I wanted to see if she was feeling better. I knocked on her door.

"Come in," Nora said.

I opened the door. "Hi, Nora. How are you feeling?" I asked.

"My leg hurts like hell," Nora said. "Well, I

guess you'll get your wish. I won't be able to travel now because of this leg."

"Maybe it's for the best," I smiled. "You're so stubborn."

"Thanks a lot," Nora smiled groggily.

"That medication's still affecting you," I observed.

"These have to be the best painkillers in the world," Nora said. "How are you this morning?"

"I'm fine. Why, Nora, you're almost pleasant today."

"Strange isn't it? I have to be drugged up in order to be cordial to my sister," Nora laughed sluggishly.

"I suppose so," I smiled. "Why don't I get Miriam to bring breakfast up to you?"

"She already did. I've eaten, and she's come and taken the tray away. What time is it?"

"It's almost 10 a.m."

"Are you just getting up?" Nora asked surprisingly.

"Yeah. I didn't drift off to sleep until after three this morning. I'm entitled to at least six hours of sleep, aren't I?"

"I suppose. So, I guess it was pretty peaceful with me in La-La Land all night, huh?"

"That's putting it mildly. The kids went to see a movie after dinner, so it was pretty quiet around here."

"Are my sisters still not speaking to me?"

"I thought it was the other way around," I challenged.

220

"Nonsense! I'm the easiest person in the world to get along with," Nora smiled.

"We really need to get you more of those painkillers," I joked.

"Maybe so, Millie, maybe so," Nora smiled. Her eyes seemed to be getting heavy. She was dozing off, so I decided to let her sleep.

I went downstairs where Ellen, Jim, Rhonda, Gina and Alex were sitting and talking. It was such a beautiful day, so we planned to spend it out on the beach. I needed to cheer Rhonda and Ellen up. Nora would be sleeping for the better part of the day, so, maybe this was the break we all needed. The kids had already gone to the beach, with exception of Tim. He had to volunteer at the hospital. While waiting on Clayton, we sat downstairs talking while eating breakfast. When he came down, we gathered our things and walked to the beach. We had such a wonderful time that day. Small miracles like this made me glad that Clayton called all of my sisters together. When we got back, Nora was sitting in a lounge chair on the patio with her crutches resting beside her. She was drinking iced tea and eating a salad. We were all laughing as we walked onto the patio.

"Well, I see my presence wasn't missed," Nora said.

"No, actually, it was. It was so pleasant, until we all realized it was due to your absence," Rhonda said.

"Rhonda, please. Let's not start," I said.

"No, it's okay. What are you mad about,

Rhonda? That I slept with your husband, or that you think I treated him better in bed than you?"

"Too bad you didn't break your neck when you fell," Rhonda said, walking away into the house.

"Why do you do that?" Ellen asked. "It's bad enough that you've broken your leg. Why must you alienate everyone around you?"

"First of all, it's none of your business. Secondly, I didn't start with her; she started with me. Now, get away from me, Ellen. The pain in my leg is rapidly moving further up to my ass at the mere sight of you."

Ellen looked as if she wanted to cry as she and Jim walked away. Gina and Alex saw how upset Ellen was and followed them into the house. Kyle and Erin were going to stay for dinner, and Robert was going to join us once he got off of work.

Everyone else went into the guest house until dinner time. Clayton and I were about to go inside as well, when I told Clayton that I wanted to talk to Nora. As he walked off, I looked at Nora.

"Mind if I join you?" I asked.

"Why not? It's your house," Nora retorted.

"I guess the medication has worn off," I said, as I sat down.

"It doesn't last forever. I got tired of lying in bed, so I managed to make it downstairs, which was no easy task, that's for sure," Nora smiled slightly.

"I'm going to have Miriam to prepare the downstairs maid's quarters for you, so that you won't have to go up and down the stairs."

"Me, stay in the maid's quarters? No thanks.

222

I'll manage," Nora said in a condescending tone.

"It was just a suggestion," I said.

"I'll be gone in a couple of days anyway," Nora said.

"Have you talked to Bill?" I asked.

"No, he hasn't called. And neither have my children. They don't care about me. After all I've done for them, they desert me. I've been a good wife and mother!"

"Listen to yourself, Nora. Here you are, once again, feeling sorry for yourself. Quite honestly, I'm sick of it. Now, you need to quit blaming everyone for your problems and take responsibility. If you want to work your marriage out, you have to call your husband and apologize for the things you've done. It's only fair."

"I don't want to be fair. Life's never been fair to me. Why should I yield to him?"

"Because he's a good and God knows patient man, who deserves your respect. Do you think that it would seem like you've lost a battle or something if you yielded to him? Is your marriage nothing more than a game to you?"

"No, it isn't. How come you insist upon taking my husband's side? You take everyone's side but mine. You take Rhonda's side over mine, you take Ellen's side over mine. You hate me, don't you, Millie?" Nora pouted. "Or do you still have feelings for my husband?"

"Of course not! We had this argument already, Nora, and now you are really pouring it on thick, aren't you?" I stood up and sighed. "Call your

223

husband, Nora."

I walked into the house, wondering how much longer this would go on. She was becoming more and more a pain. She sat out there for a while, sulking like a spoiled child who'd had her favorite toy taken away. I was not going to continue to beg her to get along with her family. If she wanted to behave this way, then so be it. I went into the kitchen to check on Miriam.

"Miriam, Mrs. Riley hasn't been too much trouble for you, has she?" I asked.

"No, ma'am. She's been fine. I've handled the likes of her before. Is she ready to go upstairs?"

"No, she's still on the patio. I'll see if she wants to join us for dinner. She may want for you to bring her tray to her."

"Yes, ma'am."

"Thank you, Miriam, for being so patient with my sister," I smiled. "I know she's been a bit of a handful for you."

"It's no problem, Mrs. Welby," Miriam smiled.

Kyle had gone to pick up Tim from the hospital that evening. That night, we all had dinner together, with exception of Nora. She didn't want to join us, so Miriam took a tray to her. All of my sisters had so many issues going on with them. I wanted terribly to solve all of their problems, no matter how unrealistic that wish may have been. The dinner was notably once again less strained without Nora there to argue with everyone. Why did she always have to be so difficult? She had it in her to be a good person, yet, somehow, she made it hard for people to get close to her. I was so worried about her marriage to Bill. I knew it wasn't my business, but I was tempted to call and talk with Bill, to see if he would be willing to talk to her. Then, I realized that Nora needed to call him herself. She was already paranoid about my history with Bill. He was a good husband who didn't deserve the treatment he received from her. It would serve her right to wonder for a little while about her marriage. I was lost in my thoughts until my son stood up and tapped his glass with his fork.

"Excuse me, everyone. I have an announcement to make," Kyle said.

Everyone stopped talking and looked at Kyle.

"Well, what is it, Son?" Clayton asked.

"It's taken a year, and after many, many nights of hard work," Kyle grinned, "we've finally done it."

"Kyle, what are you talking about?" Kirsten asked.

"Erin and I are going to have a baby!" Kyle beamed.

"Oh, Kyle, Erin! That's wonderful!" I exclaimed. Everyone started to clap.

"Congratulations, you two," Clayton smiled, hugging Erin and Kyle.

"Congratulations, big brother!" Kirsten smiled.

"So, when are you due?" Alex asked.

"The doctor said I'm due February 4th," Erin smiled.

"Well, that's wonderful! Congratulations you two! My nephew is going to be a father!" Ellen said.

"And I'm going to be a grandmother," I smiled.

We all sat around giving Erin unsolicited advice on what to expect over the next few months, not to mention the horror stories about giving birth, and the baby not sleeping all night. I thought back to finding out I was pregnant with Kyle, and how Mama always told me exactly what to expect during my pregnancy. I wondered if I would live to see my grandchild come into the world. I wanted to be there through the whole thing, but I had no idea at this point what to expect. As everyone was crowding around Kyle and Erin, a very observant Shauna came over to me.

"You don't think you'll be here to see the baby, do you Mom?" Shauna asked.

"I hope I'm here," I smiled.

"But you don't think you will be?" Shauna asked, with tears in her eyes.

"I didn't say that. Sweetheart, we've talked about this. Maybe I've asked you to be more brave than you're ready to be, and that's not fair to you. But, I'm not sure how much longer I'll be here. Can you understand that?" I asked gently.

Shauna slowly nodded her head and mustered a smile through her tears. "I-I'll be back," Shauna said, walking out of the dining room. I was going to go after her, but before I could, Kirsten came up to me.

"Let me try, Ma. She's just hurting," Kirsten said. Kirsten went upstairs to talk to Shauna.

This was such an unjust thing for my little girl to have to endure. My baby was hurting and I didn't know how to handle it anymore. I was at wit's end with everything at this point. I almost wished my children didn't even know about my illness because this was so hard on all of them, and they didn't deserve it. At least Clayton would be there with them. They were going to need each other.

The next morning, we all got up and went down to the patio for breakfast. Kyle called and said that Erin wasn't feeling well, so that they would see us later that day. He was going to go to work and they'd stop by that evening. After breakfast, we sat out by the pool talking, once again, minus Nora. Miriam came out to the patio and told me that I had a visitor. As I excused myself and walked in with Miriam, I asked who it was.

"A Mrs. Katie Spearman," Miriam said.

Katie had come. What was the meaning of this? Did she know something after all?

"Katie," I said.

"Hello, Millie," Katie said sheepishly. "I guess you're wondering how I found you."

"It crossed my mind," I said. "After yesterday, I didn't think I'd ever hear from you again."

"Well, I got your number off of my caller ID and you know, you can do anything on the internet these days, even find out people's addresses," Katie smiled slightly.

"Why are you here, Katie?" I asked.

"I think you know. I really needed to talk to you and apologize."

"About what?"

"About the way I talked to you."

"You didn't have to travel two states over to do that. A simple phone call would have sufficed," I said.

"No, this is something I needed to do in person.

227

Millicent, I'm sorry. I had no right to act the way I did yesterday. You were trying to talk to me about something so traumatic, and I was very insensitive."

"Is this something that Ellen should hear?" I asked.

"I wish she could. But, I don't even have the courage to face her."

"Maybe you should find the courage somewhere, because Ellen's out on the patio."

"She's here? Now?"

"Yes. Why don't you come on out?" I said, walking towards the patio.

Ellen and Rhonda were engrossed in a conversation when we got there. Ellen looked up.

"Oh, my gosh! Katie?!" Ellen smiled.

"Hi, Ellen!" Katie smiled back. The two of them embraced.

"I don't believe it! Millie and I were just talking about you the other night!" Then Ellen's smile faded as she looked at me. "Millie, you didn't?"

"Didn't what?" I asked.

"Call Katie and tell her to come here?" Ellen said angrily.

"No, I didn't tell her to come here," I said.

"Ellen, I came on my own. I have something I really need to talk to you about."

"What is it?" Ellen asked.

"Yesterday, your sister did call me, but it was to ask me about something."

"Ask you about what?" Ellen asked.

"About something I witnessed years ago,"

Katie said sadly. As Katie was talking, Nora came out to the patio on her crutches

. "What's going on here? A meeting of the minds? Am I invited?" Nora said.

"Nora, I'm glad you're here. Maybe you need to hear this," I said.

Clayton came up to me. "Honey, what's going on?"

"I'm not sure yet," I said.

"Well, it looks like your entire family is here," Katie smiled slightly.

"Actually, we are having somewhat of an impromptu family reunion," I smiled.

"Maybe I'm not as brave as I thought, because now, I don't really feel too comfortable saying what I came to say," Katie said.

"Just say it, Katie," I encouraged. "God knows, our family has had a lot to deal with, but I think that what you may have to say might help."

"Um, Nora, Ellen, I owe the two of you an apology."

"Why, whatever for?" Ellen asked, surprisingly.

"This is really hard for me to say," Katie sighed, as tears welled up in her eyes.

"Just say it," Nora sighed annoyingly.

"Years ago, I witnessed something that changed my life," Katie started. "You remember how baseball was everything to us during the summer?"

"Yeah. We had some great memories," Ellen smiled.

"Well, not all of them were so great for me,"

Katie said.

"What do you mean?" Ellen asked.

"One day, we were in my back yard practicing for the game. Ellen, you were pitching and when Felicia hit the ball, it went over the fence, right into your back yard on the other side of the house."

Katie then described exactly what happened:

"Felicia! You hit the ball over the fence again! You know it's the only one we have left!" Ellen said.

"I'll get it!" Katie said, as she climbed over the fence. She looked around and spotted the ball underneath a back window at our house.

"Help! Somebody please help!" It was clearly Nora's voice. She ran over and looked through the window. Daddy was on top of Nora. Nora was fighting against him, but he was too strong for her.

"Oh, my God!" Katie whispered. Nora looked right at her.

"Ellen, p-please help me! Daddy, don't do this!" Nora pleaded.

Nora thought Katie was Ellen. What could she do? Was he hurting her? Katie stood there frozen, not knowing whether she should help her or not. She grabbed the ball with shaking hands, and ran away. When she got back to the other side, she was in such a daze. Ellen looked at Katie as she ran up to her.

"Hey, what's wrong with you?" Ellen asked.

"Uh, nothing. Maybe we should finish

230

practice later? My arm's a little sore," Katie lied.

"Okay. Are you sure everything else is okay?" Ellen asked.

"Um, yeah. Everything's fine. I just want to finish practicing later. Let's meet out at the field in a couple of hours. My backyard isn't really big enough anyway. The ball keeps going over the fence."

"Well, you go take care of that arm, and the rest of us will go on over to the field now, okay?" Ellen said.

"Okay," Katie said, slightly smiling.

At that point, Ellen walked away with the other girls on the team, not once knowing what Katie had witnessed.

"Nora, Ellen never witnessed your being raped by your father, I did," Katie said, with tears in her eyes. "I was only 14, and I had no idea how to handle things."

"What?" Nora yelled. "You watched Daddy do that to me and you never said anything?!"

"N-Nora, I'm sorry. I know I could have said something, and I didn't! I've never forgiven myself for that. I've lived with this guilt for so long!"

"Oh, yeah! And that's a lot worse than actually going through it! I've spent 24 years hating my sister, not knowing that you were the coward who saw my father do that to me! Do you know what my life has been like?" Nora spit out.

"I know it hasn't been easy," Katie said apologetically. "But, I truly am sorry."

"What are you, some sort of simpleton? Do

you think apologizing makes up for the 24 years of pain I've endured?" Nora said.

"Nora, please!" I said. I went to Katie and grabbed her hand. "Katie, it took a lot of courage to come here today. And we appreciate it."

"It was the least I could do," Katie said.

"No, the least you could have done was help me when I was being attacked, you cowardly bitch!" Nora yelled.

"I-I can't believe you saw what Daddy did to Nora," Ellen whispered. "And you never said a word!?" Ellen's voice was rising.

"Ellen, I'm sorry," Katie said.

"It's your fault! H-he never would have gotten the chance! It's all your fault!" Ellen screamed hysterically.

"I-I don't understand," Katie said, shaking her head.

"H-he r-raped me four times! H-he never would have g-gotten the chance if you'd said something!" Ellen cried.

"What?!" Nora yelled, looking at Ellen.

"Oh, my God!" Rhonda said, covering her mouth.

"D-daddy got me pregnant!" Ellen yelled.

"Oh, Ellen!" Gina cried.

"I-I never deserved that! I was only 15!" Ellen cried.

"I-I can't believe it!" Nora said, in disbelief. She limped over to Ellen without the use of her crutches. "Ellen?"

Ellen looked at Nora, with tears in both their

eyes, the two of them embraced.

"Oh, Nora! Had I known, I never would have let Daddy get away with it! I would have stopped him!" Ellen said.

"I-I'm so sorry, Ellen! I should have known! You are my sister and I've been so terrible to you over the years!" Nora cried. "And you've gone through so much more! To be pregnant for our father! W-what happened to the baby?"

"He made me have an abortion. That's when I started drinking," Ellen said.

She went on to tell them all about what had happened to her over the years. Jim held his wife, as he found out for the first time since they'd been together what happened to her. After all that had gone on, Katie felt that she'd outstayed her welcome.

"Oh, Ellen. I'm sorry you endured such pain," Katie said softly. She touched Ellen's shoulder.

"You stay away from me!" Ellen jerked away from her. "Katie, I never want to see or talk to you again! You helped drive a nail into my coffin and I'll never forgive you for that. Maybe had you yelled, or said something, we could have helped my sister!"

"We were young, Ellen. I know that's no excuse, but we were only 14," Katie argued.

"Just leave, Katie," Ellen said calmly. "Your silence ruined my life. That's a huge price to pay for a friendship with you."

"I really am sorry," Katie whispered as she turned and walked into the house. I followed her.

I took Katie into the sunroom, to make an

233

attempt at helping to alleviate some of the pain she was feeling. Ironically, she'd lost a childhood friend, but helped to rebuild Ellen's relationship with Nora. Katie was so young at the time and didn't understand what type of impact what she'd witnessed would have.

"Katie, Ellen just needs time to absorb it all," I encouraged.

"I know. She has every right to be angry. I mean, had I said something, maybe she wouldn't have had to endure the same thing. And to be pregnant? How terrible that must have been for her!"

"It's a lot to deal with, but she's strong. Both of them are."

"Well, I'd better head back to the hotel. I think I've done enough here."

"Do you have to go back now? Can't you stay for a couple of days?"

"I don't think so. My plan was to leave tomorrow morning after saying what I had to say."

"But, you and Ellen need to work through this."

"Not yet, Millie. My silence nearly destroyed her. She needs time. She'll talk to me when she's ready."

"You're welcome to stay."

"Thank you, but I don't think that's a good idea. I have a suite at the Richfield Hotel. If Ellen wants to talk to me, that's where I'll be until tomorrow morning. If she's not ready, I'll understand." Katie stood up to leave.

"I'm sorry, Katie," I said sympathetically.

Katie touched my arm. "There's no need to

234

apologize. I owe the apologies."

I walked Katie to the front door. "Take care of yourself," I said, hugging her. "And thank you for giving me my family back."

"No, Millie, thank you for being so understanding." Katie then turned to walk out. When she got to her rental car, she turned around. "And tell Ellen that I've always thought of her as a sister and that I will always love her." She had tears in her eyes as she spoke.

I smiled at her and waved goodbye. I went back onto the patio to see how things were progressing between Ellen and Nora. The two of them were talking.

"Ellen, I can't tell you enough how sorry I am," Nora said.

"That's okay, Nora. I really would have never watched Daddy do something like that," Ellen said. I walked over to where they were sitting.

"It's so wonderful seeing you two getting along," I smiled as I sat down.

"What made you call Katie?" Ellen asked.

"When we were talking the other night, I noticed how much the two of you resembled. I guess I'd never paid attention to it before. Without telling you, I called information, got her number and called her yesterday."

"Did she tell you yesterday?" Ellen asked.

"No, she didn't. When I questioned her about it, she became very upset and denied it."

"Some friend. Even when confronted with the truth, she denies it," Ellen said in a frustrated tone.

"But, she came forward today. That has to mean something to you," I said.

"Yeah, it means she's a lying coward who ruined both our lives," Nora said.

"How do I forgive her, Millie? Her keeping quiet made all the difference in the world," Ellen said.

"Katie wasn't thinking like that. She was young and scared. Witnessing something like that must have devastated her," I said, defending Katie. "I mean, you say you would have said something, but the same thing happened to you and you never said a word. Why weren't you brave enough to come forward? I'll tell you why. Because you were young and scared," I said.

"That's different. My silence only hurt me and me alone!" Ellen said.

"No, your silence hurt your husband and your daughter. Think about it, Ellen. You too, Nora," I said. I got up to leave. As I stood, I told her, "Oh, by the way, Katie is staying at the Richfield Hotel until in the morning. She told me to tell you that she loves you, no matter what you think of her."

Ellen looked at me, but didn't say anything else. I knew my words affected her. Deep down, she knew I was right. I just hoped her desperation to work things out with Nora wouldn't cost her a friendship with Katie. I went into the den where Clayton was reading the newspaper. I sat next to him and sighed. Now that Nora and Ellen were finally getting along, I felt we were finally getting somewhere. After almost a week, it was about time. Clayton looked at me, as he folded his paper.

"Are you okay?" he asked.

"I'm wonderful! My sisters are speaking again and I couldn't be happier for the two of them. I'm hoping Ellen will talk to Katie before she leaves," I said.

"One thing at a time, Millie," Clayton advised.

"I know. You know, every one of my sisters has had a deep, dark secret to reveal. Have we really been so out of touch to the point where we have no idea about what's going on in each other's lives?"

"That's not too unusual. You are all adults, in different states," Clayton said. "Plus, you all haven't been together in 10 years since you buried your father."

"You have a point," I smiled, leaning on him. Then my smile faded. "Daddy's death brought us together while his actions tore us apart."

After Clayton and I had a few moments of quiet together, we joined the rest of the family. We went out to the art museum and to see a Broadway play on tour in town. During the whole outing, Ellen looked extremely distracted. I knew she was upset about Katie. Although she and Katie hadn't talked in years, she was still a friend. Ellen couldn't get past her betrayal. When we got home, she and Jim had talked about it, and she decided she wanted to see Katie. Jim offered to drive her to Katie's hotel, but Ellen insisted upon driving. Clayton invited Jim to go with him, Kyle, Robert and AJ to a sports bar. I insisted to Jim that he should go and have a good time. I told him that Ellen could use my car if he wanted to use their rental car.

The guys left that evening around six, and Ellen left shortly afterwards. She knew where the hotel was, because it was located close to the airport. Maybe now would be a good time to work on Rhonda and Nora. The two of them still weren't speaking. God knows, I didn't want another 24 years to go by filled with animosity. Gina, Alex, Nora and I were playing cards in our game room. Rhonda was out by the pool with Kirsten, Ginny and Erin.

"Looks like I win again, so pay up," Nora smiled. "You three really should learn how to play."

"You'll need the money more than any of them, considering your husband will be leaving you penniless," Rhonda said from the doorway.

"Here we go again," Gina sighed, as she gathered up the cards.

"Can we please give it a rest?" I said. "It's time to let it go."

"You know, you're not exactly swimming in marital bliss, now are you?" Nora replied.

"Are you two going to gripe at each other for the rest of the week?" Gina asked.

"I'm not mad. I've tried to apologize to her!" Nora yelled.

"I just have one question, Nora," Rhonda said, walking close to where Nora was sitting. She looked down at her seriously. "Why?"

Nora sighed and looked apologetic. "Rhonda, I wish I knew. I was so stupid. You'd welcomed me into your home and that was the way I repaid you. I'll never forgive myself for that. For so many years, I've blamed every problem I've ever encountered on my

238

childhood problems. I've been so awful! I've been jealous and spiteful. But, after finding out about the agony Ellen has endured, I know now that what I suffered was a mere drop in the bucket." Nora touched Rhonda's arm. She looked up into her sister's eyes. "Rhonda, I'm truly sorry for what I did. I hope one day that you can forgive me. I got one of my sisters back, only to lose another one. I need you too much. I need you all too much," Nora said, looking around.

Rhonda stood there with tears in her eyes. "Nora, that's the first heartfelt, sincere apology I've ever heard from you in all of your 39 years. My little sister's finally growing up," Rhonda smiled.

"Does that mean you're ready to forgive me for being such a bitch?" Nora smiled.

"Well, you'll never stop being that," Rhonda laughed. "But, I do forgive you for what happened with Aaron."

"I love you, Rhonda!" Nora said, standing from her seat.

"I love you, too, Nora," Rhonda cried. The two of them embraced.

"Finally! Boy, it's about time! We might actually have a full twenty four hours with no fighting!" Gina smiled.

She was right, because there was harmony at last between all of the McAlray sisters. We were sisters again. Now it was a real reunion, despite the initial reason they came to see me. We all sat in the game room and talked about all the things we'd been too angry with each other to discuss over the course of the past few days. This was the first time we were able to communicate without one sniping at the other. It took almost an entire week, but it paid off.

"So, when are you going to put your pride aside and call Bill?" I asked.

"I don't know. I'm not even sure he'll even talk to me," Nora sighed. "We haven't exactly been on the best of terms. We were all but in divorce court before coming here."

"Will counseling help?" Gina asked.

"I don't know," Nora said, shaking her head. "I haven't exactly appreciated my husband. I can't believe I'm about to admit this, but, I've cheated on him, I've been mean to him, and I've blamed him for every problem in our marriage. If I were him, I don't know if I'd forgive me."

"Give it time," I said. "Bill loves you, Nora."

"You know, I really believe he does," Nora smiled. Then, her smile faded. "But, what if this was the last straw? What if I've destroyed that?"

"Nora, I have to know. Is Jessica Aaron's daughter?" Rhonda asked.

"No. In my heart, I know she's Bill's," Nora said.

"Forget your heart, what about DNA?" Gina commented.

"I've never tried to find out, because I never wanted to think about it," Nora said.

"I have to know, Nora," Rhonda said.

"Right now, I don't even know. Neither my children nor my husband want anything to do with me," Nora commented.

"What about you, Rhonda? Are you going to divorce Aaron?" I asked.

"As soon as I can," Rhonda smiled. "It's been a long time coming."

We were interrupted by the phone ringing. I suddenly remembered that Miriam had left already.

"Hello?" I answered.

"I'm trying to reach Millicent Welby," a man answered.

"This is Millicent Welby."

"Mrs. Welby, this is Sgt. Rickman with Myrtle Beach Police."

"Yes?" I placed my hand on my chest. Why would the police be calling my house unless something had happened?

"I'm calling in reference to a woman claiming to be your sister who was driving a black Mercedes registered to you."

"Yes, my sister was driving my car. What's happened?"

"We've pulled a Mrs. Ellen Loweman over for reckless driving."

"What?"

"She was driving while intoxicated."

"Is she okay?"

"She's fine. She had a slight fender-bender that could have been a lot worse. Your sister is in jail, Mrs. Welby."

"Oh my goodness!"

"Millie, what is it?" Rhonda asked, standing from her chair.

"It's Ellen. She's been arrested for drunk

241

driving," I told my sisters. "What precinct are you calling from?"

"The downtown precinct."

"Can I bail her out?"

"Probably so, but it's up to the judge. There will be a bail hearing tonight within the hour."

"I'll be right down," I said, hanging up the phone. I turned to my sisters. "We have to go downtown to bail out Ellen."

"How much is her bail?" Gina asked.

"I don't know. There will be a hearing within the hour."

"I'll drive you," Alex volunteered.

"Thank you, Alex," I said.

"I thought she was going to talk things over with Katie," Gina said.

"That's where she said she was going," I said.

We all walked out of the game room. I didn't want to let Amanda know what happened. I was hoping we could get her home before Clayton and Jim. Maybe she could sleep it off and Jim wouldn't have to find out. I knew there was no way that would happen since she's been arrested. Just when things were starting to go so well. Alex, Gina and I went to the precinct together. The judge set her bail at $5,000.00, and required that Ellen would still have to go to court concerning her DUI. She was being let out on bail because she had no priors in the state of South Carolina. She was probably going to be required to attend a class, but we wouldn't know that until she went to court. I was afraid that they would keep her because of her other charges in New York, but they never came up, thank goodness. I paid my sister's bail and we managed to get a drunken Ellen home. She was in a complete stupor. We got her up to her bedroom thankfully before our husbands got home. I knew that either way, it was only prolonging the inevitable.

Out of concern, I called Katie at her hotel. Katie told me that Ellen never arrived. Not only that, Katie had no idea that Ellen was even supposed to be coming to see her. I wondered why did Ellen lie to us. What happened to deter her? Did she have any intention of even going to see Katie? Why would she do such a thing? I knew now that Ellen's problems were too big for us to handle. Our husbands didn't arrive home until almost two a.m. By that time, Ginny and Kirsten made sure that Erin got home safely. They called me about 15 minutes before Clayton's arrival to let me know they were safely home. I was in the sunroom reading when Clayton came in.

"I figured I'd find you here. I saw the light on when we pulled into the driveway," Clayton smiled, putting his keys on the table.

"Where are Kyle, Robert, AJ and Jim?" I asked, after my husband kissed and sat next to me.

"Kyle, AJ and Robert left already, and Jim went upstairs." Clayton looked at the expression on my face. "What? Is something wrong?"

I mustered a smile. "Everything's fine."

Clayton looked at me seriously. "Now, why don't I believe you?" Clayton asked, as he caressed my face.

"Nothing's wrong," I insisted.

"Millie, you're a terrible liar," Clayton commented.

"Sweetheart, everything's fine. I'm just tired, that's all. So, how was your 'guys' night out'?" I wanted to change the subject quickly.

"We had a nice time. It felt good to bond like we did. Especially with Kyle. I think he and I needed that time."

"I'm glad you went."

Clayton looked thoughtful as he smiled. "Kyle's so excited about becoming a father. It was like seeing myself when you were pregnant with him." Clayton looked at me as his smile faded.

"What is it?" I asked.

"Nothing, just a strange feeling," Clayton said somberly.

"A strange feeling about what?" I asked.

"I don't know. But, I felt like tonight had to be extra-special for some reason."

"Maybe it's because you and Kyle haven't had time to spend together in so long. I mean, you travel so much on business, not to mention my illness that's consumed our lives over the past year. It's understandable that you wouldn't have time to devote to going out with him like you'd want."

"No, that's not it. We talked, and it's as if we both had so much to say to each other. As if we didn't want to take a chance that the opportunity would never present itself again."

"I don't understand," I said, confused by his words.

244

"It was as if we'd never get the opportunity to spend that precious time together again," Clayton said.

"That's such an ominous thing to say, Sweetheart. It scares me to hear you say things like that," I said.

"Oh, Millie," Clayton smiled, rubbing my shoulder. "You worry too much. It's just me being sentimental about becoming a grandfather. He's not going to have as much time for his old man once the baby arrives."

Clayton was making a feeble attempt at appeasing me after his dispiriting words. It wasn't working. It was as if my husband was having a premonition. Maybe he felt that I needed to spend more time with the children for fear that I might not have much time left. Clayton drew me to him. I leaned over, as we both put our feet up on the sofa. Clayton's words left me a little uneasy. I knew my time was limited, but something in the way he spoke, made me very uncomfortable. He held me so close that night, as if he couldn't get close enough. I loved my husband so much. I was so glad that I was going to go first. I couldn't take one day without him. Lost in my thoughts, I fell asleep in my husband's arms.

****

The next morning, I awoke with my husband to see the sun rise.

"Why don't we just move our bed down here? We fall asleep down here so much, until we may as well turn it into our bedroom," Clayton joked.

"Then we'd spend more time upstairs," I

245

laughed.

"You're probably right," Clayton smiled, leaning over to kiss me.

"I love watching the sun rise," I sighed.

"It is beautiful, isn't it? It's something that happens every day, but each one is more mesmerizing than the last," Clayton said.

"How long do you think we'll have moments like this?" I asked.

"I'd like them forever," Clayton commented strangely.

"Clayton, are you okay?" I asked, looking serious.

"I'm fine. I'm just ready to be alone with you, without all the company. The kids are old enough to take care of themselves, so we should go off to the lake house for a weekend, just the two of us," Clayton smiled.

"I drive you crazy when we go off alone. You said I worry about the children too much, even though they're not 'children' anymore," I smiled.

My smile faded, as Clayton looked at me. "Millie, honey, what's wrong? Something's been wrong since last night. And don't think I didn't pick up on your sly attempt at changing the subject," Clayton chastised.

"I don't know how to tell you this," I started.

"Just tell me, Sweetheart."

I took a deep sigh and sat up. "Ellen was arrested last night for drunk driving."

"What? Why didn't you say something last night?" Clayton said, sitting up beside me.

"I didn't know how to tell you," I said.

"You can't be serious about this," Clayton said.

"I'm very serious. She was supposed to be going to visit with Katie."

"Didn't Katie know she was an alcoholic? Didn't she know better than to let Ellen drink?" Clayton was clearly upset.

"It's not Katie's fault. Ellen never made it to Katie's hotel. The police called, and I went and bailed her out," I said.

"Arrested? And of course, Jim doesn't know since he was out with me."

"Maybe we should tell him, to smooth things over for her," I suggested.

Clayton sighed. "No, it's her responsibility to tell him. Does she have to go to court?"

"Yes, next week. At that point, a judge will make a decision concerning her case. Um, honey, I didn't tell you everything," I said.

"There's more?" Clayton asked.

"Yes. Um, Ellen had an accident in my car," I said. The Mercedes had been a birthday present from Clayton.

"What?! Millie, why didn't you tell me? Was anyone hurt?"

"Calm down, honey. It wasn't major. It was a minor fender-bender. She hit one of those concrete markers, which is what made the police pull her over. The car can easily be fixed and she wasn't hurt," I reasoned.

"Well the result could have been very

different! Ellen could have killed someone! She could have killed herself!"

"I know that, Clayton, but she didn't!" I yelled. "No one else was involved!"

"Millie, at what point were you going to tell me? I'm your husband!" Clayton yelled.

"I'm telling you now!"

"But if you thought you could keep this from me, you would. And now you want to protect her from her husband by our intervention to 'smooth things over.' When are you going to let them grow up?"

"What's that supposed to mean?" I asked defensively.

"Your sisters have been here all of a week, and you've been playing 'mother hen' to them the whole time."

"That's so unfair of you to say! We're family. Shouldn't I be here for them?" I cried.

"Of course you should, but I see it. I've seen it every day how they don't even care about how all of their problems might be affecting you. All they can think about is their own self-importance. It's ridiculous," Clayton said, shaking his head.

"They're my sisters, and I love them! They're going through so much right now, and I have to be here for them," I said.

"They're grown women! Let them be adults! Stop feeling like you have to constantly come to their rescue," Clayton said.

"I don't want to have this conversation anymore!" I said, standing abruptly. "You have a lot of nerve expecting me to just turn my back on my family!" I shouted.

"What? Millie, I'm your husband! I love you and I've been here for you for over 26 years! Can they say the same? You act like I'm telling you to turn your back on small children. Even though they act like children, they're not. Stop babying them!"

"'Babying them'? How dare you? You're the one who picked up the phone and called them to come here! Now, you have a problem with them being here?"

"Millie, you're taking it all out of context," Clayton said.

"No, I don't think I am. You obviously have a problem with my offering my sister a place to live, so maybe she and I will move out together! At least she'll be there for me when I die!" I shouted.

Clayton looked so hurt by my words. "I'm going to leave now, before I say something I'll regret! You are the most important person in the world to me, and all you can say to me is that someone else will be there for you when you die? I've had it! When you can find my rational wife, please return her, because this person standing before me, I don't even know! I rue the day I picked up the phone to call them! It's either me or your sisters because you obviously don't have room for both! I'm leaving!"

With that statement, Clayton picked up his keys and stormed out of the room.

I followed him. "Where are you going?" I asked.

"As far away from here as I can!" Clayton

shouted.   He was still dressed from the night before, so he stormed out to the garage.

"Clayton Drew Welby, don't you walk away from me!" I demanded.   He ignored me.   "Clayton!"

I stopped at the door leading into the garage. He pushed the remote to let the door up, cranked his car, and he was gone.   My God, what have I done? I've driven my husband away.   How could I be so stupid?   I stood there and cried.   Was I slowly losing the best thing to ever happen to me?   What was I thinking?   I had to go after him.   I turned to go back so that I could get the keys to the SUV.   I must have turned too quickly, because everything became very blurred, and I blacked out.

Chapter Twelve

When I awakened, I was in the hospital, with an IV hooked up to me. At first, I wasn't sure if I was even still alive. The voices around me were muffled and hollow, comparable to an echo. I could hardly keep my eyes open. Was this the end for me? I suddenly thought about the argument I'd had with Clayton. Where was he? I soon realized there was an oxygen mask on my face.

"Clayton," I whispered.

As my eyes focused better, I realized Clayton wasn't there, but I saw three faces looming over me whom I'd never seen before. One of them shined a light in my eye.

"Millicent? Millicent, can you hear me?" the voice asked.

I slightly nodded. Who were these people? Where was my husband? "Clayton," I repeated.

The man looked at one of the other people in the room.

"Clayton's her husband," the woman clarified for him.

He looked back at me. "Clayton's not here right now, but your sisters and children are out in the waiting area. You gave us quite a scare," this nameless person smiled. "I'm Dr. David Copeland, and I'm one of the physicians in the ER here at Lakeland Shores Medical Center. Dr. Tracer has been paged, and she should be here shortly."

I nodded my head weakly. So many thoughts were swimming through my head. I'd desperately upset my husband, who wasn't here with me. These could very well be my last moments, and I'd run off the one person who'd been here with me through it all. Shortly afterwards, I saw Dr. Tracer.

"Millicent? How are you feeling?" she asked in a concerned tone.

"I've been better," I smiled weakly. "Can they please take this mask off my face?" My voice was muffled to my own ears from the oxygen mask.

"We were about to shortly," Dr. Copeland said.

"What happened?" Dr. Tracer asked Dr. Copeland.

"Well, according to her sisters, she fainted in her kitchen. Her maid found her. They called 911, and the paramedics rushed her here. I've done a Chem 18 on her, along with an admission panel. According to her chart, she's a candidate for a bone marrow transplant," Dr. Copeland said, looking at Dr. Tracer.

"Unfortunately, we haven't found a viable donor yet," Dr. Tracer said. I laid there, listening as they talked over me. During that time, a woman who I assumed was a nurse removed my oxygen mask.

"Is that a little better?" the nurse asked, smiling at me.

"Yes, thank you," I whispered.

"Keep an eye on her SATS level. Since the mask seems so uncomfortable, we may need to put her on nasal oxygen if they go below 90 again," Dr. Copeland instructed.

"Yes sir," the nurse nodded.

The two doctors commenced to talk in what I will affectionately refer to as 'medical jargon.' I'd always been one who hated not knowing what was going on. With that in mind, and my total ignorance about what they were talking about, I blurted out before I knew it.

"Would you please stop talking about me as if I'm not here? I want my husband," I said weakly.

"She's been asking for him," Dr. Copeland told Dr. Tracer.

"Okay, Millicent, we're going to try to contact Clayton," Dr. Tracer said.

"I'm going to go out and talk to your family, and let a few come back at a time. Then, we're going to get you admitted," Dr. Copeland said.

I shook my head fiercely. "No! I don't want to be admitted again!" I cried.

"Millicent, calm down," Dr. Tracer said.

"Dr. Tracer, please don't let them admit me!" I pleaded as tears rolled down the side of my face.

"David, go on out and talk to her family. I'll calm her down." Dr. Tracer ordered the nurse to give me a sedative.

"No! I don't want to be sedated! Dr. Tracer, let me do this my own way!" I said.

"Millicent, you are my patient, and I have to take care of you. Just calm down, okay?"

"Please, Dr. Tracer! I'll go home, I'll rest. I just need Clayton here to take me home. I promise I won't get stressed out," I pleaded.

"I really think you should be admitted," Dr. Tracer sighed. "I have to think about your well-being."

We disagreed back and forth for the next few minutes. Then I felt really relaxed all of a sudden. Apparently, they'd put something in my IV.

"Please, Dr. Tracer," I said weakly.

"Letting you leave here today would go against my better judgment. How about if you stay overnight? Just for observation? Then, tomorrow morning, you can leave if you want to," Dr. Tracer suggested.

"Just overnight?" I asked, starting to feel groggy.

"Just overnight," Dr. Tracer reassured.

I looked at her. She'd always been a doctor that I felt the utmost confidence in, so if she wanted me to stay overnight, the least I could do is stay. . . . . .I didn't remember anything beyond her trying to reason with me.

****

The next thing I remember, I woke up feeling rested. I thought it was the next morning. I looked around, and there were all of my sisters, but no Clayton. Was he still angry with me? Had I driven my husband away? How could I choose between the love of my life and my family? That was such an unfair decision to have to make. I truly don't think Clayton ever expected me to choose, but he'd gotten so fed up with the way everyone was acting, until his hands were tied. I realized that he was only looking out for my best interest. I've loved him for too long. We've stayed together through so much. How could a reunion ruin 26 years of marriage? Would my sisters be the cause of the demise of my marriage? It seems almost unfair that it could end in separation or divorce before we are parted by natural means.

"Clayton," I whispered.

"He's not here, Honey," Rhonda whispered, holding my hand.

"Where's Clayton?" I asked.

"I don't know. We've tried to contact him, but he's not answering his cell phone," Rhonda said.

"What day is it?" I asked.

"It's Saturday afternoon," Gina said.

"What time is it?" I asked, my head starting to clear. "It's 3:30 p.m. Dr. Tracer said you needed the rest," Ellen said.

"3:30? And Clayton's not here?" I asked.

Rhonda suddenly looked at Ellen, then back at me. "We're still trying to reach him. What happened exactly?"

"We had an argument, and he stormed out of

255

the house. But, he usually goes off for a drive, calms down, and comes back so that we can work things out. He's not at home? Has my husband even been home?" I asked, clearly becoming upset.

"Sweetheart, you need to calm down," Rhonda soothed.

"I'm lying in a hospital bed, where I've been all day and my husband's not even here? And you expect me to calm down? Where's my husband, Rhonda?" I asked sternly.

"We don't know. Clayton hasn't been back home yet," Rhonda said quietly. "Maybe he's still upset. You know if he knew you were here, he'd be right by your side." Rhonda tried unsuccessfully to reassure me.

Tears immediately ran down my face. I couldn't believe Clayton would do something like this. He'd never desert me. But where was he?

"Where are my children?" I asked.

"Kirsten and Kyle went down to get something to eat. Shauna and Tim are over in the corner sitting down," Ellen said, motioning to them.

I saw the welcoming sight of my two youngest children. They stood and walked slowly towards my bed as I smiled at them.

"Hi," I said.

"Hi, Ma," Shauna said. She looked as if she'd been crying. My sweet little girl.

"Have you been crying?" I asked, reaching up to caress her face. It was at that point when I noticed I still had an IV in my arm.

"Just a little," Shauna smiled.

"Sweetie, there's nothing to be afraid of. I just got a little tired, okay? I'm still here," I soothed.

"I'm scared, Mama! What if you die? Please don't leave me!" Shauna cried.

She laid her head down on me. As I looked around, I could see each of my sisters had tears in their eyes. I felt as if my life was spiraling out of control. No one knew where my husband was, my baby daughter was so afraid that this was the end for me. And what could I do about it? Absolutely nothing. I rubbed Shauna's back as she laid on me.

"Shh, it's okay. I'm coming home today," I whispered. I looked up at Tim, who was trying to maintain his composure, but I could tell he wasn't far behind his little sister. "How are you holding up?" I asked, looking at him.

"I'm okay," Tim smiled slightly.

"Are you sure?" I asked.

"I'm just ready for you to come home," Tim said.

A few minutes passed and Kirsten and Kyle came back. They immediately came over to my bed when they realized I was awake.

"Mom, how are you feeling?" Kirsten asked, stroking my forehead.

"I'm fine," I smiled. "Just ready to go home. Have you not heard from your father?" I asked.

"No, we haven't," Kyle said. "I've tried him on his cell phone several times, and Miriam knows to contact us the minute she hears from him. You just need to concentrate on getting well."

"I'm going to do that," I said.

Moments later, the phone rang. Kirsten was standing right beside it, so she answered it.

"Hello?" Kirsten said. She smiled. "Oh, hi, Miriam. Have you heard from Daddy?" Kirsten listened intently as her smile suddenly turned into a serious frown. She looked as if she was about to cry. She looked at me, hastily gaining her composure. Something was wrong. I could tell because I could feel it. What was going on? "Okay, I'll check on it," she said, as she hung up the phone.

"What's wrong?" I asked, as a strange chill went over me.

Kirsten mustered a smile. "Nothing. You just concentrate on getting better like Kyle said. I'm going to go out to the desk to see if you're going to have to stay overnight," Kirsten said. Then, she looked at Kyle and slyly motioned for him to follow her.

"I'll be right back; I'm going with Kirsten to talk to your doctor," Kyle said.

Kirsten was not telling me something. My God, what had happened? Was it Clayton? Had something happened? Every since I'd awakened, I could feel that something was wrong. What was it? I hated for my children to keep things from me.

Gina came over to the bed. "Are you sure you're feeling well enough to go home?" she asked.

"I'm much better," I said distractedly. "Gina, what's going on? The way Kirsten left out of here, I know something's wrong. Please find out," I said starting to cry hysterically.

"Please, Sweetie, everything's going to be

258

fine," Ellen said.   She buzzed for the nurses' desk.

"May I help you?" a voice came back over the intercom.

"Can you send a nurse in here please?   My sister's very upset," Ellen said.

"Someone will be there in just a moment," the voice said.

The nurse immediately came through the door. She tried to help settle me from hysteria.

"Mrs. Welby, you have to calm down," the nurse said.   I saw her withdraw medication into a syringe from a small vial.   She was going to give me a shot.

"No!   No more sedatives!   Please!   Don't do that!" I yelled helplessly, watching her inject the medication into my IV.   I was too weak to pull away.

"This is to help you to relax," the nurse said.

My worst fear was coming true.   They were drugging me up during the last days of my life.   I had no idea what was going on around me.   I didn't want to sleep.   Why were they doing this to me?

"Please!   What's wrong?   Has something happened to Clayton?" I asked.

"Honey, don't worry about anything. Everything will be fine," Nora reassured, rubbing my hand.

"W-why are y-you doing th-this to me?" I asked, suddenly fading again.   My vision became blurred, as I saw Kirsten and Kyle come into the room. They motioned for my sisters to go into the hallway with them.   Was Kirsten crying?   I was completely helpless.   This was not how I wanted to live my last days. What were they keeping from me?

****

When I awakened this time, there were tear-stained faces looking at me. Kirsten and Robert were there, along with Kyle and Erin. Shauna and Tim were both crying. My sisters were also there, but there was still no Clayton. I had the eerie feeling that something had happened.

"Clayton?" I said. I looked up, and suddenly there he was, smiling at me. I smiled. "Finally. I've been so worried about you."

"I'm always here with you, Millie," Clayton said soothingly, stroking my hand.

"I knew you wouldn't desert me in my time of need. Please, take me home. I'm sorry about our argument earlier. I wasn't being fair to you," I smiled.

"Shh, it's okay. All's forgiven. I'll wait on you; it won't be long now," Clayton smiled. He started to fade. What was going on? Why couldn't I feel his touch any longer?

"Clayton!" I screamed. "Don't leave me!" Tears streamed down my face. Where was he? He'd left me!

"Mom, please! You have to try to relax," Kirsten pleaded as tears rolled down her face.

"Where's Clayton? He was just here," I cried.

Kirsten looked at everyone else in the room. "Wh-what?" she asked surprisingly.

"Clayton was just standing here talking to me,"

I said. "Where did he go?"

"Mom, Daddy's not here," Kirsten said, crying.

"Where is he? Where's your father?" I asked, pleading with my daughter.

"Mom, please settle down. We have something to tell you," Kyle said.

"Wh-what is it? Where's Clayton? Please! He was just here!" I cried.

"We don't know how to tell you this, but," Kyle suddenly broke into tears.

"Just tell me," I whispered. I looked at my sisters and my children around me. "Please!" I yelled.

"Daddy's dead!" Kirsten sobbed. "I-I'm so sorry, Mom! Daddy's gone!"

Suddenly, I felt as if I was having an out of body experience. I wasn't hearing my daughter right. It was the medication. It had to be. No, I was still asleep, having a nightmare. She couldn't have been right because Clayton was just talking to me. He wasn't gone. He couldn't be. Why were my children playing such a cruel trick on me? Why were they keeping Clayton from me? He was just still upset with me. He wouldn't leave me. Clayton loved me too much. But deep in my heart, I knew it was true. My husband. My life mate. My lover. My best friend. The father of my children. Gone. Gone and never to return. My life was over. I began to sob loudly.

"NO! No, it's not true!" I cried. "P-please don't say things like that!"

"Mom, I wish it weren't true," Kyle said.

"H-he w-was just here! Please! Bring him back! He was here!" I protested.

I cried and cried. My heart was shattered in a million pieces. I never got to say goodbye. Oh, my God, my husband was dead, and I never got to tell him how much I loved him, how much he meant to me.

"Millicent, I know you're upset, but you have to think about your health," Dr. Tracer said. I didn't even realize she'd entered the room.

"I-I want to see my husband!" I cried. "I need to see him!" I was so distraught. I pulled the IV from my arm and tried to get up from the bed.

"Mom! No!" Kirsten protested.

Dr. Tracer tried to stop the bleeding from where I'd pulled the IV out. I saw her reach for the call light, calling for the nurse to come in to assist her. No, not more drugs. I needed Clayton. I needed to be with him. He needed me. I had to see for myself that he was truly gone, because my husband loved me, and he wouldn't leave me. What could I do? They were holding me down.

"Please! No more drugs! Don't keep me from my husband! I-I have to see him!" I cried.

"Millicent, please settle down," Dr. Tracer said.

"Wh-where is he?" I said, trying desperately not to fall to pieces.

"He was brought into the morgue a couple of hours ago. By the time the paramedics got to the scene, he was already dead," Dr. Tracer said.

"What happened?" I asked.

"He was in a car accident this afternoon," Dr. Tracer said.

"H-how? Where?" I asked.

"He was driving around a deep curve on Beckerman Road, and apparently lost control of his car and it flipped over," Dr. Tracer said.

"Oh," I whimpered, covering my mouth with my hands, as if that could stop the tears from coming.

"I'm sorry, Millicent. There was nothing they could do to bring him back," Dr. Tracer said apologetically.

"I want to see my husband," I said firmly.

"Mom, maybe that's not–" Kirsten started.

"I want to see my husband!" I yelled. "I don't believe any of you! Take me to him! Clayton would never leave me! He promised!" I cried. "Now, I want to see him!" I demanded.

"Millicent, I'd advise against it," Dr. Tracer said.

"I'm his legal next of kin. I have a right to identify my husband's body, don't I?"

"Yes, you do, but you're in such a fragile state. Are you sure you're up for it?" Dr. Tracer asked.

"I want to see my husband," I said calmly.

"Okay. I'll call down to the morgue and arrange for you to see him," Dr. Tracer said.

I lied there, staring at the ceiling. Tears uncontrollably ran down the side of my face. I was numb. Clayton always said he wanted to go first; that he didn't think he could bear living without me. Well, he'd done it. He'd selfishly left me first. Now I'm left to live the rest of my days mourning, waiting for the day we will be reunited. God, had I truly disappointed You to this degree? Why did You take my Clayton away? I need him too much. My thoughts were interrupted by Dr. Tracer.

"Okay, Millicent," Dr. Tracer said, as she hung up the phone. "I'm going to take you down to say goodbye. Then, I'd like to keep you for a day or two."

"No," I said monotonously. "When I see my husband, I want to get dressed, and I want for my family to take me home."

"Millie, maybe you should–" Rhonda started.

"I want to go home," I said quietly, interrupting her. "There's nothing any of you can do to stop me. You have no right to keep me here."

"You're right about that, Millicent. I can't make you stay, but I wish you would change your mind," Dr. Tracer suggested.

"I want to go home," I said.

"Okay, Millicent. Leaving like this will be against my medical advice. You have to sign a form saying that you are refusing treatment. If you change your mind after we get back from the morgue, you can let me know," Dr. Tracer said.

"I won't change my mind. I've lost everything. At least grant me the choice of being able to mourn in my own home," I said.

"Fair enough. Let's go," Dr. Tracer said.

The nurse brought in a wheelchair for me. They also gave Nora a wheelchair so that she wouldn't have to put so much pressure on her leg. Dr. Tracer decided to keep the IV out, so she bandaged my arm. Kirsten and Gina helped me into the wheelchair.

264

Kyle rolled me down to say goodbye to their father. The closer we got to the morgue, the more of a reality everything became. Maybe this was all just a bad dream. That I'd wake up and still be in Clayton's arms like I'd been for 26 years. Dr. Tracer pulled the curtain back, as Kyle wheeled me in. Shauna cried out, Tim ran off. Kirsten cried silently, as Ellen held her. Robert was about to go after Tim, but Kirsten stopped him. She told him that Tim needed time alone. The voices around me seemed to fade, as I held my head up. I'd not realized until that moment that I'd closed my eyes, praying that it wasn't my beloved Clayton. Kyle wheeled me next to him, as the attendant pulled the covers back. There he was.

As if my heart couldn't break anymore, I felt it break a hundred times more. I stared at him. I'm not sure if I kept hoping the lifeless body before me would change into another person, but I knew I couldn't take my eyes off of him. I reached up to uncover his hand. His knuckles were bruised with small shards of glass still embedded in them. His forehead had a large gash immediately above his left eye. That handsome face. That face I fell in love with all those years ago now lay before me battered, bruised and lifeless. My life mate was gone. I gently stroked his lifeless, cold hand, a hand that had held me just a few short hours ago as we watched the sun rise together.

"Clayton," I whispered. "Oh, God, it's true! Clayton!" I yelled hysterically. "I prayed and prayed that it was all a mistake, but it's not! It's not a mistake! H-he's really gone!" I broke down and cried.

I clenched his hand, as if to hold onto it for dear life. I felt someone hug me. I had no idea who it was. I didn't even care, because I knew it wasn't my husband. I'd never feel his embrace again. Never see that handsome smile I fell in love with so many years ago. I'd never wake up beside him again.

I sobbed loudly. "How could you leave me!? I-I wanted to go first! Please God, send him back to me! Please!" I pleaded.

"Daddy, why did you have to die?!" Shauna cried as she looked at her father's body lying on the table.

While I yearned to comfort my youngest daughter, how could I? I was in so much pain. I suddenly felt a terrible pain in my stomach. Had I not been in a wheelchair, I would have passed out onto the floor. I had no idea about what was going on around me. I knew that I was still holding on to Clayton's hand. I couldn't let go. I had to stay connected to him, somehow, some way.

****

"Millicent? Honey, wake up. Sweetheart, wake up."

I stirred slightly. I looked around me, and I was lying in our own bed, in our bedroom. I looked up and I was staring into Clayton's face. I smiled a sigh of relief. It was just a bad dream. I'd dreamt the whole thing.

"Oh, Clayton! I had the worst dream!" I said, sitting up suddenly. I was smiling, because my

266

Clayton was here with me. "I dreamed you'd left me; that you'd died."

I reached up to touch his face. It was real. It was really him. No bruises on that gorgeous face of his. He smiled at me, and caressed my hand with his own. He turned his face to gently kiss the palm of my hand. I was looking into his eyes, I was touching him. As my hand held his cheek, he started to fade, right before my eyes.

"No! No! Clayton, come back! Please, come back!" I cried. He was gone. Gina came into my room, followed by a limping Nora.

"It's okay," Nora soothed, hugging me. I cried in her arms.

"He was here! I know he was!" I sobbed. "H-he was just talking to me!"

"Sweetheart, Clayton's gone. He won't be back," Nora said, crying.

"Nora, he was here! My husband was here!" I screamed.

"Shh, it's okay," Nora whispered. "We'll make everything okay."

"I'll go and get her some chamomile tea," Gina offered. She left the room while Nora continued to hug me, slowly rocking me back and forth.

"Nora, please tell me Clayton's not dead! Please! I'm begging you!" I cried out.

"I wish I could, honey, but I can't," Nora whispered.

"Then it's true," I whimpered. "He's dead."

"I'm afraid so," Nora said.

I slowly pulled away from Nora. I turned my

back on her, and gently lied down. I covered my head and cried profusely. I wanted to shut out the world. How could I go on with my life? For the first time since finding out about my illness, I was really looking forward to death. Then, I could be with Clayton. As I lay there crying, I started to wonder what kind of mother did that make me. I wanted to die so that I could join my husband, not giving thought to the fact that my children would be left without either of their parents. I was tormented. This wasn't the way it was supposed to be. Gina brought me tea, which I refused to drink. I didn't want to feel better; I just wanted to be left alone. By then, Rhonda and Ellen joined in the sympathetic huddle. My sisters were crowding me, and I hated it. This was their fault. Clayton would be here if it weren't for them.

"I don't want anything, from any of you!" I shouted. "My husband left because of you! I hate you all! Especially you, Ellen. If you hadn't had that accident in my car, my husband and I never would have argued."

"Millicent, you don't know what you're saying," Rhonda said.

"Yes, I do! We were arguing about you! You all are just as responsible for his death! Well, I hope you're all happy! You finally succeeded at making me as miserable as the rest of you! Now, get out!" I shouted through my tears.

"Millie, please," Gina pleaded.

"Get out! I don't want to see or talk to any of you! Just leave! Please just leave!" I cried.

My sisters all looked at me, and respectfully

left. They felt there was no need in arguing. Ellen looked so hurt by my words. A part of me knew I was being unfair, but I didn't care. What was fair about my husband being taken from me? What was fair about my having to suffer an illness that would inevitably kill me? I wanted to shut out the whole world. After crying for a long time, I eventually drifted off to sleep. As I slept, I dreamed once again of Clayton, and our life together. How happy he'd made me. I dreamed of the births of each of our children. I dreamed of that horrific day I found out I had cancer. So many things went through my head. Then, my husband came to me again.

"Millie, don't blame your sisters for this," Clayton said.

"But, our argument about them took you from me," I said.

"They didn't make me get behind the wheel of my car. Sweetheart, it was fate. It was simply my time. You always knew I couldn't handle losing you first. God knew it as well. You've always been the stronger of the two of us. I'm better off. It was simply my time to go," Clayton's voice said.

"How can I handle this? How could you leave me?" I cried.

"I haven't left you. I'll always be in your heart. My body's just not there. I'm still with you where it counts. I know you'll never forget me, but you have to let me go," Clayton said.

"When will we be together again?" I asked.

"When the time's right," Clayton said.

"But when will that be?" I cried.

269

"I don't know, Millie. It's not for me to know. All I do know is that we will be together again, someday. I love you, Millie," Clayton said. His image started once again to fade.

"No, Clayton! Wait! I need to talk to you! I-I never had a chance to say goodbye! Clayton!" I cried, desperate for him not to leave.

Once again, vanished.

Chapter Thirteen

I awakened the next morning to the dull splash of raindrops pattering against my window. The weather really fit my mood. I looked at the pillow beside me. I caressed it and was once again hit with the reality that Clayton was gone. Gone forever. As I pulled his pillow close to me, I could still smell him. This was all I had left: his scent on his pillow. I cried as I held it to me. I'd not even realized that Shauna was at the foot of my bed and Kirsten was asleep on the sofa. They awoke when they heard me cry out.

"Mom? Mom, we're here," Kirsten said.

"Oh, Kirsten! It's true, isn't it?" I cried.

Kirsten had tears in her eyes. "Yes, Mom, it is," she whispered. "I wish it weren't."

"Where are your brothers?" I asked.

"Kyle and Erin stayed in the maid's quarters,

271

and Tim fell asleep downstairs in Daddy's chair. I tried to get him to lie down in bed, but he refused to move. I felt it was better not to argue," Kirsten said.

"How are you holding up?" I asked.

"About as well as can be expected," Kirsten said.

I looked at Shauna, and held out my arms. "Come here, Sweetheart," I said, embracing my youngest child.

"Mom, what are we going to do without him?" Shauna cried.

"I don't know, honey. We'll get through this together, as a family," I said.

"Mom, we don't want for you to do a thing. Kyle and I will handle everything," Kirsten insisted.

"No. This is the last thing I will ever get to do for your father. It's something I have to do."

Kirsten smiled through her tears. "I know there's no need to argue with you."

I immediately pulled the covers back to get out of bed. "I need to take a shower. W-we h-have a lot to do!" I cried. I broke down into tears as I sat on the side of the bed.

"Mom, you're not ready yet," Kirsten said, hugging me.

"I-I can't do this! P-please just leave me alone for a little while," I cried, covering my face.

"I don't know if that's a good idea," Kirsten argued.

"Sweetheart, I'll be okay," I said, touching Kirsten's hand. "Both of you, go downstairs and check on your brothers." I hugged my daughters.

"I'll finish making calls," Kirsten said.

Shauna and Kirsten left my room. I looked at the clock. It was 8:30 a.m. Only a little over 24 hours before, I woke up with my husband. Now, I'd never wake up with him again.

"Why, Clayton? Why did you leave me? Why now? How do I live without you?" I cried, looking up.

I glanced over at our wedding picture, which was resting on my night stand. We were so young. We had a lifetime ahead of us. Who would have guessed a lifetime would only last 26 years? We talked about having children and spoiling our grandchildren together. Together. Not anymore. All because of my husband's desire to reunite me with my sisters. They'd single-handedly destroyed my life. I tried so hard with them. I hated them for what they'd done. I cherished my marriage, yet mine was ripped away from me much too soon. They took their marriages for granted, yet their spouses were still with them. I just wanted for them to all go home. I didn't want to see either of them. Let them go back to their miserable lives and leave my children and me alone. My thoughts were interrupted by Gina. She knocked as she entered my room.

"Millie?" Gina called out gently.

"What do you want, Gina?" I snapped.

"I wanted to talk to you," Gina said, as she closed the door behind her.

"I told you I didn't want to talk to any of you! Now will you please leave?!" I shouted.

"No, I won't." Gina sat beside me on my bed.

273

She put her arm around me.

I abruptly stood up. "I don't want comforting from you, Gina."

"Well, that's too bad, because you're going to get it whether you like it or not." Gina stood up and walked over to me, touching my shoulder. "Don't try to be strong, Millie," she whispered.

I jerked away from her. "You just don't get it, do you? You all killed my husband! You may not have been driving the car, but you all are equally accountable! I'll never forgive either of you for this!" I cried.

"Millie, you don't mean that," Gina said.

"Like hell I don't! Go home, Gina. I don't want nor need either of you here. Your 'being here for me' is not going to bring my husband back."

Gina turned me towards her. "You will not run us away, dammit! Now, no matter what the circumstances, we came together for you. So, you'll just have to deal with the consequences of having four sisters who will love and support you whether you like it or not!" Gina yelled.

I looked at my little sister. She was giving me a dose of my own medicine. She was right. Despite the fact that I didn't initially want them around, once they were here, I'd refused to give up on them, and it worked. We were all together again. But, why did it have to be at the cost of my husband's life?

"Why did he leave me?!" I screamed. I broke down and my sister held me. I needed her. I needed her desperately. "H-he promised he'd never leave me!"

274

"I know, I know, Sweetheart," Gina whispered as she held me. "Just let it all out."

"I-I don't know if I can live without him, Gina!" We sat down on the sofa as I cried in my sister's arms. "Oh, Gina, I'm so sorry for what I said to you!" I exclaimed.

"Shh. There's no need to apologize. You're in pain, Millie. You have a right. You've always been so strong and I've always admired that about you. Now, it's our turn to be strong for you. I love you so much, Millie," Gina cried. "I'll be here to help you through this as long as you'll let me."

"Thank you, Gina," I smiled through my tears. "My little sister. I love you, and I'm so glad you're here with me." Gina hugged me tightly, as we sat there for a few moments.

"Is there anyone I can call for you, Millie?"

"No, Dear. Kirsten is taking care of that. I-I hope she has the right phone book. Clayton never kept up with addresses and phone numbers. He'd have addresses and phone numbers scribbled all over the place. I-I'd always," I said tearfully. "I'd always find them and put them in the book we kept in the study. I-I used to tell him that he'd lose his arm if it weren't attached," I smiled, then suddenly looked serious. "Now, he's lost his life," I whispered. I stood up again.

"Millie," Gina started.

"I have to pick out his suit. Clayton's favorite was his dark gray suit. That's the one; that's the one he should wear." I looked in Clayton's closet.

"Maybe you should do this later," Gina

suggested.

"I need to call Grayson Funeral Home." Then, I smiled and turned to Gina. "Oh, I guess the hospital already took care of that."

"Let me help you, Millie," Gina offered.

"No, I h-have to do this myself!" I yelled. As if on cue, my other sisters came in.

"Millie, what can we do?" Ellen asked.

"I'm fine. Everything's under control. I'm okay, really," I smiled, hugging Clayton's suit. "Maybe you all could check on the children? They're downstairs."

"Well, I have a bum leg, so I'll stay with you," Nora smiled.

"That's a good idea," Rhonda chimed in.

My sisters were not going to give me the one thing I so desperately wanted, which was to be left alone. Maybe they were right. Maybe the last thing I needed was to be alone.

"We'll be downstairs," Ellen said.

I walked around the room tidying up. I looked into Clayton's closet again. He'd carelessly thrown his shirt and pants onto his closet floor. I leaned down to pick them up. Clayton hated putting his clothes into the hamper. I smiled as I thought of how I used to chastise him constantly. It never mattered because I always had to come behind him. Deep down, I never wanted him to stop. It was one of those annoying habits about him that I loved so much. Now, he'd never leave clothes lying around again. I sobbed as I leaned against the door of his closet, hugging his clothes to me. Nora came over to me.

She hugged me. I had to get the strength from somewhere to get through this. I had no idea how, but I had to for my children.

"I need to get his shirt, to go with the suit," I cried. "I keep telling Clayton not to throw his clothes on the floor. I mean, how hard is it to put them into the hamper?" I sobbed.

"Let me get this for you," Nora said, gently taking the clothes from me.

After crying for the next few minutes, I wiped my face. "I need to get Clayton's cufflinks to go with the shirt he's going to wear." I picked up Clayton's suit again off of the bed. I was trying to maintain my composure. I'd been crying all morning.

"Millie, let me take care of this. Why don't you lie back down?" Nora offered.

"N-no! Th-this is all have left of him!" I struggled to hold on to his suit as Nora gently pried it from my arms.

"It's okay," Nora whispered. She laid the clothes on the sofa. "Come on, Millie. Let's sit down for a minute."

"No, you go ahead. I know your leg must be hurting you by now," I said. "I need to keep moving. Did you call Bill yet?"

"Yes, I called him last night. He and the kids will be here tomorrow."

"So, are you and Bill going to work things out?"

"I don't know. Right now, I'm worried about you."

"Why would you be worried about me?"

"Because of what you're going through," Nora said, in a confused tone.

"What am I going through?" I smiled.

"Millie?" Nora looked at me strangely.

"What? Everything's fine. Now, you need to clear out while I lay out Clayton's suit for church."

"Church?"

"Of course, Silly! What else would we do on a Sunday morning? Clayton will be back in a minute," I said. I didn't know it at that moment, but I was becoming more irrational with my thoughts, totally isolating myself from reality.

"Millie!" Nora shook me. "Look at me."

"What, Nora?" I smiled.

"Clayton's dead, Honey. He's gone," Nora said gently.

I shook my head slowly as tears ran down my face. I backed away from Nora. "St-stop it, Nora. D-Don't say that! It's not true!" I yelled. "No! H-He p-promised he wouldn't leave me!" I fell onto my bed and sobbed once again.

Nora made her way over to me and held me. What happened to me? What caused me to blank out like that? I never knew why it happened, but I do know that for a brief moment, my turmoil and denial ran so deep to the point where I lost touch with reality. I refused to let my husband be dead. Whatever it took, I was willing to do anything to make the past 24 hours go away. I was falling apart inside and I didn't know how to fix it. The one pillar of strength I always leaned on was no longer here. My sisters provided gentle shoulders, but they weren't my husband. As I lied there, I tried to make sense of it all. We always did everything together. He was my best friend. His job sometimes took him out of town, and on some occasions, before I got sick, I would travel with him.

My husband always got along well with others. I kept thinking of all the people who would be affected by his death. Clayton's death. It was too soon for those words to co-exist. Now, they were hand in hand.

After convincing Nora that I just needed to be alone, I went into the shower. Only one week had passed since my sisters' arrival. I was a happily married woman that day; now a week later, I'm a widow. My, what a difference a day makes. As I stood in the shower, I let the water envelop me as I thought of the 26 years I'd been married to my life mate. My Clayton's life was snuffed out much too soon. One memory that stuck with me was Clayton's proposal. I'll never forget that night. . .

"Clayton Welby, where are we going?" I smiled.

"You'll see Millie," Clayton said.

It was a warm, spring night in Alabama. It was on a Saturday and the fair was in town for spring break. Clayton knew I was terrible at carnival games, a point I'd proven over and over during the two years we'd been dating. We'd been walking around hand in hand all night, getting sick off of cotton candy, hot dogs and popcorn. I was 17 and Clayton was 19. We'd come back to the fair that Saturday night as a reward from Daddy for chaperoning Nora, Ellen and

279

Clayton's little brother, Andrew to the fair the night before. Andrew and Ellen were the same age. My soon-to-be brother-in-law had a major crush on my little sister Ellen. But, if it wasn't about baseball, Ellen didn't notice. When I spotted the Ring Toss game, I got excited. Clayton knew this was one of my favorite games. The first time we went, I won a huge stuffed animal.

"The Ring Toss! Come on, I have to play it," I said. I was almost as excited as most of the little kids.

"Millie, you play this one all the time," Clayton sighed.

"Oh, come on. It's the only game I'm any good at." I grabbed Clayton's hand and dragged him along with me.

"Okay, fine," Clayton said. "But, I get to pick the prize if you win."

"It's a deal," I smiled.

When we got to the booth, I noticed Clayton's brother Greg was manning it.

"Hey Greg. Working here again for Spring Break?" I asked.

"Just like every other time," Greg smiled. "You ready to play?"

"I'm always ready," I smiled.

It only took a couple of minutes for me to play a perfect game. As per my deal with Clayton, I allowed him to pick the prize. To my dismay, he picked an ugly green frog. Clayton knew I hated frogs, so I tried to protest.

"This is perfect!" Clayton smiled.

"You know I hate frogs.   Why would you pick that?" I argued.   Then, I looked at Greg.   "Greg, I want something else."

"No deal," Clayton said, shaking his head. "You said I could pick it."

"I lied.   Greg, give me that cute little stuffed puppy," I said, pointing to another prize.

"That's not available," Greg said, shaking his head.

"What do you mean it's not available?   It's one of the prizes.   I won a perfect game, and that's what I want," I argued.

"The frog will be fine," Clayton said, retrieving it from Greg.

"Greg!   I don't want the frog!" I protested.

"I'm sorry, Millie, that's all that's available," Greg shrugged.

"What?   But, that's not fair!" I said.   I almost had tears in my eyes.

"Come on, Millie," Clayton said, dragging me away.   "Let's get on the Ferris Wheel.

I was livid.   I couldn't believe he was going to make me keep that ugly frog.   I was silent the next few minutes.

"Are you mad at me?" Clayton asked, as we got on the Ferris Wheel.

"I'm not speaking to you," I pouted, as the ride started.

"Here, hold the frog.   You might like him more than you think," Clayton said, holding it out to me.

"I don't want to hold it," I protested, pushing it

281

back.

"Millie, trust me," Clayton whispered.

"What's so special about it?" I asked. When I looked a little closer, the frog was holding a little black velvet box. I smiled slightly. "Wh-what is this?"

"Well, if you'd quit yelling at me, you'll find out," Clayton said. "I fell in love with you on this Ferris Wheel a year ago. And, I think if you'll let me, we can have a hell of a life together. Millicent Reece McAlray, will you marry me?"

"Oh, Clayton!" I whispered with tears in my eyes. I hugged him excitedly. "Yes, I'll marry you!"

I didn't even realize the ride had stopped as he kissed me.

That was the best day of my life. My Clayton and I were engaged. Greg knew all about his plan, and apparently everything went perfectly. Clayton was always full of surprises. Needless to say, I kept the frog.

After slowly being brought back to reality, I turned the water off and got out of the shower. When I stepped out, I looked at the vanity area. I saw Clayton's toothbrush and razor. I picked up Clayton's razor and I turned it on. I needed to hear the familiar whir of his razor. Anything to take me to a time and place when my husband was still here. The hypnotic drone offered me a small consolation.

"Snap out of it, Millie. Clayton would want for you to be strong," I told myself. I put the razor back into its cradle and got dressed. When I stepped out into my bedroom, all of my sisters were there waiting for me once again.

"I didn't expect to see all of you in here," I said.

"You need us," Ellen said. "And we want to be here for you."

"Thank you, but I'm tired and I just want to be alone," I said.

"Miriam sent up some soup for you," Rhonda said.

"I don't have much of an appetite."

"You need to eat to keep up your strength," Nora said.

"You know what? Maybe I need to get out of this room. The walls are closing in on me."

"Whatever you say," Ellen said.

We walked downstairs into the foyer leading into living room. I looked at the clock and noticed that it was only 9:30 a.m. Already, there were colleagues and friends gathered at the house. This was going to be awful. Kyle was talking to one of the other executives in Clayton's office. Clayton had been a top executive for many years. It was quite an accomplishment for him to be in his position at one of the top brokerage firms in the country after only few years. As I stood there, Miriam came up to me.

"Mrs. Welby, I'm so sorry about Mr. Welby," Miriam said, with tears in her eyes. "He was a good man."

"Thank you, Miriam. We're going to have a lot of people coming through over the next few days. Maybe you can call the agency and get some help," I suggested with no emotion.

"Yes, Ma'am," Miriam said, looking at me strangely.

I walked into the living room and everyone stopped talking. The room was too quiet, and all eyes were on me. I had to be strong. Clayton would want me to be strong. But, how could I? I just wanted to get this over with.

"Millie, is there anything we can do?" Diane was our neighbor of 15 years. She and her husband Edward were always so kind. Our families have practically grown up together.

"I'll be fine, Diane," I smiled.

"Mom, I talked with Uncle Andrew and Uncle Greg. Uncle Greg will be here this afternoon and Uncle Andrew will be here tomorrow. Aunt Vivian will be here tomorrow morning because the earliest flight she could get isn't until then," Kirsten said.

"What about your grandparents?" I asked.

"We felt it best not to tell them over the phone. Uncle Andrew is going to tell them and bring them here," Kirsten said.

"That's good thinking, Sweetheart," I smiled. I was totally numb. I had no emotions, just business to take care of.

"We've already talked with Grayson Funeral Home's director. We have to go by tomorrow to pick out everything and finalize the arrangements," Kyle said.

As Kyle was talking, I started to cry. Someone handed me a tissue, as Kyle held me. I sat down, trying to gain my composure. It was something about Kyle telling me we had to 'finalize arrangements' that seemed to turn this terrible nightmare into a reality. A reality I was fiercely trying not to accept. After crying for what felt like hours, I knew I had to pull myself together. I was worried about my children. Shauna was there, but Tim wasn't. I needed my children with me, all of them.

"Where's Tim?" I asked.

"He's out at the guest house," Kyle said.

"I-I need to see him," I said. I stood and walked out to the guest house. It had stopped raining, but the clouds were still dark and gray. Tim was playing a video game. "Tim?"

"Oh, hi, Ma," Tim said, barely looking up from his video game.

"How are you handling things?" I asked.

"I'm fine," Tim said, shrugging his shoulders.

"Do you want to talk?" I sat next to him and put my arm around him.

Tim stopped playing his video game and jumped up. "No, I don't need to talk."

"Honey, I think you should," I suggested.

"There's nothing to talk about. I'm fine," Tim insisted.

"Well, I'm here for you, Sweetheart," I whispered.

"Ma, would you leave me alone!? I don't want to talk about anything! Dad left me, end of discussion," Tim murmured.

"He didn't just leave you. He left all of us," I said.

"I hate him for doing that!" Tim yelled as he

clenched his fists. "I just want to hit something!"

"Sweetheart, that's just your hurt and anger talking, but it's good you're getting your feelings out in the open and not keeping them bottled up," I said.

"Dad left us. All the hurt and anger in the world won't bring him back," Tim cried. "Why did he have to leave us?" Tim broke down, and I held my son as we cried together.

"It's okay. Just let it all out," I soothed. He held on to me so tightly, as if he was afraid to let go.

"What now? How do we make it? I've been so afraid of losing you! Now, I'm going to lose both my parents! He wasn't supposed to leave! W-who am I going to talk to?! Dad was always there for me!" Tim cried.

"I know, Sweetheart. I miss your father, too. But, we're going to get through this. And, I don't plan on leaving here too soon," I said.

A chill went over me the moment I said it. Was I offering empty promises to my child? My children had already been through so much. Every time I think we're headed in the right direction, something bad happens. We sat there and talked about how we were both feeling.

The week before my sisters' arrival, Tim and Clayton had gone out to the lake house to go fishing. Tim had so much fun with his father that weekend. Clayton told me that Tim had confided in him about a girl he liked. Clayton said he was so glad he had the time to do that with just Tim. Tim was always able to talk to his father about anything. He told his father things that most teenage boys didn't tell. Clayton never told me everything they talked about, and I was glad he didn't. Tim always needed to know that he could confide in his father about things he may not have wanted me to know. Clayton was a wonderful father, so I trusted that Clayton would never advise him wrong.

The more Tim and I talked, the more I realized that Clayton had managed to spend time with each of the children individually. He and Shauna had gone to a Father-Daughter dance with her camp on the Saturday the week before his and Tim's fishing trip. Shauna told me that she didn't know her father could dance as well as he did. What Shauna never knew was that Clayton had learned the latest music and dances, so that he wouldn't embarrass his daughter. He'd worked on it for almost a month, right up to the night of the dance. Clayton and Kirsten had gone to see a movie together the Friday before Shauna's dance. It was a horror movie, which was something Kirsten and Clayton always shared. Kirsten insisted upon treating her dad to a night out. They went out to eat that night as well at Kirsten's favorite restaurant. Clayton told me how proud he was of Kirsten. He'd always secretly wanted her to major in marketing and finance so that she could come to work with him, but Clayton never said a word. He always said he wanted her to make her own decisions about what she should do. He was just as proud bragging to everyone that his daughter was a nurse.

It finally dawned on me that Kyle's night with his dad when they went to the sports bar, was special to Clayton because he must have had a premonition. It was as if Clayton knew he was going to die. It didn't make sense until then.

I was really going to miss my husband. This wouldn't be easy, but I couldn't avoid it. Tim and I sat there for almost an hour talking about his dad. When he was ready, we went back into the house to join everyone else. I have no idea how many people were even there, but I was touched that so many people loved and respected Clayton. When Tim and I went into the main house, I went into the den and sat in Clayton's chair. I felt closer to him, like he was right there with me. There were people all over the house, offering a helping hand with anything I may have needed. I felt a small degree of comfort as I listened to various family members and friends reminiscing about my husband. I cried as each one of them smiled about the wonderful memories they had of him.

At times, I felt myself getting weaker. A part of me knew it was all because I was in mourning. I was torn because I no longer cared about myself, but I was worried about my children. I almost preferred to die so that the fear of losing me would be over. They could get on with their lives after mourning for me and their father. But, would that be too much for them to handle? Only God knows what they can handle and what they can't. Clayton and I had done a great job raising them. Neither of them had ever gotten into trouble, which we were proud about.

Later that afternoon, Clayton's older brother, Greg arrived with his two daughters. He'd been awarded full custody of Carolyn, who was 14, and Gretel, who was 17. Greg had been divorced for five years. He looked so lost when he came through the door. Greg and Clayton were so close. He lived a little over 30 minutes away. He'd retired from the air force, which is what brought him to South Carolina. He didn't enlist in the air force until after he'd graduated from college with a degree in aerospace engineering.

Greg was the reason Clayton and I moved here. We came to visit Greg and his ex-wife one summer almost 18 years ago. We fell in love with Myrtle Beach almost instantaneously. We packed up and moved from New York, where we'd been since Clayton's graduation from college, and his career began on Wall Street. Ironically, we were the reason Ellen and Jim moved to New York. It was like a chain reaction of sorts. I never understood why my little sister wanted so desperately to get so far away from Alabama. Now, unfortunately, I know the real reason. When we decided to move to South Carolina, Ellen and Jim had become loyal New Yorkers. Clayton's brokerage firm had an office in South Carolina, so it couldn't have been more perfect if we'd planned it that way. I looked at Greg, and noticed how he was almost the spitting image of Clayton. It was as if I was looking at my husband. Greg hugged me tightly.

"Millie, I'm so sorry," Greg said with tears in his eyes. "I miss him so much!"

"I know. I miss him, too," I said.

"I can't believe it. I-I just saw him yesterday. I had no idea that would be the last time I'd see my brother."

"Y-you saw him yesterday?" I said

surprisingly.

"Yeah. He said that the two of you had a disagreement, and that he felt really bad about the way he'd acted."

"H-he was with you," I said, with tears in my eyes.

"When he left, he said he was heading home. Before leaving, he'd tried to call you here at the house, but there was no answer. So, he tried your cell phone, and left you a message."

"A-are you sure? Clayton left a message for me?"

"Yes. I heard him as he was talking. Didn't you get it?"

"No," I said, running to my purse.

I looked at my cell phone. It showed that I had one message, and the last number to call had been Clayton's cell number. I went into the sunroom and closed the door. I don't know why I wanted to be in the sunroom, but it just seemed fitting that I hear the last words my husband said to me in the room where we'd parted.

"Millie, it's me. I'm at Greg's. Honey, I'm sorry about running out on you like I did. It was unfair of me to do that to you. I would never expect you to be anything but the wonderful, loving woman you are. I'm on my way home, so put on your best outfit so that I can take my beautiful wife out to dinner. We're going to have an evening together alone. I'll be home in a couple of hours. I love you, Sweetheart."

The time of the call was at 12:38 p.m. I

wondered exactly how long after that was my husband killed. So far, all I knew was that he'd had the accident that afternoon. I immediately saved Clayton's message.

"Thank you, Clayton," I whispered, hugging the phone to my chest.

I need to hear those words from him. My husband didn't die angry with me. Knowing that offered a little comfort to my broken heart. Shortly thereafter, I heard a knock on the door.

"Millie?" Rhonda called out. "Are you okay?"

"Yes, I'm fine," I murmured.

"Is there anything I can do?" Rhonda asked, putting her arm around me.

"No, I just heard a message from Clayton. He forgave me for our argument," I smiled through my tears.

Rhonda smiled. "How does that make you feel?"

"Like I can put my husband to rest with peace of mind. I knew I'd spend the rest of my life blaming myself." My smile faded. "Rhonda, how am I going to get through these next few days?"

Rhonda held my hand while my other hand still clutched my phone as if I were holding on for dear life.

"With a lot of love and support from a family who will be here for you as long as you need us to be."

I hugged my sister. "Thank you."

As we stood there talking, we were interrupted by Greg. "Millie?"

"Oh, Greg," I smiled. "You remember

Rhonda."

"Yes, I do," Greg smiled slightly. "Still as beautiful as ever."

"Thank you," Rhonda smiled.

Greg and Rhonda had graduated from high school together. I watched the two of them closely. There was an awkward silence as Rhonda and Greg stared at each other.

"Well, I'm going upstairs. I need to be alone for a while," I said.

"Do you need any help?" Rhonda asked.

"No, you two stay and talk. I'll be fine," I reassured.

I went upstairs to talk to my husband. I wanted time alone with my thoughts. He'd been such a big part of my world. I had so many important decisions to make. I was so accustomed to making decisions with him, but now, I had to make the most important decisions for him. I went into my bedroom to look through pictures. I wanted to find the perfect one for his obituary. I decided to use the one we'd taken a few months ago. As I looked through all of the pictures, I decided I wanted to do a collage in his honor. Was I being overly pretentious? Then I realized that I was celebrating the memories of the love of my life. There was never enough I could do to express what he meant to me. As I sat there quietly, I could still hear the subtle murmur of our company downstairs. I'm not sure if they noticed my absence, but I knew I needed to get away to be by myself. This second night would be as hard as the first. Would this pain ever go away? Would my heart ever stop breaking?   I hugged Clayton's picture as I cried silently.   I eventually cried myself to sleep.

Chapter Fourteen

Bill arrived the next day, along with Jessica and Matthew. Jessica and Nora had time to sort some of their problems out by talking things through. There was a lot of anger, but they respected my grief by remaining cordial. Bill had venting to do as well, so the four of them spent a great deal of time together talking about what they were feeling. Nora told me later that they were going to go to counseling as a family. She knew she still had a lot of demons to fight, but with a loving and forgiving husband, she could do just about anything. Before Bill's arrival, he had no idea that Nora had even broken her leg. He sensed a positive change in her, as she opened up to him about what happened to her as a teenager. Bill listened and confided in her that he felt closer to her than ever before. Nora even acknowledged her indiscretions, but Bill already knew. Jessica knew about her indiscretions, and she told him everything out of anger. He was just glad to know that Nora had finally grown enough to take responsibility for her own actions.

During the time when Bill, Jessica and Matthew went home, he had a DNA test done to prove whether or not Jessica was his daughter. The tests confirmed that Jessica was truly Bill's daughter. Bill stated that nothing would change the way he feels about Jessica, but he had to know. This helped to ease a little of Rhonda's pain as well.

I talked to Ellen about all the problems she'd endured over the years. I knew she had a long way to travel with her problems, but I also had the greatest amount of confidence that she could do it.

"Ellen, I need to know. What happened that day?" I asked, as we were going through some of Clayton's things. Ellen had wanted to help me, although I felt I needed to be alone to do it. But, she insisted, so while Nora, Rhonda, Gina and Alex were out, we sorted through Clayton's belongings together.

"I don't know, Millie," Ellen sighed. "I was heading for the hotel that night, and I passed a bar. I couldn't help it. I thought it would help me deal with Katie a little better. The trap was set, and I walked right into it. I feel like this is all my fault."

"No, no, Ellen, it's not," I said, touching her hand. "You just need help. I don't blame you for Clayton's death."

"But, you two were arguing because I'd had an accident in your car," Ellen said, with tears in her eyes.

"It was wrong of me to tell you that. I was angry and I needed to lash out, but Sweetheart, you are

295

not to blame for Clayton's death. Clayton left me a message. He was on his way home when he had his accident. He'd apologized, so he wasn't driving in anger."

"I still will never forgive myself. You trusted me, and I let you down."

"No, Ellen, you let yourself down. My car is being repaired, so there's no permanent damage. I just want to see you get the help you need. I've forgiven you, Honey," I said, hugging her. "No matter what, I'll never hate you. You are too special to me."

"I love you, Millie," Ellen cried. "I mean, here you are in mourning, and yet you're having to be supportive of me and my problems, trying to comfort me. I'm supposed to be comforting you."

"You are, simply by being here," I smiled through my tears. I'd finally made peace with my sister over this whole ugly mess.

****

The next few days were hard, but keeping busy was therapeutic for me. As we approached Clayton's funeral, which was scheduled for the Friday after his death, I became filled with an exorbitant share of anxiety. I knew once we put my beloved husband into the ground, that would be it. There would be nothing else to do, but live the rest of my life without him. I'd picked out what he would wear. I wrote a special poem to him for his obituary, and the kids and I each picked out the pictures to go on his collage.

Although it wasn't healthy to do so, I'd been to the funeral home every day because I needed to be close to him. During that time, I started to notice how close Rhonda and Greg had become. They'd spent just about every waking moment together. I didn't know whether to be happy about this or concerned. If my sister could finally find happiness, then a part of me felt that she should go for it. I just didn't want either of them getting hurt. Both of them had been through bad marriages and I was afraid that one would become more serious than the other. I knew that there was a time when Greg really cared a lot about Rhonda. He'd been her escort when she became homecoming queen, because Aaron was in college and couldn't come home. I'm a true believer that if something is meant to be, it will be, even 30 years later. But realistically, although Aaron treated her terribly, she was still in love with her husband. I guess my biggest wonder was if Rhonda would actually divorce Aaron.

Early the day before Clayton's funeral, I got my answer. Rhonda was served with divorce papers at my home. It was painfully obvious that my brother-in-law wasted no time in filing. He must have started the proceedings the moment he arrived back in Colorado. Despite his hastiness, Rhonda seemed in good spirits about it. Although I'm sure that no matter how difficult the marriage may have been, I can't imagine it being easy to be faced with the reality that it was over.

"Are you okay?" I asked as Rhonda read the papers.

"I'm fine. It's something I should have done a

long time ago. I have to ask myself sometimes if I would have ever really done it on my own. I know I left him when I came here, but, what if I'd gone back? If I'd never found out about his affair with Nora, I might actually have gone back to him."

"I meant what I said about your staying here. You can stay as long as you like," I said.

"So we can grow old together?" Rhonda smiled.

"Exactly," I smiled back. My curiosity was getting the best of me, so I had to ask. "So what's going on between you and my brother-in-law?"

Rhonda blushed. "What makes you think there's anything going on between us?"

"Oh, come on, Rhonda. It's me you're talking to."

"Greg is very sweet, but he's just a healthy distraction."

"'Healthy distraction'? So, who are you trying to convince, me or yourself?" I challenged.

"Funny, you asked me the exact same question two weeks ago about my marriage to Aaron. But to answer your question, Millie, there's nothing going on between us," Rhonda said, looking half embarrassed.

"There's nothing to be embarrassed about. From the papers you just received, you're almost divorced, and he is divorced."

"It's not that. I'm just not going to fall in love again. So, if you have some crazy notion about our getting together, forget it," Rhonda said, looking down. "We're not in high school anymore."

"But you once were, and if I recall, Greg was

quite fond of you. Why didn't you date him?" I asked.

"Because for some reason, I thought Aaron Harmon was the greatest thing God ever created," Rhonda said, rolling her eyes.

"Well, at least you know now."

"Yeah, thirty years later."

"Better late than never," I laughed.

Rhonda smiled as she looked at me. "It's so good to hear you laugh. I haven't heard that sound in a week."

"I have to keep my mind off of tomorrow."

"Why, Millie? That's not going to make it go away," Rhonda reasoned.

"I know," I sighed. I looked at Rhonda. "Does Aaron know about Clayton's death?"

"Yes, he knows. I called him and told him about it. He offered his condolences, and in the same breath told me not to use that as a way to get him to come back so that I could try to 'get my hooks back into him.' Can you believe the arrogance of that man?"

"Yeah, I can," I smiled. "So, I take it he won't be back for the funeral."

"No, he won't. Which is fine with me."

We sat there in the kitchen drinking coffee that morning to have a little 'quiet down time.' Miriam had gone shopping, so the kitchen was empty. Bill and Nora had gone to the doctor about Nora's leg. Alex and Gina were out getting something to wear to Clayton's funeral. Ellen had to be in court, so Jim went with her. Ironically, Clayton's death seemed to reunite and strengthen my sisters' marriages. Why did it take such a tragedy? Amanda and Ellen even seemed closer. Ellen talked to her about what she'd gone through in her life and vowed to be a better mother. After Ellen's admission about what happened, Amanda found a way to forgive her mother. Amanda had matured over the past week or so, although I knew that her problems were far from over. She promised her mother that she was going to do better in school, and stop getting into trouble.

Kyle and Kirsten had been amazing. They pulled even closer together to deal with our terrible tragedy. They were out taking care of last minute details and picking relatives up at the airport. Clayton's parents, along with Andrew and his family were staying with Greg. They drove up to our house every day. Vivian and her husband John were staying at a nearby hotel. As Rhonda and I sat there, lost in our own thoughts, the phone rang.

"Hello?" I answered.

"Millicent?" Dr. Tracer responded.

"Yes?"

"This is Dr. Tracer. I wanted to offer my condolences once again," Dr. Tracer said.

"Thank you, so much," I smiled.

"You're welcome. The main reason I was calling was to let you know that our gamble paid off," Dr. Tracer said.

"I'm afraid I'm not following you," I said hesitantly. "One of your sisters is a viable match," Dr. Tracer said.

"One of my sisters? But, they haven't been

tested," I said, glancing in Rhonda's direction.

"Yes, Millicent. They were tested the Monday after you were released from the hospital," Dr. Tracer said.

"But, how? I don't remember their being tested," I said.

"They came in without your knowledge. Clayton was with them, and they each submitted samples to be tested as a possible donor," Dr. Tracer said.

"Are you serious?" I smiled.

"Yes. Your sister Nora is a viable donor for you," Dr. Tracer said.

"Nora?" I responded, astonished.

"Yes, she is. Now, I know that Clayton's funeral is tomorrow, but, if Nora can get in here Monday morning, we can finish the screening process," Dr. Tracer said.

"I don't believe it," I said quietly. "I'll talk to Nora when she gets back."

"Good. Millicent, this was Clayton's idea. He refused to give up on you. That's why he got all of your sisters to come to visit, so that they could be tested. Now, granted, they could have been tested from home, but he wanted them here for you."

"I really had a wonderful husband, didn't I?" I smiled.

"Yes, you did," Dr. Tracer said. "I plan to attend the funeral tomorrow, so I'll see you then, okay?"

"Okay, Dr. Tracer," I said. "I'll see you tomorrow. Goodbye." I then hung up the phone and looked at Rhonda. I smiled at her. "You all were tested?"

"Yes, we were," Rhonda smiled. "When Clayton called me, he didn't ask originally. He just asked me to come and visit you. But, I found out later that day, that due to the kind of cancer you have, that a bone marrow transplant could save your life. I'd already decided before coming that I was going to be tested."

"Oh, Rhonda," I smiled, with tears in my eyes. "When did all of you decide to do this?"

"That Sunday night. When you went upstairs to your bedroom, and Clayton went up to check on you, we all were so worried about you. When he came back downstairs a little later, he got all of us together and asked us would we be willing to be tested. He told us about how you felt guilty about not telling us about your cancer in the first place, and didn't want to burden us by asking. No matter how at odds we were with each other, we all agreed that you were important to us. We made plans to go early Monday morning to be tested," Rhonda sighed.

"I remember that day. Everyone was gone but Alex. She and I had a real heart to heart talk that day. I wonder if she knew what was really going on."

"Probably," Rhonda shrugged. "I'm sure Gina told her."

I smiled slightly. "You know, I like Alex. I never thought my sister would be in an alternative lifestyle, but, I like her. I have to wonder though."

"Wonder about what?" Rhonda asked.

"Is this what Gina really wants? I mean, Alex

302

is sweet. That day you all were gone, she revealed to me that she'd lost a sister and a brother three years ago."

"Really?" Rhonda gasped. "How?"

"Her brother needed a bone marrow transplant and her sister was killed during a robbery. Her sister was a viable donor, but, before she could donate, she was killed. Her brother died eight months later."

"How terrible! Poor Alex! That had to be awful to lose her siblings like that. What about her parents? Did she mention anything about them?" Rhonda asked.

"While we were making our scrapbook, she commented that she and her mother used to be really close before her mother found out she was gay. Her mother's now embarrassed by what her friends will think, and her father has disowned her. She's really been through a lot. I mean, is it really worth it? She's lost a sister, a brother, and pretty much her parents as well. She seems all alone. But, what I don't want is for Gina to stay with her out of a sense of obligation or guilt," I said.

"You think Gina would do that? I mean, Gina's always been her own person. I really think she'll follow her heart, even if it means ending things with Alex if she's not comfortable with it," Rhonda said.

"I know you're right." I shook my head, as I sipped my coffee. "Sometimes, I feel like we're living a soap opera."

"So, who's the evil villain?" Rhonda smiled.

"That would be Nora, hands down," I smiled.

303

"Somehow, I knew you'd say that," Rhonda laughed.

"But, the evil villain might turn out to be the heroine. Dr. Tracer said Nora was a match," I said.

"I'm glad," Rhonda smiled, touching my hand. "I know it's in Nora to be a good person, and I know she'll welcome the chance to help you."

"I love all of you so much," I smiled.

Rhonda and I sat there talking a while longer, when we heard the doorbell. I knew that it was probably company arriving. Everyone who came by brought food. I had no appetite, so it didn't really matter to me. Our front door was a virtual revolving door, thanks to floral deliveries and loved ones and friends coming in and out that day. A lot of them came to pay respects because they wouldn't be able to make it to the wake. The wake was a last minute decision I'd made because Kirsten was adamant about it. A part of me felt like it was going through a funeral twice. For me, once would be way too many. But, I had to consider my children. Their feelings were very important when it came down to final plans for Clayton's funeral.

****

The wake was planned for 6 p.m. We were still expecting more relatives from out of town. Several colleagues from New York had gotten in the night before. We had so many flowers from loved ones already at the house, and the funeral home was flooded with floral arrangements as well. I was touched to know how much my husband meant to so many people.   Although I was a truly blessed woman to have almost 30 years with him, it still seemed as if I was cheated.   I wanted more time with him, but now my life with him was a thing of the past.   When we all gathered for his wake that evening, reality hit hard.   All week, I'd been handling our business affairs and making arrangements.   There was some focus, despite the reason for it.   Now, I had to sit here with family and friends in the presence of my husband's body.   Life couldn't get more torturous.

I sat there and stared at Clayton's casket.   I got up, and went to get a closer look.   He looked so peaceful, as if he were sleeping.   I'd given them the gray suit to put on him.   He had a handkerchief in his pocket, and his favorite tie clip.   I reached down to hold his hand.   It was cold and soft.   I caressed his face, wanting desperately for him to open his eyes, but he never did.   He lay there peacefully, despite my wishes.

"Oh, Clayton.   I need you so much!" I cried. "You have to help me through this!"

My children were immediately attentive. Kyle put his arm around me as I cried.   I was so weak, and I would surely have fainted if he'd not been there to hold me up.

"Come on, Mom," Kyle said, gently, leading me back to a bench.

As I sat there, my oldest son held me.   Kirsten sat on the other side of me, and held my hand.   She had tears in her eyes.

"Maybe I shouldn't have insisted on a wake,"

Kirsten said.

"No, Sweetheart. I'm glad you did. I just miss him so much!" I cried.

It took everything in me that night, to be there and think about my husband. To see him in the room, and know that he couldn't come to me, and be there for me. I just hurt all over. I had such a conglomerate of feelings: sadness, illness, fear, weariness, and believe it or not, relief. I felt relief because I knew that this would soon be over. I wasn't sure how much more I could take. It helped to have people around, but, there was going to come a time when that would be over. Everyone would go home, and the house would be almost empty.

As we all sat around in the funeral chapel, we reminisced once again about Clayton and how he'd touched our lives. Clayton's sister Vivian fondly remembered, as she smiled through her tears, about the times when they were younger, and how much mischief they would get into together.

"Clayton and Payton always kept us on our toes, even when they were babies," Clayton's mother, Nina smiled. "They were identical, so they always tried to pull a fast one on us."

"That's the truth! It was 'double-trouble' all the time," Jacob, Clayton's father chimed in.

"I'll never forget the time when Clayton talked Vivian into putting glue in my hair while I was sleeping," Greg smiled.

"And I got into a lot of trouble! I can still feel the spanking I got for that one," Vivian smiled.

We all laughed. I almost felt guilty about

laughing at my husband's wake. But, wasn't that what this was all about? Remembering him? Didn't that make my laughter acceptable? He was the life of the party, but he wasn't there to share in it.

"He always pulled some sort of prank. Don't think he got away with it; he got into trouble for doing that, too," Jacob smiled. "He tried to say it was Payton who convinced you to do it. But, your mom and I knew better."

"How old were you when that happened?" Kirsten asked.

"Gosh, Clayton and Payton were about 9, I believe," Vivian smiled. "Mom, weren't they about 9 when that happened?"

"I believe so," Nina smiled. "It was right after their 9th birthday because Greg was 10 at the time. So, you were only eight, and always their scapegoat."

"I remember hearing about that! I was only two when that happened," Andrew said.

"Yes, you were just a baby. Too young for Clayton to put the blame on you. Although he was going to let Vivian and Payton take the blame for the entire thing, we knew he wasn't totally innocent! Clayton was the brain behind the operation, but he denied it until the bitter end!" Nina smiled.

"The bitter end," I said softly.

"Now, it seems that I've lost both my boys," Nina sighed.

"Honey, we don't know that Payton will never return," Jacob said.

"I love all my sons," Nina cried. "I refuse to believe that Payton would leave me and never look back, but if he's alive, he's made it clear he wants nothing to do with us."

Everyone suddenly became quiet, lost in their own individual thoughts about Clayton. Clayton's twin brother had left when we were still in our teens. It was always a touchy subject with the family, so no one ever mentioned Payton.

"You know, I knew about it when it happened," Vivian said monotonously.

"W-what?" I asked, astonished.

"I guess I should say I had a strange feeling the day he was killed. The day it happened, I felt a strange chill all over. It went on for almost an hour. Then, it went away almost as suddenly as it came," Vivian said.

"What time was this?" I asked.

"It was around 1:15 p.m.," Vivian commented.

"Clayton's cause of death was a blow to the head. They were able to estimate from his bleed that he probably lived about an hour before dying. According to the police report we got a couple of days ago, his estimated time of death was between two and three p.m.," I said. "Why didn't I feel it? Why didn't I feel my husband slipping away?"

"Because you were fighting for your own life at the time," Nora commented.

"What?" Nina said.

"We had to rush Millie to the hospital that day," Ellen said.

"Millie, are you okay?" Nina asked. "In the midst of everything that's happened, I haven't even asked about how you're feeling health wise."

308

"What are you all talking about?" Andrew asked.

"I guess everyone will find out soon enough. I have cancer," I said.

"Millie, I had no idea," Greg said. "Mom, did you know?"

"Yes, Dear. Millie needed to talk to someone about it. You were so sweet that day. You said you needed a mother to talk to," Nina said, with tears in her eyes. "You've always been like a daughter to me, Millie. You were one of my best students, and you gave my son an unexpected challenge when he fell in love with you. I was glad he chose to spend the rest of his life with you. You made him so happy."

"Thank you, Nina. I needed to hear that," I said with tears in my eyes.

"Do you need anything?" Vivian asked.

"No, you all have done so much. I just want to get through tomorrow. I just feel so sad all the time. Sometimes, I wish I would have died that day," I said, sadly.

"Honey, you don't mean that," Nina said.

"I mean, I know that's a selfish thing to say, but Clayton was my life," I cried. "Then, I think of my children and how much they mean to me. They're who've kept me going this past week."

Everyone stared at me silently. What could they say? Who could console me? Then, I thought about how Nina and Jacob were feeling. They say that the worst feeling in the world is to have to bury a child of your own, no matter how old they are. This was their son. They loved him, just as much as I did.

But, their concern was for me. As we sat there talking, I felt sick to my stomach. I wasn't sure if it was because I hadn't eaten, or if it was the anxiety from everything that was happening. I didn't know how much longer I'd be able to hold on without running from the room.

"Millie, are you okay, Dear? You look a little pale," Nina said, in a concerned tone.

"I-I'm not feeling too well," I muttered. I stood up, and walked to the bathroom. I became nauseated, having to throw up.

Afterwards, I looked in the mirror. My eyes were still puffy from crying so much over the past few days. Any amount of make-up I had on was a thing of the past. I looked at my reflection and wondered how I went from a vibrant, healthy, loving wife and mother, to a sick, mourning widow who wanted to die. I was being attacked by cancer and suffering from a shattered heart, but I had to have the strength to give my husband a proper goodbye. Tomorrow would be hard, but I could do it. I stood there and cried.

"How am I going to make it through this, Clayton? You have to help me here. I'm so torn about what to do," I whispered.

"Millie, you can handle it. You're the love of my life. Just hold on, Sweetheart. I'll be there to hold your hand, the whole time," Clayton's voice said.

It startled me, as I looked around. There was no one there. I was starting to think that I was losing my mind. I kept vaguely remembering Clayton coming to me in a dream when he first died. Was it a dream? Was my husband really reaching out to me?

310

I'd never believed in supernatural beings, but this wasn't the first time I could hear and feel Clayton's presence.

"Clayton?" I called out.

"I'm here, Millie." Clayton's image appeared before me. He touched my cheek, just as I'd done to him a few minutes before when I was standing by his casket. "Our children are going to need for you to be strong, Millie. There are some rough roads ahead for them, and you have to be there for them, especially Tim and Shauna. They'll both need you the most." He held my hand.

"What, Clayton? Will I be able to be here for them? They're not going to lose me too, are they?" I suddenly became frightened.

"Just be there for them now. They need you." Clayton then kissed my hand as he faded. Was I losing my mind? Why did I keep seeing him?

"What were you trying to tell me, Clayton? Please don't leave!" I cried.

Nora came into the door, still on crutches. "Millie? Are you okay?"

"I-I'm fine. Clayton was here," I said.

"Sweetheart, Clayton will always be in your heart," Nora said gently.

"No, Nora, it's more than that. He keeps coming to me. It has to be something. It's like he's reaching out to me. There's something he's trying to warn me about," I said.

"Like what?" Nora asked.

"I don't know. I'm sure I'll know soon enough." I looked at my sister.

"Millie, I'm worried about you," Nora stated seriously.

"Do you think I'm losing my mind?" I asked.

"No, I don't. You just lost your husband. It's understandable that you would be missing him enough to think you're hearing his voice, or even seeing him," Nora said gently.

Translation: 'Millie, you're a total nutcase.' Although she didn't actually say those words, but I could tell by the look in her eyes that was what she was thinking.

"Nora, I don't know what to think. But, I do need to talk to you," I said.

"About what?"

"Dr. Tracer called today. It seems you're a match for me."

Nora smiled. "Finally, I can do something for you."

"Are you still willing to do it?"

"Millie, you're my sister," Nora said, holding my hand. "I would do anything for you. I may be a brat, but, I love you. I'll be here as long as you need me to be."

"Thank you," I smiled. "I love you, too, Nora. Come on. Let's go back out to the chapel," I said.

"Are you sure? We can stay in here for a little while longer if you want," Nora said.

"I'm sure. I need to be close to Clayton again," I said, opening the door.

The moment we walked back in, everyone looked at me, wondering if I was going to break. How could I go on like this? Everyone was handling me with kid gloves and I hated it. They all wanted to help, but no one understood that I couldn't be helped. I just needed to get past losing my husband. Question is, would I ever get past it? I was in a lot of pain, physically and emotionally. One more day, just one more day.

We stayed at the funeral home for a couple of hours. Before leaving, I requested that everyone else go on ahead of me. I wanted to spend time there, with him alone. Kirsten and Kyle were totally against the idea. Kyle told everyone to go back to the house, and that he would stay with me. I tried to protest, but he insisted. He agreed to stay in the lobby area to give me some privacy. I walked back to Clayton's casket.

"Look at you," I smiled. "Still handsome as ever." I touched his hand again. "You've left me a legacy, Clayton. Four beautiful children, and more wonderful memories than I ever could have hoped for. It was just too short," I said, as tears ran down my face. "I was all set, Sweetheart. I wanted to go first. I was ready. You're my rock, Clayton." I sighed. I walked around to look at the flowers that were surrounding his casket. I read some of the cards.

"Here's one from your college roommate, Jack. When was the last time you saw him? Probably not since your class reunion a few years ago. You always said the two of you mixed like oil and water at times, but he turned out to be one of the best friends you had in college," I smiled. I read another one. "This one's from your old supervisor at the grocery store you worked at during your senior year in high school. Orchids. Remember how you'd always

313

give me orchids? You knew I loved those." I walked around his casket and stared longingly at some of them, touching the soft petals gently. "Ironically, you've never even liked flowers. You always said that was the beauty of living at the beach. Less grass to cut, less flowers to plant. Let's face it, you've never had a green thumb." I walked back over to his casket and looked lovingly at my husband. "I love you, Sweetheart. Sleep well, my love." I kissed my fingers and gently touched his lips as I cried. "Goodnight, Clayton." I turned and walked out slowly, part of me hoping that I would now wake up from some horrid nightmare. But, as I continued on my journey to the door, I knew it wouldn't happen. Kyle was sitting in the lobby area.

"Mom? Are you okay?" Kyle asked, as he stood up.

"Yes, yes, Dear. I'm fine," I reassured. "Let's go home."

Kyle and I walked out in silence, never once looking back. I didn't want to look back. Why was I being forced to be without the love of my life? I kept trying to make sense of it all, and so far, I came up with nothing. I knew that I'd never marry again, because I'd never love a man the way I loved Clayton. He was my lifeline.

We got back to a full house of people. Everyone wanted to be there when I got back, to offer support of some sort. While I appreciated it, it was getting tiresome. I felt as if my life was now under a microscope. The next day was coming whether I liked it or not, and no amount of support or comfort would prevent it. It was inevitable that I would have to bury my husband. The last of our company finally left around 11 p.m. that night. A part of me resented the fact that everyone else would go on with their lives in the next few days as if nothing had happened.

The next day was going to be one of the hardest days of my entire life. It would be the day I'd have to say goodbye to Clayton forever. I wondered how I would get through this without dying. How could I watch them lower him into that cold, dark ground? The service was scheduled for 11 a.m. I had a sleepless night, waking up constantly. I roamed the halls of my home throughout the night. Everyone else had managed to get to sleep. The house was still full with all of my sisters and their families, but I'd never felt so alone. No one could begin to relate to what I was going through. I had a hard time falling asleep in our bed that night for some reason. I even took something to help me sleep, but nothing worked. I got back up and went downstairs to the sunroom, making a detour into the kitchen for my usual cup of hot milk. As I sat there in the kitchen, my thoughts were interrupted when Gina came in.

"Oh, I didn't know you were here," Gina said. "I came down for a glass of juice."

"Help yourself," I smiled.

Gina pulled a glass from the cabinet. She looked at me as she poured her juice. "How are you holding up?" she asked.

"I can't sleep," I said.

"Obviously. Want some company?"

"I welcome it," I said, offering her a chair.

Gina sat at the table with me, looking quite distracted. She sighed heavily.

"Want to talk?" I asked.

"Huh?" Gina said, seemingly in another world.

"Gina, what's wrong?" I asked.

Gina stood and walked to the window. That was a sure sign something was wrong. My sisters and I always had a knack for staring out of the window when we were deep in thought about something.

"I'm late, Millie," Gina sighed.

"Late? Late for what?" I asked, dumbfounded.

Gina looked at me. "Millie, I'm *late* late."

"Oh, *that* late. Well, it's probably stress. You couldn't be pregnant," I said. I looked at my little sister as she remained silent. "Could you?"

Gina let out a heavy sigh. "I don't know."

"But, you're involved with Alex. Now, I know I don't know a lot about your type of lifestyle, but, last I checked, it takes a woman and a man to make a baby," I said.

"I know that," Gina said.

"Gina, are you seeing someone besides Alex?" I asked.

"No, not anymore," Gina said.

"What's that supposed to mean?"

"Millie, I was engaged a few months ago," Gina said.

"What? To whom?" I asked, standing to walk towards her.

"Mark Carlisle. He works at my architectural firm."

"Well, why haven't you mentioned him?" I

asked.

"Because we weren't meant to be," Gina sighed.

"Gina, what happened?" I said. "Why did you call off your engagement?"

"It's a long story. You wouldn't be interested," Gina commented.

"Yes, I would," I said.

"Let's talk about something else," Gina suggested.

"Gina, talk to me," I encouraged.

"About what?"

"Why did you call off your engagement? My goodness, it's like a tennis match with you!" I smiled.

Gina smiled, and then looked serious. "I guess I got a case of cold feet," Gina shrugged.

"What woman doesn't? But, that's still no reason to call it off if you love him. How long were the two of you engaged?"

"Two months."

"Do you want to talk about it?" I asked, looking at her.

"Millie, Mark is an arrogant jerk who cheated on me," Gina cried, leaning on me.

"Gina, what exactly happened?"

She pulled away from me and sighed. "Three months ago, we'd been together for exactly a year. I wanted to plan something special for our one year anniversary. First, maybe I should tell you who Mark is. Mark's father owns the architectural firm where I'm employed. His dad started out as an architect years ago and managed to build an empire. Believe me when I tell you, they are some of the richest people in Beverly Hills. I knew his dad already, fleetingly when he'd come up to the office. But, I'd never met his mom until a week before our one year anniversary. We were going to go ahead and announce our engagement to them, so we went to their house for dinner."

"How long had the two of you been engaged when you told his parents?"

"We wanted to keep things very quiet, so we'd been engaged almost two months."

"Two months? Well, I guess it's not too hard to believe, since you didn't tell us either," I stated.

"Can I finish, please?"

"I'm sorry," I smiled. "Go ahead."

"Anyway, we went to his parents' house for dinner, and everything went really well. His mother and I got along really well, she even told me about a wedding coordinator that their family had used before. The day of our anniversary fell on a Saturday. I guess I didn't want to remind Mark because I felt he'd remember it on his own. While I was there getting prepared for a romantic evening with my loving fiancé, my cell phone rang. I answered it, and it was a woman asking for Mark. Apparently, Mark and I had gotten our cell phones switched by mistake that morning when he left to go and play basketball with his brother."

"What did the woman say?"

"Well, I asked who she was, and she told me her name was Nikki, and asked who I was. I told her I was Mark's fiancée."

318

"What was her response to that?" I asked.

"She told me that the Mark Carlisle she knows is not engaged, and that she's been seeing him for over a year. At first I thought she was just some bitter woman out to hurt him because he'd rejected her."

"How do you know that's not the case?"

"Because the woman told me that she'd been to our apartment, and she described our room down to the sheets on our bed," Gina said matter-of-factly.

"Are you serious?" I asked incredulously.

"Oh, yes, very serious. She told me that Mark had mentioned that he had an ex who he couldn't get rid of because she was always running in behind him," Gina smirked. "Apparently, that would be me."

"Oh, how awful! Did you confront Mark?"

"No. That would have been too easy, too many ways for him to lie his way out of it. We came up with a plan and I invited Nikki over. I didn't have to give her the address because she already knew it. Not long after hanging up with Nikki, Mark called me when he realized we'd gotten our phones mixed up. I think he was trying to figure out if he'd gotten any calls and if I was mad because I'd caught on to him. But, I played it cool, like everything was normal."

"So, you invite Nikki over, and what happened?"

"She got there before Mark, so I had her to hide in the guest bedroom when I heard his car pull up. Before then, she and I had a chance to talk for over an hour about things, mostly comparing notes. She accounted for a lot of the time when Mark was telling me he was out with friends or working late or whatever lie he could pull out of a hat. She told me that she saw my picture in Mark's wallet once, and she asked who I was. He told her I was his cousin from Alabama. Can you believe that? His cousin."

"So, what happened when Mark arrived?"

"Oh, it wasn't pretty at all," Gina said, shaking her head. "I was very sweet and loving to him when he walked in, all smiles. He sat on the couch, and I poured him a glass of wine. Even had the jazz playing in the background. I massaged his shoulders, and let him get really relaxed. Then I leaned over and whispered in his ear, asking him who the hell was Nikki."

I laughed. "Oh, I love it! What did he have to say?"

"At first, he acted as if he didn't know who I was talking about. When I mentioned he'd gotten a call when our phones were mixed up by mistake, he feigned vaguely remembering someone named Nikki. Said she was some woman at the jewelry store where he'd had my ring custom made. Said she must have been calling about the anniversary surprise he had for me."

"Wow, that was a good one," I smiled.

"Yeah, he was smooth. That was the quickest, most creative lie he'd come up with yet. I asked him was he sure, he insisted that was who she was, telling me that he thought that maybe she had a little crush on him, but he'd never give a girl like that the time of day. At that moment, Nikki immerged from the other bedroom, and his eyes became as big as silver dollars," Gina laughed.

"I'll bet they did," I said. "What happened after that?"

"Oh, he jumped from the seat. Nikki walked up to him and slapped him. Right then and there she confronted him, telling him that he'd brought her back to our place apparently when I was out of town for a few days. Then, she dropped an even bigger bomb, one I wasn't aware of. She pulled out a picture of a little boy about two months old, asking if he'd forgotten his son. He stood there looking stupid, saying that wasn't his son. After lying himself further into a corner, he finally admitted that the baby was possibly his, but that Nikki was a whore and didn't mean anything to him. Nikki left in tears. I told Mark that I wanted him out of the apartment and that I never wanted to see him again. I started pulling his things from the closet and tossing them out over the balcony. We got into a huge argument, and he almost hit me. I wouldn't stand for it, even if he didn't actually do it, so I knocked the hell out of him with my fist. I didn't take those self-defense classes for nothing."

"And after what Rhonda has gone through, the last thing I want is for anyone in my family to be in an abusive relationship. So, where does Alex fit into all of this? What made you make such a drastic turn in your lifestyle?"

"I met Alex a week after breaking up with Mark," Gina stated. "A mutual friend invited me to a party she was hosting. I went, against my better judgment. I met Alex, and we started talking. That night, I had no idea that Alex was gay. We exchanged

321

numbers, but I didn't think anything of it. She started calling me, and coming over all the time. She finally admitted a couple of weeks later that she was gay and had fallen in love with me. I was still trying desperately to get over Mark. I figured it would be worth it to try it, so I did."

"And, how do you feel about your decision?"

Gina looked serious, and then she smiled. "I care about her, Millie. She's great for me. At first, to be honest, I wasn't comfortable with it, but, she's a good woman, and I'm happier than I ever was with Mark. She's trustworthy, and I know she loves me."

"So, you're happy leading this life?" I asked earnestly.

"I'm very happy. Millie, don't worry about me. You all wanted me to find the right person, right?"

"Well, of course we do," I said.

"I did, Sis. It may not be a man, but, I'm still happy. Isn't that what's most important?"

"I suppose so," I smiled. "If Alex makes you happy, I won't stand in the way of it."

"Thank you, Millie," Gina smiled, hugging me.

"You're welcome. You know, you never needed my blessing. You're an adult and you make your own decisions."

"I know, but, your opinion means so much to me," Gina said.

"Don't let anyone's opinion define who you are, Gina."

"How do you always know what to say?" Gina smiled.

322

"Just lucky, I guess," I smiled.

"What would I do without you?" Gina asked.

"You'll be just fine, Gina. I know Alex cares for you, and for that I'll always be grateful. Do me a favor though," I said.

"What's that?"

"If you ever get to a point where you see that this isn't the relationship for you, don't be afraid of getting out of it. What I mean is, don't stay with Alex just because you don't want to hurt her. Fair enough?"

"Fair enough," Gina smiled.

"But, now, I still think we need to talk about the fact that you're late. Obviously, you've been with Mark pretty recently," I observed.

"The day Clayton called me and told me about your illness, I was understandably upset. Mark came by my office that evening, and one thing led to another. I slept with him in a moment of weakness."

"Are you sure that's all it was?" I asked.

"Yes, I'm sure. Now, I don't know what to do," Gina sighed.

"Well, if you're pregnant, you're going to have to figure it out," I said. "Would you have the baby?"

Gina smiled. "I've always wanted a child. Yes, I'd have the baby."

"Well, Sweetie, I hope everything works out the way you want it to," I said.

"But, what if this hurts Alex? That's the last thing I want to do."

"Gina, you said you care about Alex, right?"

"Yes."

323

"Does she want children?"

"Yes, she does."

"Well, this may be a way. Although, Mark probably won't go away to easily once he finds out you're carrying his child."

"I know," Gina sighed desperately. "So, what do I do?"

"Gina, I'm afraid that's a decision you'll have to make for yourself," I said.

"What if it's the wrong one?"

"It won't be. But, let's just wait and see. How late are you?"

"A day," Gina said.

"Only a day? Sweetheart, give it a couple of days, at least."

"Usually, I'm like clockwork. I'm never late," Gina said.

"Sweetie, this has been a stressful couple of weeks," I said. "Give it time."

"You think I'm being too presumptuous?"

"Yeah, that's a safe bet," I said. "Now, why don't you go on up to bed and stop worrying about this?" I suggested.

"Aren't you coming?"

"I will in a little while," I smiled slightly.

"I love you, Sis," Gina said, hugging me again.

"I love you, too," I said.

I sat there a few more minutes after Gina went up to bed, and then I got up and went into the sunroom. Upon instinct, I went to my keepsake box to retrieve the letter I'd written to Clayton several months before. I'd made a conscious decision at that moment to bury it with him. I opened the box and saw an unfamiliar envelope. There was a letter that I'd never noticed before with Clayton's handwriting. It had my name on the front of it. When did he have time to write it? This letter had not been here when I wrote the letters to my sisters. I opened it and read it:

Dear Millie,

I know you've been writing letters to everyone, trying to prepare for a time when you won't be here. I saw the letters in this drawer, and I realized that while you've been so busy letting everyone know what they mean to you, I'd not written you to let you know how much you mean to me. I wish I knew where to begin. Millie, I don't even know what life was like before I met you. You've brought out something in me that I didn't even know existed. Twenty six years. That's how old I really am. The day you looked into my eyes and said "I do" was the day I was born. You breathed life into this empty shell by those two simple words. You've given me four wonderful children, and the opportunity to wake up next to the most beautiful woman in the world every morning for twenty six years. You've brought so much to my life, Millie. When I'm away from you, I can't wait to see you, to hear your voice. Something to connect me to you in some way. I know you've gotten prepared to leave the children and me. Knowing that brings tears to my eyes. I know that one of us has to be here for our children. Honey, to be honest with you, I'm hoping to go first. I don't think I could live a second of my life without you. Does that sound selfish? I know it

does. But, Millie, I can't handle losing you. So, either you'll have to fight hard and give me another 26 years, or I'll have to go first. When I think of all that we've gone through. Getting on our feet financially, four children, your illness. You've been the pillar of strength through it all. You've never made demands of me, except for me to love you. I can't thank you enough for that. It's as if you were telling me that my love was enough to sustain you. You've been such a blessing to me, Sweetheart. You're everything that I ever hoped for and then some. So, I want for you to fight, Millie. Don't let this thing win. My sweet, sweet Millicent, I love you.
Love,
Clayton

"Oh, my," I sighed, looking up. "Now what? Clayton, did you know? Did you know you'd leave before me?"

I folded the letter up and put it back into the envelope. I held it close to my heart. I picked up the letter I'd written him and put it in my robe's pocket along with his letter to me. I looked in the downstairs hall closet and retrieved a blanket and pillow. Maybe if I fell asleep in the last place I spent with my husband, I'd sleep for the rest of the night. I imagined Clayton with me, as I laid there on the sofa and re-read his letter to me. It was one of my ways of having him right there with me. I imagined his arms around me. It seemed so real, as something warmed me all over. My husband was lying next to me. Eventually, I drifted off to sleep at almost three a.m.

Chapter Fifteen

The day finally arrived. The day I'd been dreading for almost a week. Clayton's funeral. Although my night was restless, I awoke at 6:30 a.m. when I heard Miriam arrive. I laid there looking out of the window, transfixed by the gentle trickling down of rainfall. Every drop seemed to pierce into my soul, as it paralleled to each tear I'd shed over the past week. I was lured away from my trance when I started to hear the constant ringing of the doorbell. I looked at the clock and noticed it was almost 7 a.m., so I went upstairs to my room to escape the constant sympathetic attentiveness of family and friends. I ran a hot bath, wishing I could simply drift away. While my water was running, I pulled out the black dress I'd chosen to wear. It was one of Clayton's favorite, and this day was all about him.

"I want you to see me at my best, Sweetheart,"

I smiled.

As I was about to take off my robe I realized I still had the letters in my pocket. I read Clayton's letter once again, and put the letter I would leave with him in my purse. I took my bath, and as I came out in my robe, Ellen and Nora, who was still on crutches, came in to assist me.

"Do you need for us to do anything?" Ellen asked.

"No, I'm fine," I smiled slightly. My sisters looked at me.

"I'm going to fix your hair," Nora said.

"And I'll help you get dressed," Ellen volunteered.

"I'm not a child. I've been dressing myself and doing my own hair for years. I'm not too fragile to do something as simple as that! I don't need you all babying me as if I can't manage to do anything for myself! Just leave me alone!"

"Fine, we'll be downstairs," Ellen said quietly.

"Wait," I sighed. "I-I'm sorry! I didn't mean it," I cried.

Nora reached out her arms and held me as I cried to her. "It's okay, Millie," Nora whispered.

"I don't know what's wrong with me! I'm such a mess!" I cried.

"Sweetheart, you just lost your husband. Stop trying to be strong for everyone else," Ellen advised.

"I-I know," I said. "This is just so hard to deal with! When will it get easier? Will I ever get over losing my husband?"

"It takes time, Millie. I know we're not in a

position to tell you that, but, I can promise you that it will be better some day," Nora said.

At that moment, Gina, Alex and Rhonda came in. I felt as if I was being treated like an invalid. A part of me just wanted to be left alone, although it was the last thing in the world that would happen. Everyone stayed with me for a little while, then they went to their respective rooms and got dressed. I looked in the mirror. I picked up the black hat I was going to wear and placed it on my head. I was a widow. I looked the part. I had tears in my eyes, as I realized the veil over the black hat I wore was a lot like the white veil I'd worn on my wedding day. Totally different occasion. Same cast, different script. I recalled crying on my wedding day as well. Yet, those were tears of joy and anticipation. Now, these tears were of pain and loneliness. I thought back to my wedding day. . .

"Mom! Where's my garter?!" I yelled, looking frantically through dresser drawers.

My mom came into the room. She smiled calmly as she walked to the chest and pulled it out.

"Here it is, Sweetheart," she smiled.

"Thank you!" I said with a big sigh.

"I know you're nervous, but there's nothing to worry about. Everything will be perfect."

"What if I trip and fall as Daddy's walking me down the aisle? What if no one comes? What if I forget what I have to say?" I said, shaking.

"Those are normal concerns for your wedding day, Millie," Mom smiled. "Trust me, you'll be a

329

beautiful bride, and everything will fall into place."

"What if I'm not a good wife?"

"You'll be a wonderful wife," Mom reassured, holding my hand.

"What do I do? This is my wedding day, that means tonight is my wedding night. Mom, what should I expect?" I whispered nervously.

"Oh, my little Millicent. You're still so innocent," Mom smiled, as she stroked my hair. "Do what comes naturally. I've talked to you about what to expect. It will be beautiful because you'll be with the man you love."

"But, it'll be my first time."

"Will it be Clayton's first time?"

"No."

"Well, let him teach you. Trust me, it'll be fine. One day, you'll be having this same talk with your daughter."

"Not if I don't get through today," I sighed.

"Oh, Millie. You have a life time ahead of you to look forward to with Clayton. You'll have children and grandchildren," Mom said. "You'll grow old together."

"I-I hope so," I smiled through my tears.

At that moment, Rhonda, who was my matron of honor, walked in. "Knock, knock," Rhonda smiled. She looked at me. "Oh, Millie, you look beautiful!"

I'd decided to wear my mom's wedding dress, just as Rhonda had for her wedding. Mom wanted for all of us to wear her dress when we got married.

"Your sister's nervous. I've tried to calm her,

330

but it seems to be in vain," Mom said.

Rhonda hugged my shoulders playfully. "Trust me, little sis, you've nothing to worry about. The worst thing to happen is that you'll trip going down the aisle, or no one will show or you'll forget what you have to say," Rhonda laughed.

"Rhonda!" I pulled away from her. I was frustrated enough and now Rhonda wanted to make fun of me.

"Rhonda, please!" Mom laughed. "Don't make things worse."

"Don't worry, Millie, I was listening at the door," Rhonda smiled.

"This is not the day for jokes! It's my wedding and I'm nervous enough already!" I said.

"Now, is that any way to talk to someone who came in to give you a present?" Rhonda said.

"What are you talking about?" I asked in an irritated tone.

"I brought you something blue," Rhonda said, handing me the handkerchief Mom had given her for her wedding day.

"Oh, Rhonda! Thank you," I said hugging her.

"And I have something old," Mom said, as she pulled out her pearls. "My mother gave them to me when I married your father, and Rhonda wore them for her wedding. Now, I'm passing them to you for your wedding."

"Oh, I think I'm going to cry!" I said, through my tears.

"You still need something new and borrowed,"

331

Rhonda said.

"Well, let's see. Kristen loaned me her earrings, so that's borrowed. Where is Kristen by the way? I thought she was coming over." Kristen was my best friend since grammar school who was killed seven years after I got married. She was there when Kirsten was born, and I gave her name to Kirsten, but I switched the 'i' and the 'r.'

"She's going to meet us at the church. Her dress had a slight tear in it, so her mom had to fix it," Rhonda said. "Trust me, she'd never miss an opportunity to be a bridesmaid in her best friend's wedding."

"Okay, good. The last thing I need is for something to happen to my wedding party. I guess something new would be my purse. Clayton's mom gave it to me. So, it looks like I'm all set," I smiled.

"Looks that way," Mom smiled.

Nora peeked her head in. "The limo's here," she said.

"Okay, we'll be out in a minute," Rhonda said.

As we were about to walk out of my bedroom, I took one last look, as I pulled the veil over my head. "Goodbye, Millicent McAlray," I smiled.

I was brought back to reality as I pulled the black veil over my head. "Goodbye, Millicent Welby," I cried.

At that very moment, Nora poked her head in the door, just like she had 26 years before. "The limo's here," Nora said quietly.

"I'm on my way," I said. I picked up my

purse, and walked out of my room.

When I got downstairs, everyone was there waiting. All of my sisters, two brothers-in-law, Alex, my nieces and nephews, and my in-laws. There were a lot of our extended relatives and friends there as well. We had three family cars. The director came inside to talk to us. After a beautiful prayer with us, he got everyone lined up for the car they were to ride in.

"Okay, Mrs. Welby. In your car will be you, your four children, your daughter-in-law and your future son-in-law," Mr. Grayson said. "We will be lining up outside, in approximately 10 minutes." He was the owner of the funeral home. I was glad he was able to handle everything himself. Everything had to be perfect. This was the only chance I'd get to do this for Clayton.

"Okay," I said.

"In car two, will be parents of the deceased, sister, brothers, sister-in-law, and brother-in-law. In car three, will be sisters-in-law of the deceased, and brothers-in-law," Mr. Grayson continued.

I looked at Gina, as I noticed Alex. "Alex should ride in that car as well," I stated.

Gina looked at me, and mouthed "thank you" to me. Ginny was going to drive Kirsten's car, and AJ was going to drive Kyle's car.

We assembled in our designated cars for the journey to the church. The church was exactly five and a half miles from our home. The grave site was another three miles from the church. This was going to be the most agonizing ride of my entire life. It was a rainy, cloudy day, much like the day after Clayton's death. I looked out the window as we rode along, thinking about my life with Clayton. He would want for me to be happy, to live life to the fullest, I knew that. The question was, how could I live life to the fullest when I felt so empty?

We arrived at the church at 10:30, and the church parking lot was completely full. Even the lot across the street was filled with loved ones' cars. Knowing how much I love my husband, it's not surprising that so many people would love him as well. I learned later that there were over 500 people at my husband's funeral. We went into the church for the processional and I got one last chance to see my beloved Clayton. I cried as I approached his casket. Kyle had his arm around me and Erin was immediately behind us as we walked in. I reached into my purse and pulled out the letter I'd written him. I paused, and for some strange reason, I couldn't put the letter in his casket. Maybe a part of me refused to let go, because despite my initial desire to put the letter with him, I couldn't do it.

"Oh, Clayton!" I cried. I became lightheaded, and almost passed out.

Kyle noticed it. "Mom, are you okay?"

"Yes, I'll be fine," I said through my tears.

When we finally got to our seats, I stared at Clayton. I couldn't take my eyes off of him. After everyone was seated, the service started. I never thought I'd have to witness something like this so soon. Since finding out about my cancer, I didn't think I'd have to witness it at all. I'm not sure how we got through the funeral, but we did. Everything was so beautiful, as close friends spoke such kind words about my husband. It made me even more proud of him than I already was, if that was possible. As he was taken out, I felt a piece of myself going with him. We followed behind, as we loaded back up for the journey to Clayton's final resting place. We'd already picked out our plots, which were right next to each other. At least we'd be together in the afterlife. I listened as our pastor did the final ceremony at the grave site. I had an orchid that I gently placed on top of his casket.

"Goodbye, my love," I whispered, as tears flowed down my face. I stood there, unable to move. I wanted to watch them lower him into the ground.

"Mom, let's go," Kirsten said.

"No, I want to see them lower him," I said.

"I don't think that's a good idea," Kirsten protested.

"I know it's not. I just want to make sure he's safe," I said.

"He's safe, Mom. No harm can come to him," Kirsten said gently.

"Leave me alone, Kirsten," I said calmly.

"Kirsten, come on. Let's give her a moment," Kyle said.

I stood there for what felt like an eternity, as loved ones came up and hugged me, commenting about how good Clayton was, and that they'd be there for me if I needed anything. These were just empty words to me. Words people feel compelled to say during a funeral. I acrimoniously wondered what any of these people felt they could possibly do to make me feel better about losing my husband. I watched the ground workers lower Clayton's casket as I felt a part of my heart tearing away and going with him. The way I felt that day was indescribable, as I realized that I'd never forget seeing that casket descend into the ground.

"I'm going to miss you, Clayton," I whispered as I stood there crying. A sharp pain hit me in my stomach, causing me to double over. My children had been waiting patiently on me at the car. When they saw me, Kirsten and Kyle came to my aid.

"Mom, are you feeling okay?" Kirsten asked.

"I'll be fine. Just the reality of it all," I said.

"I think it's more than that," Kirsten protested.

"We'd better get you home," Kyle said.

My children walked me back to the car. I was in a great deal of pain, but I didn't want to worry them so I felt it better to keep quiet. They'd gone through enough already without having to worry about me. We needed to just get through this day together as a family. The car took us back to a house full of waiting guests for dinner. Countless faces watched me as if I were a time bomb ready to explode. I was sitting on the sofa in the living room, pretty much tuning everyone out, consumed with my thoughts, when Shauna came and sat next to me. She leaned over and I held her.

"Mom, you're not going to die, are you?" Shauna asked.

"No, Sweetheart, I'm going to be fine," I smiled, reassuring my youngest child.

"We didn't think Daddy would die, and now

he's gone," Shauna said.

"We can never predict these things, Honey. I promise you, I'll be here for you as long as I can, okay?" I said.

"I love you, Mom," Shauna said, hugging me.

"I love you, too, Shauna." This is the sort of thing that was tearing me apart. My children pulling me in one direction and my husband pulling me in another. I didn't know what I wanted to happen.

After sitting there listening to endless stories about Clayton, I got up to go to the restroom. As I was about to come out, I felt nauseated. I started coughing up blood.

"No, God. Not now," I whispered. "My children need me."

It took a lot for me to get my bearings before leaving out of the bathroom. I was met at the door by Ellen.

"Are you okay? I thought I heard you coughing," Ellen said.

"It was just a little cough. I'm fine," I smiled slightly.

"Are you sure?" Ellen asked. "Dr. Tracer is in the living room."

"Yes, I'm sure. Please don't bother her. I'm going to the kitchen to check on things."

"Why don't you let me do that," Ellen volunteered.

"No, Dear. I have to do something to keep my mind occupied," I said.

"Okay, Millie," Ellen said, as she hugged me.

I walked into the kitchen where I was greeted

by Miriam. She tried to get me to eat something, but I simply didn't have an appetite. I longed for a bottled water and she immediately retrieved one for me. I wanted to go to my special place in the sunroom. When I got there, I stood and looked morosely out over the backyard. My mind wandered to Clayton playing football with Kyle and Tim on so many occasions. Several of their friends would come over, and they'd have a ball. I sadly thought about the fact that those times were now forever gone, leaving only memories of the past.

I was brought back to reality when I heard some of my guests laughing. They were probably remembering another funny anecdote about Clayton. Although I wanted hopelessly to be alone, I knew that wouldn't be possible at this moment. I despondently thought about the fact that I would have all the time in the world to be alone now that Clayton was gone.

Sometimes, I didn't know whether I was coming or going. I was tired. I'd been fighting for my life, now I was suffering twice as much because I'd lost the one individual who gave me the support I needed when I felt like giving up. There had been so many times when I'd been in the hospital over the past year, when I was at death's door. Clayton stayed vigil by my side the whole time. He wouldn't let me give up, no matter how much I wanted to. A part of me feels like I set the wheels in motion to my husband's destruction because of my illness. He was desperate to save me, so he contacted my sisters. I knew it was ridiculous to feel this way, but it seemed like such a chain reaction. I mean, maybe Clayton never would have left home that morning if it weren't for something one of my sisters had done. He'd been so patient with everyone. He was caring, loving and supporting, despite the fact that my family had more than its share of psychotic episodes since arriving. How do I thank him for that? I argue with him, defend them to him, and accuse him of not wanting to be there for me. No, it wasn't my sisters' fault that Clayton was gone, it was mine. Let's face it. No matter how much he'd gotten over his anger by the time he left Greg's house, he wouldn't have been there had I not ran him off in the first place.

I wondered how long I would blame myself for my husband's premature death. This could go on for the rest of my life. I thought back to the letter and the phone message. While they provided a degree of solace, they couldn't replace him. No amount of pictures, letters or memorabilia would ever do that. The best thing for me to do was to figure out a way to pick up the pieces to my life, and go on without him because my children needed me. I went back out into the living room where there were still a lot of guests. Some of them had left, but the house was still pretty full so I circulated, to thank as many people as I could for their love and thoughtfulness. I handled things just the way Clayton would have wanted me to. With a smile. Everyone ate, socialized, and eventually left by 7 p.m. The only ones left with me were my children, my sisters and my in-laws. The house was full, but it still seemed so empty. While the extra hired staff was cleaning up, I noticed that it started to rain again. The whole day had been cloudy and gloomy, raining sporadically. We all sat around quietly, when Nora broke the silence.

"I think the service was beautiful," Nora said.

"It really was," Ellen chimed in.

"And the flowers! There were so many of them!" Rhonda said.

I started to shake my head fiercely. "Please! Please don't do that!" I screamed.

"Don't do what?" Rhonda asked.

"Don't try to make small talk to keep conversation going. You don't have to occupy my mind every moment," I said.

I listened to the rain as it sprinkled against the windows. I sadly thought about the fact that it was such an ominous day already, only to be peppered by a constant downpour.

After an hour or so, Vivian and her family left for the hotel. They'd be leaving the next day heading back home, so they wanted to turn in early. Andrew and his wife headed back to Greg's house, with their parents, because like Vivian, they were leaving the next day. Everyone was slowly going back to the life they'd fleetingly left behind. Everyone would be able to do that except for me. Greg stayed around to visit with Rhonda, but used me as an excuse.

That night, after everyone had gotten settled, I went into my room. I stared around the room silently, and thought this was the first day of the end of my life. I noticed Clayton's obituary lying on the bed. I picked it up and read it. I'd been so busy planning, until I didn't even know what I'd written about my own husband. I read through the entire thing, over and over again. It didn't change the fact that he was gone, and it only offered a temporary comfort. I looked over at his pillow, and I caressed it softly. Never again would his head touch it. I lied on his pillow, as tears began to flow once again. I wondered how many tear-filled nights I would experience. As I lay there, I heard a knock at my door.

"C-Come in," I said.

"Mom?" Kyle called out, as he and Erin entered my room.

"Hi, Sweetheart," I smiled, sitting up.

"Erin and I wanted to come in and say good night. We were about to leave."

"Mom, I'm so sorry about Dad," Erin said, holding my hand. I was seeing an impressive side of my daughter-in-law.

"Thank you, Dear," I said, hugging her. "How are you feeling?"

"I'm fine. Just eating everything in sight," Erin smiled.

"That's understandable! Clayton was so proud when he found out about the baby," I said.

"Did you know he sent us a dozen balloons the next day? Six blue, and six pink. He enclosed a note card that said, 'Just covering both bases. Thanks for making us grandparents. Love, Mom and Dad,'" Erin said, with tears in her eyes.

"Why, I had no idea," I smiled.

"He called and asked if we received the delivery, and then he offered to pay to decorate the baby's room," Kyle said.

"We wanted to let you know that we'd like to

name the baby Drew," Erin said.

"Oh, Clayton would love that," I smiled. I suddenly started to cough.

"Mom, are you okay?" Erin asked.

"Yes, just this nagging cough."

"Maybe we should call your doctor," Kyle suggested.

"No, I'll be fine," I insisted. "Now, you'd better get your wife home so she can get plenty of rest."

"Are you sure? We can stay longer," Kyle offered.

"No, that's okay. I'm tired. I was about to make an attempt at getting some sleep when you came in."

"We're sorry. We'll let you rest," Erin said, hugging me again.

"Okay," I smiled. "I'll see you both tomorrow."

Kyle and Erin got up to leave. I tried in vain to muffle a cough as they walked to the door. The two of them looked at me, as I began to cough profusely.

"Mom, I'm going to page Dr. Tracer," Kyle offered.

"No, Kyle. She just left here a little while ago. I'll be fine," I said between coughs. "I just need some water."

Erin went to the bathroom for a glass of water. "Here you are," Erin said, handing me the glass.

"Thank you," I said.

They waited until they knew I was feeling better before leaving. Before I could drift off to sleep,

Kirsten came in, supposedly to say goodnight. Obviously, they'd decided to take turns watching me. I suppose I couldn't blame them. After all, they'd just lost their father. Kirsten sat vigil by my side throughout the night. Despite what I said, it was so good having her here with me. I needed her. I needed a part of Clayton. What better part than one of our children? We talked for the rest of the night about so many things. My daughter was making an intrepid attempt at keeping my mind off of everything. I brought up to her about the wedding, which was scheduled for the first Saturday in November. My daughter was having her dream wedding. Everything was going according to plan. As we were talking, and I was remembering my own wedding, Kirsten became sad.

"I wish things were different," Kirsten whispered.

"I know, Kirsten, but your father will be with you in your heart," I said.

"I know he will, but I'd much rather he was here to walk me down the aisle."

"So do I, Kirsten."

"Mom, since Daddy's not here, will you walk me down the aisle?"

"Are you sure you want for me to?"

"I couldn't be more sure," Kirsten smiled.

"Well then, I'd be honored," I smiled. "Talk about a change in tradition."

"I know," Kirsten smiled.

Chapter Sixteen

M y sisters had made the unanimous decision to stick around for a few more days. Alex wasn't able to stay, so she caught a flight home the day after Clayton's funeral. She had to get back to work. As I talked more and more to Alex, I became more and more impressed. She really was a great girl. It was my little sister's decision, and if Alex made her happy, I would find a way to be happy for them.

Ginny and AJ were going to fly back home the next day, because Ginny had to get back to work, and AJ had to get home and finish packing for medical school in Arizona. They'd talked to their father, and decided that they wanted nothing more to do with him after the way he'd treated their mother. Bill explained that he wouldn't be able to stay but a couple of days because he needed to get back to his office, so

Jessica and Matthew decided to leave with him on Tuesday. Nora was going to stay for the next couple of weeks to finish screening to be my donor. Then, she would fly back in a couple of months for the transplant. I didn't want the transplant before Kirsten's wedding, because I wanted to be able to be a part of it all. So, we planned the transplant for the Monday after Kirsten's wedding. Jim was going to fly back home on Monday. Amanda wanted to stay with Ellen, which I think was good for her. She was going to have to attend a class about drunk driving, which was a mere slap on the wrist. It could have been a lot worse. The judge took into consideration that she wasn't from South Carolina. He ordered her to attend the classes before leaving, which would be three times over the next week. If she failed to do so, he would have her picked up, because he knew of her trouble in New York. Clayton's death seemed to be a 'scared straight' tactic for Ellen, because during the course of the week, she'd not taken one drink.

Rhonda was going to fly back in another week so that she could pack her things and move out. She and I talked about it again, and she refused to impose on me. I desperately wanted her to stay, but Ginny offered for her to stay with her. My big sister was leaving me when I needed her the most. But, I had to respect her for doing so. She deserved to be happy, not to have to babysit me during my mourning and illness. So, she and I came to an agreement. She'd stay with me for a couple of months, and then go back to Colorado. I wondered how much of her decision was based on me, and how much was based on my brother-in-law. She still denied anything between them, but I knew better. I think that maybe she wanted to test the waters before diving in. I got the feeling that the two of them would end up together, despite Rhonda's protests. I could tell she had feelings for him, but was too scared to admit it.

Gina was going to stay with me for another week, then she'd fly back on the next Saturday. It looked as if our little reunion had been extended another week. Maybe it was a good thing. So much of the visit had been about animosity and planning Clayton's funeral. Maybe now, we could concentrate on our relationships with each other.

Those next few days were not as bad as I'd anticipated. My sisters were extraordinarily loving and supportive during the following week. We caught up with so many things, things that we'd been putting off because of anger or mourning. Although I was still missing my husband, they helped to ease a little of the pain I was feeling. With most of my sisters' families gone back to their respective homes, we acted like teenagers. It was good to feel young again. I felt healthy, even if only by a mild standard. I wanted to gain a new lease on life. I wasn't sure if I could, but I at least needed to try. I'd never spend another living day not missing and loving my husband, but at least I had almost 30 years of memories to sustain me for the rest of my life.

We'd had a wonderful few days, and on the Wednesday night after Clayton's funeral, my sisters and I rented a few movies and sat around in our pajamas. All of their husbands as well as Alex had gone home, so it was just us. Amanda was with Tim and Shauna. Our family reunion was dwindling down, but it was still nice to have them with me. This is the type of reunion that Clayton would have wanted. Clayton. The thought of him still saddened me. My sisters would get to go back to their husbands. I'd never be able to do that again.

I watched how well Ellen and Nora got along. Such a waste. All those years of complete misunderstanding. They were so healthy for each other. If only they'd realized it years ago. Looking at them now, you'd think they'd never had an ill feeling for each other. My thoughts were interrupted by Rhonda.

"What's going on in that head of yours, Millie?" Rhonda asked.

"Nothing much. Just thinking how wonderful it is that we're all together, as a family. I have my sisters back," I smiled.

"You know, if someone had told me a month ago that Ellen and I would be happy in each other's presence, I would have told them that they were crazy," Nora smiled, looking at Ellen. "I've been so stupid for so long. I should have just opened up a long time ago. Not that I'm discounting what Daddy did to me, but every time I think about what he did to you, Ellen, mine seems small by comparison. I'm going to be here for you, Ellen. I want to help fight those demons with you. Will you let me? I know it by no means will make up for the way I've treated you over the years, but I owe you at least that."

"Nora, your saying that to me has been the best

therapy I could ever hope for," Ellen smiled. "It would be easier having someone to hold my hand throughout this thing. I'm looking at a rough road ahead of me, and I just want for all of you to be patient with me."

"We will. That's what we're here for," Gina smiled. She then sighed heavily and closed her eyes, seeming to be thinking of the right words to say. "You guys, I have an important announcement to make."

"Well, what is it?" Ellen asked.

"I'm pregnant," Gina said softly.

"Pregnant? What did you do, use a turkey baster?" Nora asked.

"No. I'm pregnant by my ex-fiancé," Gina said.

"Ex-fiancé?" Nora, Ellen and Rhonda said in unison.

"Yes. I was engaged, now I'm not. We had a brief encounter a few weeks ago, now, I'm carrying his child," Gina said.

"How do you feel about this guy?" Rhonda asked.

"I'll always love him, but, I care about Alex," Gina responded.

"So, you and Alex are going to raise this baby?" Ellen asked.

"Yeah, we are. I called her this morning and told her the news. She wasn't too thrilled about Mark being in our lives, but she said she'd find a way to deal with it, because she loves me."

"I hope you know what you're doing," Nora said.

"I do. I'll be fine," Gina smiled.

As we sat there talking, the doorbell rang. I went to answer it since Miriam had already left for the day. It was Greg.

"Hi, Millie. I just thought I'd come by and check on you," Greg said.

I knew he was really there to see Rhonda, but he didn't want to admit it. I decided to have a little fun with him.

"I'm fine, Greg. Thanks for coming by," I smiled, closing the door in his face. I leaned against the door and laughed. Rhonda came out.

"Who was that at the door?" Rhonda asked.

"Like you don't know. It's your boyfriend," I smiled.

"I don't have a boyfriend," Rhonda smiled. "Greg and I are just friends." At that precise moment, my brother-in-law rang the doorbell again.

"How did you know I was referring to Greg?" I asked.

"Because that's all you've been referring to over the past couple of weeks, Millie," Rhonda said, as the doorbell rang again. "So? Are you going to let him in, or does he need to stand outside all night?"

I opened the door. "So, are you checking on me or are you here to see Rhonda?" I smiled.

"No, I came to check on you," Greg insisted as he blushed.

"Which you could have done by phone," I acknowledged. "Come on in. You know you're always welcome here, even if it is to court my big sister."

349

"Would you please tell this woman that there's nothing going on between us?" Rhonda sighed.

"Millie, Rhonda and I are just friends," Greg said. As he said it, he stared at Rhonda. There was a pregnant pause between the two of them which I, of course, picked up on.

"Well, Greg you're welcome to join us. We're watching a movie in the media room," I said.

"Sounds good, but I don't want to intrude," Greg said.

"Oh, it's no intrusion," Rhonda said quickly.

"Well, in that case, I'll stay," Greg smiled.

"Did Rhonda tell you that she's going to be staying with me for a couple of months?" I asked.

"Yeah, she mentioned it," Greg said, as we walked into the media room. "I think it'll be good for both of you."

"Especially you, Greg," I said slyly.

Rhonda looked at me as her mouth dropped. "Millie!"

"Hello, Ladies," Greg said, as he entered the media room.

"Hello, Greg," Ellen said.

"Hi," Nora smiled.

"How are you?" Gina asked.

"I'm good," Greg smiled.

"So, what were you talking about, when you were coming in?" Nora asked.

"I was talking about Rhonda and Greg," I said, looking at the two of them. "We all know that the two of you care for each other. When are you going to admit it?" I asked. "You've been acting like shy,

350

love-struck teenagers."

"Yeah, we've all seen it," Ellen smiled.

"What?" Rhonda asked.

"We see the way the two of you are when you're around each other. I say go for it," Nora shrugged her shoulders.

"Can't hurt," Ellen said.

"Just don't wear white at the wedding," Nora said.

"Listen to you. You all have us dating and married already. There's nothing going on," Rhonda smiled.

"So, why are you smiling?" I asked.

I knew I wasn't making matters any better, but they were both good people who deserved to be happy. They'd both been through tumultuous marriages, and they were long overdue for happiness.

"I always smile," Rhonda said.

"Okay, okay, we'll leave it alone," I said.

We all sat around after watching the movie and played cards. Greg and Rhonda couldn't take their eyes off each other. Maybe this would just be a summer romance, or maybe it would be something more. I just hoped the two of them wouldn't be too proud to let nature take its course. Greg stayed for another hour or so, and then he left. Rhonda graciously walked him out, which all of us noticed.

"So, you think it'll happen between those two?" Nora asked.

"No doubt. Those two are heading for something serious. They couldn't keep their eyes off each other," Ellen commented.

"I hope she's happy," I said.
"She will be," Gina smiled.

****

All of my sisters with exception of Nora left on the following Saturday. Gina had an early flight, so she was the first to leave. Rhonda was second, with a mid-morning flight. And Ellen was last with an afternoon flight. Although Rhonda was coming back in a few days, I was still going to miss her. My sisters provided me with a healthy distraction. I didn't want to accompany them because it would be too painful seeing them leave. Besides that, I didn't need to be in a crowded airport. I was so grateful for the three weeks we spent together; three precious weeks that signified so much to all of us. It took some time, but I realized that if it was Clayton's time, it would have happened whether my sisters were here or not.

The house was so quiet that night as I walked around. It seemed so big and empty all of a sudden. Of course, Kyle, Erin, Kirsten and Robert all came over for dinner. They didn't want for me to be alone although Nora was with me. Tim originally had plans with his new girlfriend, Krysteena, and some of their friends, but he backed out because he wanted to be there with the rest of us. They'd been dating only for a few days, and she seemed like a nice girl. They went to school together and she lived only a few blocks from our house. When Tim opted not to go out with the others, Krysteena decided not to as well and joined us for dinner.

I think Shauna enjoyed having her brothers and sister there. She was going to need all the support she could get. After all, she'd had the least amount of time with Clayton than any of us. She was so afraid that I wouldn't live much longer, and it really affected her in so many ways. She was becoming somewhat anti-social, which had never been in her character. My daughter needed my unfaltering guidance, but for the first time, I felt lost. I'd been there for all of my children's 'awkward age,' and now that Shauna was at that stage in her life, I felt that I was cheating her. Not only did I have my illness to deal with, I had to deal with the loss of my husband. How do I focus my attention on my child who needs me when I need someone? Maybe we could be strength for each other. I was saddened at the thought that my little girl would live the rest of her life without her father.

Nora and I were able to bond so well while we were alone. She was doing something for me that no one else, not even my husband or children, were able to do. This was phenomenal for both of us. I never knew how much strength my sister had until we started going for preliminary treatment and to finish her screening. It was grueling, and it was going to take a few weeks. It was so ironic that the sister we'd always considered selfish and mean, was the one who was willing and able to save my life.

Rhonda arrived back on the following Wednesday. Her attorney was going to handle everything for her concerning the divorce. She'd gone in and taken care of signing everything during the few days she was home. Rhonda decided to fight for what was rightfully hers. She felt that she deserved something for all of the pain she endured. She commented that her divorce from Aaron would be like a heavy burden being lifted. She'd visited with her children, who'd received her things. Aaron cruelly had someone to come in and pack up her things and deliver them to Ginny's apartment. Aaron was sending a message loud and clear that he didn't want to see Rhonda again. There were rumors floating around that Aaron's lover was coming by the house. Being so callous was dangerously close to playing Russian Roulette in a divorce, especially considering he didn't want for Rhonda to get a dime of his money. I suppose Aaron didn't care anymore, because he felt he'd intimidated Rhonda enough. But, he was in for a few surprises. Rhonda wasn't the weak person he thought her to be. In typical fashion, Aaron's arrogance stood front and center, causing him to lose temporary rights to their home. The judge granted Rhonda temporary dwelling rights until the case was settled.

During the time when Rhonda and Nora were at my home, they were such a big help. Nora stayed with me for almost a month after everyone else, but she needed to get back home. She actually missed Bill and her children. She didn't need to be back to do the actual donation until after Kirsten's wedding. The plan was for her to remain with me for another month afterwards.

Before Nora returned home, she and Rhonda stepped in and helped Kirsten with a lot of her wedding plans. They were able to do things I didn't feel up to doing, which I acutely appreciated. Kirsten needed a mother's help when planning her wedding. She deserved to go shopping with someone, to get a woman's opinion. When I felt up to it, I would help out a little, but it wasn't very often. Most of the time, it was a chore simply getting out of bed in the morning. Rhonda took over and was in complete mother mode for Kirsten after Nora left. If it weren't for those two, my daughter would have been cheated out of so much. I'll never forget how much they helped us. To show my appreciation, I was able to plan a special dinner to celebrate Rhonda's birthday, which was during the first week of October. Greg surprised her with a weekend getaway to a cabin in the mountains.

Kirsten's wedding was less than a month away. I was at least able to get the invitations ready to be mailed. I felt helpless, almost useless otherwise. Although there was a wedding planner, I wanted to do something. Kirsten never made me feel as if I wasn't helping, but I still felt as if I were cheating her out of what being the mother of the bride was all about.

Kirsten's shower was planned the Saturday before Rhonda was to leave, which was on the following Friday. We'd planned for thirty people to attend her shower, but we ended up with fifty-seven. I stayed seated through most of it, for which I will feel eternally guilty. Rhonda, Erin, Miriam and Robert's mom did everything. She received everything from toasters to negligees. Oddly enough, this was only one of three showers given in my daughter's honor. Her co-workers at the hospital wanted to give her a shower at work so that they could all be there. And then there's the infamous bachelorette party, complete with 'live entertainment' given by some of Kirsten's close friends. Let's just say the guest list was limited to an exclusive few. Kirsten told me later that the bachelorette party had almost as many people as the shower we'd planned for her. Who knew there were so many women interested in something like that? I'd chosen not to be a part of that because I felt that Kirsten might be a little embarrassed if I participated, and quite frankly, it wasn't my cup of tea. She insisted that I come, but I felt that she was just being gracious more than anything else. At the rate she was going, my daughter would be too 'partied out' by the time the wedding came around to enjoy the festivities.

The wear and tear from all the planning and parties was starting to take its toll on me. I didn't want to worry anyone, so I kept quiet. I knew my health was waning rapidly, but I prayed for just one more month. I at least wanted to see Kirsten marry Robert. Then, once I received my transplant, maybe my life would eventually become normal again. I knew that even that would be a long way off. The recovery time after receiving a transplant could take up to a year, and I was praying for the strength to make it through it. Clayton was no longer here as a support network for me. Sometimes I still felt so lost without him.

Kirsten and Robert were building a house not far from our home. Kirsten always loved the water, so they really wanted to stay near the beach. The property they'd chosen had a breathtaking view of the ocean that made me almost envious. All of my daughter's dreams were coming true. Everything Clayton and I could have ever hoped for in our children's lives was coming into play. They had their whole lives ahead of them. Every time I looked at Kirsten, I thought of myself at her age. By the time I was twenty-three, I already had her and Kyle.

I was starting to worry about Erin now because she and Kyle found out that they were having twins. Next step: baby shower. She was so helpful in getting everything organized for Kirsten's shower. She and Kirsten seemed to have grown much closer. After Kyle and Erin married, Kirsten and she had their share of run-ins. Kirsten felt Erin wasn't treating her brother right, and she had no qualms about telling Erin exactly what she thought of her. I was glad to see that it was water under the bridge now, and that the two of them could be there for each other. Erin had to get used to being a wife. She was an only child, and had been pretty used to getting her way, not having to share or compromise like Kyle had been used to doing. So, it was a learning experience for her. I think she eventually adapted quite well.

About a week before Rhonda was due to leave, she received a phone call from her attorney. Just as expected, Aaron countered back with an offer that was less than 1/4 of what Rhonda asked for. This meant that they would have to go back to court to fight it out, unless Rhonda wanted to settle for Aaron's counter-offer. When Rhonda asked her attorney's advice, she advised Rhonda against it, stating that if Aaron wanted to roll such a serious dice, let him. Rhonda would come out on top of this one if she was patient. Rhonda agreed to stick it out. Her attorney also advised that she move back into the house, since she'd been awarded temporary dwelling rights.

Aaron was livid over the fact that Rhonda wouldn't accept his offer. The day before Rhonda was due to leave to return to Colorado, Aaron called threatening her life. I was immensely afraid for her and I tried unsuccessfully to convince her to stay and not go back, that the house wasn't worth it, but she knew she had to face things at some point. She didn't want for AJ and Ginny to find out about Aaron's threat because she knew that AJ would confront him. I wanted to go back to Colorado with her, but she wanted to do this on her own. She felt that Aaron was just blowing off steam because he didn't expect for Rhonda to stand up to him, and that he would eventually calm down. Although she knew him better than anyone, she had to be out of her mind not to take his threats seriously. Aaron had already beaten her more times than she could even remember; what on earth made her think he wouldn't kill her? I prayed for her safety constantly, hoping that Aaron wouldn't follow through on his threat.

Greg was worried about her as well. He wanted to go back to Colorado with her for a couple of weeks, but Rhonda refused to let him. That's all Aaron would have needed for ammunition was to find out that Rhonda brought another man to their home. Plus, she didn't know what to think, whether Greg wanted to be her guardian or lover. The two of them had been seeing each other almost every day. Rhonda admitted that things were getting serious between them, but they wanted to keep things quiet for now. Although she spent many nights with Greg, she was concerned that she was making a big mistake. She didn't want for things to end up like they did with Aaron. She voiced her concerns about losing a good thing with Greg because of Aaron.

"Then go for it," I told her.

"No, I need to know that I can make it on my own first," Rhonda commented.

"What's wrong with being with Greg? Don't you want to be happy?" I asked.

"Who says it takes a man to make a woman happy? A man caused me to live twenty-seven of the most miserable years of my life. The last thing I need is a man to get too serious with. I have to do this, Millie. I have to do this for me," Rhonda stated seriously.

"I understand," I nodded. "You know you're welcome here anytime."

"I know, Sweetie. But, you need some time to yourself. You're still in mourning," Rhonda said.

"Maybe I need to focus on something else for now," I said.

"No, Millie. Trying to avoid thinking about Clayton is the biggest mistake you could make."

"I'm not avoiding it. I just know that constantly thinking about him won't bring him back to me. I have to move on without him."

"Enough said," Rhonda smiled.

The day after Rhonda left, I got a welcoming call from Ellen.

"Hello?" I answered.

"Hi, Millie!" Ellen's voice boomed. She sounded happy.

"Ellen! How are you?" I asked.

"I'm great. The question is how are things with you?"

"They're good. Just tired. I have to continue going to outpatient therapy to get ready for my transplant in a few weeks."

"So, you started back with the chemo and radiation treatments?"

"Yeah, I did. I owe it to my children to be here as long as I can."

"I'm proud of you, Millie," Ellen said.

"Thanks, Ellen. That means a lot coming from you. How's the rehab going?"

"Well, I'm on an outpatient basis now after being at the facility for six weeks. I see things in a whole new light now."

"Oh, Ellen, that's wonderful," I smiled.

"Guess who came for a visit," Ellen said.

"Who?"

"Katie."

"Really? That's great."

"Yeah, she and Michael came along with their two children. Their daughter is Amanda's age and their son is a year younger. They stayed for a week during their kids' fall break from school."

"Are the two of you okay?" I asked.

"We're better than ever. It was so nice having my friend here. We promised not to stay away from each other like that again."

"I'm glad." As I was talking to her, I stood up

to stretch my legs a little. "Nora told me she came up there a couple of weeks ago."

"Yes, she did. She came and we had a wonderful time. Gosh, I didn't realize how much I missed my sister until I saw her."

"You and Nora are good together," I smiled.

"She went to one of my counseling sessions with me. She was so supportive."

"Nora can be pretty grown up when she wants to be," I laughed slightly. "I'm so grateful to her for doing what she's doing for me."

"Donating her bone marrow is a wonderful act of love. I'm so proud of her," Ellen said. "Well, Sis, I won't hold you. I just wanted to check in. We'll be there for Kirsten's wedding. How are the plans going?"

"Great. She's not a total nervous wreck yet," I smiled.

"Don't worry. She will be by her wedding day," Ellen joked.

"You're right about that!"

"Well, I'll talk to you later. I love you, Millie."

"I love you, too, Ellen." I knew when we hung up that Ellen was going to be okay.

Chapter Seventeen

The Thursday before Kirsten's wedding, Gina and Alex arrived. Ginny, her boyfriend Keith, and Rhonda arrived that night. Unfortunately, AJ's life consisted of nothing but medical school twenty-four hours a day, preventing him from coming to the wedding. Ginny was going to be one of Kirsten's bridesmaids. Ellen and Jim, along with Nora and Bill, arrived on that Friday morning. Amanda couldn't come because of school. Ellen and Jim decided to test Amanda's level of responsibility, and left her with a friend. Her friend's mom assured them that Amanda would be fine. Jessica had midterms, and Matthew's football team was preparing for the playoffs, citing their inability to attend. Everyone seemed rested and happy. True to form, Greg came by to see Rhonda. That afternoon, Kirsten and Robert were treated to lunch by Kyle, Erin, Ginny, Keith, Gina and Alex.

"How are things since the fire?" Greg asked.

"They're getting better. Can you believe Aaron burned down the house when I was granted the right to stay there until the divorce was finalized?" Rhonda said. "I loved that house. I'd raised my children there. He was so cruel about it because he waited until I'd moved everything back in, then he torched it."

"Did you ever file charges?" Ellen asked.

"I tried to, but so far, they haven't done anything about it. I know it was arson, but it looks as if it will be ruled accidental."

"So, where do things stand?" Nora asked.

"Right now, everything's still tied up in court because my loving husband won't give up. I could be tied to this man for another year. But, concerning the house, our insurance company will probably pay it off and give us a settlement. All the money in the world can't replace the precious things I had in my home. Pictures, antiques, gifts my children made for us, everything, gone, just like that," Rhonda said, snapping her finger. "Ginny's been great, but I know I've been cramping her style for the past few days since the fire. She and Keith never have any privacy unless they go to his place. I feel like an intruder."

"Did the insurance company not offer to put you up until your settlement?" Ellen asked.

"Yeah, they did, but I'm afraid to be alone," Rhonda sighed. "So, Ginny insisted that I live with her."

"Can't your attorney put some pressure on Aaron? I mean, he's been a real son of a bitch during your marriage. Why is he so willing to risk it? He should just leave it alone and split all assets," Ellen stated.

"Because that might make life easier for me. Financially, Aaron will not be hurting for money if he has to pay me fair alimony and split assets. But, he's stubborn," Rhonda sighed. "So, technically for now, I'm homeless," Rhonda joked.

"Rhonda, it's not like you're destitute. You have money. Why don't you just buy another house?" Nora suggested.

"Technically, I don't have anything until this whole divorce thing is settled. But, I have been shopping quietly. My agent back home has set up for me to see a few places, but I don't know. I think it's time for me to consider leaving Colorado. Aaron would never do anything to the children, but I wonder would I be safe as long as I'm living there. Maybe I need to put a few states between us. Millie, does your offer still stand about my staying with you?"

"Why, of course it does," I smiled.

"The smart thing would be not to purchase anything as long as I'm in bondage to Aaron. So, I'd like to 'freeload' off you for a little while," Rhonda smiled.

"Freeload all you want," I laughed. "This house is too big anyway."

"It's just until my divorce is final and I can find something here that I like," Rhonda commented.

"No, please stay as long as you want," I

offered.

"Thank you, Millie," Rhonda smiled.

She looked at Greg and he smiled at her. Fifty states in the country, and my sister wants to stay in South Carolina. Hmm, I wonder why? How much did Greg have to do with her decision? The thought of the two of them made me smile.

"You know, the Donovans' house is for sale," I suggested. "Maybe you could look at it before you leave."

"Where is it?" Rhonda asked.

"About three houses down. It's a beautiful home," I commented. "Their daughter Lisa is a close friend of Kirsten's and one of her bridesmaids. I think their house is five bedrooms and five and a half baths."

"Oh, that's way too big!" Rhonda stated. "I don't need that much room anymore. It's just me, and even if Ginny and AJ come to visit, I still wouldn't need more than three bedrooms."

"What about when the rest of us come to visit?" Ellen joked.

"Well, I'll just send you all down here to Millie's house," Rhonda laughed.

"Hey, I've served my time. Now, it's your turn," I smiled.

"Actually, I was thinking of something a little further out, away from the beach," Rhonda commented.

"I thought you loved the beach," Nora said.

"I do, but not enough to buy a house on it," Rhonda said.

"So, where 'a little further out' were you thinking?" Ellen asked.

"Oh, I don't know, maybe in Freeman County," Rhonda said. "They have some nice ranches out there. You know I love horses."

"Uh huh, horses, right? Freeman County. Greg, isn't that where you live?" I asked.

"Um, no, actually, I live in Jemison County," Greg said.

"Which is right next to Freeman County," I said, smiling.

"Just who do the two of you think you're fooling? We all know there's something going on. The question is, when are you two going to stop denying it and admit how you feel about one another?" Ellen asked.

"We're just friends," Rhonda and Greg said together.

Later that afternoon after we'd all had lunch, we met the others at the church to see how the coordinator was coming with the decorations. Clayton and I had hired the best coordinator in South Carolina when Kirsten first started planning her wedding. The entire church looked beautiful. Kirsten had chosen the colors purple, lavender and silver. The guys were going to wear black tuxedos. There were beautiful arrangements on every pew, with ribbons linking them together. We went back to the church for the rehearsal at 3:00 p.m. The directress was like a major in the armed services. She took her job very seriously, although everyone wanted to joke around during rehearsal. There were six bridesmaids and groomsmen, and one matron of honor and best man. There were two flower girls, and one ring bearer. She wanted for Shauna to be included, so Shauna was a junior bridesmaid. After everyone knew their place, and the songs were timed perfectly, we were all ready to eat. We were at the church until 6:30, with a 7 o'clock reservation at the restaurant.

The rehearsal dinner was to be held at Delvecchio's Restaurant. Kirsten loved Italian food and it was the restaurant where Robert proposed, so it was only fitting that they wanted to host the dinner there. When we got to the restaurant, there was a private room decorated festively for the occasion. Everything was going exactly as Kirsten wanted, with exception of Clayton's absence. She and Robert gave the wedding party their gifts and got up to make speeches thanking everyone for their help and participation in making everything come together so well. Everyone toasted champagne, with exception of Nora, Erin, Ellen, Gina and me. We drank ginger ale instead. Kirsten was so happy. There were times when I didn't think I'd make it this far with my daughter as far as her wedding was concerned. God knew she needed one of her parents to be here for her. We always figured that parent would be her father, but fate has a habit of putting a twist of irony into every situation. This wasn't the ideal scenario, but I suppose sometimes we have to just play the hand that life deals us. We stayed at the restaurant until almost 10:30 talking and enjoying each other's company.

Kyle and Erin went on home because Erin wasn't feeling well. The past month had been hard on her. She was in her sixth month, and had to stop working until after she had the babies. She was not on complete bed rest, but her doctor advised because of the stress on her job at the advertising agency, that she needed to take off until after the babies were born. Her feet were swollen, so she was going to wear flats at the wedding. She had to have her dress let out because she'd gotten bigger carrying the twins. When she was fitted, they tried to anticipate how much bigger it would need to be. When she picked up her dress a week ago, the maternity bodice was a little too snug around her belly, so it had to be let out a little more. Kirsten was going to stay at our house and get ready there in her old room. Robert was going to be at his parents' house. They were both going to stay in Kirsten's apartment, since her lease's end coincided with the finishing of their new house. Robert's apartment lease was up at the end of November, so he decided to move out early into Kirsten's apartment. Everything was going perfectly according to plan. Kirsten playfully shooed Robert out of our house at 11:55 p.m. and told him that the next time he'd see her would be when she was walking down the aisle. Shauna and Tim went up to bed, but the rest of us seemed to have had a caffeine overdose. Kirsten was understandably jittery. Being with her brought back so many memories. We all stayed up really late that night, reminiscing about our own weddings.

"Ellen, remember when you got married? The best man had the hiccups," Rhonda smiled.

"Oh, I'd forgotten about that! Jim, you were standing there, and every time you tried to say your vows, Craig would hiccup," Ellen laughed.

"It wouldn't have been so distracting had he not been standing right next to me," Jim said.

"Yeah, and the preacher stopped and asked if Craig needed to be excused," I laughed.

"What did he say?" Kirsten smiled.

"He told them to hold on a minute, went to the water fountain, came back and said, 'okay, I'm ready now,'" Ellen laughed.

"The whole church laughed at him," Jim smiled.

"Mom, tell me about your wedding," Kirsten said.

"Oh, honey, we've talked about my wedding so much," I sighed.

"Millie's wedding was beautiful!" Nora said. "Mom's dress was a perfect fit for her."

"No it wasn't!   I had to lose ten pounds to get into her dress!" I spoke up.

"When?   I don't remember you dieting to lose for that dress," Ellen said.

"I used to work out every night, and I stopped drinking sodas until my wedding.   I was a fanatic about getting into that dress," I said.

"Yeah, Mom wanted all of us to wear it," Nora said.   "Too bad I eloped.   I never got the chance to wear it."

"Too late now!   You couldn't fit into that dress if we paid you!" Rhonda laughed.

"I'll bet I could!" Nora challenged.

"Oh, please!   Nora, that dress was a size eight. You've got to be at least a ten," Rhonda said.

"Okay, enough about my size. You're not exactly skin and bones yourself, Dear. Besides, it only means I've filled out in all the right places," Nora smiled.

"Excuses, excuses," Rhonda laughed.

"Well, my dress is beautiful. I can show it to you since Robert's gone," Kirsten offered.

"We'd love to see it!" Ellen said.

"We'll sit this one out," Bill said.

Sans the men, we all went upstairs to Kirsten's room. Her dress was hanging on her closet door, still zipped up.

"I had it zipped up, because Robert was up here earlier, and I didn't want for him to see it," Kirsten smiled as she unzipped it.

Her dress was white with diamond stones around the choker neck, which connected to the shoulder and long satin sleeves. The chest part was tulle, with a form-fitting satin bodice. At the waist, it was a fanned out floor-length skirt with layers and layers of tulle material. At the very bottom was a three inch satin trim, with the diamond designs identical to the ones in the choker. Her train was made of satin material with more diamond designs, with a huge bow where the train met at the waist. Her train was beautifully decorated with satin roses and diamond accents.

"Oh, Kirsten! Your gown is beautiful!" Ellen exclaimed.

I'd not seen Kirsten's dress yet, because it had been at her apartment since she picked it up a week ago. I was totally shocked because it was the dress that I liked the most when we were looking months ago.

"You got this one?" I smiled, with tears in my eyes.

"I kept coming back to it, so I knew it must have been the one," Kirsten smiled.

"Kirsten and I saw this dress back during the summer, and she tried it on then," I said. "I fell in love with it when I saw it, but I told her that she should keep looking until she found what caught her eye."

"I loved the dress too, but I know Mom. She would swear I was getting it because she loved it. So, I decided to indulge her and look at other dresses, but deep down, I knew this was the one," Kirsten said.

As we stood there talking, I felt sick. I tried not to lose composure, but apparently, the pain showed on my face.

"Millie, what's wrong?" Nora asked.

"I-I'm fine. Just tired I guess," I tried to muster a smile.

"You don't look fine," Kirsten said in a concerned tone. "Why don't you lie down?"

"It's just been a long day. I'll be fine," I said.

I suddenly felt lightheaded, and I didn't remember much after that. When I awakened, my sisters were leaning down over me, and Kirsten had smelling salts, waving them under my nose. I wasn't sure how long I was passed out, but I figured it couldn't have been too long. It looked as if we were still in Kirsten's room.

"Mom, you're going to bed, now," Kirsten said.

"H-how long was I out?" I asked.

"Just a couple of minutes. I'm really worried about you. Are you going to be up for my wedding tomorrow?" Kirsten asked.

"Of course, I am. I'll be fine. I just need to get a good night's sleep," I smiled.

"Come on, help me get her up," Kirsten said to my sisters. At that point, Kirsten and Rhonda helped me to stand. Nora opened the door, as they guided me into my room.

"Millie, maybe this wedding is a little too much for you," Ellen said, as we entered my room.

"No, I did not come this far to miss my little girl's wedding. I'm going to be there if you have to roll me in on a stretcher," I insisted, as they gently sat me on the bed.

"Maybe Kyle should give you away," Ellen suggested.

"No, because he's a groomsman, and so is Tim," Kirsten said.

"What about Greg? He's right downstairs. He'd be perfect," Rhonda suggested.

"That's a good idea," Nora said.

"But, Uncle Greg doesn't have a tuxedo," Kirsten cried.

"I don't think it's mandatory to give you away," Nora said.

"Listen everyone, I'm going to give my daughter away, just like we planned," I insisted.

"Mom, I don't think you're up for it," Kirsten said, shaking her head.

"I'm up for it," I smiled. "Now, will you

372

please let me get some rest so I can do my part tomorrow?" Everyone looked at me, as if they were afraid to leave me alone. "I know you're thinking that I won't be here tomorrow. I've been dealt some pretty raw deals, but I've not come this far not to make it to Kirsten's wedding. The wedding's less than 24 hours away. I'll be fine."

"I'm going to stay with you for the night," Kirsten said.

"You'll do no such thing. You're the bride, and you have to get a good night's sleep," I insisted.

"I'll stretch out on the sofa," Gina offered.

"Please, I'm not an invalid. I won't fade away into the night," I said. "Besides, Gina, you're pregnant. You need to be comfortable in a bed."

"Your sofa is comfortable enough. I'll be fine for tonight," Gina insisted.

"I think its best that someone be with you tonight, Mom. Now, if you won't let me stay, at least let one of your sisters stays with you," Kirsten pleaded.

"Fine, fine. Have it your way," I said throwing my hands up. I knew I was fighting a losing battle.

"I'm going to let Alex know that I'm staying in here tonight instead of the guesthouse," Gina said, standing to leave. "Then, I'll be back, okay?"

"Okay, Gina," I smiled.

"We're going to lie down. Gina, if you need anything, just yell. We're right down the hall," Nora said, as Gina was about to leave out.

"Okay," Gina said.

All of my sisters left, but Kirsten wanted to

stay with me until Gina returned. There was so much fear in my little girl's eyes. I looked at her and smiled, as I stroked her hair. She started to cry, as she laid her head on my shoulders.

"Sweetie, I'm going to be fine," I soothed.

"S-so much has happened over the past few months! Losing Daddy! And now, the night before my wedding, I might lose you too!" Kirsten cried. "What did we ever do to deserve this!?"

"It's not for us to figure out," I whispered. "You know, there were so many times after your father died, when I wanted to just give up. I wanted to go on and be with him. He used to come to me in these visions, and for a while, I thought I was going insane. I still dream of your father from time to time, but I realized that God kept me here for a reason. Yes, we'd been trying to prepare emotionally for my death, but that wasn't in God's plan. Just as it isn't in God's plan for me to miss your wedding," I said.

"Mom, I'm so scared! I keep wondering what kind of wife and mother I will be, if I'll be nearly as good as you've been over the years. I need you here to guide me. You've been so strong throughout your illness, throughout everything. I'm just scared that this could be too much for you. We've pushed the envelope so much with your health. You keep over exerting yourself, trying to do too much," Kirsten cried.

"I promise to take it easy, okay? The wedding's just about over; you and Robert will go on your honeymoon, and I'll be fine," I reassured.

"You say that, but I know you. Now, you're

going to be worried about Erin and the babies. Since she's been off of work, you've been getting Miriam to take you over there," Kirsten said.

I looked at her. "How did you know about my going over there?" I asked.

"Erin was talking about how sweet you were to come over there just about every day to check on her, and you'd always offer a helping hand. She told me that she felt guilty because you were dealing with your own illness, and that she didn't want you doing too much for her," Kirsten said.

"I was hoping you wouldn't find out about that," I smiled. "I just need something to do, Kirsten. Shauna and Tim are back in school, so I'm bored most of the day. I need an outlet. Worrying about all of you provides that outlet."

"Mom, it's time to worry about yourself. I want you to fight this cancer as long as you can," Kirsten said.

"But, don't you see? Fussing over you and Erin and the rest of my children gives me something to look forward to everyday. That keeps me going. Having too much time on my hands causes me to start feeling sorry for myself. You remember when Rhonda and Nora stayed with us a couple of months and they were helping you with the wedding plans?"

"Yeah," Kirsten said.

"Honey, I just about went insane, because I didn't have anything to do," I said. "You all have been handling me with kid gloves. I needed to get control of something again. When Erin's doctor took her off of work a couple of weeks ago, it was like an answer to a prayer. Not that I want for my daughter-in-law to be sick, but it gave me somewhere else to channel my restless energy. I've been a housewife ever since your father and I married. I've always had someone to take care of, and old habits die hard," I said cavalierly.

"You take your illness so lightly," Kirsten said softly.

"I can't let the cancer control me, I have to control the cancer," I stated.

"Just be careful, Mom. You just started back with the radiation and chemo. They're killing your bad cells to get you ready for your transplant. You have to take it easy," Kirsten said.

"I promise to be more careful," I smiled. "Nora and I will go into the hospital on Monday, I'll have my transplant, and everything will be good again. Trust me."

We sat there quietly for the next few minutes until Gina came back into my room. She'd already changed into her night clothes and brought in a blanket and pillow. I kissed Kirsten goodnight on the forehead, and she left and went to her room. Gina looked at me as she was about to lie down.

"You are so strong, Millie," Gina smiled.

"You think so?" I asked.

"Yes, I do. You've been through so much, and I honestly don't think I could do it if I were you," Gina said. "I would have given up a long time ago."

"Thank you, Gina," I smiled. "I'm proud of you, too. How have you been feeling?"

"I'm feeling fine," Gina smiled.

"Did you tell Mark about the pregnancy?"

"Yes, I did," Gina said.

"And what was his response?"

"He wanted to go ahead and get married. Can you believe that? He thought it was the answer to all of our problems."

"He doesn't give up too easily, does he?"

"No, he doesn't," Gina said.

"Did you tell him about Alex?"

"No, I didn't."

"Why not?" I asked.

"Because I don't know how long Alex and I will be together," Gina said.

"I don't understand."

"Alex and I have been having a lot of problems. Millie, I can't seem to be proud of my relationship with her."

"Why do you think that is?"

"I think you already know. Being pregnant seems to make me a little less gay."

"What's that supposed to mean?"

"I don't know. The pregnancy feels right. It feels natural. Mark and I have been communicating a lot more. He's so excited about the baby. And I also found out that Nikki's child isn't his."

"That still doesn't change the fact that he cheated on you," I reasoned.

"I know, Millie. And you're right. But, the man I fell in love with, he's still there. He annoys me half the time, but, I love the way I feel when I'm with him. It feels right."

"So, what exactly are you saying, Gina?"

"I'm saying that I'm going to end things with Alex."

"Are you sure that's what you want to do?"

"Millie, I care about Alex, but, she's not who I'm supposed to spend my life with. It's just not what I want."

"Are you saying you don't want to lead a gay lifestyle?"

"I should feel comfortable, right?"

"Well, of course, you should."

"I don't, Millie. As much as I care about Alex, I'm in love with Mark. It feels right with him. I don't feel ashamed of it; I look forward to seeing him. He comes into my office and rubs my stomach, talking to the baby as if he or she can hear him," Gina smiled.

"And you like that?" I smiled.

"I love it. My relationship with Alex has always felt so dirty and wrong. That's why I couldn't tell anyone about her. I don't have her pictures up in my office. I don't even have her picture at my apartment. Shouldn't I be showing off the person I'm with?"

"If it's right, yeah, you should."

"So, why do I still have a picture of Mark on my fireplace mantle? Why did I keep a picture of him on my desk?"

"Gina, it sounds like you've made your own decision about this. Are you going to get back together with Mark?"

"I want to. I really want to," Gina smiled.

"I worry about you."

378

"Why?"

"Because a few months ago, we stood right in my kitchen downstairs and I asked you how you felt about Alex. You told me that you cared about her and that you were comfortable with your life with her. What's happened to change that, Gina? You've never been known for being fickle."

"Alex can't accept my child, Millie," Gina sighed. "This baby is a part of me. How can she not accept someone who's a part of me?"

"Maybe because you cheated on her when you got pregnant. How did you feel when you thought that other baby was Mark's? You didn't accept that baby with open arms."

"You're right."

"Maybe Alex feels the same way."

"But, it's different," Gina said.

"How? Because both of you are women? She should understand your need to be with a man from time to time? Gina, that's not fair. If you're going to lead a life as a woman who's with a woman, you have to treat it like any other serious relationship. In other words, there can be no men in your life for intimate purposes."

"You're right, Millie. That's why I know I have to end it. I never cheated on Mark. Will you give me your blessing to do this?"

"Gina, you don't need it," I smiled. "I told you that a long time ago. If you want to work things out with Mark, do it. But, it's time for you to make damn sure you know what you want. Maybe you should be alone for a while. Don't be with anyone until you can figure out what or who you want."

"That's a good idea," Gina said. "Thanks for the advice, Millie. I'm going to let you get some sleep now."

"Goodnight, Gina."

"Goodnight, Millie," Gina said, as she turned off the lamp next to the sofa.

Chapter Eighteen

When I woke up the next morning, the sun was shining brightly. It was a beautiful fall day, and as I looked out the window, I knew it was the perfect day for a wedding. I smiled thinking about my daughter's big day. Everything was going to be perfect for Kirsten and Robert. I looked at the clock. It was almost 8:30 a.m. In 7 ½ hours, my baby would be walking down the aisle to the man with whom she was going to spend the rest of her life. I looked over at Gina lying on the sofa. She was still sleeping peacefully. She'd always been a heavy sleeper, even as a child. I'm sure it has gotten progressively worse since her pregnancy. I didn't want to disturb her, so I slipped on my robe and tiptoed out the door, down to Kirsten's room. I knocked softly as I entered.

"Kirsten?" I called out.

She wasn't in her bed. I knocked on her bathroom door. No answer. She must have been downstairs eating breakfast already. I went downstairs, and she was sitting at the kitchen counter reading the paper and drinking a cup of coffee. I'd given Miriam the day off because she wanted to attend the wedding. She looked up and smiled when I walked in.

"Good morning, Mom," Kirsten smiled.

"Good morning, Dear."

"How are you feeling?" Kirsten asked.

"I'm feeling so much better. I think I was just fatigued last night," I said. I looked at her as I observed the coffee. "Do you really think caffeine is a good idea?"

"It's decaf cappuccino," Kirsten said. "Why don't you join me?"

"Thanks, I will." I poured a cup and sat down across from Kirsten. "Are you nervous?" I asked.

"Like you wouldn't believe. This is probably going to be the most nerve-wrecking day of my entire life. I mean, all eyes will be on me as I walk down the aisle. Everything has to be perfect, Mom."

"It will be," I smiled, placing my hand on hers.

"Robert's been so wonderful," Kirsten smiled. "He's suffered through more than his share of my nervous breakdowns over the past few weeks."

"That comes with the territory," I smiled.

"Mom, how did you and Dad make it for 26 years? So many marriages end in divorce these days," Kirsten sighed.

"The best advice I can give you is to keep God first in your marriage, and like my grandmother said when someone asked her how she stayed married for over fifty years, 'don't go anywhere,'" I smiled, as I sipped my cappuccino.

"I don't get it," Kirsten responded in a confused tone.

"In other words, no matter what, stay with your husband. If you argue, don't run out. Stay and work it out. There's no staying power in the majority of marriages today," I sighed. "Everyone runs for the hills at the least little sign of trouble. The vows say 'for better or worse,' not 'for better or better.' Things won't always be perfect. But, you have to love him enough to work through things."

"But, look at Aunt Rhonda and what she's gone through," Kirsten protested.

"Sweetie, Aaron was in a class by himself," I said. "Aaron showed signs of being an abusive man before they ever married. He was always cruel to her."

"Really? I had no idea," Kirsten said.

"Yeah. I remember once before they got married, Rhonda was supposed to be meeting him at a restaurant for lunch," I said. "She was 15 minutes late, because she'd been in class and had some questions for her professor afterwards. He waited until she got there, and stood up and looked at her. He said to her loudly, 'I wanted you to feel the inconvenience I just felt for the past 15 minutes. Buy your own damned lunch.' Then, he walked off, leaving her standing there with everyone staring at her."

"Oh, my goodness! How mean!" Kirsten said.

"Oh, Honey, that was the lesser of so many evils. He was always doing things to make Rhonda look bad in front of others. He seemed to get some sort of high off of it. So, the writing was on the wall before she ever said 'I Do' to him," I said.

Kirsten looked at me slyly. "Mom, did anything ever happen between Aunt Rhonda and Uncle Greg when they were younger?"

"No, nothing serious. He escorted her when she won Homecoming Queen in their senior year. He really had feelings for her, but she wouldn't give him the time of day. She was such a fool for Aaron at the time."

"Why didn't Uncle Aaron escort her?"

"Because he was in college, and according to him, he claimed he couldn't get away in time to be there as her escort. He didn't call until one hour before he was supposed to be there to pick her up. He went to school two hours away in Atlanta, so he could have called before then," I said, shaking my head.

"Boy, he didn't give her much notice, did he?" Kirsten asked.

"No. I believe that deep down, he was hoping she wouldn't be able to find anyone to escort her in time, so that she would look bad. But, as it stood, Greg played on the football team, and the ceremony was for half-time. Greg had hurt his shoulder, so he wasn't able to play in the game anyway."

384

"How did he know she needed an escort?"

"She and your aunt Vivian were good friends. Vivian had skipped a grade, so her, your father and his twin brother Payton were a year behind Rhonda and Greg," I clarified. "She cried to Vivian that Aaron had done it to her again, and that she didn't know what she was going to do. Vivian suggested Greg because he wasn't playing anyhow."

"So, Uncle Greg felt sorry for her and took her?"

"Well, something like that. Like I said, Greg had a crush on your aunt, so he thought this would be a good way to show her what she meant to him."

"But, she forgave Uncle Aaron?"

"That's the strange part. There was a Homecoming dance after the game that night. Greg thought he'd really have a shot with Rhonda, because he was not only going to escort her out on the football field, but he was going to be her date for the dance afterwards. He escorted her onto the football field, she won the title, and he was her date for the dance," I said.

"So, things went according to plan?" Kirsten asked.

"Well, that's where it gets a little sticky," I said.

"Well, what happened?"

"Aaron showed up," I said.

"What? I thought he'd said he couldn't make it," Kirsten said.

"That's what he told her. Apparently, he changed his mind, and showed up at the dance," I sighed. "She melted like butter with a hot knife going through it. Despite the fact that she'd said she was finished with him, she was so wooed by the fact that he went through 'all that trouble' coming home for her sake, until she left the dance with Aaron, leaving Greg there looking foolish. Greg was always so mild-mannered. He didn't tell her how hurt he was by what she did, but Clayton knew. Your father told me about it when we started dating. I was wondering why she ended up coming home with Aaron, when she'd been crying over him a few short hours before."

"Boy, he did a lot to her," Kirsten sighed.

"Kirsten, you have no idea," I said. "So, unless Robert has shown signs of being abusive, cheating, or being too lazy to hold a job, then everything else, you should be able to work through."

"You always put my mind at ease," Kirsten smiled, with tears in her eyes.

"That's what I'm here for," I smiled.

As we sat there, the entourage came in.

"Well, here she is," Ellen said.

"What time did you two get up?" Gina asked, yawning.

"Oh, I've been down here for a few minutes," I smiled. "You were sleeping so well, I didn't want to disturb you."

"So much for keeping your eyes on her," Nora rolled her eyes.

"So what, am I fired as my sister's baby-sitter?" Gina smiled.

"Don't worry about it. You were tired, and you're pregnant. But, we have a big day ahead of us,"

I said, standing.

Around that time, the phone and the doorbell started to ring. We'd been getting gifts delivered to our house for the past couple of weeks. A little before 9:30, Kirsten's bridesmaids started to arrive. My gift to them was to have them to go in for pampering before the wedding. One of the local pampering spas set aside several hours to work on everyone. Everyone was going to get a one hour massage, their hair, nails and make-up done. It was going to take almost three hours, so they needed enough time. It was a rather large spa, so everyone would be able to get individualized attention without having to wait. The limo arrived to pick them up at 10:00 a.m. They were going to come back to the house around two, just in enough time to get changed and to the church.

"Why didn't you get a pampering for yourself?" Rhonda asked.

"I have a million things to do. This is Kirsten's special day, and I want for everything to be perfect," I smiled.

After the limo left with the bridal party, Kirsten and Shauna, the phone rang. It was the caterer at the hotel. They were unable to get in touch with the wedding planner, so they called me. Apparently, the delivery had gotten mixed up, and the colossal shrimp that Kirsten had been looking forward to wasn't going to get there in time. So, they wanted permission to substitute it for something else. Kirsten's one wish, out of everything on the menu was colossal shrimp.

"Well, what will it take to get it here?" I snapped.

"The earliest it can get here would be tonight, which won't be until after the reception starts," the caterer said.

"That's not good enough. My daughter specifically requested this months ago. Now, I don't care what it takes, but you find exactly what my daughter wants if you have to call every restaurant in town!" I yelled.

"Mrs. Welby, that could take a while, not to mention it could be very expensive," the caterer said.

"I don't care. We won't be paying any more money for it because we've already paid $25 for each pound. Now, this is your screw up. Fix it!" I said, slamming down the phone.

"Millie, what's wrong?" Ellen asked.

"The caterer screwed up. You know how Kirsten loves shrimp. She wanted colossal shrimp to be served at the reception. There's been some sort of delivery mix up and the caterer is saying that the shrimp won't get here in time."

"Why did they call you? Isn't that a headache the wedding planner should be dealing with? I mean isn't that what you're paying her to do?" Nora asked.

"They couldn't reach her and I was the other point of contact," I said. "They left her a message and called me."

"Well from the sounds of it, you took care of things," Nora smiled, patting me on the back. "My kinda girl! You handled it just the way I would have. There's no time for slacking off on the job."

Everyone laughed at Nora complimenting me on being hard on the caterer. It was never in my nature to not be understanding, but this day was too important to Kirsten. There was no room for mistakes. She was nervous enough as it was. I was glad she was gone to the spa when the call came in. That was just one more thing she would have been worried about. The rest of the morning and afternoon were hectic. The wedding planner called back a couple of hours later saying that the problem had been resolved, and that the caterers had gotten the shrimp we ordered. She also apologized to me for the caterers bothering me with the problem because they didn't reach her. As if that weren't enough to deal with, I couldn't find the bracelet I'd brought for Kirsten. It was supposed to be her 'something new.'

While I was upstairs, Vivian and her family, Clayton's parents, Greg, Andrew and his family all arrived. Vivian and Nina came into my room, as I was coming out of my bathroom in my robe. Nina had a pair of sapphire earrings, as her something blue for Kirsten. The something old was the antique hairpin my mother had left Rhonda. And Ellen was going to let her borrow her sixpence from her own wedding.

"Well, where is the bride?" Vivian asked, smiling.

"They're at Sophia's Spa. They should be back pretty soon," I said, looking at the clock. "It's almost 2:30 now."

"Where's her dress?" Nina asked.

"It's in her room down the hall," I smiled. "It's absolutely beautiful!"

"Millie, you look so happy," Nina smiled

389

tearfully.

"I am. My little girl's getting married today. If Robert makes her half as happy as your son made me, she's a blessed woman," I smiled, as a tear ran down my face. "Oh, I guess it's a good thing I haven't done my makeup yet," I laughed.

"We're going to leave you alone to finish getting ready. We'll be downstairs," Nina said.

"Okay, I'll be down in a few minutes," I said, hugging Nina and Vivian.

I looked at my dress hanging on the back of my door, and I looked over at Clayton's picture resting on my bedside table. It was as if he was smiling right at me. I started to think back:

"Do you, Clayton Drew Welby take Millicent Reece McAlray to be your lawfully wedded wife?" Reverend Walker asked.

"I do," Clayton said, looking into my eyes.

"Do you, Millicent Reece McAlray take Clayton Drew Welby to be your lawfully wedded husband?"

"I do," I smiled, as tears ran down my face.

"Repeat after me: I, Clayton, take thee, Millicent to be my wife."

"I, Clayton, take thee, Millicent to be my wife."

"I promise to love, honor and cherish," Reverend Walker said.

"I promise to love, honor and cherish," Clayton repeated.

"In sickness and in health," Reverend Walker said.

"In sickness and in health," Clayton repeated.

"For richer or poorer," Reverend Walker said.

"For richer or poorer," Clayton repeated.

"For better or worse," Reverend Walker said.

"For better or worse," Clayton repeated.

"Until death parts us," Reverend Walker said.

"Until death parts us," Clayton repeated.

"Repeat after me: I, Millicent, take thee, Clayton, to be my husband."

"I, Millicent, take thee, Clayton, to be my husband."

"I promise to love, honor, cherish and obey," Reverend Walker said.

"I promise to love, honor, cherish and obey," I repeated.

"In sickness and in health," Reverend Walker said.

"In sickness and in health," I repeated.

"For richer or poorer," Reverend Walker said.

"For richer or poorer," I repeated.

"For better or worse," Reverend Walker said.

"For better or worse," I repeated.

"Until death parts us," Reverend Walker said.

"Until death parts us," I repeated.

"Do you have the rings?" Reverend Walker asked.

Greg passed the ring Clayton had for me to Reverend Walker, and Rhonda passed the ring I had for Clayton. Reverend Walker then said a touching prayer, blessing our rings.

"With this ring, I thee wed," Reverend Walker said, as Clayton placed the ring on my finger.

391

"With this ring, I thee wed," Clayton repeated.

"With this ring, I thee wed," Reverend Walker said, as I placed the ring on Clayton's finger.

"With this ring, I thee wed," I repeated.

"By the powers vested in me and the state of Alabama, I now pronounce you husband and wife. You may kiss your bride," Reverend Walker smiled.

"Finally," Clayton whispered through his smile as he kissed me. Everyone in the church started to clap.

That was the happiest day of my life. It didn't get any better than it did that day, pledging my love and life to Clayton. We had our whole lives ahead of us. I sighed and smiled, as I thought of Clayton and what that day meant to both of us. Now, it was Kirsten's turn. When we had our children, Clayton and I looked forward to celebrating their weddings with them. We never knew that Kyle would be the only one who would have both of us there for his big day.

I quickly got dressed after doing my makeup. I sat down on the sofa to put my shoes on, and felt something hard underneath me. I moved the pillow over and discovered the box with Kirsten's bracelet. Thank God I found it. I'd wanted it to be a surprise for her. Shortly after I finished getting ready, I heard the girls come in, because they were laughing as they went into Kirsten's room together. After giving myself a once-over in the mirror, I walked out and down the hall to Kirsten's room. Shauna was coming out.

"Hi, Sweetheart," I smiled, hugging her. "How was the spa?"

"Mom, it was great! You should have come! They did our hair and nails! Everything! Do you like this color?" Shauna was absolutely beaming as she showed me her nails. It felt so good seeing my baby smile again.

"It looks great on you," I smiled. "And your hair! It's gorgeous!"

"I don't have on too much make-up, do I? I know you don't like for me to wear a lot of make up," Shauna said.

"It's absolutely perfect!" I said. "Where's your sister?"

"She's getting dressed. I'm about to go to my room and get dressed," Shauna said.

"Do you want me to help you?" I offered.

"Would you?" Shauna asked.

"Of course! Come on," I said, hugging her shoulders.

We went into Shauna's room, and she went into her closet to pull out her dress. It was almost identical to the other bridesmaids' dresses, but it was silver instead of purple or lavender. Kirsten wanted her little sister to stand out and be noticed. I looked at Shauna as she started to undress and I removed her dress from the hanger.

"I'm sorry we haven't spent much time together lately, Sweetheart," I smiled.

"That's okay. It's a lot going on getting ready for a wedding," Shauna smiled.

"Well, after all this madness is over and after

393

my transplant, we're going to try to do something together, just the two of us, okay?" I asked.

"Okay," Shauna smiled.

"I love seeing you smile, Angel," I said, pinching her cheek.

"Mom!   My make-up!" Shauna laughed.

"Oops!   Sorry, Sweetheart," I laughed.

I helped Shauna to step into her dress, and then I zipped it up for her. She turned around and faced me, with a smile a mile wide on her face. She was happy. Even if it was just for today, just for this moment, my child was happy. For the first time in over a year, my daughter didn't have a care in the world. She was just a 12 year old, plain and simple. Why couldn't everyday be like this? But, I knew deep down, that tomorrow would be a different story. She would go back to worrying about me and my health, and whether or not I was going to leave her, especially since I would be going back into the hospital on Monday. She had too many stresses and strains for someone her age. When I first found out about my cancer, Clayton and I debated for three days about whether we should tell Shauna when we told the rest of them. She was only 11 at the time, and that was a pretty big cross to bear for someone so young. We decided to roll the dice and tell her, and ever since then, I've regretted it. She's been living her life like a time bomb, waiting to go off. After she put on her shoes, which she was a little wobbly in, I started to worry.

"Honey, are you going to be okay in those shoes?" I asked.

"I'll be fine. I've been practicing walking in them," Shauna smiled.

"Okay, let's see you do it," I smiled.

Shauna walked slowly, trying terribly hard not to mess up. "See? I'll be okay."

"Okay," I sighed. "If you insist. But, just in case you change your mind, I have a little surprise for you."

"What is it?"

"Come with me." We went into my bedroom, and I looked in my closet. I handed her a shoe box.

"What's this?" Shauna asked, looking at me.

"'Rescue shoes,'" I smiled. "They're the same shoe, just with no heel."

"Mom, I'll be fine," Shauna smiled as she rolled her eyes.

"Take them just in case," I smiled.

"Okay," Shauna sighed.

I looked at the clock on my bedside table as were about to walk out. It was almost three o'clock. The wedding was supposed to start in just a little over an hour.

"My goodness, we'd better hurry. The wedding's supposed to start soon," I said.

We went into Kirsten's room, which was totally chaotic. Everyone was talking and laughing at once, as they all hovered around the bride. Erin was sitting in a chair, drinking a milkshake. Kirsten was standing in front of a full-length mirror, as one of her bridesmaids was putting her veil on her head. She turned around and smiled as she looked at me. I stood there frozen, as I looked at the most beautiful bride I'd ever seen. I started to cry.

"Oh, Kirsten!" I smiled. "You look beautiful!"

"Thank you, Ma," Kirsten smiled, with tears in her eyes. "I can't seem to stop crying. They've had to touch up my make up twice since we left the spa."

"Sweetie, this is one of the most important days of your life; you deserve to be emotional," I smiled. I looked over at Erin. "Erin, Sweetheart, are you okay?"

"I feel great, Mom. That spa was just what I needed. Now, if I can convince Kyle to do that for me once a week, everything would be perfect," Erin smiled.

"You're on your own on that one," I smiled. "Can I have a few moments alone with the bride?" I asked, looking around.

"Sure," Madeline, Kirsten's matron of honor smiled.

Everyone left out, including Shauna. I stood there quietly, smiling and looking at Kirsten. I hugged her.

"You are such a beautiful bride!" I smiled. "Oh, I said that already, didn't I?"

"That's okay. I don't mind hearing it again," Kirsten smiled.

"I want you to be happy. You both deserve all the happiness that I had with your father and then some. Robert's a wonderful guy, and I know you two are making the right choice."

"Mom, I'm so nervous. I mean, what if I trip up as I'm going down the aisle! What if no one attends? What if I forget my vows?" Kirsten said.

396

"Boy, talk about deja vu!" I smiled.

"What do you mean?" Kirsten asked.

"Do you know that I asked my mom almost exactly the same questions, almost word for word, on my wedding day?" I laughed.

"You're kidding?"

"No, I'm not. The only other thing I wondered about was what was expected of me on my wedding night."

Kirsten blushed slightly and smiled.

"I get the feeling you won't be questioning me about that," I said jokingly.

"Mom, you've told me about the birds and the bees years ago," Kirsten smiled.

"Yes, and you told me when you lost your virginity," I said. "But, either way, tonight will be the beginning of a whole new life for you. It'll be like no other experience you've ever had, because it will be your first time with Robert knowing you as his wife, and that makes all the difference in the world."

"Did you see the bouquet he sent me?" Kirsten smiled. Pointing to her dresser. It was a beautiful bouquet of two dozen lavender roses, with a beautiful purple and silver bow.

"Oh, how beautiful!" I exclaimed.

"He sent them to me at the spa. I was getting a facial when the delivery guy brought them in. I was so shocked! He knows how much I love purple," Kirsten said. "It was a beautiful surprise."

"Oh, speaking of surprises," I said, reaching into my pocket. "Here's something new." I handed her the box with the bracelet in it.

397

"What's this?" Kirsten smiled.

"Open it up and see," I smiled.

Kirsten opened the box. "Oh, Mom, it's beautiful!" Kirsten hugged me, crying.

"You know, if we keep this up, neither one of us will be in any shape to make it down the aisle," I said through my tears. "We'd better get ready to head to the church."

"Okay," Kirsten smiled.

"Do you have everything?" I asked.

"Yes, I think so," Kirsten said. She had a bag with everything she could possibly need: makeup, small sewing kit, her slippers, tissues, and any other emergency items she could think of. The bag was a gift from her wedding planner. I looked at her.

"Oh, dear, you don't have your earrings on," I said.

"Oh, I almost forgot! Grandma Nina came in here earlier with a pair of sapphire earrings. That was perfect since it's my birth stone and something blue. And, let's see. Aunt Rhonda gave me the antique pin, so that's something old," Kirsten said, reaching up to her head to show me the pin. "And Aunt Ellen let me borrow her sixpence, so I'm ready to go," Kirsten smiled.

"Don't you want to go ahead and put the earrings in?" I suggested.

"I guess I should," Kirsten smiled, taking them out of the box. She put the left one in perfectly, but the right one refused to go in. "Oh, dammit!"

"What's wrong, Dear?" I asked.

"I can't get the earring in!" Kirsten started to

panic.

"Calm down, Sweetie. Let me try," I offered. I took the earring from her shaking hands. I didn't have much better luck than she did.

"Ouch!" Kirsten winced in pain.

"Sorry, Sweetheart. Come on, let's get to the church and see if someone can get it in." As we walked out the door, we were met by Nora and Ellen.

"Oh, Kirsten!" Nora whispered. "You look beautiful!" She hugged Kirsten. She then looked at her and frowned. "Darling, why are you wearing only one earring?"

"Oh, Mom!" Kirsten started to cry uncontrollably.

"What did I say?" Nora asked.

"Kirsten can't get the other earring in," I said, hugging Kirsten.

"Is that all? Hush with all of that crying! That's what we're here for! We'll get the earring in," Nora said.

With every effort being made, no one was able to get the earring into Kirsten's ear. Her ear was starting to get sore. This was not good. Kirsten was frantic enough. The last thing she needed was for something like this to happen. Then, one of her bridesmaids had an idea.

"There's an accessory shop in the mall on the way to the church. Why don't we stop by and let them put it in?" Trista suggested.

"What time is it?" I asked.

"It's 3:20. The wedding's due to start in 40 minutes," Rhonda said, looking at her watch.

"Well, they can't start without the bride," I said.

"Mom! I have a defective ear! I-I'm going to be without my earring!" Kirsten cried, shaking her head.

"No, Kirsten, your ear isn't defective. The hole's just closed up. Come on, let's go," I said.

"Let's just call the whole thing off! I can't go down the aisle like this! What will Robert think?" Kirsten cried.

"Sweetheart, we'll buy you clip-ons if we have to," Rhonda laughed.

"N-No! These are the earrings I want to wear because Grandma gave them to me!" Kirsten continued to cry.

"Honey, you're going to ruin your make up," Ellen said.

"Everything's ruined already!" Kirsten cried. She was turning red in the face, and her make-up was pretty much a thing of the past.

"Kirsten, calm down. We're going to go to the accessory shop and have them to re-open your ear, okay?" I said.

"W-What if they can't!? What if m-my ear is closed forever!?" Kirsten cried.

My little girl was falling apart. I wanted terribly to laugh because she was being extremely ridiculous, but, the sad part is, she was completely serious. She really felt as if everything was falling apart. I hugged her as she cried.

"Good thing she didn't know about the shrimp," Nora said.

"Nora!" Ellen said, shushing her.

Kirsten lifted her head from my shoulder in alarm. "What? W-what happened to the shrimp?"

I glared at Nora. I could have committed bloody murder right then and there for Nora opening her mouth.

"Nothing, Kirsten. The shrimp is fine. Everything's fine," I soothed, cutting my eyes at Nora.

She looked at me and shrugged apologetically. She mouthed the words "I'm sorry."

"D-Did something happen to the shrimp?" Kirsten asked shakily.

"Sweetheart, everything's fine. The shrimp will be there. But, if we don't get going, you won't be there," I said, smiling.

I walked with her down the stairs. The bridesmaids were going to ride in the limo with Kirsten. The groomsmen and the groom had a limo as well. Kirsten's was white, Robert's was black. Kirsten wanted for me to ride with her. I got into the car with her and we headed to the mall on our way to the church. Lisa tried to touch up Kirsten's make up during our journey to the mall. When we got to the accessory shop, Madeline and I got out with Kirsten, helping her with her gown. We'd thankfully detached the train so that she could move around a little better. As we were walking through the mall, we got plenty of stares from people wondering why we were there, with Kirsten in a wedding dress.

"Mom, everyone's staring at me," Kirsten was about to cry, again.

"No, no, Sweetheart. They're just looking at

401

how pretty you look in your gown," I tried to reassure her.

"That's right, Kirsten. You're such a beautiful bride," Madeline said.

"Oh, you're just trying to make me feel better about looking foolish walking through a mall in my wedding gown!" Kirsten cried. "This day is ruined!"

"No it isn't," I sighed, as we arrived at the accessory shop.

Kirsten's gown was too wide to get through some of the aisles, so Madeline and I both had to lift it for her. The saleswoman as well as several customers looked at us strangely.

"May I help you?" the saleswoman asked skeptically.

"Um, yes. Obviously, my daughter here is about to get married. But, she can't get this earring into her ear because the hole seems to have closed. Can you help us out?" I asked, handing her the earring.

"Um, sure," the saleswoman smiled slightly. "Come on, sit over here."

She guided us to a chair. We looked at Kirsten's gown and then at the chair. It was too big to try to maneuver so that she could sit down.

"Can we do this standing up?" I asked.

"Sure," the saleswoman smiled. "So, what time's the wedding?"

"It's at four," I said.

"Ooh, that's cutting it close," the saleswoman said. Kirsten looked at her alarmingly.

"No, we have plenty of time," I said, eyeing the saleswoman. She caught the hint.

"You're right. And you're such a beautiful bride. It's not as if they can start without you," she said, as she sanitized Kirsten's ear.

"Th-Thank you," Kirsten said.

"So, how many attendants do you have?" she asked, as she put the earring into the gun.

"S-six bridesmaids, th-this is my matron of honor, a-and my little s-sister is a junior bridesmaid," Kirsten said in an almost vacillating tone.

"Oh, that's a pretty big wedding!" she commented, as she positioned the gun onto Kirsten's ear. She was obviously trying to keep Kirsten distracted while she worked. "He must be pretty special for you to go to all this trouble for an earring."

Kirsten smiled. "He is. We've been together for over three years."

"How long have you been engaged?" she asked, as she shot the earring through Kirsten's ear.

"Almost a year now," Kirsten smiled. She didn't even realize that the earring was in her ear. She was starting to calm down a little.

"There we are," the saleswoman said, as she finished up. She turned Kirsten's face towards her and observed her work. The saleswoman smiled. "Perfect."

"Thank you so much!" I said, as I pulled out the money to pay her.

She stopped me. "Consider it a wedding gift," she smiled.

"Thank you," I smiled. "But, please, take it as a tip if nothing else."

"No, it's quite alright," she smiled, refusing to

403

take the money. She looked at Kirsten and smiled again. "Best wishes to you."

"Thank you," Kirsten smiled.

"Come on, we'd better get going," Madeline said.

We helped Kirsten with her dress, and left out. We got to the car, and from that point on, we headed to the church. I looked at my watch. It was 3:45, but at least the church was only another five minutes away. We sat in the back and toasted with sparkling grape juice. There was a bottle of champagne for the happy couple when they left the reception. As we were all talking, the limo came to a stop. We assumed that he was simply stopping at a red light. Kirsten was talking and laughing, so she didn't notice that we still weren't moving. Several minutes had passed, which indicated that something was wrong. I was sitting against the glass immediately behind the driver. I pushed the button, as the glassed moved down.

"Why aren't we moving?" I whispered.

"There seems to be an accident up ahead. Looks pretty bad," the driver said.

"Oh, boy," I sighed. Just what I needed. To tell my frantic daughter that an accident was going to cause even more of a delay. "Okay, thank you." I pushed the button to move the glass back up. Kirsten looked at me, and stopped smiling.

"Mom, what's wrong? Why are we still sitting here?" Kirsten asked.

"Nothing's wrong, Sweetheart. Everything's fine," I smiled slightly.

"N-No it's not. We're not moving. We've

404

been sitting here for five minutes!" Kirsten started to cry.

"Sweetheart, it's just a little accident up ahead. That's all. It just has traffic moving a little slow. Everything will be fine, Kirsten," I tried to reassure her.

Kirsten began to shake her head. "M-My wedding's ruined!" she cried.

"No, Kirsten, it's not ruined. It's not even four o'clock yet," I said.

"Robert's going to think that I deserted him!" Kirsten cried.

"Oh, Kirsten," I sighed.

"Kirsten, everything's going to be fine. Very few weddings get started on time," Trista said.

"But, mine was supposed to! Th-This is a bad sign!" Kirsten cried.

"No it's not," Greta, one of her other bridesmaids, said. "My wedding didn't start on time, and I'm still married."

"That's right, Kirsten. Don't panic. Everything's still going to be beautiful. Just think, this will only make Robert more anxious to see you. Make him wait a little," Ashley, another bridesmaid, said.

"Wh-what if we're stuck here for hours!?" Kirsten cried, burying her face in her hands.

"I'll call over to the church to let them know what's going on," I suggested as I pulled out my cell phone. I decided to call Rhonda's cell phone.

"Hello?" Rhonda answered.

"Rhonda," I said.

"Millie, where are you?"

"We're stuck behind a bad accident. Just let everyone know that we're on the way," I instructed.

"Okay. Is Kirsten about to fall to pieces?" Rhonda asked.

"Like you wouldn't believe," I sighed.

"Well, were they able to get the earring in?"

"Yes, they were. It's perfect. Hopefully, we'll be there in a few minutes. We're only a couple of minutes from the church." As I was talking, the limo started to move. "Oh, it looks like we're moving. We should be there shortly."

"Okay, bye," Rhonda said.

I hung up the phone. "See, Kirsten? We're moving, and we're only a few blocks from the church."

"W-Was Robert okay?" Kirsten asked.

"Robert was fine. Don't worry," I reassured.

We pulled up to the church at 4:05 p.m. The church was packed. It was a good thing we'd already gotten ready before leaving the house. We'd been trying to debate about using the church dressing rooms, but so we wouldn't forget anything, we figured it was best to dress at home, and do any final touches once we got to the church. We went into the dressing room, where the directress was barking out orders. She wanted the bridesmaids to line up as soon as everyone checked their hair and makeup. Lisa worked on Kirsten again to perfection. Someone handed me a beautiful corsage to put on. I was starting to get a little nervous myself at this point.

A few minutes later, the directress came in to

direct us out to the hallway. Everyone was lined up, as we saw the hostesses go in and take their place. Greg was going to escort me to light the unity candle and then to my seat after I got Kirsten to the pulpit. It was one of those duties that was kind of thrown at him at the last minute. We heard the soft music playing, and shortly thereafter, our male and female soloists started to sing a beautiful duet. I looked at Kirsten, who was shaking. I put my arm around her, to calm her.

"And it's only 4:30," I whispered to her.

"Thank you, Mom," Kirsten smiled.

"For what?"

"For being sane," Kirsten smiled. "Let's face it, you had to be sane enough for both of us."

"Anytime," I smiled, hugging her.

"You're really a pretty bride, Kirsten," Shauna smiled, looking at her sister. "I hope I'm as pretty as you when I get married." I looked at Shauna's feet and smiled. She'd decided to wear the flats after all.

"Thanks, little sis. Trust me, you're going to be a beautiful bride, too. Look at who we take after," Kirsten smiled, looking at me.

I looked at Shauna, as my thoughts drifted to the day when she would marry. I probably wouldn't even be there for it. I held back the tears that stung my eyes. I looked ahead at Tim. One of Kirsten's bridesmaids was about to be escorted in by him. I probably wouldn't be around for his wedding, either. As I stood there, my chest became heavy, and I found it hard to breathe. I didn't want to alarm Kirsten. This day was too important for her. I could do it. I could get through this. I had to, for Kirsten's sake. She'd looked forward to this day for so long. Every girl dreams of her wedding day, and I refused to let Kirsten's be filled with bad memories of something happening to me. She deserved better than that. I silently prayed to have the strength to get through it. 'Just one more day, God,' I prayed. I closed my eyes for a moment, in hopes that the pain would pass. As if I were talking directly to God, He answered my prayers and the pain went away. Maybe it was just a panic attack; I'll never know for certain. The important thing was at least Kirsten's wedding wouldn't be stained with something bad happening to me.

"Okay, it's time," the directress smiled.

I looked at Kirsten as we walked forward slowly. I had my right hand holding her by the elbow, as we walked to the door of the sanctuary. Everyone stood and looked in our direction. Robert was standing up front smiling, and Kirsten smiled at him. From the looks of it, they felt as if they were the only two people in the world. I knew that feeling all too well. I looked at Kirsten, as I saw the tears fall down her face. She was trembling as she smiled through her tears. Robert told her he had a special surprise for her, and as she started walking down the aisle, Robert began to sing to her. He'd written a song for their day, had the music composed for it, and planned it as a surprise for Kirsten. He'd told me about it a few weeks back. The night before, Kirsten commented that she didn't recognize the music the pianist was playing at rehearsal. But, the directress insisted to her

408

that it was a beautiful wedding piece that was fairly new. Kirsten almost stopped walking as she heard Robert singing.

"Now's not the time to stop," I whispered.

"Th-this was my surprise?" Kirsten whispered softly as she smiled through her tears.

We continued our journey down the aisle. It was probably the longest walk of Kirsten's life, but the destination was worth it. When we got to Robert, Greg was waiting for me, as he escorted me to light the unity candle, and then to my seat. It was a little out of sequence, but considering the circumstances, it was fitting. The pastor performed an absolutely beautiful ceremony, as Kirsten and Robert both cried during the exchanging of vows. I cried too, as I watched my daughter marry her soul mate. For some reason, her wedding affected me more than Kyle's did. I guess because he was my son, and daughters are just so different when it comes down to things like that. At the end of the ceremony, Robert kissed his new bride, and the pastor announced that they were Mr. and Mrs. Robert Shane Martin. Everyone stood and applauded as the bride and groom walked briskly down the aisle, followed by the entourage of bridesmaids and groomsmen. Greg escorted me out, as Robert's dad escorted his mom out. Everything went off without a hitch.

After the photographer got the wedding party back into the church for pictures, we headed to the reception to convene with waiting guests. The reception was to be held at the Wyningham Hotel. It was a five-star hotel, because our little girl deserved the best. There was a band, and the lighting was spectacular. We'd been anticipating 350 people, and once again, we missed our mark. There were almost 400 people there, but the wedding planner assured me that the caterers could handle it. They knew they had no choice after the coronary they nearly gave me over the shrimp earlier. The whole night was beautiful. Everything was perfect as Kirsten and Robert were greeted by well-wishers. The reception lasted for over three hours. We'd rented a suite for them to have for the night, so that they could catch their early flight to Hawaii the next morning. All of their things were already at the hotel. Kirsten's luggage was brought over earlier by Madeline and Robert's things were brought over by Carl, his best man. I'd instructed that a bottle of champagne and roses be put into the room as well.

When they got ready to toss the bouquet and garter, my curiosity got the better of me. I nudged Rhonda to try and catch it. As a joke, she got into the crowd of single women wanting desperately to catch the bouquet. As luck would have it, Rhonda caught it. She stood there, completely shocked over the fact that she'd caught the bridal bouquet. When the garter was tossed, who better to catch it than Greg? Which is exactly what happened. It couldn't have gone better if I'd planned it myself. Well, fate was telling the two of them to get together. Now whether they'd listen or not was a completely different thing.

The cakes were beautiful. Kirsten had chosen to have eight separate layers, with the smallest layer sitting the highest with the bride and groom on top.

The descending layers got larger, with equal sizes on each side. They curved around to meet up at a large round layer cake at the base. There were lavender flowers on it of course. The groom's cake was a set of chocolate, large square cakes, with grapes cascading down each one. The setting was exactly like the bride's cake. But, instead of eight layers, there were only six.

Everything was wonderful. It was truly a storybook wedding. My princess had her prince, and they had their whole lives ahead of them. This was a day I'd remember for the rest of my life. I was able to forget my troubles, even if it was just for one night. The smiles on my daughter and new son-in-law's faces were enough to last a lifetime. The only thing missing was my husband. I had to believe that Clayton was smiling down from Heaven at his little girl. I smiled as I watched them dancing together. It brought tears to my eyes.

Kirsten and Robert had already said goodbye to all of their guests and retired to their suite in the hotel. Most of the guests had started to leave by 9 o'clock that night. Eventually, I started to grow tired as I sat in a nearby chair and removed my shoes. I yawned as I tried to rub the tired lines from underneath my eyes. I looked towards the doorway and was startled by who I saw. He smiled at me.

"Clayton?" I whispered.

Chapter Nineteen

Everyone was stunned, to say the least. Who was this person? Surely, it wasn't the love of my life. I'd buried him just a few months ago. This wasn't making sense. No, I'd died and I was with him. There was no other explanation.

Everyone looked at me, wondering what to make of this. This couldn't be Clayton.

"Wh-Who are you?" I cried.

"Sweetheart, it's me, Clayton. I've been in the hospital."

"N-No! I just buried my husband! Y-You couldn't be him!" I screamed.

"Who the hell are you?!" Kyle yelled.

"Kyle," Clayton smiled. He tried to hug his son.

"Get away from me! Who are you?" Kyle

asked, pushing him forcefully.

"What is going on? Why don't any of you believe me?" Clayton asked.

"Because this is a sick joke! Now who are you?" Kyle asked. He held me because I became lightheaded.

"D-Daddy?" Shauna cried.

"Hi, Sweetie," Clayton smiled, hugging Shauna.

"Oh, Daddy! I missed you!" Shauna cried in her father's arms.

"Shh, it's okay. I'm here now," Clayton whispered.

"Get away from my sister!" Kyle said, pulling Shauna away from Clayton.

"This can't be true," Tim said. "Our dad is dead!"

"No, Son. I'm alive and well," Clayton smiled.

"I'm calling Kirsten," Tim said, pulling out his cell phone.

I was stunned. Was this really my husband? Was this a sick joke? Everything in me wanted to believe it was Clayton, but did I dare do such a thing?

"This can't be true," I whispered.

"It's true, Millie. I'm here and I'm alive," Clayton smiled.

A few minutes later, Kirsten and Robert came down and Kirsten was as shocked as everyone else to see Clayton.

"Oh, my God!" Kirsten cried, covering her mouth.

"Hi, Sweetie," Clayton smiled.

"Oh, my God!" Kirsten said again, as Robert held her.

"I know this a shock to everyone. I'm here, though," Clayton said.

"Who are you and what are you trying to do to our family?" Kirsten asked.

"Sweetie, it's me, Daddy," Clayton said, approaching Kirsten slowly. He smiled at her.

"Who are you?!" Kirsten repeated, as Robert held her.

"I'm your father. Look, this is obviously a shock to all of you. I think I can explain what happened if you will give me a chance."

I went to a nearby chair and sat down. My heart was racing. This couldn't be my husband. If it was, then who did we bury back in July? I looked at him, and something about his eyes. No, it was wishful thinking. This was some con artist trying to take advantage of our vulnerability. If this was Clayton, there were certain things that only Clayton would know. He came and sat beside me. Kyle tried to pull him away.

"No, don't," I stopped Kyle. "If you're Clayton, tell me something only Clayton would know," I challenged.

"Okay. I wrote a letter to you. I put it in your keepsake box with all the other letters you'd written," Clayton said.

"Wh-What?" I responded. I had tears in my eyes. No, this was too easy. There had to be more proof. "Anything else?"

414

"Millie, I can explain everything. The person you buried that you thought was me was my twin brother, Payton," Clayton said.

"Payton? But, Payton hasn't been around for years," Vivian said.

"I know. I found Payton not long after Millie got sick," Clayton said, looking at his sister. He sighed, and went on to explain. "I'd brought Payton here from Tennessee. He was down on his luck and broke. I helped him get an apartment and a job here. He didn't want anyone in the family to know I'd found him, so we kept it quiet for a while."

"Clayton would have told me," I said.

"Sweetheart, you had a lot going on. I kept Payton's secret, but I'd finally been able to convince him to let me tell the family he was alive and well," Clayton said.

"This doesn't make any sense!" I shook my head fiercely.

"I know it's a lot to take in," Clayton sighed. "That morning, when I left home after our argument, I went to Greg's house. We talked, and I told him that I was wrong. He agreed with me and told me that I should put my stubborn pride aside and call you. I did, and I left you a message that I was sorry and that I wanted you to put on your best outfit because--"

"You were taking me to dinner," I finished for him. "How did you know about that phone call?"

"Because I'm the one that made the call," Clayton said. He then took my hand in his. "Honey, I know this is a lot to take in. After I left Greg's, Payton called me. He needed to run a few errands.

415

I'd wanted to buy him a car, but his license had been revoked because of some problems he had in Tennessee. I tried to convince him to get his license back, but he wanted to wait. When I got to Payton's apartment, we left. When we got to the store and picked up a few things, Payton had 'conveniently' left his wallet and cell phone at his apartment. A fact he decided not to tell me until we got to the register. I paid for his items and we left. I was mad by the time we got back to the car. I confronted him about trying to use me when all I did was try to help him."

"What happened after that?" I asked.

"Well, I was mad. I got on Beckerman Road, and we were arguing about it. He told me that he'd been treated unfairly by the family, and he was determined to get as much from us as he possibly could. He told me that he'd been cheated out of the good life, and he wanted his share. We were yelling back and forth and I lost control of the car. When we went off the ravine, I was thrown from the car. We didn't have our seatbelts on. I had no memories of anything, and I stumbled away. This man and his wife rushed me to Fairmont Hospital. I didn't have my identification on me, so I was admitted under 'John Doe.' I'd apparently slipped into a coma for three months. When I awakened yesterday, my memories were still fuzzy, but I wanted to see you. I kept trying to tell them I had a wife and four children. I just couldn't remember your names."

"How could you forget us?" I whispered.

"Sweetheart, I'd never forget you. My memories were just clouded. But today, I knew

416

exactly who you were. Everything came flooding back like a tidal wave. I remembered you and the kids, the fact that I had a grandchild on the way, and my daughter was about to get married. I refused to wait another moment, so I left the hospital and came here."

"How did you get here?" Kyle asked.

"I caught a cab. Apparently, I had $47.00 on me when I had the accident, and I called the cab from my room. I snuck out and came directly here. I remembered that today was Kirsten's wedding day," Clayton smiled.

"Payton? H-how did you find him?" Nina cried. "I-I thought my son was dead."

"Mom, so did I," Clayton said, smiling at his mother. "But he wasn't. Payton was living in a shelter when I found him. I'd hired a detective a while back."

"Why didn't you tell anyone? Why wouldn't you tell me?" Greg asked.

"Because Payton was ashamed of how he turned out. His pride played a huge factor in things. He left when we were 17 and didn't look back. Because of it, he thought we'd ridicule him. I told him that we'd never do that. It looks like Payton was just trying to use me, though," Clayton sighed.

"So, are you saying we buried Payton and not you?" I asked.

"I was with Payton. I was thrown from the car, and my wallet wasn't on me. Since Payton didn't have his wallet in the first place, it would stand to reason that he was mistaken for me. I mean, we're identical," Clayton said.

"Well, how do we know you're not Payton trying to muscle in on Clayton's family?" Greg asked.

Clayton looked thoughtful. "Greg, ask me anything, something you know for a fact that there was no way I'd ever tell Payton."

"Okay. Only Clayton would know my PIN number to my checking account for emergencies. If you're Clayton, what is it?"

"It's 2972," Clayton replied.

Greg looked surprised. "Clayton?"

Clayton smiled. "I told you it was me, Big Brother."

"Wait a minute. It's going to take more than a four digit number to convince me," Kyle said.

"Kyle, when you were sixteen, you told me about losing your virginity and the fact that your girlfriend Lucy thought she was pregnant," Clayton said. "Is that enough for you?"

"Well, what about me? What's something only Daddy would know about me?" Kirsten challenged.

"When you were twelve, I caught you sneaking a sip of wine from the bar in the den at home. You were punished for a week, and you had to do a two-page report on the dangers of drinking," Clayton said.

"My God, that's true," I said. "Everything you've said is true. Clayton?" I said, standing. "Is-Is it really you?"

"Yes, Millie, it's really me," Clayton smiled as he stood next to me. He took my hand in his again and placed my hand on his chest. I was trembling as I

418

felt his heartbeat. "On our wedding night, you wore a white negligee and--"

"Okay," I smiled, stopping him. "Let's keep some things to ourselves."

"Now do you believe me?" Clayton smiled. "Even though Payton and I share the same DNA, our fingerprints are different. Remember my first job with the government? I had to have fingerprints done, so there's a record of it on file. We can compare them."

"We'll do exactly that," Kyle said.

"Kyle, this has to be Daddy," Kirsten said. She ran to Clayton hugging him. "Daddy! I thought you were gone! I-I missed you so much!"

"I missed you too, my little peppermint," Clayton said.

"Only you would know you used to call me peppermint," Kirsten smiled with tears in her eyes.

"It was after your favorite bedtime story *The Peppermint Fairy*," Clayton smiled. He suddenly looked serious. "I meant what I said. I'll do the fingerprints to prove who I am. I don't want for there to be any doubts in anyone's mind. If you buried Payton, we can have his body exhumed. His fingerprints are different, not to mention he's been in a lot of trouble in Tennessee. He has prints on file, too. Millie? Is that okay with you?"

"I know it's you," I smiled. "Why didn't I know you were still alive?"

"Sweetheart, all the proof pointed towards my being dead. I can understand why. Trust me, if there was any way for me to be with you, I would have never let you suffer like that," Clayton said.

I gently took his hand in mine as tears streamed down my face. I reached up to caress his face with my hand. This was the man I'd spent the last 26 years of my life with. This was my Clayton. We had so much to talk about. But, if it would put my children's minds at ease, I wanted the fingerprints done. My heart was whole again. All those nights I'd cried myself to sleep thinking he was gone forever, that I'd never be in his arms again, were wiped from my memory. My husband was home, safe with me. I looked into his eyes again and the eyes looking back at me were from a man I'd taken vows with; that I promised to be with forever. Everything he said was true. There is no way anyone but Clayton would know the things he did.

"Thank you, Millie," Clayton smiled. "I'll do whatever it takes to put my family's mind at ease. I know Kirsten's wedding was today. I'm just sorry I missed it."

"Oh, Daddy!" Kristen cried. "It's all been recorded! Don't worry! You'll have plenty of time to watch it," Kirsten smiled.

"Well, listen, let's not all just stand here. We need to get home!" I smiled. I held on to Clayton for dear life, wanting to make sure this wasn't a dream.

He had on a pair of hospital scrubs. Everyone else went back to the house, while Clayton's parents, Kirsten, Robert, Kyle and I left there with Clayton and went back to the hospital where he was admitted. When we got there, the nurse was relieved to see him walk in.

"Sir! Where have you been?! We've been looking all over for you!" the nurse said. "Nicole, call off the search for our John Doe," she instructed the clerk.

"I had to go to my family," Clayton said.

"We could have contacted your family," the nurse said.

"I couldn't wait," Clayton smiled. "I want to go home."

"Sir, the doctor hasn't signed your discharge orders yet," the nurse said. "Why didn't you let us contact your family for you?"

"I was anxious. The minute I remembered everything, I had to leave," Clayton responded.

"We've been searching for you for over two hours," the nurse sighed. "I'll page the doctor to see what he wants to do."

"Andrea?" Kirsten said. "Andrea Weston?"

"Kirsten!" the nurse smiled. "Do you know him?"

"He's my father, Clayton Welby," Kirsten smiled.

"Well, I had no idea!" Andrea smiled. "I've been his nurse for the past three months."

"It stands to reason that you'd never seen him. You graduated a semester before I did, so you weren't at my graduation," Kirsten said.

"Look, let me contact the doctor. He's well enough to go home, so maybe he can leave tomorrow," Andrea said. "Wasn't your wedding today?"

"Yes, it was," Kirsten smiled.

"I'm sorry I wasn't able to make it, but I

421

couldn't get off of work," Andrea said.

"That's okay. I understand. My daddy being alive is all I need."

"Hold on. Let me see what he says." Andrea then dialed the paging operator. "Yes, please page Dr. Edmonds to ext. 4024. Andrea Weston. Thank you."

"Even tomorrow morning would be good if it's necessary," I smiled. "It's after 9 p.m. so it'll be almost impossible for him to go home tonight."

"Not necessarily. Mr. Welby has been well enough, and the doctor was going to discharge him pretty soon. If he's still in house, I'll see if he can come by to see him," Andrea said.

"Thank you, Andrea. That would be a big help," Kirsten smiled.

"Anything to help," Andrea said.

"Andrea, the doctor's on the phone," the clerk said.

"Thank you," Andrea smiled, picking up the phone. "Dr. Edmonds? Our John Doe's family is here. We have a positive ID on him. Is there any way he could go home tonight? Okay, I'll let the family know." Andrea hung up the phone. "He thinks Mr. Welby is well enough to go home, but he's home already. He told me to get all the paperwork together and he'll sign it first thing tomorrow morning."

"Thank you for all of your help, Andrea," Kirsten smiled.

"Anytime," Andrea smiled.

"Oh, Clayton! You can come home

tomorrow!" I smiled.

"I'm ready, Sweetheart," Clayton smiled, holding my hand.

"I'm going to stay with you tonight," I said.

"That'll be fine. The doctor will round pretty early tomorrow morning, so he should be discharged by 9 or 10 a.m.," Andrea said.

"Thank you so much," I cried.

"You're welcome," Andrea smiled.

"Robert, can we postpone our flight?" Kirsten asked.

"You'll do no such thing!" Clayton smiled. "I'll be here when you get back. This is your wedding night. Go on with your plans, and I'll see you when you get from Hawaii."

"But, Daddy, we have so much to catch up on!" Kirsten smiled.

"And we'll catch up on it all. You will go and enjoy your honeymoon and you can catch up with your old man when you get back," Clayton said.

Kirsten kissed Clayton on the cheek. "Okay, Daddy," she smiled. "I love you so much!"

"I love you too, Kirsten," Clayton smiled, hugging his daughter. "I'll see you when you get back."

"Okay," Kirsten smiled. She then hugged me. "Bye, Mom. Take care of him."

"You know I will," I smiled. "I love you."

"I love you, too," Kirsten said.

"Bye, Robert," I said, as Robert hugged me.

"Bye, Mom," Robert smiled.

After Kirsten and Robert left, the rest of us

went into Clayton's room. He sat on the bed, and I sat next to him, holding his hand. I would never let him go again.

"I still can't believe all of this," Nina said.

"I wish I could have helped him more," Clayton said.

"I can't believe I didn't know which one of my sons had perished," Nina cried.

"Don't blame yourself, Mom. The only difference between us is this mole on the back of my neck," Clayton said pointing it out.

I looked at his neck. "My goodness! It's there!" I smiled.

"That was the way we could tell Clayton and Payton apart when they were babies," Nina smiled with tears in her eyes. "I'm so sorry, Clayton."

"Mom, you had no idea. All evidence pointed to it being me. I'm sorry I didn't tell any of you about my finding Payton, but he wanted to keep it quiet. Millie, I should have told you," Clayton sighed.

"Clayton, I don't care as long as you're here now," I said.

"Our son is alive," Nina said, with tears in her eyes. "I-I don't know how to feel. I've still lost a son."

"Sweetheart, Payton stopped being our son a long time ago," Jacob said. He held his wife.

"I'm sorry, Mom and Dad. I tried to help him. I feel like I cheated you by not telling you that I'd found him."

"No, son, you were being loyal as usual. Payton could have contacted us long ago. He'd turned his back on his family years ago," Jacob said, with tears in his eyes. "I'm so glad you're back, Son."

"It's good to be back," Clayton said, hugging his parents.

"I still loved him, Jacob," Nina said. "No matter what, he was our son. One loss is just as great as the other to me."

"Nina, Payton was raised to be a man, not to run out the minute things were tough," Jacob said. "Now, we all know the reason he ran away. If he'd have waited, he would have found out that the girl lost the baby. He wasn't man enough to stick around and mourn the loss of his own baby. As far as he knew, he had a grown child, but it didn't stop him from trying to use his brother!"

"I told him about the baby, Dad," Clayton said. "He seemed really hurt by it."

"See, that's just it. You shouldn't have had to tell him something he should have been man enough to stick around and find out firsthand," Jacob said.

"You sound like you're not hurt in the least that our other son is dead!" Nina cried.

"I loved him, too, Nina. I loved him just as much as I do my other children. If he'd given us a chance, we could have shown him. Payton had just as many opportunities as Clayton, Greg, Andrew and Vivian. He chose to throw his chance away!" Jacob said.

"Look, everyone's a little tense," I said. "Why don't you all go on back to the house, and I'll stay with Clayton."

425

"Okay, Mom," Kyle smiled. He looked at his father. "Dad, I'm glad you're back."

"Thank you, Son," Clayton smiled as he stood up. "I love you."

Kyle then hugged his father.

"I love you too, Dad," Kyle said with tears in his eyes.

Kyle then hugged me. "Mom, I'll be back to pick you two up first thing tomorrow morning."

"That'll be fine," I smiled.

There were hugs all around as Nina, Jacob and Kyle left. I looked at my husband, praying I wouldn't wake up from a magnificent dream. I smiled as we sat on the bed together.

"There's so much that has happened, Sweetheart," I said, caressing his face.

"We have a lifetime," Clayton smiled.

"Oh, speaking of lifetime, Nora was a match," I smiled.

"I knew it! I knew one of your sisters could save your life!" Clayton said. "Have you done the procedure yet?"

"No, we're going to the hospital Wednesday. I wanted to get Kirsten's wedding behind us before doing the transplant," I said.

"My sweet Millie," Clayton said, as he caressed my face. "Always putting everyone else's needs ahead of your own. I love you so much!"

"I love you, too," I cried.

At that moment, our lips met. My husband was here with me. We were together, and nothing and no one would ever tear us apart again. It was like a dream as we were connected once again. We lied on his bed together in each other's arms. I didn't want to fall asleep. I wanted to revel in the fact that he was alive and well. I was so afraid if I fell asleep that I'd wake up to find I'd dreamed the entire miraculous event. That night, we talked about everything. I caught him up on everything that had transpired in his absence. We knew that I'd be in the hospital for a while after my transplant, but knowing Clayton was alive gave me the strength I needed to withstand anything. Despite my being so excited, weariness soon took over. Around 4 a.m., we fell asleep in each other's arms.

The next morning, Andrea came in before her shift was over.

"Mr. Welby?" Andrea called out.

I yawned and stretched. I looked beside me and smiled. It wasn't a dream. I was really with my husband. I sat up slowly as Clayton awakened with me.

"Good morning, you two," Andrea smiled. "I was about to get off in a little while, but I wanted to come and tell you I hope you do well and I'm going to miss having you around. I'm so glad you found your family."

"Me too," Clayton smiled, never once taking his eyes off of me.

"Well, Dr. Edmonds should be here within the hour. Your nurse, Grace, will be in shortly to see you. Mr. and Mrs. Welby, I wish you all the best," Andrea smiled.

"Thank you for taking care of him," I smiled.

"It was my pleasure," Andrea said.

It was almost 7 a.m., and as we were talking, Kyle came in with a small piece of Clayton's luggage.

"I figured you'd need something to wear home," Kyle smiled.

"Thank you, Son," Clayton said.

"Well, goodbye, Mr. Welby, Mrs. Welby, Kyle," Andrea smiled, as she left out of the room.

Afterwards, Clayton got up to take a shower. His dayshift nurse came in and we told her that he was in the shower. She explained that the doctor had just arrived and would be in shortly to see us. After Clayton came out of the shower, the doctor came in a few minutes later. He talked with us in great detail about Clayton's recovery. Clayton had been walking with a slight limp due to an injury to his leg during the accident. The doctor prescribed for him to use a cane to assist him for a while. He signed all of the necessary paperwork, and we were leaving the hospital by 9 a.m., heading home. We arrived back at our house by 9:30 that morning. I was so happy. My Clayton was home, and all was well again. When we walked in, there were a million questions from everyone. It was a little overwhelming, but we welcomed it. That morning, we talked with our families to answer any questions. We had so much to do. Clayton was declared dead, which was a mistake I was all too happy to correct. I contacted Dr. Tracer to tell her about Clayton's miraculous return. Our transplant was scheduled for Wednesday, so on that Monday morning, we were able to start the process for Clayton's death being null and void.

Even though we told him it wasn't necessary, Clayton insisted upon proving beyond any doubt that he was Clayton and not Payton's. When we did the fingerprint match, it proved 100% that he was my husband.

Chapter Twenty

The Wednesday after Kirsten's wedding, Nora and I checked into the hospital with Clayton right there by my side. The procedure Nora had to endure lasted about an hour, but, she would suffer some discomfort for the next couple of weeks. Bill had taken time off to be with her during the time she was healing. My prep conditioning lasted for almost a week before my transplant. My healing process was just beginning after my transplant. It would take several months, and I'd be sensitive to just about everything around me. I couldn't eat fresh vegetables, I couldn't be around fresh flowers. I couldn't even be around small children if there was a risk of them having a cold. Given my immune system was practically non-existent, a common cold could kill me. I was going to have to be in the hospital for at least a month, which meant I would miss Thanksgiving at home.

   After Kirsten and Robert returned from their honeymoon, Thanksgiving was only a few days away. Nora was able to go back to DC to spend time with her children for the holiday. I missed my sister, but I knew she missed her family. The bone marrow transplant unit was prepared for those of us who wouldn't be able to be home for the holiday. So, they had a big celebration, inviting all of the patients' families to be there. I felt as if I were being blessed twice. I had so much for which to be thankful. Not only did I find a donor, my husband was back with me. It was wonderful despite the fact that I couldn't be home. Greg came to the hospital with Rhonda. After the celebration dinner with the other patients, I was able to spend some time with my family in one of the activity rooms. While there, Greg stood up and announced that he'd proposed to Rhonda and that she'd accepted. My sister looked so happy; both of them did. She'd confided in me a few short weeks before that she wanted to stop living in fear. She loved Greg and this marriage was almost three decades overdue. Finally, the two of them would receive the happiness they both deserved. There was still the not-so-small detail about Rhonda's divorce not yet being final, but she felt confident that everything would work out fairly soon.

   I was able to go home the week before Christmas, but, I had to really be careful. Clayton and I had always made such a big deal about Christmas. Ironically, I did a lot of my Christmas shopping months ago because I didn't think I'd be around for it. Because of my immune system, I wasn't able to go into the attic with Miriam to pull out decorations. So she, Kirsten, Clayton and Rhonda brought everything downstairs. I had to wear a mask, but, at least I was able to participate. As I was going through some of the things, I noticed a box with gifts inside. I didn't recognize it, because I knew I'd not left it there.

"Clayton, what's this?" I smiled.

"Hmm, you found out my secret," Clayton smiled.

"When did you shop?" I asked.

"Well, I shopped quite a while ago. I've done it that way for years," Clayton said.

"Beat the Christmas rush, huh?" I smiled.

"Something like that," Clayton said, as he playfully leaned in to kiss me.

"I'm so glad you're here. You know, a few months ago, I was dreading this being the first Christmas without you. I'm so blessed to be given another chance with you."

"I'm the blessed one, Millie," Clayton whispered.

On Christmas Eve, Kirsten and Robert along with Kyle and Erin came by the house. As a long standing tradition, we pulled names as usual. Rhonda, Greg and his daughters participated as well. Ginny and AJ were able to be there also. They'd brought their gifts to exchange with Rhonda and their new-found family. I pulled Greg's name, and at first, I had no idea what to get him. Then, remembered how he was always talking about how he wanted a new air compressor for his workshop. I assumed my big sister would want to get him something more romantic, so I decided to get that for him.

That night, Kyle sat at the piano and started playing Christmas music, as we all gathered around. After we'd song several songs, it was time to open gifts. I glanced at the tree and noticed all of the beautiful Christmas ornaments with our names on them.

"Everyone, I have something I want to say," I said.

"What is it, Honey?" Clayton smiled.

"When I thought of this Christmas, a part of me wondered if I'd even be here to enjoy it. Back in July, I was dreading the thought of spending such a special holiday without my husband. Clayton, the thought of all those times I'd mourned you still saddens me. But, I've been given such a precious gift to have you back. We're a family again," I smiled. "So, I want to propose a toast. To miracles and blessings," I said, toasting my glass in the air.

"Miracles and blessings," everyone repeated together.

"My wife is so sentimental," Clayton smiled. "Of course, there's reason to be after the kind of year we've had. I almost lost all of you. But, I'm here now, my beautiful wife is on the mend, I've gained a new son-in-law, and I'm about to be a grandfather to twins. Life doesn't get much better than this!"

"Oh, Clayton," I smiled. I looked under the tree at the box with my name on it from Clayton. "Why don't we open up gifts?" I smiled looking around.

After getting my gift from Clayton, I sat down by the fireplace. It was wrapped beautifully, which I'm sure was courtesy of a gift wrapping department. My Clayton could barely wrap a sandwich, let alone a gift. I opened the box to reveal two open first-class tickets to France, along with a brochure about the villa he'd planned on renting when I was ready to go. He had a beautiful card inside telling me that he wanted us to go back to a time when we first fell in love. When we first got married, we couldn't afford much of a honeymoon, so we spent three nights in a little cabin in Gatlinburg, courtesy of his parents' friend who owned the place. He always said that one day he'd take me to Paris for a real honeymoon. I cried as I thought of what my husband had done for me. All those years of working hard, never having the time to take a real vacation. Clayton traveled so much, and although I'd accompany him quite frequently, it was never a vacation. It was always work. I enjoyed it, simply because we were together. We tried to make it a family thing during the summer when the children were out of school.

"So, what did you get?" Kirsten asked, sitting down beside me.

"Paris," I smiled, holding up the tickets.

Kirsten looked at the tickets. "Open-ended first class. Daddy, you really know how to shop."

"Well, it's only fitting. Your mom and I never had a real honeymoon. Now's the time for it," Clayton smiled.

"Sweetheart, I don't know what to say," I

smiled with tears in my eyes. I kissed my husband tenderly. "Thank you. Come on, open yours next," I said to Clayton.

"Okay," Clayton said, tearing off the paper. "Oh, Millie, I love it!"

"Oh, Daddy! What a gorgeous watch!" Kirsten said.

"Thank you, Sweetheart," Clayton said, kissing me.

"Me next!" Kirsten smiled, tearing into the gift from her father. "Daddy! A new laptop computer."

"Oh, Kirsten! That looks top of the line!" I smiled.

"Only the best for my little girl," Clayton smiled.

"Kyle, what did you get?" Kirsten asked.

"A new leather jacket. It's just like yours, Dad," Kyle smiled.

"I knew you'd love it," Clayton smiled. He seemed to be enjoying seeing other people opening his gifts. "Okay, Tim. You're next."

"Okay," Tim smiled, tearing into the paper. "Thanks Dad! It's a digital camera," Tim smiled.

"What did you get, Sweetheart?" I asked Shauna.

"New ice skates," Shauna smiled.

"Robert, did you see your gift?" Clayton asked.

"You got me a gift?" Robert asked, surprised that his new father-in-law would think of him.

"Yeah, here it is," Kirsten said, retrieving it from under the tree.

Robert opened the box to reveal a new pair of

sneakers. "Man, these are top of the line," Robert smiled. "Thank you, Sir. I'm ready to whip you on the court, now, Kyle!"

"No pair of shoes can do that!" Kyle laughed. He looked at Erin. "What did you get, Honey?"

"Wow! A designer handbag," Erin smiled.

"Well, you thought of everything," I smiled.

"I tried to," Clayton shrugged. "Now, we need to decide when we're going to take this trip."

"Honey, I'm ready to go whenever you want!" I laughed.

"Wow, Paris. That sounds like a lot of fun!" Rhonda said.

"Rhonda, Greg, why don't you join us? We can plan it for after you get married."

"No, you two need some time alone, and so do Rhonda and I," Greg smiled.

"Maybe you're right," I smiled. "I guess I was being a little presumptuous by assuming my sister and brother-in-law would be interested in joining us."

"No, it's a beautiful thought. But, you and Clayton need some time to yourselves. Besides, Rhonda and I had our mind set on Italy for our honeymoon," Greg said.

"Well, that settles it. Sweetheart, we'll plan the trip for February, maybe around Valentine's Day," Clayton smiled.

"That sounds perfect," I smiled. "Honestly, your being here is all the gift I needed. Having my family here with me is priceless. Nothing will ever amount to what you've given me," I said with tears in my eyes. I sighed and looked around. "Well, let's eat," I smiled.

"It's about time!" AJ said.

We all gathered around as Clayton said the blessing. We had a wonderful Christmas feast. As I looked around at my children, I realized that I was truly blessed. That entire holiday was wonderful.

After everyone had gone, Clayton and I went to our bedroom. We'd not made love since his return because of my transplant. I'd bought a negligee that I knew he would love. Miriam had helped me get the room ready. I had candles and a jazz CD playing. I went into the bathroom to shower and get ready for bed. When I stepped out, my husband couldn't take his eyes off of me.

"Wow," he whispered. "You're beautiful."

"Thank you," I smiled.

Clayton reached out for my hand and kissed me passionately. I yearned for my husband to make love to me. We'd been waiting until the perfect moment to know each other again intimately.

"Oh, Millie! I've missed you!" Clayton whispered passionately.

"I've missed you, too. Make love to me, Clayton," I whispered.

My husband immediately picked me up in his arms and laid me gently on the bed. He began to get to know my body all over again as we made love. It was truly a homecoming, because now we were complete. Afterwards, we lied in each other's arms, consumed with the fact that we were together again.

When we brought in the New Year, it was wonderful, just as Christmas had been. We went to church to bring in the New Year. Like every year, I'd organized the breakfast we typically had after service. This was no ordinary New Year considering the way it could have been. A year ago, we brought in the New Year together, not knowing whether it would be our last one because of my illness. We tried to make the most of the holidays the year before then, because we felt as if I were living on borrowed time. But, not only was I blessed to be here for another New Year, Clayton was brought back to me as well.

By the first week in January, Erin was getting restless. Then, it finally happened. On January 3rd, Erin had come over along with Kirsten to help Clayton and me put away Christmas decorations. We were in the den and Erin was putting ornaments into their boxes.

"Ow!" Erin yelled, closing her eyes in pain.

"Erin, what's wrong?" I rushed to her.

"Ma, it hurts!" Erin cried.

"That's okay, Sweetheart. It's time!" I smiled.

"But I'm not due for another month!"

"Sweetie, you're carrying twins. It's okay for them to come a few weeks early," I reassured.

"Ma, I'm scared!" Erin cried.

"It'll be fine," I soothed. "Kirsten! Clayton!" I yelled. They'd been upstairs putting some things away. "I'm going to call your doctor."

I immediately went to the phone and looked on our list of emergency numbers and called Erin's doctor. They instructed me to get her to the hospital immediately. After hanging up, I called Kyle at work.   He said he'd meet us at the hospital.   Kirsten came rushing into the den.

"What's wrong?"

"Erin's in labor," I said, hanging up the phone.

"It's okay, Erin.   Mom and I are here." Kirsten rubbed Erin's back.   "Let's get her to the hospital.   I'm going to pull my car around."

"Where's your dad?" I asked.

"He's still upstairs in the attic," Kirsten said.

"What's going on?" Clayton said, walking into the room.

"We're about to become grandparents!" I smiled.

"Oh, okay!" Clayton said. "Um, okay, let's get her to the hospital.   We need to call Kyle!"

"I've already done it.   Kirsten, go ahead and get your car pulled around and we'll meet you out there," I said.

"The SUV will be more comfortable," Clayton suggested.   I'll pull it around."

"Okay, either one is fine.   We just need to get to the hospital," I smiled.

We pulled up to the Women's Center at the hospital where someone was waiting with a wheelchair.   Clayton went to park in the parking deck once we'd gotten out of the car.   Kyle was pulling up, coming to a screeching halt as they were about to roll her in the door.   He jumped out of his car, leaving his door open.

"Wait!   I'm the father!"   Kyle yelled.

"Kyle!   Help me!"   Erin screamed.

"I'm here, Sweetheart," Kyle said, holding her

439

hand. "Rebecca, her contractions are about six minutes apart," Kirsten told her co-worker.

"Thanks, Kirsten," the nurse said. "How much has she dilated?"

"I haven't checked her yet," Kirsten commented.

"Kirsten, don't leave me!" Erin begged.

"Shh, I won't, Erin," Kirsten soothed, holding her other hand, briskly walking with the wheelchair.

I suddenly remembered that Kyle had left his car door open. I went to his car and realized he'd also left the motor running. I smiled at his nervousness behind becoming a new dad. I turned the car off and locked the doors. I went to labor and delivery after calling Erin's parents. I remembered that in the rush, I'd forgotten to call them. Clayton came in a couple of minutes later. While we were in the waiting room, Kirsten came out in scrubs.

"How's Erin?" I asked.

"She's fine. Still waiting. She hasn't dilated enough yet for an epidural, so her pain is probably still pretty intense. Are her parents here yet?" Kirsten asked.

"Not yet. They're on the way."

"She's asking for her mom and you," Kirsten said.

"Do I need to dress out?"

"Yeah, if you don't mind," Kirsten advised. "Wear a mask. I don't want to take a chance with your immune system still being so vulnerable."

"Okay," I smiled. I looked at Clayton. "I'll be back shortly, Sweetheart."

"Okay. Give them my love," Clayton smiled.

A few minutes later, I found myself trying to calm my daughter-in-law's nerves. Kyle was a real trooper with the way he handled things. He never left his wife's side. Shortly thereafter, Erin's parents arrived. This was truly a time when a girl needs her mother. Finally, after another eight hours of labor, Erin delivered my first two grandsons. One was 5 pounds 6 ounces, the other was 5 pounds 10 ounces. They named one of them Drew Carrington Welby and the other one David Channing Welby, after Erin's father. Both babies were strong and healthy, and she had no complications. When I saw my first two grandchildren, I knew I had to be a blessed woman to witness something so precious.

A week after the twins were born, I got a phone call from Nora. She'd found out that she was pregnant. Apparently, she'd gotten pregnant right after our procedure, because she was already six weeks when she called with the news. My thirty-nine year old sister was going to have a baby. She commented that maybe this time she could do it right. Oddly enough, she and Bill were very excited about the baby. I, of course, was worried because of her age, plus she'd donated bone marrow to me. I knew that was silly because the doctors assured us that her bone marrow would replenish itself. Her age and health were the least of her concerns, and she ecstatically said so. Jessica and Matthew were both happy for their parents, and looked forward to having a little sister or brother. Jessica started dating a guy she'd known for a couple of years, who attended Yale with her. My niece was finally happy, notwithstanding the comprehensible reservations she'd originally undergone. They were all going to counseling together to try and slowly piece their family back together. Although things were much better, they still had a way to go.

That February, Clayton and I went to Paris. We had a wonderful time. I was able to forget about everything and so was he. We'd never been so relaxed. For the first time, we allowed someone else to pamper us. We were like lovesick teenagers during the entire time. We fell in love all over again.

A couple of weeks after our return home, around the first part of March, Rhonda received great news. Her divorce was finalized. My sister didn't do too bad. Since the house burned down, she received a check for the full value of the house and contents, which equaled out to $2.5 million, she was also awarded their vacation home in Florida. She'd been awarded mandated alimony payments of $6000.00 per month. Plus, she got her car and all personal assets. All of the stocks and bonds were to be divided equally, and he couldn't sell them without her permission. She wanted nothing to do with Aaron and he wanted nothing to do with her, so the two of them agreed to sell them, and she received another $1.5 million from that. My brother-in-law was getting exactly what he deserved. Unfortunately, the alimony could be stopped if she remarried, or lived with another man. Rhonda didn't care. She wasn't going to let that stop her from being happy with Greg. So, Aaron still got off pretty good. He didn't have to come through with the alimony payments.

REUNITING SECRETS

Rhonda and Greg didn't want anything too big, so the third week in March, they had a very small ceremony, with just our families. My sisters flew back in to witness Greg and Rhonda marry. The second marriage in a few months' time, and they were all able to be here for both of them. I'd never seen Rhonda so happy. The look in her eyes said it all. There wasn't any sadness there anymore. They took the well-deserved trip to Italy after they got married, and stayed there for 2 weeks. Greg already had a buyer for his house. So, he and Rhonda bought a ranch about 20 minutes from my house. Things were good for them.

That particular spring seemed to be good for all of us. Kristen and Robert were happy, and that April, we got yet another pleasant surprise. Kirsten was pregnant. I suspected as much, but I didn't say anything. She'd told me that they'd wanted to wait a year before trying to have a baby. She was absolutely stunned, because she confided in me that they'd taken precautions. I explained that taking precautions doesn't always guarantee not getting pregnant. It seemed as if my family was rapidly growing.

Gina was finally getting her life together. After going back and forth for a few months, she finally made a decision. She and Mark eloped in mid-April. It was just in time, too, because she gave birth to a little baby girl a week later on April 24th. She weighed 7 pounds 10 ounces. They named her Kendall Millicent Carlisle. I was surprised, yet proud that they gave her my name. When I met Mark, I was immediately charmed. He would be good for my little sister. She and Alex remained friends despite their breakup. Alex finally found someone who was good for her, someone who was proud to be in a relationship with her, which was what she deserved. I had a great deal of respect for Alex because of how sweet she was to me during their visit. I was glad she found the right person, and I was glad my little sister found her way finally.

Tim turned 16 a week after we found out about Gina's elopement, and had gotten his driver's license. In light of his new-found privilege, he begged and begged for a car. Clayton and I were planning on getting him one, but after Clayton's accident, I was terribly afraid of my son possibly suffering the same fate as his father. Clayton told me I was overreacting, and that we couldn't protect him from every little thing. It took a lot of thinking about the pros and cons, but eventually, I conceded and we got him one a few weeks after his birthday. He deserved it, because he'd always proven responsible, although the past few months had been trying. He'd started hanging around Anthony a little too much for my comfort. He had a few rebellious episodes, but he eventually found his way back to being himself. All it took was one conflict with the law to make him change. Anthony convinced him to ride with him one night, to try and buy alcohol. Tim went along and as luck would have it, the police pulled them over and searched Anthony's car, finding marijuana and the beer they'd convinced an adult to purchase for them. It was a wake-up call for Tim, and he knew he never wanted to feel the fear he felt that night when he thought he'd go to jail for something Anthony had done. Tim swore to his father and me that he didn't know Anthony had drugs. We believed our son, but we told him that he would have to earn our trust again for even going along with Anthony to buy alcohol illegally in the first place. As much as I wanted for him to remain the innocent little boy he always was, I knew my youngest son was growing up.

Shauna turned 13 on May 12, and along came her cycle on the Saturday following. I'd feared that I wouldn't be here for her when she started. I knew that Kirsten knew how to handle it, but I still felt it was something I should help her through. We had a mother-daughter day, so that she could ask any questions that she might have felt shy about at some point. I explained to her what it meant, and the changes her body would go through because of it. She told me that she didn't want it, that she wanted to be a little girl again. I gently explained that there was no turning back. If it were left up to me, she would remain a little girl forever, but neither one of us could control it.

Life was good; almost too good. Kirsten and Robert enjoyed the thought of parenthood once they got used to the idea. They'd moved into their house already, so they were ready to start decorating the baby's room. Just like we did for Kyle and Erin, our gift to Kirsten and Robert was to have the baby's room done. I jokingly told her not to throw us any curve balls and come up with twins like her brother did. Deep down, I wouldn't have cared. The more the merrier. Although I get the sneaking suspicion that my daughter and son-in-law might not share my views.

During Nora's last two months of pregnancy, her doctor put her on complete bed rest. Her blood pressure kept going up, and it was hard to keep it under control. On July 8th, Nora gave birth to a beautiful baby girl. She weighed 5 pounds, 2 ounces. The baby was born a little over month early, but, she was healthy and a decent weight. The doctors told her this was a possibility because of Nora's age. She proudly named her Tiffani Ann Riley.

Things were going so well between the McAlray sisters until we'd decided to have another family reunion around the same time as before, so we planned it for late July. I wanted to host it again. Nora was so excited about the baby, until she was determined to be there even though she'd just given birth a couple of weeks before. Oddly enough, our family had grown by four babies and three in-laws, and it was continuing to grow. Everyone arrived on the third Saturday in July. The sleeping arrangements were pretty much the same as before, with a couple of changes here and there. Everything was going along smoothly.

We were having a cookout, laughing and enjoying each other's company. Miriam handled everything as usual. Nora was a proud mom, Erin was a proud mom, Gina was a proud mom and Robert swore that he could feel his and Kirsten's baby kicking, although she was just in her fourth month of pregnancy. I was so glad we'd made up for lost time. Over the past year, we'd been reunited several times after the last reunion. I was sitting in a lounge chair, looking around at my family.   I smiled as I thought of all that had happened to make our bonds stronger.   All the trials over which we'd prevailed.

A couple of days later, Clayton accompanied me to the doctor's office.   I was so nervous, even though my husband tried to reassure me that everything was fine.

"Hi, Millicent, hi, Clayton," Dr. Tracer smiled. "I've got wonderful news for you."

"What is it?" I smiled.

"All of your tests have come back.   Millicent, you're cancer free," Dr. Tracer said.

"Oh, Dr. Tracer!   S-So I'm going to live?" I said excitedly.   "I'm not going to die?"

"Oh, not for at least another thirty or forty years," Dr. Tracer shrugged.

"I'll take it!" I smiled.   "Oh, Clayton!   I'm going to be well!"

"I heard her!" Clayton had tears in his eyes.

"We still want to keep an eye on you, so as long as you come in regularly for checkups, you'll be just fine," Dr. Tracer smiled.

"Not a problem!" I exclaimed.

When we got back home, I couldn't wait to share the news with the rest of the family.   We'd bonded so closely, and they'd been my strength when I wanted to push them away.   As we celebrated my news, I looked around at my family.   Such a beautiful family.   All those years of conflict, secrets and misunderstandings; now we were whole again.

A year ago, my illness brought us together. Without Nora, I might not have survived.   Now, I could live with the hope of seeing my other two children getting married and having families of their own. For so long during my illness, I thought I was going to leave them. Now, to know that I'm well again, I was filled with a new hope.

The years passed, and we still came together as a happy family. The children grew, and Tim got married when he was 27. He was a mechanical engineer. He worked for one of the top car companies in the country. He'd relocated with his wife and their baby to North Carolina. Shauna graduated from college and immediately got ready for law school. She and her boyfriend dated pretty seriously in college. After law school, Shauna married her boyfriend of five years. Two years later, the two of them had a baby boy.

My children were happy, and so were Clayton and I. My sisters were happy, my nieces and nephews were happy. Things were wonderful. I thought back over the years how blessed I truly was. Clayton had retired from his firm, and we were going back and forth to our vacation home in Aspen. I've been cancer free now for over twenty years. I appreciated life more when I found out about my cancer, because I thought my time to enjoy life was limited. After I was cured, I knew that I was being given a second chance. My children are happy. Kyle and Erin had two more children after the twins were born. Kirsten and Robert had one more child after their little girl was born.

This was what life was all about. What could possibly be better than being able to be with the ones you love?   The appreciation I now had for my life was priceless.   There was no longer that stoic belief that I could handle things on my own.   My husband taught me that, and for that, I'll be forever grateful to him. We're growing old together, surrounded by our grandchildren and children.   As we watched Shauna's little girl playing with her toys, I came to the realization that life doesn't get much better than this.

Made in the USA
Columbia, SC
21 August 2024